NECROLOGY

NECROLOGY
MEG RIPLEY

Creature Publishing

Brooklyn, NY

Copyright © 2024 by Meg Ripley
All rights reserved.

ISBN 978-1-951971-14-4
LCCN 2024934786

Cover design by Luísa Dias
Spine illustration by Rachel Kelli

CREATUREHORROR.COM
 @creaturelit
@creaturepublishing

For Victoria and my mother's mothers,
My sisters, Brooke and Kate,

And especially Stephen, who helped me roll this curse.

CONTENTS

Prologue: Salem, Massachusetts Bay Colony, 1693 · 1

Chapter 1: Andrews House Orphanage, Blackmoor, New York, 1894 · 7

Chapter 2: The Train · 19

Chapter 3: Let Me Go · 33

Chapter 4: I'm Here · 43

Chapter 5: What Evil's in This Place? · 52

Chapter 6: By the Fire · 58

Chapter 7: Wet Sheets · 75

Chapter 8: A Bang on the Door · 87

Chapter 9: Meeting Sr. · 97

Chapter 10: Liberty · 109

Chapter 11: The Train Again · 115

Chapter 12: Who Stands as Tall · 125

Chapter 13: The Tin · 132

Chapter 14: The Wolves · 142

Chapter 15: Confessions · 155

Chapter 16: The Rocks You Got · 172

Chapter 17: Meet the Doctor · 187

Chapter 18: Milk · 195

Chapter 19: Her Crown · 201

Chapter 20: By the River · 211

Chapter 21: The Judge · 221

Chapter 22: Animals in the Yard · 231

Chapter 23: Alone with the Tin · 239

Chapter 24: Marble · 245

Chapter 25: Don't Forget Milk · 253

Chapter 26: Dirty Sympathizer · 259

Chapter 27: Proof · 268

Chapter 28: Divining Rods · 276

Chapter 29: Time to Go · 284

Chapter 30: You Need Me · 292

Chapter 31: Biggest Dirty Sin · 304

Chapter 32: Back Aboard · 310

Chapter 33: Trial · 316

Chapter 34: The Truth · 328

Chapter 35: And What Do *You* Say? · 337

Chapter 36: Sixty-Four · 349

NECROLOGY

Barefoot and proud, Mad Dog marches unceremoniously up the long dirt road toward the courthouse, considering destiny and her lost wife Tituba's prophecy: *Revolution will rise in the jaw of a waking beast.* Whether it was a promise of an eventual change, or a conjuring to make her task today conscionable—how could any one woman, even an elected leader such as herself, sign a contract swearing off women's innate magic for the sake of safety from unmagical men?

Stars consulted, any clarity on the protection of her bodily autonomy had remained eclipsed by dead women. Now, escorted by guards in black hoods, marble in her pocket and stick slung atop her shoulder, she's here on behalf of a reluctant majority vote.

Windows in town remain shuttered with pity or fear. On a street corner, a lone sinewy man jeers, waving a black flag. He and an unkindness of ravens are the only ones to bear witness to her and these guards' pilgrimage to the courthouse today.

As the moss-colored sky turns to mud, the phantom scent of twenty-four women burned, casualties of just the last fortnight, and the fate of her wife, materializes on the breeze. *Storm's brewing.*

Arrived, two grand black doors open, forcing a shift in air pressure that makes her ears pop. A shrill gasp sounds as restless

1

spirits rush past her, indoors and up onto the ceiling of the courtroom. A central table with a lone scroll sits partially obscured by six men. Their roving eyes trail from her face, down to her dirty bare feet, and halt at various stations on the way back up.

Five of these men are judges presiding, the brothers Dodd. They're wolves. She can tell by their curious nostrils flaring. They're out for blood, and find it too. Their snouts wrinkle as they note it running down her pant leg. She's left it visible on purpose—as proof to the world she's thinking clearly. They avert their eyes. The sixth man, Supreme John Freemen, steps out front of the pack, extending a hand in her direction.

"Mrs. Hull," he says with a smile. It's a cruelty. He knows full well that he should address her as a superior, Omega. At the very least, by her birth name. She hasn't even resigned yet.

She refuses his hand.

His enduring smile, his posture tell he believes he's being helpful today. A self-appointed leader of an exploded faction of fundamentalist Blackbook devotees, his charisma, finances, and demand for unwavering allegiance from his followers has brought the cancerous mindset of her gender needing management to every doorstep, ocean to ocean. Patriarch of unmagical men, he's proposed this contract.

Looking behind himself, he nods to a seventh man, someone Mad Dog hadn't registered at the back of the room.

Flooded with relief, she says, "Alpha Bloom?"

Thank summer, the country's counter advisor has historically been a diplomatic man. Balance is possible today, long as the potentials of Freemen's pocketbook for campaigning and reelection don't cloud Bloom's judgment. Blinking once, she questions why Bloom remains seated. He smiles meekly, cemented to his chair.

She can't offer any courtesy in return. Delivered or withheld, a woman's smile might be her most powerful hex. The ability to ease an entire room with maternal serenity? Play coy, seduce, dominate, or ridicule—uncontrolled, it's capable of prompting an otherwise loving partner's backhand. It's why she's here today.

"Shall we?" John Freemen leans in.

Bloom's unengaged look at the floor is so curiously craven, Mad Dog's speechless. Freemen will function on the Alpha's behalf? Her cheeks flair with heat, sympathy for Bloom's forsaken supporters. It's clear, Freemen are in charge of his party now. Of the country.

The wind claps a shutter closed to her right before it slams open again. Dust hits the window glass on her left with a tinny crackle. Some leaves fly by in a gust. Then more. Fresh restless spirits wiggle in through the window's weep holes as the wind picks up. The window frames wheeze. Light in the room shifts, and midday outside looks more like night. The storm has landed.

Winds gust, and there's a high-pitched whistle from under the heavy doors at her back. A few two-toned howls sound before pressure builds and a full-blown siren's scream is unleashed. Dust plumes from between floorboards. A liquid flash of lightning flares outside, and a rumble of thunder vibrates under her heels. The Dodds look at one another as Freemen's hand flies up to feel the back of his neck, electricity in the air making everyone's hairs stand on end. This meeting, this pact—will bring balance? She nervously drums her toes on the wooden floor.

Rotating the stick off her shoulder, she lays it tenderly on the desk. Retrieving the small marble from a satchel woven of her foremother's hair, she lays it down next to the stick. The offering cues her resignation, but she holds her chin high.

"No magic, no violence," Mad Dog whispers.

Acid flares in her throat as she picks up the contract, scanning the agreement's terms. Today, she'll sacrifice two religious artifacts. They're security in the joint endeavor for balance for mankind, 'Librium—or what Freemen refer to as control.

Orthodox Blackbook believers know that the rock, the Necrology, is an impression of women's magical history. That the Woodfeast, the stick placed between Mother's clenched jaw during the birth of the world, encapsulates women's autonomy. Sacrificing these artifacts stings, but if nature is cyclical, relics will come and go. Second happenings are possible. According to Tituba, inevitable, even.

"This is for the best." John Freemen's self-assuredness falls away with debris hitting his cheek. Alpha Bloom's head is bowed so low, he might as well have nodded off.

More dust hits the windows, on her right this time. She watches another hair of lightning lick amber into the sky. More leaves hit the window, but stick this time. She realizes it's moths, not leaves, as a boom of thunder rattles the building. The doors at her back fly open with a *crack*. A Dodd stumbles, falling to one knee. Another, shaking, mimics the first. Moths, thick and heavy, scatter into the room, bringing rain. They dart, then land on the walls, wings testing. *Harbingers of great change.* She gulps. It's either reassuring, or a sign of dark times.

"Sign," Freemen yells over the din, face hard as he hands her a pen. The scroll before her is threatening to take flight, so he secures it with both hands. Dust or impatience makes his eyes tear.

The Dodds have all tipped over, cowering. Red hands on their faces. A tempest of grit blasts through the room. The screaming wind grows to a penetrating howl.

The bottom line awaits her signature.

Next to it, she sees John Freemen's scrawl. Pen on paper, she pauses to think of her wife. Their last embrace. Tituba's want for this moment. For the sake of the daughter Tituba had planned to conceive one day. What could have been their little girl's smile. Free of judgment in a world that revered her strength. Respected her age. Acknowledged her wisdom.

A moth flits across the room, landing on her hand. The building bumps once on its foundation. Scratching out Mrs. Mary Hull, she scrawls her real name, Mad Dog.

Leaves and sticks circle the room, but she remains untouched. Turning on her heels, and without a look back, she marches straight out into the dark and rain. It feels like the end, but it's only the beginning. Whatever funnel clouds await her, she welcomes them. May they wake that beast. Make her yawn, jaw distend in a gruesome sneer. May they stir unfiltered hopes and dreams in little girls. The daughter she's now determined to bear. Her daughters' daughters.

And oh, ignite all the change they'll bring.

*

Focused on the hammer in his grasp, a man in black takes but a few strides across the courthouse's steps before he's forced to contend with what remains of the plague—the slick, caked bottom of his boot. Indelicately he scrapes the carcasses of dead moths off his sole, leaving a hunk of macabre mash behind on a low ledge. He curses the inconvenience before hammering a nail into each of the four corners of a declaration on the courthouse wall. A notice, also distributed by raven, to all colonies and points west:

THE SEPTEMBER CONTRACT
Salem Convention 5th of September, 1693

IN ATTENDANCE:
Freemen representative, Mr. John Freemen
Judges, Brothers Dodd
Dirty representative, ~~Mrs. Mary Hull~~ Mad Dog

REPRESENTATIVES OF BOTH PARTIES DO HEREBY AGREE TO:
1. *The ban of all Dirty magic by all cunning women including teachings and history*
2. *The ceasing of all violence against Dirty women by Freemen for circumstance of their sex*

TERMS:
1. *The surrender of the Wood and the Marble to the Freemen so they may not forget past wrongs against the Dirty while Dirt prospers. Dirt shall work and play quietly.*
2. *A plebiscite will convene if ever evidence surfaces of this contract being broken.*

X. *Mad Dog, Dirty*   X. *John Freemen, Supreme General*

Chapter 1

Andrews House Orphanage, Blackmoor, New York, 1894

Rabbit and Rook kneel in the dirt playing at a cursing. The knees of their trousers are soaked through with cold damp, and their stooped shadows sit midday small under leafless maples. Rabbit wiggles her loose tooth, praying to summerland that her inexperienced feet are connecting her to the dirt and all her potential magic. She's eight, a little girl still learning, but if Rabbit rolls this curse right, she'll stop the arrival of the most terrible person she's ever known, a man she and the other orphans call "the Beard."

As Rabbit rolls, the die collects flecks of mud in its grain as it travels along the ground. Black and inlaid with gold dots, the die's face shows six.

"Good focus," Rook says, his dark eyes sharp.

With icy fingers, Rabbit moves her marker, a gray piece of slate, six spaces. Notch fifty-two, *Saw, the destructor.* Today she's asking the wilds for notch sixty-two, *Bury.* She's on track to disappear the Beard entirely, if only she can focus and roll with purpose, with clarity, the way her teacher, Whitetail, does. She's rolled nine times and has two more rolls.

Rook has drawn a spiral with his finger in the dirt, notching it with sixty-three slashes. They'll need to work together to make the curse. To ask the wilds to blow a new future in the Beard's direction. March is here. His train is due any minute. Or not, if Rabbit can derail it by cursing a mudslide, or rock fall.

Now, they two kneel, staring down at the drawing on the ground like a secret flame they'll have to nurture to keep warm.

Rabbit fantasizes that today could be her day. To prove to Whitetail she's grown. She'd witnessed Whitetail use Sixty-Three to curse water from a rock when she'd been thirsty. Used it to heal Rook's split toe too. She's ready to connect directly to the dirt, pray to the wilds for safety from a man who, for reasons not entirely clear, threatens her family.

Two players for the game Sixty-Three. Her, representing the will of man, him, the wilds. Just because she can ask the wilds to turn the sky black doesn't mean they'd ever allow it. It's a matter of balance. Play the curse alone, there's none of nature's design, just the will of a person. And Whitetail says curses made without "the consent of the will of the wilds" is for the bold . . . or stupid.

Rook snatches up the die, rolls it in his dusty palm, then tosses it. Forty-seven, *Snake eye.* He moves his marker, a twist of wood, two spaces.

Rabbit's turn. Rolling the die, she tosses it. Moving her marker to fifty-seven, *Smoke,* she huffs an impatient breath. Looking over her shoulder, she checks to see that Whitetail hasn't emerged from the house looking like a ghost. These days, Whitetail has become withered, consumed by the newest orphan, Mouse, who's always exempt from chores and ever by Whitetail's side.

"If you cost me bedtime parables, I'll hate you five seasons," Rabbit warns. *A night without Whitetail's stories would be like a morning with no yawn.* But if she's caught, she'll deserve the end. Sixty-Three isn't off limits, but its ritual is always, always led by Whitetail. Because somewhere in the time between the ritual's creation and today, the last five notches got iffy. And messing with the wilds, the energy field connecting all living things, can muddy balance. Whitetail says you can't go running around sticking "ifs" in balance. Balance is important.

"Think they'll grow bigger?" Rook asks, taking up the die in his fist. He plays this game well. Rabbit supposes that's why he always enjoys practicing with Whitetail. He's better at casting than Rabbit. Though Rook was born without magic in his bones like her and the other girls, he can will the die to go this way or that.

Rabbit seals her lips together and holds her breath. She knows exactly what Rook is asking about but can't let on. It's an uncomfortable subject for all the orphans. Whitetail has grown antlers. She checks again to see that Ms. hasn't come outside looking.

"Rabbit?" Shaking the die in his fist, he doesn't toss it. Instead, he wraps his elbow around his long shin bone, waiting for her answer.

Rabbit shrugs. Running out of air, she exhales with a puff and sees stars.

"Dunno. Who cares?" she says. Whitetail is perfect, antlers to toes. She's the only mother Rabbit's ever known.

"'If you don't spit the truth out at the start, it'll find a way to make a hole and come out on its own.' That's what she's always saying," he says, finally putting his marker down.

A secret? Rabbit knows Whitetail's principles and the dangers of oppressing truths. The antlers' appearance speaks of an otherness that makes Rabbit scared to look Whitetail in the eye. Appearing the same night as Mouse—not there one night, there the next morning—seems unnatural. At first appearance, they were the size of pussy-willow pods in spring. One on either side of her head. In just three months, they've grown fast as shadflies to the length of a fillet knife.

Nothing grows overnight except mold. But Whitetail claims the antlers aren't like mold. Supposedly, neither are her blackening eyes, hands, or feet.

"You think she's got a greater truth to tell? She didn't do nothing wrong. She claims the antlers are proof she's nearing summerland."

"You believe that?" Rook sits back on his haunches. "Something seems off. And the Beard's not gonna like it one bit." Rook shakes his head. "She's so Dirty looking. And her belly! She looks with child! I think, I think . . ." Rook's round, glassy eyes shoot to the ground. He's four years older and, like all the children, eerily wise. ". . . that something's gone off with her."

Rabbit furiously shakes her head. She can't bear the thought. Whitetail's devotion to the wilds may have kept her lookin' young—a leaf frozen midwinter—but at a hundred and fifty years old, she says she's near for death. Afterlife. Summerland. That's a good thing, and she's deserving for how strong and devout a Dirty woman she's been.

"She cursed herself someway. That night. In the kitchen. She willfully played Sixty-Three alone. No input from the will of the wilds. Mouse showing up naked in the middle of the night in a January snow squall. Whitetail brought her someway. The antlers are the effect. She did something muddying. She was bold. Or stupid. He delivers to both summer and winter, you know." Rook points to line sixty-three, *the Grimm*.

Blinking up at him, Rabbit's stomach drops.

Rook believes that Whitetail is destined for winter because of some mud she's made? If the woman who so vigilantly cared for them, fed them, and taught them—who *saved* them—is destined for anywhere but summer, it would be tragic for a woman so wholly bound to her principles. Her going to winter seems an impossibility. *But.*

She's breathless, overwhelmed, and backtracking. "You said 'Dirty' just now like it were a swear—like they do." She throws a finger at what she can't see beyond the mountains: humanity that has forgotten truth. Most of the Dirt stopped worshipping the wilds over two hundred years ago, since her foremothers signed the contract denying women access to the power they can tap from it.

"Who are you to speak of the will of the wilds? And to decide that anyone's too Dirty looking? You think Dirt deserves to hide? We can't help we're born female. Or want to worship what those women out there have so easily cast aside. You think Ms. owes anyone a reason for the way she looks? She don't."

"I . . ." Rook holds his hands up defensively. His mouth hangs open; he's silent.

"You think that because you're male, you know everything? You don't know. You can't even curse. Just assist. In fact, you don't know anything, you son of a Freemen," Rabbit spits.

Not a matter of genitalia—a spectrum exists. Where Rabbit had been born with a limitless crop of potential power, Rook has but a few seeds to sow.

Rook leans forward, lowers his hands. "Everyone's wrong sometimes. Everyone makes mistakes. Even her. Even you."

In Rabbit's eyes, Whitetail has never, ever been wrong.

The confidence in Rook's mouth falls away, and it makes Rabbit's heart ache. She knows he isn't a son of a Freemen. Those are made, not born. There are Dirty men out there, but most don't show themselves. They're hiding, Whitetail explained, to save themselves from incarceration and persecution, same as the women Dirt. Almost his entire life, Rook has spent under Whitetail's supervision. Just because he is male, unable to directly ask the will of the wilds for anything, doesn't make him an enemy. He is Dirty like her, but what he'd said about Whitetail's misstep, it'd scared Rabbit. Because deep down she believed it might be true.

Rook is right in thinking the Beard won't like how Dirty Whitetail looks. Magic being illegal means Dirty beliefs are kept secret in front of Freemen authority. Whitetail has coached the children to never, ever speak of summer or winter, or the wilds—of Dirt—in front of strangers. The looks Whitetail got, back even before the antlers; her height, her black fingers, their length! Coal color of her eyes. The way callers stared at her when they came to the door. Shivered at the sound of her two-toned voice. The way those thieving men ran, pants' seats wetting as she scared them out of her crops last fall—it told Rabbit that Whitetail's appearance was upsetting to people. Even more upsetting than for the children. *Rook is right—she looks positively Dirty.*

What will the Beard do to Whitetail, to the children, if she's outed today?

"You think I'll grow up to be one of them." Rook's voice is soft. He crosses his arms, and his face goes dark. "That's what you're saying? I'm destined to be a Freemen?"

Whitetail once showed the children a strange paper, a drawing of Freemen blackhoods at a rally. Men gathered in fields, dressed in black masks, in olde Salem. Their beady eyes proudly stared off the page and made Rabbit's stomach hurt. Square hoods and blazing torches, stomping and swarming like bees, they'd been working to keep women's magic muzzled, like Sarah, the orphanage's nippy goat. In Salem, they burned witches, Dirty-kind, stabbed them, strangled them, and beat them. Those were old times when blackhoods were in the open, before, Whitetail says, Freemen began pretending they weren't supporters of violence. Since the September Contract, Whitetail claims men of that kind only gather in secret, illegal-like.

This boy before her is too wise to ever become one of those men. Birth isn't destiny, is it? Rook may never be what Rabbit is or could be, but unlike the Freemen, he seems okay with that, and doesn't want to stone her for their differences.

"It's not true. You're Dirty through and through." Rabbit puts a reassuring hand on Rook's shoulder. In fact, every worship, every study, Rook has jumped in even deeper than her. "You're one of us. Forever." She winks, trying to build a bridge between them. He is her other half. A part of her heart. Always will be.

He glances down at the unfinished curse.

"As for the will of the wilds. The sun is high. We better hurry! Try. Focus on the roll," Rabbit says. "I can't do it without you."

Rook's grin comes back with the challenge. Whitetail has a fancy lacquered Sixty-Three board they'd play after dinners. Back before Mouse came, and the board stayed hiding, anyway. Regardless, the children know Sixty-Three so well they don't need a board anymore. They know its spaces on the timeline like they know each other.

Finally, he lets loose a three. Rook moves his chunk of wood to notch fifty.

"*Duration*." Rabbit taps her bottom lip, then narrows her eyes to check he's paying attention. Rook should know, notch fifty is *Goose*. *Goose* permits a player to double his steps, unlike *Duration*, which makes you skip a move altogether. Other notches on the spiral can have you backtracking fast as a hummingbird. Roll too many sixes, pass sixty-three, you can wind up recycling to one, or two, which send you elsewhere. The lower numbers on the lifeline are baby steps. Sometimes two steps forward only to take a step back. If she hits the right combination of numbers, meets Rook on their chosen notch where they're allowed to align, she can cast her first real curse and not have to accept what the wilds deliver in Rook's roll.

Rook shakes his head, dismissing her direction, and dutifully doubles his steps, progressing to notch fifty-three. *Owl, roll again.* He does so without speaking.

Rabbit licks her lips as she commits to casting a five. Condemning the Beard to engrossment, concealment, or entombment, it would make Whitetail proud of Rabbit. Evil in a black hat wouldn't be coming today.

Rook rolls. His die shows a four. As he places his stick atop her rock at notch fifty-seven, *Smoke,* her smile falls.

"Yield," Rook commands. He has landed on *Smoke* too. It not being their eleventh and final roll means her marker gets bumped forward to notch fifty-eight, *Reckoning.*

But she's rolled ten times already and had just prematurely committed to casting the five. Ms. always says that timing is everything. With only one roll left, it will be impossible to ask again, for a four, instead. Rolling a five would get her to sixty-three, *Grimm,* the master of death and deliverance. What would that bring to this situation?

She dared not . . .

"You can't just move in there and take that, I was there first," she argues, to stay on *Smoke.* "*Reckoning* is a lie of a notch, anyhow. A reckoning can't even exist on its own without an original grief of some kind, a flame which is missing from the lifeline entirely. Smoke? *From what?* I shouldn't have to move out of the way just so you can take the space. We both stay."

She was so close to landing on sixty-two. She wants to disappear the Beard. If she argues hard enough—

"Rules are rules. Move one notch." Rook's eyes deliver a warning. He shakes his head at her stubbornness when she refuses to surrender.

Lifting her slate, he moves her piece for her. *The first Dirty consent: If it's not yours, don't touch it.* Her jaw tightens. "You want the same outcome as me. How can you take my space? You're the one that convinced me to come out here!" Reaching out her hand, she grabs his wrist and stops him.

"Because there's no use cheating the wilds. It only brings mud. You mustn't."

"How dare you! Let us roll from here as though there's a—a—"
She searches for what she means to say. "Some kind of a light. Or
a flame on the board. Otherwise, why would there ever be smoke?
Reckoning for what? Let's see who meets sixty-two first from this
moment. Let's roll as equals. And stop the Beard!" Something feels
so wrong. *The second Dirty consent: If it's yours, defend it.*

The consents, Dirty commandments, ethics devised by her
foremothers at the dawn of time, are easy to remember. Rules to live
by are simple in principle, but hard to know when to implement.
She'd never experienced a time when giving someone power didn't
feel like relinquishing some of her own.

Rook hesitates a moment, then frowns. "We started as
equals . . . at the start. You step aside. Play this wrong and you'll
bring mud. Disaster. You know this." The wind whistles through
the trees above. It blows Rook's wild hair up and back. He
watches her a moment, then puffs a regretful huff.

Today Rabbit feels desperate. To grow up. To help the only
mother she's ever known. Be loved as much as Mouse. Impress
Whitetail with how hard she's practiced talking to the Dirt.
Control something. Anything. Show Rook she can do it. But she
can't, because at notch fifty-eight, she's already lost a chance at
meeting him on sixty-two.

Instead of taking her last turn, Rabbit crosses her arms. From
fifty-eight she could roll the five she'd been trying for, but the
Grimm would bring the coach. The coach would summon ghosts,
like a divining rod for specters. Most spirits, when they die, go to
the coach willingly, but some red-boned wraiths make a run for it,
evading collection 'cause they've got a vicious score to settle before

they rest. Her feeling uneasy might make her roll another number altogether, and at this point all she thinks is that she'll never be good at commanding the die like Whitetail, and she'll meander through this life like a dandelion seed with no agency of her own.

"Last roll. Finish the asking." Rook eyes her small marker.

Looking down at her stone, like a claw on the ground, she can't help but pout.

She closes her eyes and tries to focus. Her stone was a gift from Whitetail. Not all markers are created equal; there are many magical stones in the world. Hers is not terribly powerful, but it's her most prized possession. It was trusted to her with the unspoken promise that it never be used to make mud. Always balance. Always 'Librium. If she doesn't roll, mud will come.

"No," she says, feigning courage. Taking up her stone, she grips it to her chest. She can't bring herself to finish the curse. A breeze blows, and she ineffectively tries to rub goose pimples away, the slate cold in her fist.

Rook pauses, his mouth twisting. He glances at her apologetically.

Her heart races. She loves and loathes him.

Rook nods sternly; he takes up the die and hands it to her. "If you don't roll, neither can I, and you'll make me a part of your mess." He eyes her, the corners of his mouth turning down. He'll need to roll last to close the curse. She can ask the wilds for an outcome, pray, but as the direct representative of the wilds, he'll have a final say on the Beard's landing place.

Wind blows the tears of frustration in her eyes, making them feel cold.

"Hey!" Rook's brow furrows angrily. "One player for will, the other, wilds. You can't call to the wilds for help and then not listen." His quoting Whitetail grates on her nerves. She knows they need to close out the game. For balance. *Don't be stupid.*

Still, she shoves the stone marker into her pocket. "It's a dumb game, anyway." She feigns indifference. What does an unfinished curse mean? Mud could mean a couple of flower heads knocked off in a far-off field—or all Earth's birds grounded for good. Might be nothing a'tall. She has no idea.

"It isn't just some game! Give it—" He reaches out for her wrist with tears in his eyes. Plunging his hand into her pocket to steal her stone, she opens her mouth to yell. But before she can summon enough air, a shrill holler sounds.

They both freeze.

The scream of the A&O steam engine's whistle echoes through the mountains. Rabbit's mouth goes dry as her heart restarts.

"It's too late," Rook warns, turning to look back toward Andrews House. "The mud's made."

Chapter 2

The Train

H e's probably descending the A&O's train steps by now!" Rook's eyes are darting off to the surrounding woods. "I'll kill him. I'll kill him if he . . ." Though they're still alone in the woods with no one to fight, his stance is defensive, feet dancing.

"Hush! You're scaring me. If he what? What will happen when the Beard sees Whitetail, you think?" Rabbit pleads. She hears her own voice tremble at Rook's mention of murder.

Murder, wrongful death, makes restless spirits. Rabbit's chest freezes and her hands tingle.

"Rook! What are you afraid of?" She raises her voice to get his attention. What makes this Freemen more worrisome than the rest? She's still not sure what threat the Beard brings.

Rook shakes his head at her ignorance.

Memories of the last time he visited fly through Rabbit's mind like a hatch on the river in spring. He'd come three times before; only once was she old enough to remember. The other two times were regaled by Rook and Snake in whispers that Rabbit devoured like myth. He'd come once when Andrews House was being built. Once to stand for a photo when the papers came to take a picture; she'd been a babe. And then the last time, which was not so smiley and friendly as the first two times. He came carrying flowers, not the milkweed and bee balm found locally, but roses, the biggest Rabbit had ever seen in her life.

"The Beard, well, you can tell he's sweet on Whitetail."

Rabbit nods her head. Who wasn't sweet on Whitetail?

"In love with her looks—her old looks anyway," he adds.

Rabbit knows what he's getting at. Whitetail has explained the difference between "sweet on" and "in love." Genuine love is to know someone like you know yourself. Where the third Dirty consent—*Don't become confused over what's yours*—isn't an issue because what's yours is theirs. Family above all else. The orphans love each other. Rabbit loves Rook best of all. The Beard doesn't seem to know anything about anyone other than himself.

"But Ms. turned him down," Rook explains. "Remember last time, the Beard left spitting swears every which way that he'd 'be back next time' looking for 'the right answer.'"

"Sure." Rabbit remembers his dissatisfaction. He tossed the roses he'd brought over the porch rail on his way out. Rabbit's stomach turns cold at the prospect of "*or else*." "What are you afraid the Beard will do?"

"I'm not sure. Something very wrong. Hurt her spirit." His voice is flat, and his eyes search the ground. They stare at the game.

"Wrong" is a foggy explanation. She traces Rook's gaze, now trained on the hills. Though it's impossible to see the train from where they stand, Rook seems resigned to try. The tip of his nose and cheeks are bright red. He's cold, like her. Rabbit reaches for Rook's typically warm hand, but today he shakes her off. As of late, his hands have become harder to cling to. And right now, he's upset with her.

Huffing, he bends down and grabs his marker, his twist of wood.

His eyes scan, lost in thought as he roughly drags a filthy foot through the Sixty-Three spiral in the dirt, destroying evidence of it. "We need to get back to Whitetail. We need a plan. I can hear the devil's steps already. Whatever happens, today is your doing, Rabbit," he warns, grabbing her wrist and shaming her for not completing Sixty-Three. Lifting her hand, he plunks the die in her palm.

Rabbit drops the die in her pocket next to her slate marker.

Rook licks his lips and eyes the path that leads down to the main road. Beyond the raspberries, skeletal in this season, stands the orphanage. Windows stand in pairs along both stories of the home with X's crisscrossing them. The big wooden planks of siding wrapping the building are black with rot. Mold has taken over so aggressively along the roof eave that the decorative filigree that once adorned it looks more like coal these days. There's a big wraparound front porch that has a hole you've got to watch for. Rabbit was running up the steps one day when her leg struck it right through.

"Here's what we do," Rook says. "You round up the others. You all take Whitetail, hide in the deep wood. I'll hide in the brush to jump out, stop his heart. If it doesn't stop, I'll tell him she's gone, run away." He looks at the height of the sun veiled by gray clouds. "It'll be less than an hour before he gets here."

He looks at her standing there.

"Go!" Rook says. "Do as I say, damn it!"

Rabbit's jaw drops. The swear sends her feet running. Swearing is for those in cahoots with the devil or, in special cases, the artful. Artful is what Whitetail is, and when she swears it's okay because she was born with the Dirty ability to read the stars with her naked eyes.

"Whitetail!" Rabbit screams as she runs. "Ms.!" When she hits the front steps, she makes all four in just two bounds, hopping over the hole in the boards. Whitetail comes to the rusting screen door and steps out onto the porch, her face pained with worry.

"Rabbit?" Whitetail says, shielding her eyes against the already muted sun. She's spent too long indoors and is withering like a daisy in the cellar. Her antlers have grown even bigger since this morning. Long as bear claws, they make her look mean, even though Whitetail's never so much as raised her voice to the children since they'd fallen into her care. Rabbit wants to believe, like Whitetail, that these antlers are proof of a final transition, but they seem to draw from Whitetail's spirit when they should be proof of its overflow. There are dark blue circles under her eyes that sit cavernous on her ashen complexion. The shadow of the antlers' reflection forces a ripple through the otherwise composed waters of her face.

This is bad. And not just for Whitetail either, but for all of them. Their caretaker's trouble could only mean theirs. Take away a dandelion's head, all the seeds come loose, untethered on the wind. Rabbit can't stand the thought of Whitetail dying someday, destined for summer or winter. But winter would be devastating. Rabbit herself would become untethered on the wind.

"He's coming, Ms.! Beard's train has come! We heard the A&O holler. Rook says that I'm to take you and the others to the deepest part of the woods for safekeeping."

"Rook says that. And what do *you* say?"

Rabbit blinks speechlessly up at Whitetail. She fights the urge to cry a little. Whitetail seems to not understand the urgency of Rook's plan. As Whitetail rolls her black fingers into fists and places them on her hips the way she always does, Rabbit's stumped by her own lack of opinion. Self-loathing seals her lips shut because stupid mud-making girls shouldn't have opinions.

"Would you have me hide?" Whitetail asks.

Rabbit shrugs. "Yeah. That's the plan. Rook says—"

"What, dear girl, will we do tomorrow when he comes back?" Whitetail leans forward, raising her long dark brows over her black-marble eyes.

Rabbit thinks about it a moment. "Oh! Rook says he's going to hide. He'll kill the Beard. You'll be free."

Whitetail smiles lightly. Opening her mouth to say something, she stops. Brows creasing with a new seriousness, she pushes past Rabbit and squints into the afternoon sun in search of something off the porch.

"Rook?" Whitetail's voice is hard as she calls. She stands still a moment, listening. Rabbit notes there's nothing but the sound of dry leaves in the wind. Birds, crows in the distance. Water rushing lightly beyond that. Rook is terribly good at concealing himself. He can stealthily slip into branches, behind trees not ten yards off, and still, you'd never know he was there.

Whitetail's mouth twists. Taking her cigarette tin from a pants pocket, she opens the lid, letting it rest on its hinge, and narrows her eyes at its contents: their parents' blessings.

As a keeper, a Dirty woman, Whitetail protects lost children, young and old. Legacy of the original forest dwellers, she's a human with gravitational pull, and a spiritual advisor to the children, same as she was to their parents. A natural guardian, she keeps Rabbit's eight sisters from believing they're innately evil and her brother from thinking the Dirt owes him fruit.

Their mothers gave Ms. a shock of hair, a piece of spirit, from each of the children's heads. As ancestors of the forest and avoiders of industrialization, unpracticing Dirt didn't swear off culture and customs, Whitetail's explained. Their quiet Roscoe commune always kept lingering respect for the Dirt. Barefoot and like-minded, they held fast to one another. Whitetail, their leader, had trained her eyes on the stars. When she'd admitted to foreseeing crumbs of tragedy, perhaps surrounding the children, it prompted their parents to seek the children's security.

The hairs help her keep track of them and are what allowed her to save the children the night of the fire that killed their parents.

Rabbit was swaddled, and in Whitetail's arms; they smelled smoke. Whitetail sought her collection of the town-children's hair, each swath lying tied with a ribbon. The children looked warm, cocooned with midnight slumber, so she blew on them.

With her chilly breath, the hair samples rolled over, showing her that each child in their parents' apartments nearby stirred. Alerted, she trusted they'd smell smoke. Inexplicably, but by her command, they ran, Pheasant and Goose being carried by Snake, Mole crawling to the street, to safety.

Whitetail lifts a bundle of black hair. *Rook's*. It's tied with a strap of leather. She twists it between her thumb and pointer, rolling it back and forth to inspect it.

Rabbit shivers.

Looking up, Whitetail puts the hair back inside the tin and closes the lid. Re-pocketing it, she walks to the far end of the porch. Leaning over the rail, she gazes down into the hedge.

"I'll not call you twice," Whitetail announces to the hedge.

After a crackle of branches, Rook emerges from the brush looking irritated.

"Yes, Ms. Whitetail?" A quick reproachful look from Rook shows Rabbit that somehow, someway, she'd done the message delivery all wrong. She was supposed to be stronger? Less pleading, perhaps, and more authoritative, but this was Whitetail she was speaking to. A force! Rabbit believes the woman could keep summer from following spring if she so desired.

"Rabbit has just warned me that I am to flee with the children to the woods to escape the man you call Beard. That *you'll* be taking care of him for me? That right?"

"Yes, ma'am." Rook looks redeemed, verging on hopeful. He stops glowering at Rabbit and straightens up.

Whitetail stoops, bending down over the rail to look at Rook more closely. His big, dark eyes widen as her proximity brings her long black braid over her shoulder in his direction like a snake. Rabbit feels like pulling the braid back like a rope that would keep Whitetail focused on her for once. Set a bell ringing that Rabbit played a huge part in this master plan too. Not just Rook.

"I thank you, Rook. Your offer is selfless. But know this, a woman who needs a man for protection is forever kept in his shadow. You know, well as anyone, that your shadow is not where I'll wait. Besides, you could plan to kill the Beard. But remember, you can ask a man to accompany you to the Grimm's doorstep, but he'll invite you *both* in for tea. Are you ready for death to offer you tea?"

Rook's eyes glass over. "I don't want your spirit hurt."

"This situation, like any, requires being seen through to the end. And if I've told you once, I've told you a thousand times, boy, it's amazing what the spirit can cope with to preserve the body. My spirit is a mighty oak that just won't fall. Now, take this bread. Don't come home until after dark." Handing him a bundle wrapped in a cloth, she knocks her chin in the direction of the hill that leads down to the river. She raises an eyebrow. "I believe the Beaverkill is loud enough this afternoon to cover all your chatter."

Rook looks unconvinced, and, taking the bundle, tucking it under an arm, he doesn't move. His glassy eyes stare up at Whitetail, squinting.

"Have a nice day of it, will you?" Whitetail says, her tone softening.

"But—" Rook bites his bottom lip.

The house's screen door opens with a squeal, and Mouse emerges from the shadows. As always, her shiny black hair is braided to match Whitetail's, and the way she carries herself, the tilt of her face, the movement of her hands, the way she sometimes blinks in pairs, is uncannily similar. Since the wintery night three months ago when Mouse, with her beautiful eyes and perfect hair, arrived on their doorstep, Whitetail's been consumed with only *her*. At breakfast, *Oh! That porridge will be too hot for our liking, Mouse.* In the rocker by the fire in the kitchen, *We don't like the heat on our shins.* It seems Whitetail anticipates Mouse's every whim without the child speaking, almost considering Mouse another limb or part of herself. Her child. Even though Whitetail's stomach is bulging, she's never birthed a child. The bump she carries is just her twin sister, who she swallowed years back. It's a secret that Hyena's in Whitetail's belly. Rabbit almost gags at the thought of Hyena rifting around Whitetail's body. Imagines her peering out Ms.'s eyes.

As Whitetail's distracted by Mouse, Rook's eyes roll up to note Whitetail's pregnant-looking belly and her antlers. His shoulders slouch, and the corners of his mouth turn down. Rabbit knows he wants to stay here and protect their adoptive mother, but an order's an order.

"I charge you both with protecting the others. Take them down to the water. Rabbit, take special care with Mouse."

Special care.

This statement grates on Rabbit. Always "special care" with Mouse. Why does Mouse necessitate special care? Both Rabbit and Rook nod. Mouse looks hurt, reading Rabbit's annoyance. Mouse is six, so Whitetail believes, but she's so much more coddled than Rabbit had ever been. Than Pheasant or Goose had ever been. So much more nurtured than any of the others. Mouse is more important, or more fragile, but Rabbit can't fathom why. It makes her loathe the girl.

Rabbit lets out a sigh. It garners a reproachful look from Whitetail.

After Whitetail turns to walk away, she grabs the screen door handle and, opening the door a crack, she adds, "Don't come back until dark." Her demeanor is complicit in the Beard's coming, and it's mystifying.

"Yes, Ms.," Rabbit manages.

Rook is quiet.

Whitetail walks inside, letting the screen door creak and bang behind her.

"C'mon, you take Mouse and get Pea and Rat," Rook says. "I'll round up Goose, Pheasant, Dove, Bear, and Mole. Meet you at the big rock. Hurry!"

He takes off, carrying Whitetail's bundle over his shoulder. The big rock is the children's meeting spot. It serves as a seat for picnic lunches, paper on which to draw with chalk rocks, and an altar at which to kneel for prayers to the Dirt. It's where they met when there was any kind of gathering, and Ms. always claims it is a chip off the mother rock, a fragment of Earth's history, and that's why she requested the men build Andrews here in the first place.

Whitetail's call to action, combined with the fact that Rook is still talking to her despite Rabbit's someway foiling his original plan, has Rabbit running even faster than before. Imagining the wheels of the carriage the Beard has acquired, churning out their grease, rolling down the long dirt road, is all the fire she needs to fuel her legs. Looking back over her shoulder, she spots Mouse, her little legs trotting, but too slowly.

"Oh, for summer's sake, hurry up, Mouse!" Rabbit's breathless when she finds Rat and Pea, red hair glowing, out back trying to hoe the still semi-frozen soil. "Hey, girls! Beard's coming. We have to go to the river till dark. We meet the others at the rock right now."

The two girls turn to look at Rabbit. Rat, then Pea, drops her hoe, and they both come running. Mouse plunks down, beginning to happily twist old grass into a new doll.

"*Ughhh!*" Rabbit groans. "Whitetail's orders. You disobey her, and you'll never forgive yourself. Get up. I'm in charge of you."

Mouse's shoulders drop. Slowly she stands up, dusts off the front of her trousers, then takes off running. Rabbit follows, then passes her, leaving the others behind as she leads them all around the house, down the backyard, and toward the rock. Rook and the others are waiting, ready to depart. Her stomach is rumbling for the bread in the sack Rook is carrying. She sees he's got it in hand as her party arrives at the big rock.

Crossing the road together, the children pause at the far side, atop the ravine that leads down to the river. They look down. A freezing wind picks up, blowing dirt at their fronts, and they're all forced to rub dust from their eyes. Rabbit listens, but there's no carriage within earshot on the road. The temperature has dropped. Rabbit feels little Mouse's hand grab hers.

She shakes it off.

She doesn't want to hold it. Rabbit imagines letting the little girl tumble down the hill to eventually be eaten by raccoons or foxes.

"I'm scared," Mouse says. It's something in her brow and the unique texture of her hair, more like grass, that makes it conceivable she could be Whitetail's very own daughter.

"You may look like Whitetail, but you sure don't act like her." *Whitetail's not afraid of anything.* "We've run down this ravine a thousand times. I think you could sprint it with your eyes closed. What's different today?"

Mouse can see things Rabbit can't. Hear the echo of times past. Future too? The child is artful in a way Rabbit only aspires. Born with the ability to read stars, just like Whitetail. As Mouse turns to look over her shoulder, back at the porch, back at the house with its dark windows, she looks withered, and it's impossible not to take pity on her.

"No smoke." Mouse points to the chimney. "No breath. It's a shell, Rabbit."

Looking back at Andrews, it looks desolate. Erected in remote Blackmoor after the nearby Roscoe fire eight years ago, Andrews House was never finished. Had the workmen who'd first shown up in droves, charitable in nature, grown wary of the eerily unyielding forest? Or had it been Ms.?

The siding has lost most of its oil, revealing grayed patches of wood underneath. A black vine has aggressively taken over and wrapped itself repeatedly around an eave as though it would like its territory back. The windows, some of which are cracked, one never installed, are boarded up to keep the cold out. From this angle, it's plain to see the porch is warping and the black mold is taking over.

"Let's go." Rook's voice is far off as he calls from downhill. There's the muffled noise of branches cracking in the distance. He's taken the lead, and one by one, all the other orphans are following him, sidestepping, off the road down toward the river. Their marching is kicking up dried grass seed, and it's drifting up into the air as they travel.

Rabbit and Mouse are left alone. Rabbit yanks Mouse's hand, but the child isn't moving. There's a noise on the air. *A whinny?*

Rabbit leans back on her heels to see if he's come. There's nothing on the road.

"Come on."

Blinking away the start of some tears, Mouse looks up at Rabbit, her face round and pale.

Rabbit's angry, but her heart breaks a little. If only she could be as cherished as this creature by Whitetail. If only she could be as perfect to her mother as this child. Be as skilled. As beautiful. See whatever pieces of the future Mouse saw just now when she looked back at the house. Rabbit's stomach turns.

"It's a scary day, isn't it, Rabbit?"

Though Rabbit agrees, she remains stoic. The Beard. The mud she's stirred in the wilds. "We'll all be fine. Everything's going to be fine." The comfort Rabbit's offering is only half-hearted. Mouse's mouth shows she's disbelieving.

"*You'll* all be fine." Mouse's eyes blink out tears. Her little bow-pout pinches, stifling a gasp. Her chest heaves a single shudder.

As the far-off echo of hooves sounds, Rabbit's heart is in her throat. The other children have completely disappeared into the brush. Rabbit delivers a pleading look to Mouse. Her use of "you'll" stays with Rabbit a moment. She's not sure what to say. Why always Mouse apart, separate from her, from the others? But here Mouse's tone is the one sounding stung. An unmistakable bitterness is bothering Mouse.

Rabbit yanks Mouse by the wrist. Even so, the child doesn't move.

"He's coming. I think I hear him. Whitetail's fine," Rabbit snaps. "She'll know what to do. With him."

"But that's just it. We don't know what to do with him," Mouse whispers. Rabbit has always known that Mouse was like Whitetail, but in this moment, Mouse seems to be curiously implying they're one person.

Rabbit's stomach drops. She's worried too. "You're safe with me, Mouse. I'll keep you safe." Rabbit takes her hand more gently. "I'll always keep you safe, okay?"

"Hur-ry!" Rook's voice is small and echoing with the distance he's gained.

"Okay?" Rabbit repeats.

Rabbit pulls Mouse's hand even harder. The girl's fine soft fingernails slip partway through Rabbit's grasp.

The rumble of the Beard's carriage is so loud now, Rabbit knows it's getting close. The pattern, the *clip-clop* of hooves, is so distinct, it drives Rabbit forward a step. Looking back over her shoulder at Mouse's doubtful stare, Rabbit's wanting to leave her behind.

Please, Rabbit mouths. And finally, the little girl stumbles begrudgingly over the ravine's edge, gripping Rabbit's hand so tight it hurts.

Chapter 3

Let Me Go

The man Whitetail's children call "Beard" has a proper name. It's the same name that's engraved on the wooden sign that hangs out front of the orphanage: Andrews House. Mr. Johnathan Andrews Jr.'s beard is his most notable feature and the first thing Whitetail sees when he visits. It precedes him through every doorway at which he never knocks.

Although her pantry and cold room are rich with potatoes, turnips, and dried trout, Whitetail hasn't a penny and very little use for money. The children are right to be afraid of Andrews. His every visit is a threat to the family they've nurtured here. His allowing them to stay is charitable. She doesn't need Andrews's support for anything but this roof. For this roof, she is grateful. This family is all she's got and the only thing she seeks to protect. One disapproving crinkle of Andrews's brow will make it disappear. She's always known his investment was in her, not the children.

Lifting the right half of her apron to wipe her brow, she lets it fall to land beside the left. She's sliced the apron vertically up the middle and hemmed the slit so it doesn't hang like a skirt over her trousers. Make no mistake, it's two long, sturdy legs she stands on. Not withering stems. Able legs, the same as any man.

Cracking open her cigarette tin, she evaluates the children's shocks of hair and sees they're moving along the river. Black hair bound with sinew; Rook is leading with Pea. Brown hair bound with red ribbon; Rabbit, as directed, is helping Mouse. Begrudgingly holding her hand even. During hide-and-seek, at bedtime, and during early morning hours, Whitetail can see each child's movements down to every sigh and blink. Her observing the bundles of hair lets her observe the kids' spirits—location, mood, motives, no matter how far they drift. Even Snake, having grown up and gone off to work in service at Andrews Sr.'s house, is still occasionally under her third eye. After all, despite their differences, Snake is kin. The day the child bullishly boarded the train for Syracuse would forever pain Whitetail's spirit. She'd never had to say goodbye to one of her children before. Had to watch them make a choice beyond comprehension and depart for a land so despicable and a future in a service she'd been trained to avoid.

Saddling up to the kitchen table with dinner's potatoes and a bucket of water, she's forced to scrub them at an arm's length from the table's edge. Her belly grows. Her shadowy sister compacted to the size of a bean when Whitetail swallowed her, but has since grown to an undulating mass the size of a pumpkin, making Whitetail's back pain and ankles swell. The weight of her sister has begun burdening her every fiber.

After years of conversing with restless spirits from across time in search of the stone, twenty dead sisters mysteriously showed up in the middle of the night and whispered the Necrology's location in Hyena's ear.

Hyena's determination to travel to New Amsterdam, infiltrate Freemen secret society, while posing as some Blackbook devout named Morgan, and steal the rock—the Necrology—was precisely what brought the fire that killed the children's parents, making Whitetail a mother of ten.

The night of the fire, Whitetail located Hyena's shadowy form cornered by flames inside a dark wall, pitifully crying for help. Whitetail peeled back the wallpaper, stabbed a hole in the wallboard with a knitting needle, and after wrapping her lips around the hole, drew her sister in like tobacco smoke, and swallowed. First to save Hyena from burning, Necrology still in her belly, but eventually to keep her safe. From herself.

Although Hyena's residence was supposed to be temporary, Whitetail's circulatory system, like a maze with no end; brain; and, eventually, stomach had proven a fine holding cell. After Whitetail realized that it was her sister's intention to summon the list of Dirty dead, publish a memorial for dead battered women, shining a light where none was allowed, she put a hard stop to it. It was what invited Freemen torches to the children. She couldn't let her sister, recklessness incarnate, run amok. Noble but angry to a fault, Hyena was keen on action but so . . . imperious.

At five years old, Whitetail had had her lunch stolen by a boy and wound up grateful she'd, at the very least, had breakfast. She accepted that the boy had simply needed the meal more. The same boy mocking Hyena's schooling at home, her evening-time-only emergences, and preference for shade? At midnight, he'd curiously have a bedroom lantern that wouldn't turn on whilst a shadow stalked his room. Schooled on passivism, Hyena could only ever turn the other cheek *after* a last clap. And now—children hung in the balance of Hyena's initiative.

Twins, they were born during a thunderstorm. While Whitetail had crowned during a flash of positive lightning, cloud to ground, Hyena, a rifter, had been born second, and during an almost imperceptible instance of dark lightning—the invisible kind. She possessed a sensitivity to light only tolerable by her ability to become a massless shadow. Their mother often claimed a rifter's negativity, their intolerance to light, could be neutralized by a positive charge, but the discomfort of it all had kept Hyena shadow-bound.

As a newborn, Hyena squirmed under candlelight. The singular time she'd ever crossed their cottage's threshold by day, she was swaddled in their mother's arms. A sliver of sunlight met her chin, scorching her so badly she was reduced to bucking, writhing screams before—*poof!* Hyena slipped into a crack in a floorboard, and mother cried, distraught half a day before the baby was finally recovered. Mother said the smell stayed in all their hair for days. A scar remained on Hyena's chin. And from then on, venturing out of doors required Hyena's slipping into their mother's pocket, or flask, else she'd pitch a fit.

Their mother claimed it was being born on either side of a leap year's waxing and waning moon, a day apart, that did it. Made her the way she was. Whitetail believed it was more likely their mother'd been cursed.

Over the last eight years, Hyena has become riddled through with parasitic anger. The Necrology's a piece of ice in hot water, embedded in Hyena like a cellular-level branding. Hyena's evolved from less a captive creature to more a force of unadulterated vengeance. She's absorbed the marble's wisdom, every murdered woman's name. Whitetail fears that her own positive charge, the positive connection to the ground that's allowed her to hold Hyena this long, could have altered Hyena's onetime physical vulnerability. It could have made Hyena resilient, maybe even in daylight. What's inside her could be a monster, the likes of which the world has never seen. She grows like a storm. Pure war incarnate.

She's angry and tired of containment. Her demeanor, while never a particularly patient woman, has turned to rot and resentment. Her restlessness is understandable and physically painful.

How was Whitetail to know at the time she swallowed Hyena that she would become this, this . . . thing? Despite their being kin, Whitetail would've rather spent the last eight years this close to anyone else. For the sake of the children's safety, Whitetail has taken the task of jailor to bare toes.

Today, Whitetail needs to fix the impossible. If she releases Hyena, granting her sister her wish to be cast out into the cold light of day with the marble that would let her air the names of the wrongly dead, she'll get the rest of Whitetail's little family killed in the Dirty extermination it would bring. Blackhoods, roving Freemen puritans, blackcoat police confederates, and stranglers, haunted and guilty, would be at their door in an instant. Dirtiness alone would condemn her coven. Her family would be dead before any interrogations over having harbored a terrorist like Hyena occurred. Worse, the voices of the murdered, concealed in the

Necrology, would be perhaps forever silenced if Hyena were killed before having the chance to air them. And the world would never have 'Librium. Someday will be the right time for Hyena to be free. But right now, the Dirty numbers are too small to make gains. More death might eradicate them as a kind entirely. As it stands, their dwindling troops are relegated to woodland shadows, disbanded in foreign countries.

If Whitetail keeps guard of Hyena and the Necrology, she'll be burdened with this pregnant appearance. The way she looks right now will sabotage any sympathy or dreaded engagement to Andrews Jr. this afternoon and force her eviction. She'll lose the house and the children. *My children.*

Whitetail feels her sister chuckle, like irritating gas under her ribs. The delivery is cruel. Hyena's been listening to her thoughts again.

Let me go, then. Hyena's voice is quiet but stern. *I'm tired. I'll disappear, I'll hide, I'll keep the list of dead safe. Please.*

The sun is sinking. She dares not hope that Andrews isn't coming. She'd gotten the telegram. Eventually, he'll be here. His carriage driver is weaving him through the redeveloped remains of what was once her tiny village, the children's hometown, the town never re-formed after the great fire that sought to destroy Hyena. The fire that subsequently resulted in no one, certainly not the children's parents, left alive to petition the Andrews empire's A&O railway lines.

Andrews Jr. is about to see what he wants to when he looks at her swollen belly. There'll be no disguising it this time with dress or positioning. Last visit, he asked her to marry him. Strong-armed her by saying he'd need a commitment to let her stay. When she bluntly turned him down, he was sour. She doubts there'll be any reasoning with him. Belly aside, her antlers are a permanent fixture thanks to her muddying balance. After years of warning the children against ever playing Sixty-Three alone, she'd boldly gone and done the very thing and begged the wilds for the ability to contain Hyena after her own death. Hyena leached a little more of her energy every day. And soon, there would be no energy left. A sunset would cue Whitetail's passing. Only the wilds could grant a dying woman the power to hold her sister after her own death.

The wilds delivered beloved little Mouse on the orphanage's doorstep, but simultaneously cursed Whitetail with antlers. Velvety, the length of a goat's horn and growing, they are unmaskable and bring increasingly painful headaches. She hopes her lifelong commitment to the Dirt will offset the imbalance she's brought. The abomination the wilds have delivered in Mouse is curious. Whitetail can't decide if her prayers have been answered, or if she's invited a nightmare.

I'll disappear, I'll hide. Please.

Hyena's lying, of course. Whitetail knows she has no intention of staying quiet or playing the long game. "Keeping *you* safe is what needs to be done. It's difficult for both of us," Whitetail says aloud.

Ha! Hyena's deep, angry laugh wells up into Whitetail's mouth and into her ears, hollow like a jar. *Ugly and stupid. You don't have the right to hold me. What do you know of easy? I sit here, caged. It goes against the will of the wilds, keeping me prisoner. I've served the Dirt. Always. There's no good time for a revolution, there's just a time. Why delay it?*

Whitetail raises her chin and steels her resolve. "There's more than just you and me at stake, and you know it. You're right; history, truth will need to be told. But timing is everything. What's the point of speaking if the world's not ready to listen? I lose you, and all the sacrifices the Dirty have made to keep one another safe will have been in vain. We wait—the prophecy waits—for the beast who will bring the change. It's the least deadly path." She'd seen bloodshed in the stars. Potential for harm to the children too. If only the future were immutable, and she had the whole picture.

Fool. You're a woman of faith but have none in me. The change can't come to fruition if you're actively working to subdue it.

"You, dear sister, are a beast, not *the* beast." Neither was Whitetail. Their mother clarified this point repeatedly to her dying day. Her consultation of the stars had been thorough.

The truce has long been broken, why—why tamp a flame to save some leaves when the tree is actively being felled? Truth finds a way. Keep me, and a change will still blow. Keep a secret too long, and it will make a hole and find a way. I'll claw a way . . . Hyena's voice crackles. There's a growl.

Whitetail is struck by a terrible pain in her stomach. Like a wringing towel, her gut twists, and she staggers. Holding the table's edge, she waits for the pain to subside, only it doesn't. Her head throbs and as she lowers her chin, grunting in search of air, she feels the antlers' weight on her neck. She's exhausted.

"Stop. Please," Whitetail whispers. Her gut flinches in pain again.

Then let me go. Let me out. Or I'll . . . Hyena's fervid laugh bubbles painfully in Whitetail's ears before she opens her mouth, and it slips out.

Hyena's words stop Whitetail's heart. Her sister's sadness brings tears to her eyes and makes her hands shake. Hyena has always been difficult. Even though close, they have never gotten along, and Whitetail regrets the deterioration of their relationship. She did love her sister.

Hyena delivers another blow to Whitetail's gut before rattling up into her chest and throat, choking her.

I can't stay here. I'll not stay. Hyena's voice grows more frantic and higher pitched. *Change only comes from change. You can't stop what the wilds have meant to be in me.*

Whitetail's frozen until the neigh of a horse outside startles them both. Hyena rattles her way back down to Whitetail's stomach, and with a groan, she rolls over.

Leaving the counter, Whitetail sees through the front window that a carriage has stopped at the road. *He* has already descended the carriage stair. Turning to appraise the property, he starts up the walk toward the house. His sign, his territory.

There are, Whitetail notes, no flowers in his hand this time. His steps up the path speak of a mission. Her heart falls as she breathlessly wishes for a miracle. That he's found another paramour. But as a hand pats his coat's breast pocket, she knows. He's still looking for the right answer.

Will you marry me?

As the screen door opens with a squeal, Andrews Jr. brushes his shoes on the doormat, then marches into the front hall.

"I'm here." In an instant of his calling, his cologne wafts down the hall and under her nose, making her gag.

"Ms. Elizabeth?" She loathes him for calling her that. After the fire, men from New York City gave her the surname Whittle out of frustration. While settling the papers for Andrews House, the men dug, almost interrogating. *Well, what are ya? You Munsee? Or Mohican?* She's none of these. She's from the Dirt, and that's the only explanation she'd given them, though they stubbornly refused to believe it. Elizabeth Whittle is not her name. It's just a name that makes Mr. John Andrews Jr. feel more comfortable around her.

Though he ought not be.

Chapter 4

I'm Here

Mr. Andrews," Whitetail responds, shoulders falling as she fills a clay cup with water from a pitcher. "I'll be right with you." Her voice, despite her want to seem cheery, comes out lifeless. She feels a cold ache in her chest. A floorboard groans underfoot as she idles a beat. With any luck, he'll find her utterly repulsive and not ask for her hand. She isn't sure why he ever wanted her in the first place.

He is wealthy. The heir to the A&O railway, no less. Handsome, young, and likely fawned over by many a beautiful shadow willing to lurk in his wake. She? She smokes. Prefers pants. She's never been made up. Never worn gloves except mittens for the cold, and never found use at any meal for more cutlery than a knife and spoon. The children are the only thing that saves her from scandal. After all, she's not a mother, a wife, or any relation to God. She lives alone with no man for assistance. And assists no man. She spends as much time teaching the little girls at Andrews angling, farming, and gathering as showing them how to cut or sew—women's work, as Freemen call it. It is all work in her mind—man's, woman's; around here it's simply what needs to be managed.

As she walks around the corner and into the parlor, she finds him standing, not sitting as she instructed.

43

"No," he gasps.

His smiling eyes and high chin sink as he looks her over. A handkerchief lies across his palm with a gold band set with an achromatic stone displayed on top. Aventurine, the concealer's stone, she notes. Quickly wrapping the handkerchief around the ring, he retracts his arm and tucks the ring into his coat's breast pocket. His mouth is a hard line of fury.

She extends the cup of water in his direction.

"I say—" He ignores her offering. His eyes flit from her extended stomach up to her antlers and back again. "What is this?" The pain in his eyes is undeniable. She pities him because he's stupid, but pathetic as he may be, he's still dangerous.

"Welcome, Mr. Andrews." She looks at the glass and offers it up. "Would you like some water?"

"Sorry?" He blinks with irritation.

She raises the glass higher. "Would you like to inspect the residence, or just the property?" She waves a hand at the lawn strewn with dead leaves beyond the windows as she sets the glass down carefully on a small unvarnished table at the end of the sofa. Nearby is a collection of fairy books, entertainment for the children once donated by well-meaning Freemen. Though she refuses to read them, she's decided that the kids' literacy, fostered by Snake, is an acceptable growth.

He blinks at her stomach.

"You're a monster. You—you—*cow!* You whore." He looks at her bulging belly again and blows out a chest full of exasperation. His mouth trembles with helpless fury.

Ignoring him, she tries to press on. "I can assure you the orphanage and its tiny residents"—she gulps at the sight of Mr.

Andrews's face reddening—"are flourishing . . ." Her voice falls off as heat rises to her cheeks.

He hates her now. Hates her just as much as she hates him.

His lungs full again, he lets loose, "You're disgusting. Your head . . ." His mouth trembles. "Come here." Dropping his black hat onto the couch, he walks toward her. She takes a cautious step back. She's never shied from confrontation in her life, but there is much at stake here. As not to engage him, she looks at the floor, ignoring his proximity.

"Get over here." Grabbing her by both biceps, he picks her up and holds her aloft, inspecting her. "Look at me."

She gives in. His eyes are wild and his mouth drawn. Whatever empathy she once felt for him blows away with his breath grazing her cheek. She eyes him. *He's half drunk.* A drink to build nerve, perhaps, or in celebration of his perceived accomplishment?

"Such. A. Shame." He drops her like his hands have been burned. "Such a goddamned, bloody shame." He spins once, taking in the room. He lifts his hands up, smoothing back his disheveled, greased hair. "Was this . . . all to avoid my proposal? This was not our arrangement."

The only arrangement they ever spoke of was him building this roof and posting the sign on the lawn with his family's name on it in return for her getting to keep the children safe. Subtext wasn't something she felt accountable for here. Why the Freemen have such a hard time understanding the third Dirty consent—*Don't become confused over what's yours*—when it would be so easily remembered if they had any respect for the fourth: *If you're confused over what's yours, ask!*

He comes in close again and her back goes rigid. She sets her jaw in a clench so he won't see it trembling.

"Your intention is to make a fool of me, is it? Cast a spell, make me fall in love with you. Give you . . ." His chest heaves, and he drops his head. "All of this, all that you wanted." He looks around at the orphanage walls. "You're a Dirty con woman."

Dirty? Unmistakably. Not that he even knows half the whole truth. But conning? No.

Although she'd known all along Jr. was sweet on her, the development of Andrews House was more of a strategic play from him and his family than any swindle on her part. Thousands of acres' land rights were being disputed before the fire in Roscoe. Andrews, A&O, wanted to build a rail line, and locals wanted to keep their homesteads, not be relocated. But after all the defiant homesteaders died, collateral damage in the Roscoe fire, what citizen would protest orphan's housing funded and built by the rail company? Would condemn the raising of a roof over their precious, motherless heads? Jr.'s being smitten with Whitetail had nothing to do with his family manipulating what little was left of a distant community, and certainly nothing to do with the promise she'd made to the children's parents that she'd keep them safe.

She knew the day they met who Andrews Jr. was. Who his father is—the most influential man in the country. The orphanage being erected in the Andrews name meant the Andrews family laid claim to the ruins of Roscoe and this plot of Blackmoor territory. With the children living here, the Andrews family had less friction over land rights.

"My wants have always been simple. To care for the children.

I am grateful for all—"

"Your gratitude was supposed to be proven in your marriage to me!" he snaps. Pausing a moment, he takes out the handkerchief from his pocket and mops his brow. The ring topples out of it, rolling onto the rug. Face red, eyes glassy, he looks lost. Silence fills the room.

"I'm married to the children, then after they're grown, to myself alone."

"*To me!*" he screams, stomping a foot, making the glass of water on the end table tremble. Rattled, unsure of what to do, Whitetail walks briskly toward the kitchen to escape him. *Let him leave with some dignity.*

Instead, he follows her.

His hulking stance speaks of battle. In the kitchen, he flips over her table, breaking her large handmade clay bowl and spilling all her goat's milk and the potatoes she'd been scrubbing across the floor.

Whitetail turns her back on him. Covering her mouth with a fraught hand, she leans over the hearth and wills the wilds to intervene. *Make him go.* She's so tired. Too tired for this. Heart racing, her anxiety courses through her hands, and they shake. After taking a deep breath, she conceals them in her pockets.

"I am grateful," Whitetail whispers. "I am grateful." And she is. Her chest heaves as her mouth summons foreign words. "You're a good man," she says, trying to smooth. She's grasping at hairs. Due to her lifestyle, placating isn't a skill she's ever needed to hone. It feels harder than swallowing rocks. Impossible, even.

Hyena releases a loud gurgle out of Whitetail's chest, then a burst of laughter erupts from Whitetail's mouth. She wants to reach for the mantle over the fireplace before her, but her arm is not hers anymore.

"What?" Andrews says. "What's so funny?"

She feels him at her back. The light shifts in the room and with it, her weight. She feels lead-heavy and immobile. Whitetail's never felt so caged in all her life. She doesn't want to turn around. But slowly, by someone else's want, she does, grinding clay chips of her broken bowl into the floorboards with her hard-calloused bare feet.

Mr. Andrews stands hulking, vibrating with rage. Greased hair's hanging low in his eyes. His coat's disheveled. He's sweating. Looking her up and down, he licks his lips. Darting forward a step, he slaps her across the face so hard her cheekbone feels broken, and she wonders momentarily if she's lost an eye.

"It runs in your veins," Hyena stammers between Whitetail's clenched teeth. "Just like your father. The fear. Like a disease. Fear that someone won't be there to flatter you at the end of the day. Serve you. That you'll have no one to support you without them being obligated to you. That you might have to stand on your own two feet and be happy with your own decisions and accomplishments without a trophy on your arm as proof of it to other men. Someone to always nod when you ask. To dominate when you want. You can't stand how we look or act because you fear us. You can't have us."

"Have you lost your—I say, you look like a ghoul!"

"Even looking like a ghoul, you still don't deserve us," Hyena growls, her voice animal. "You don't get to have us."

Mr. Andrews launches, pushing her backward toward the fireplace. As Whitetail bangs her head on the mantle, knickknacks and kitchenware slip. Her giant cast-iron pan crashes to the floor with a *clang*. Her Sixty-Three board slides off the shelf from behind it and smashes on the floor, too, some of its wood fibers disintegrating at an edge. Scanning, she sees some of the children's markers, but no die. No twist of Rook's wood. No piece of Rabbit's slate. *No!* She should have been watching the children more closely. What have they done?

As Mr. Andrews spots the board, recognizing it, his face pales, and his chest heaves. "I should have known. How could I not have known you were Dirty?"

As he mutters to himself, Whitetail fights to regain control of her own body. Only half-accomplishing smoothing her apron.

"You witch!" As he turns, he punches Whitetail in the face and then beats her chest with the side of his fist. "I loved you. I loved you, you Dirty witch!"

As she collapses on the floor, she scrambles for footing, but his fists keep her down. She's helpless. Paralyzed by her anger over her lack of action. But what wouldn't she physically survive if it meant saving those children? Her spirit can endure anything if it means they're safe.

He takes a minute to watch her, perhaps waiting for tears that never come. His chest heaving, he unbuttons his jacket. Cumbersomely, he goes down on his knees and climbs on top of her, grunting, his teeth bared. He puts one forearm over her arms overhead. His other hand is free.

She asks herself what she's done to deserve this. The answer is nothing.

He single-handedly pulls her apron aside and pulls down her pants, then begins prying at her undergarments. His weight on top of her is suffocating, and her belly hurts. It feels as though Hyena is squeezing to stuff into her lungs.

"P—" Whitetail breathlessly searches for what she wants to say. "*Pha!*" She'll not ask for forgiveness. For mercy. She can't. Not even to save herself because it would be a lie. She'd like to explain that it was Hyena disrespecting him just now, not her. But it would just confirm his opinion, that she is nothing but Dirt.

As he gets his own trousers down, there's a sickening bang. It's a singular thunderous *clang*, the noise of which makes Whitetail wince. She spots a hand. Her hand. *No!*

The silence is deafening, and it takes what feels like an eternity for time to click back into anything like regular. Whitetail tries to summon some breath.

Mr. Andrews looks dumbfounded as it comes into view, his face changing from red fury to surprise as he sits back up on his knees, shakily scanning the room, his chest still heaving. Quickly and gingerly he raises a hand to the back of his head. Whitetail drops the cast-iron pan in her hand, letting it fall to the floor. With Mr. Andrews's weight off her chest, she can breathe again.

Mr. Andrews's jaw falls open and as he tests it, stunned, his eyes close a moment. She can see how pained he is. Clumsily he staggers to his feet and slowly unfurls to standing. Again, he lifts a hand to feel the back of his head. Blood marks his shaking fingertips when they come away. His shoulder is crimson, and there is a light tapping noise. Blood is cascading to the floor. Adjusting himself, he re-buttons his jacket and smooths the hair off his slick forehead.

Something moves at the windowsill. The light in the room changes. Whitetail sees them. The children. They've come home against orders. Their eyes are round, and their mouths hang open with fear. Mr. Andrews sways unstably, then squints, looking at the window, then down at her, still lying there on the floor, apron divided. He tucks his shirt back into his trousers, and his lip trembles furiously.

"Whitetail?" Rook whispers as Whitetail slowly gets up off the floor.

Her head's pounding. Whitetail's entire body rumbles as she seeks control. *Hyena's power.* Whitetail has never experienced her take over like that before. Make her say something, do something she didn't want to do—would never have done. It leaves her feeling so, so powerless. Whitetail shoots a hand out for a tea towel. Snatching it up, she hands it to Mr. Andrews to help with his bleeding.

"Don't hurt me," his voice squeaks. He flinches as she comes close.

Whitetail's chest fills with pain. After a warning look at the children, they fall away from the window, and she notes the peepers along the river have stopped chirping.

"Let me—" she urges, offering the tea towel.

But with a quick turn, Mr. Andrews does an about-face. Blood is visibly running down the back of his neck into his shirt collar. He disappears from the kitchen. She follows him to the living room where he snatches his hat. He carries it in his hand as he marches for the front door.

The front door squeals as it opens. Slams on his way out.

Falling to her knees, she prays to the wilds, but she just can't hear them answer.

Chapter 5

What Evil's in This Place?

R abbit knows what she saw from the window. Him on top of her. She'd seen frogs coupling, dragonflies, too, but this was not joyous as those instances had been. Mr. Andrews was trying to hurt Whitetail. Steal part of her spirit. When he did, Whitetail's face turned dark and corroded. The black of her fingers spread up her wrists and forearms. Her arm holding the pan bent at an unnatural angle. Her mouth twisted, and for a second, Rabbit thought she was going to explode with an inexplicable pressure. Rabbit has never seen anything like it before.

Rook drops the stick he's been carrying into the dead, brown grass and leaves it at his feet. Idling on the lawn below the window ledge, he looks lost.

"You go tend to Ms.," he says to the others. "Get her up. Help her right that kitchen. Go around the back way now, you hear? He's coming out the front."

Rabbit understands from Rook's darting finger that she is not included in these directions.

"Okay," all the girls say as they scatter.

Rabbit is certain they did not see what she and Rook had at the window. Quickly they scuttle around the back of the house,

52

disappearing with purposeful steps. With marching orders, as Whitetail calls them.

Rook's hands grip his waist hem anxiously. "You and me, we'll go tell the Beard not to come back again, or else." Rabbit knew just as much as Rook that Whitetail dismissed this plan earlier.

But what else could be done?

"All right." She feels electric. Rook's plan is better than no plan, and he is an ally, as Whitetail always said.

Following Rook around the side of the house to the front yard, they catch up to the Beard quickly. He's shaking and disheveled, wandering off-kilter down the path toward the road. Toward his carriage. Rook snatches up a large rock and hurls it, knocking the man in the calf.

He stumbles.

Rook hurls another rock. This one beans the man in the back. "Don't you come back here!" he warns.

The Beard pauses. Whether it is renewed composure or the recognition of these small-scale avengers, he looks at the two of them with a flash of fire in his eyes.

Rabbit's bold steps cease, and she stops in her tracks, hesitant to get too close. She hadn't expected him to turn around. She realizes just how close she is to him.

Rook stands poised, knees bent, ready to run as he glares at the Beard. The Beard could never catch him, and he knows it. Rook stoops, grabs another rock, and tosses it hand to hand, a scrappy look on his face.

"That name up there yours, boy?" Beard asks.

Rook keeps his stance but eyes the sign.

"This—" As Beard's eyes scan the building, he seems at a loss for words. "This—" He stands, hulking. "This—" He looks down searchingly for the driver, who is waiting, obliviously engrossed with his pocket watch, by the carriage. Finally recalling his words, Beard spews them. "This is *my* place. Don't you forget it." His eyes flit down to Rabbit. Chest heaving, his face freezes.

He is pale, and his eyes are dark. He's still huge and scary, but clearly disoriented. Disabled. Rabbit forces a smirk onto her face.

"You son of a Freemen!" she says. "Git!"

Rabbit feels victory is upon them all. The Beard is leaving, told off and wounded, hopefully never to return. As he lunges, taking a threatening step in her direction, Rabbit darts back a hop, and, laughing playfully, turns around. A look to Rook says she's taunting the man just enough. But then Rook's eyes grow round.

She hasn't got time enough to even fully turn around before the Beard catches her by the throat. Lifted up by her neck, she hangs. Her legs try to kick him, but they mostly dangle. Her hands, her nails, can't fight him; they only grip his wrists. The weight of her shoulders stretching her neck hurts like fire.

"*Guk*" is all she gets out. *Rook!* She wriggles like a lagomorph.

"Let 'er go!" Rook screams from farther back in the yard.

"Sir?" The driver who was waiting by the road is now on the lawn. "Mr. Andrews!" he says indignantly. The man's eyes narrow when he sees Rabbit's predicament.

But the Beard's eyes stay trained on hers. There is pressure behind her eyes, and the sound of her pulse in her ears. She can't breathe, and he knows it. He knows he's got her. She tells herself war is wrong. *It's amazing what the spirit can cope with to preserve the body. My spirit is a mighty oak that just won't fall.* She's certainly succumbing to the lack of breath left in her chest and so, as Whitetail has instructed, instead of fighting for her spirit to remain whole, she sacrifices some and lets her arms dangle limply at her sides to show him she gives up. She sees the evil in his eyes. Anger in his jaw. He is a monster. Ms. always warned her, she'd need to spot a mean man before he got her. Blackness fills Rabbit's vision.

She wakes up dizzy on the ground. As she peers up, her eyes struggle to make out the light, the trees, and the Beard. He kicks dirt on her, some of it landing in her mouth, before he walks away. Rolling over, she rubs her throat and summons courage. Stubbornly, she feels she can't let him walk away. Not after what he's done to Whitetail. To her. No matter Whitetail's teaching her to always step aside for the sake of the family's safety. Rook is standing over her, watching the Beard's back as he walks away. Rook helps her to stand, and she sees stars.

Any man who hurts me shall forever be looking over his shoulder. Rabbit's eyes narrow. She once heard Whitetail utter these words.

He doesn't turn around. He simply staggers after the driver, who occasionally looks back over his shoulder. At her. At Rook. At the Beard.

"Winterland's curse is upon you," Rabbit croaks, her voice gone. Having to sacrifice a sliver of her spirit for the sake of a breath just hadn't been worth it. The screen door opens behind her, and someone's on the porch.

With her utterances, the Beard stumbles. After another step, he falls with a thud, flat on his front in the grass. His face lies offside, askew at a terrible angle. The wind whistles through the trees around them, and the sun has almost set. The Beard doesn't move again. Rabbit's posture, poised for a fight, isn't necessary. Something's happened.

Aghast, the pale, stumbling driver circles back to kneel beside the Beard. After trying to right him, the driver only gets the Beard rolled onto his back. The Beard's face is white as the moon. His eyes are vacant.

"What have you done, children? What have you done?" the driver asks. His eyes widen at Rabbit.

Rook takes a step forward and grabs Rabbit by the wrist. They move a step closer to the Beard, to the driver.

"Back!" the driver hollers. "You get back! Stay back!" He slowly drags the Beard toward the buggy down the lane. After arduously dumping the Beard's limp body in the back, he turns to look back at the house, at the windows. His eyes never cease their darting.

"You've killed him! You Dirty wraiths!" His eyes scan the porch, then the house's windows and roof. As his eyes settle back on the porch, he whimpers.

Rabbit looks up at the porch to see what he sees. It's Whitetail. She's emerged from indoors, surrounded by the other girls, who've all laid their hands on Whitetail's folded arms. The other children look like ghosts with big black eyes shining through the near dark. The mud they're still covered in from the river has dried white. Rabbit's struck by an overwhelming, inexplicable fear. She's never had a marker-free curse work before. Is she ready to read hair? The Beard looks . . . He looks . . . Dead.

The world is quiet save for the wind that's tireless. Rabbit's knees are shaking, not from cold but sadness and shock.

"Leave this place," Whitetail commands. Mouse peers from behind her skirt like a mini-Whitetail.

The driver's horses prance as the driver climbs back into his carriage. They take a step back as the cab lurches back a foot. He turns, tears in his eyes.

"It's not Andrews House, it's the devil's house," he says, snapping his horse's reins.

"It's my house," Whitetail says, though the carriage is out of view, sprinting for town.

Chapter 6

By the Fire

All evening, Whitetail has kept her eyes trained out the window and her ear on the road. So far, there's been no coming horses. Policemen, crooked blackcoats. Dinner was just a few potatoes and broth. It's what the children could make on their own. They're cleaning up nearby. Unstacking plates, they wash each in a tub. Everyone except Rabbit, who's still staring at her plate. What happened between Hyena and Mr. Andrews earlier was damning for them all.

Her appearance, the driver's furtive glares at the house, at the children, a dead man riding home in his cart—this would surely shift tides and draw the attention of authorities and Freemen. Still, she can't bring herself to reprimand the child. Rabbit's glumly set the die she'd apparently borrowed earlier on the table and is staring at it. Had she made mud?

Hyena's aware of Whitetail's stress. Like an eel, she rolls over in the shadows of Whitetail's ribcage, pressing against her lungs, making it difficult for her to breathe.

"You didn't eat, Ms.," Mouse says, her dark eyes gazing up at Whitetail where she stands by the window.

Whitetail can only smile as she stoops. The little girl reaches up from her tippy toes to press her small, cool hand against the hot spot on Whitetail's cheek. It still throbs where Mr. Andrews slapped her. He'd knocked out one of her teeth too, for summer's sake. It still sits in her pocket, and she plans to bury it in the garden after dark as a gift back to the Dirt.

"Let's sit," she says to the room. Whitetail slides her chair toward the hearth. Hyena doesn't like the fire, of course. Terrible memories. And regardless, it usually irritates Whitetail's legs through her slacks. Keeping cool typically helps Whitetail feel young and responsible for her own spark, but tonight she is all but withered to dust and needs to steal the fire's pulse. Oh, how her bones ache over what's occurred and what it will bring. Whitetail will use what little freedom she's got left here and now to choose: cool or warm. To contain Hyena and converse with the wonderful children she swore to keep safe all those years back. She's not sure how much time they'll have left together.

These children are still spring's cherry blossoms. So very young. These gentle buds would all be withering in the coming season. The children's roles, with tides turning, would take years to prove as good or evil. She'd taught each of them of 'Librium, the possibility of equality in the world among all things, and would leave them to prove whether they could solve balance, achieve 'Librium in their lifetimes. She'd schooled them but neglected to warn that some of them would die for or against this cause. She's not a fortune teller, it's just the law of finding 'Librium—justice's scales can't level themselves without both sides losing some.

"Did your mama have antlers, Ms.?" Mouse asks innocently. Climbing onto Whitetail's lap, she rests a small hand on hers. Together they rock lightly.

"No, my mother didn't have antlers," Whitetail says. When she asked the wilds for help to contain Hyena after her own death, she'd been blessed or cursed, not only with Mouse, but this crown.

"Why are they growing larger each day?" Mouse asks.

"I can't say for sure. But my mother grew all the more magical as she reached summer. When she died, she was the most powerful woman I've known."

"Will you become as powerful as her? Before you die and go to summer? These tell of your magic?"

"Again, I can't say. Depends how long I live, perhaps. My mother lived to one hundred and forty-nine. That was a rarity, but I'm older than that now. So maybe my journey to my ideal is needing more steps, and these will help." In a world where each man casts a shadow, devout Dirt have always lived to the long length of early evening's light. If devotion to the wilds, piety, and a purpose means a slowing of a person's seasons, she's been living but one season a year. Her longevity in this realm matters little compared to her want to persevere as the children's guardian.

"You're like a mother to us," Mouse says.

"Yes," Pea says, her heavy expression beaming with sincerity.

Whitetail pauses a moment, lost in thought. "When I think of my mother, I think of magic. I remember her hands, bony and marked by sun scars from working in the river. She was of the Dirt and stayed true to it until her dying day."

"And your papa?" Pheasant whispers from across the room. Whitetail hopes the girl's shyness won't be an obstacle in her future.

"My father?" She's surprised by the question. "I had one, I suppose, but never that I knew. My mother always claimed me and Hyena came to her like a crack of thunder from a very nice man who was fun for a night, not a lifetime. Born on either side of the leap day amidst a storm, we've always been so different from one another." She pats her stomach. "Some children are born of husbands, others by free-spirited women, children. You'll learn that in time." She raises her eyebrows.

Mouse looks in Rabbit's direction. Rabbit's still sitting at the table with her back to the rest. Whitetail can't help the corners of her mouth turning up. Funny how the two seemingly bonded today. Mouse crosses her arms in disappointment that her new friend is sitting elsewhere.

"Her mother died too," Mouse says about Rabbit with a somber whisper. She looks down at the ground thoughtfully. "But not my mother, right?"

"Right." As a paradox, Whitetail's unsure who she'd consider Mouse's mother to be, or whether they're dead. "The wilds never die." It's all Whitetail can admit. *The issue of Rabbit's parents is, perhaps, more complicated still.*

Rook scowls.

Whitetail smiles at Rook, cueing him to calm down. He understands that speaking of death and loved ones can be difficult. He's protective of Whitetail. And of Rabbit.

A dish smashes on the floor as Dove fails to pass it to Pheasant. Pheasant's skittish on a good day, but today her hazel eyes water with stress. The girl's scared of her own reflection.

Whitetail feels Hyena rattle around in her chest with irritation at the loud noise, letting loose an exasperated staccato laugh. Whitetail's hands shake uncontrollably a moment, and she realizes it's Hyena taking hold again. Hyena's never liked the children, and the plate falling seems to have made her edgy. Whitetail's hand inexplicably raises, and she struggles for control. Her fingers curl, hand balls into a fist behind Mouse's head. Biting her lip, she tries to curb the sudden want to violently grab Mouse's hair. To hurt her. Whitetail's eyes tear. Preoccupied little Mouse is *like* a daughter to her, unlike the others.

She loves them all, would die for them, but Mouse is different.

Pheasant carefully takes Rabbit's plate, the last to be cleared. Placing a comforting hand on Rabbit's shoulder, she offers grace. Her hazel eyes stare into an unknown space a few moments before she returns to her chore.

Rabbit remains at the table, seated alone. Rabbit hadn't even touched her dinner, though she's usually the first one done, unless it's turnip. Born hungry. She ate solids young. Her teeth came in at just a month old. Whitetail remembers because she was there, holding the baby in her arms. She was carrying Rabbit in circles, trying to comfort her teething the night she smelled smoke, the night of the fire. Oh, how her teeth just had to be free.

Breathing deeply, Whitetail feels Hyena's rage simmer down and her awful impulse ebb.

"You're an orphan too? Like us, Whitetail?" Dove asks, as she clears the broken plate with a broom. Her thick digits grip the floor brush handle as she sweeps. Stooping with sturdy legs, her wavy blonde mop cascades in her face. She blows it away from her eyes with a puff.

The subject of abandonment brings Pheasant to sit near Whitetail's feet at the hearth.

Rabbit looks back over her shoulder at Mouse, at Whitetail, then back to her own lap.

"Pheasant, your parents were lovely folk. Hornby's Liquors was a favorite spot of mine. It was a little shop. I would buy whisky from your parents' store once a year on the anniversary of my mother's death so that I could sip it and talk with her in the dark pasture under the stars." Her mother would come to her on a chilly breeze and together they'd recall the old days.

Pheasant and Goose were six months old at the time of the fire. Bear, currently pulling faces from the corner, trying to get Rook's goat, hardly older. But Rook, now twelve, Pea, and Rat, each eleven, occasionally spoke of their parents. Sometimes with correct details, other times with fantasies that would make Whitetail chuckle to herself.

"After a certain age, we're all orphans," Dove says across the room, tossing the shards of broken plate in a bucket, then flopping down on the floor. Rook moves a trout's length to his right to make more room for her.

Whitetail unbraids Mouse's ratty hair, first combing it with her fingers, then re-braiding it for her. Chores complete, the rest of the children sit by her feet like chicken feathers clinging to her slacks.

"Is it always summer in summerland, Ms.?" Pheasant asks.

Snake had always been so harsh on Pheasant. Though Whitetail is sad Snake's gone, and without her actual name, she is comforted that Pheasant will have the chance to come into her own. Without Snake, Pheasant isn't being bossed around.

"Not the hot-as-heck part of summer, but the warm breeze and sweetgrass part, yes. After the Grimm decides you're ready to rest, you're delivered."

Pea tilts her head at the back of the group. "Who goes to winter?" she asks quietly. Resting her long, thin face in a pale hand, her freckles and red hair glow like embers.

Rook turns around. "The bad people, like Freemen government. Stranglers and military who've murdered; blackcoats, police who enforce the unjust law; blackhoods who are cruel to the Dirt—they hold persons down, so they go down. Dragged into the ice and cold forever."

"How does the Grimm know who's good and bad? You always say we're born set for summer. How does he know which person is set for winter?" Pea asks, her voice a little louder now. As with all the children's futures, she worries for Pea's. Curiosity, fact-checking, can so easily be misconstrued as interrogation. Nowadays, asking questions can get you killed.

"Well, Rook's mostly right. Not all Freemen are necessarily delivered to winter. Not if they don't know their own ignorance. It's the conscious effort to hurt others that damns you. Ignorance is damaging, but forgivable. Some women, vultures, women against women, get sent to winter. In the end, it's your intentions versus damage."

"What if someone makes a mistake?" Mouse asks, touching Whitetail's hot cheek again before looking across the room at Rabbit.

Rabbit's cursing Jr. was a big mistake. Perhaps so was Whitetail's holding Hyena this long.

"Does the mistake hurt someone?" Whitetail clarifies.

Mouse nods, yes.

"And the mistake has been made with malice in the heart?"

Mouse shrugs, then nods again. "But you're a very good girl otherwise," she says. She curiously rubs, then pats Whitetail's hand in a comforting way. It dawns on Whitetail that, although she and Mouse can both read the stars, one doesn't always see what the other sees. If every woman is unique, each stargazer is too. If all the women in the world united, they'd see their future as a whole. But until then, she'd have to accept fragments.

"It would be for the Grimm to decide. Sometimes the Grimm must call it. Some bad, some good, the Grimm calls it. Steal from this man, give to those men, save a cat, but throw stones at a bear; burned at the stake so the Grimm can't smell your soul definitively? Then he calls it. Then for those who have no spirit left to sort, it gets even more complicated."

Mouse's bottom lip pops out, and she looks at her lap. "No spirit!"

"You think Beard has enough spirit to be sorted?" Rabbit glumly gets up from the dinner table, finally coming to join Mouse and the others. She's left the die behind on the table like a peace or penance offering. Mouse climbs off Whitetail's lap, choosing now to sit in Rabbit's.

"Will the Beard haunt me for my curse before I die and go to winter?" Tears well up in her eyes, but she doesn't cry. *Rabbit's always been so strong.*

"Indeed, it's true," Whitetail says. "Ghosts rise from the murdered and run from the Grimm, Rabbit. He'll not catch them until they've had their injustice heard by the living. But Mr.—" She couldn't say his name. His family's history. His parents. She dared not weigh in on what this all meant for Rabbit. "He had but a seed remaining of an apple. I don't believe we'll see his spirit in summer."

Either way, in Freemen's terms, summer meant deliverance by a horned psychopomp named Death to Father John's knee and being permitted to sit quietly in a black room called After.

"Besides him hurting Rabbit, he acted out against the September truce," Rook clarifies to the room. "He was going to hurt you, Ms." The sorrow in Rook's eyes makes Whitetail's chest swell. He's paid attention all these years.

"Even Mad Dog, if she were alive today, would have commended your actions." Rook wipes frustration from his eyes and looks at Rabbit, who's slouching, head bowed in shame.

Rook's the most sympathetic boy Whitetail's ever known. She trusts he will grow up and make her proud.

"Mad Dog," Pea barely whispers in adoration. "Your mother's mother."

Whitetail smiles at Pea's awe. "You remember my grandmother's story?" Whitetail asks. "How she stepped down as the last Omega?"

"She signed the truce," Mouse says, puffing her chest up with pride. A mannerism unmistakably like the one Whitetail's just made.

"Mmm." Whitetail nods. "Her signature was supposed to bring 'Librium."

"Promised Dirt would stop their magic because it was too scary for blackcoats." Pheasant almost whispers it as her dark eyebrows raise behind her curls.

Mouse pouts a moment before she leans back, settling into Rabbit's chest. Rabbit's forced to lift her chin and rest it on Mouse's shoulder.

Whitetail smooths her shirt over her enormous belly. Whitetail's sympathy for Mad Dog knows no bounds. The woman's taking the reins, signing the contract on behalf of all Dirty. It extinguished a powder keg. It was what the people wanted and her wife Tituba's, dying wish. It was strategy. Whitetail wants to devise the same. Hyena's war will be necessary—but Whitetail's unwilling to accept a body count. She's fallen in love with the children . . . *Maybe even more than the cause.* After Mad Dog resigned, no one rekindled the post as Omega. Dirty had become so scattered by then, there was no way to organize.

"And . . . since we've been Dirty," Pea admits from the back, "we've broken the truce too?" Pea shrugs in apology as all eyes in the room fall on her. Though Whitetail's always preached truth, she's surprised by Pea's directness.

"Correct," Whitetail says, "but an entire history of women shouldn't be erased to keep 'Librium. If the wilds granted women magic, who are bitter men to will it away? How will future women know they are magical if no one tells them? It would be like telling people to eat with their palms when the wilds gave them fingers."

The children chuckle.

"How long's the world been imbalanced?" Mouse asks.

"Well, people have always worked together for their survival. But the day a person realized they were with child, the split happened that day. The day labors divided, and the wilds bestowed new power, magic to women, in recognition of their very arduous task: birthing man's most prized possessions."

"Children," Rook clarifies from the back.

Whitetail nods. "But a very few men, not all, or even most, grew jealous. These called out 'unequal power,' thinking it unfair they should support the privileged, not recognizing childcare as work. Blackbook ideology, with its religious trappings and rigid political hierarchy, was built around a single goal: control of inherent magic. Like poison, Freemen's book spread. Now, our government, America's current Alpha, Sanderson, is more a puppet advised by ghostly forefaders, wraith-remains of the country's forefathers, and their eldest living Freemen heir, the Supreme, than an actual leader. Sanderson may be elected by majority vote, but he's a pawn. It's the Supreme, the son of the Freemen—those who die clutching misogyny to their breasts, whispering, 'Rational thought before magical rot'—who is the actual law-leader of our nation.

"Someday, America will have a new order," she says. "Dirty dead will have their injustice heard by the living." Whitetail thinks of the Grimm once more.

As Whitetail rocks in her chair, gathering hard-to-find breath, she sees pain in Rook's eyes.

"There *are* Dirty male allies. Oh, yes," she says reassuringly. "Wonderfully good men, but they live in fear. As they should. Holesome Prison is a bitter winter here on earth. Most professed Dirty men in this country wind up in jail for heresy. The others are unwilling to step out of the shadows for the cause. Because shadows are safe. Not only do these men feel magic is not their battle to fight, they also have no stakes to lose in the game; they've grown complacent and accustomed to the way things are. He makes his living. Goes home to a woman who treats him like a master. And his wife has all but forgotten the old ways. They've been told to wear shoes—shoes! Say it takes covering your neck to be a lady. *Poof!*" Whitetail's stamina falls off. "They've lost touch with their Dirt. Forgotten that Dirt need not benefit a man to be permitted. As simply women's nature, there can be no expectations of it—for her, for him, it simply always has been. And need not be regulated by outside forces."

"The Dirt owes us nothing. The magic can't be owned," Pheasant says, looking around the room for affirmation.

"The Dirt owes us nothing, and magic *can be* owned," Whitetail corrects her. "And worse, erased by unintentional forgetfulness or explicit lawmaking. Magic is owned by every woman. But in a world where Freemen own the Dirt, demand it bear them fruit, there is no balance. Laws over women will change, or we'll all be lost. Your natural self is magic, my loves."

She feels a pull in her chest, drawing her forward. Rigid with shock, a painful growl comes out of her mouth. Her voice slips out between clenched teeth. "For peace, power must be returned to where it was first stolen from. But Freemen would never allow— th-th-at until we use the Necrology to reveal the list of murdered, there will be no cha-ange, no ba-lance," Hyena painfully blurts in a low guttural voice. "There's no way to reconcile a future without recognizing the p-p-ast. And Freemen won't take part willingly-y. There will be a war."

The children stare a minute, their little mouths open. Eyes wide. Mouse jumps up and darts to hide behind Rabbit, who's looking unsure. The other children look around at each other, noting a change in Whitetail.

The room falls silent, save for the crackle of wet wood in the fireplace.

"I'm sorry," Whitetail whispers, a regretful hand on her chest.

Rabbit shifts uncomfortably. She looks at Rook.

"They say the Necrology is the very same marble mounted in the kept woman's staff." Rook is breathless. The Supreme's wife's cane has always been a point of fascination for Rook.

"Mmm. That's what they say." It is easier to let the children believe Freemen propaganda on the whereabouts of the Necrology than explain the stone being absorbed by Hyena, or Whitetail's determination to keep both locked away. The Freemen never publicly admitted after Hyena's so-called murder that the indestructible stone, fabled to be one of Sarah's rocks from parable fifty-eight of the Dirty texts, was never recovered.

Everyone assumes Freemen have it since no one's proved otherwise. Whitetail has no idea what stone is in the head of the Supreme's wife's cane. Or what happened to the Woodfeast.

Mad Dog's having handed over the Necrology when she signed the contract remains bitter fruit. The most powerful marble, an artifact containing all Dirty history, even magic from those long dead and those yet to be born—centuries, back and forth—was so painful a loss that Hyena demanded it be righted. If only Mad Dog had handed over alabaster when she signed the contract, anything else, knowing the Freemen wouldn't have been able to tell the difference. Although Hyena's stealing the Necrology from the catacombs of the Blackbox, the Freemen capital church in New

Amsterdam, was a well-intentioned endeavor, it had been reckless, costing innocents, these children's parents, their very lives.

"Remember, Dog signed the paper and handed over the marble and Wood, intending to keep us safe, not rid us of our entire identity," Whitetail says. "After Dog handed the Necrology and Woodfeast to the Freemen, she explained to our foremothers what her wife, Tituba, had prophesied: *The marble was precious. It emblemized our history. But our legacy is not lost. We're all children of Mother . . . a chip off the same block as her.* According to Dog, our mothers' mothers' ancestral power is accessible in every single one of us when we're born." Years after Tituba's death, Mad Dog birthed the daughter they'd always sought. Whitetail's mother.

Whitetail has no idea what the message means, or whether any part of her would produce a marble—birth a chip off the Necrology—would she ever consider willing it. But she's certain: the prophecy is true. "Same as the chip off the mother rock out back, you're a chip off your mothers. And since everything buried rises in time, as Tituba prophesied, *Revolution can't be buried. It will rise in the jaw of a waking beast.* Nature is cyclical. There will always be second happenings."

Rook looks unconvinced. "So, a chip? Where's the beast sleeping? If I found the beast and won a piece of the marble back for you, you could force the Freemen down the road to 'Librium and reconciliation." He looks around the room. "Let's wake the beast. Revolution."

"Mmm. The beast and the unearthing of a chip could be a tool with which to beg for balance, but even with the sage of Mad Dog's blood flowing through my veins, I'd have no intention of inviting you to the Grimm's door." Whitetail rubs her bulging belly.

Rook gulps, eyes flashing at the prospect of danger. "I don't see what's wrong with war. Who knows how long the beast will sleep. It would be so easy to just steal the kept wife's cane."

They're practically begging for it, Hyena's voice rattles in Whitetail's ears as she delivers a painful blow to her ribs and then thrusts up into her throat. As she swallows pain, Whitetail shuts her mouth. Recovered but tired, she scans the children's worried eyes.

"We'll not speak of the Necrology any further. Or war." Whitetail's reduced to a growling whisper. "Someday. Not today." She believes with all her spirit someday it will happen, but refuses to choose war now for these children. She's sacrificed too much to keep them safe so far.

Hyena wins her tongue. "If you keep something, anything, down, it will always rise in time." Whitetail sees Mouse gulp and pinch her eyes shut.

Whitetail groans, wincing with the effort to regain control of herself, her mouth. "But timing, timing is everything, children. It's what will minimize loss. And it's the loss—of you, of the dwindling Dirty—I cannot, will not, allow." Whitetail leans back, pausing in her rocking chair. Her hands, fingertips ever blackening, grip the chair's arms firmly. Gritting her teeth, her eyes cloud with tears.

The seated children all bolt to their feet when they note her body language. Turning toward the door, for bed, safety— it's clear Whitetail's change in voice has rattled them. The fresh distrust in their eyes pains her spirit. For the first time in her life, she questions just how much of her spirit will be left to travel to summerland. Hyena can't stay in her belly any longer. The spirit it has cost, sliver by sliver, spent through the years to keep this body upright, forge on like this, a mother, to keep this husk functioning as Hyena's prison, is almost gone.

The spot between Whitetail's shoulder blades aches. The weight of what has grown on her crown is compressing the bones in her neck. She needs rest at this time of her final sprint.

Hyena's reminder hits her harder than Johnathan Andrews's fists: *If you keep something down too long, it will always rise. And there will be destruction. And death.* Whitetail had lost control of Hyena for the second time today. This near to death, Whitetail has no time to waste. She cannot, will not, let Hyena escape—launch a war that would have all whom she loves lost like late frost landing on early blooms.

"Never forget," Whitetail says, inexplicably panicked by the sight of the children's departure. "Your path is yours to forge." She hopes the path she's treading will leave no damage. "My love will see its way around any mountain, travel any distance, over any surface and time. It will find you, no matter how far downriver you roam."

Looking across the room at the children's little faces, flickering amidst firelight, she wants to tell them how proud she is of them. *Even of their mistakes.* As she looks at Rabbit, her fingertips fly up to her mouth in an attempt to hold back an overflow of emotion.

Mouse nods fervently before turning to eye Rabbit too.

"Proud." Mouse nods sharply, staring Rabbit in the eye.

Putting her fingertips to her mouth, same as Whitetail, Mouse lets it evolve into a kiss, lightly blown in Rabbit's direction.

Rabbit looks ashamed and Mouse's kiss remains unacknowledged.

"Off to bed, my brave little warriors," Whitetail whispers, in a voice she isn't positive is hers. And all the children scatter like katydids after the last song of summer.

Chapter 7

Wet Sheets

Restless, Rabbit tries to get back to sleep, but she can't. She's wet. *Sweat?* No, urine. The acrid smell hits her nose as she sits up and lifts her top sheet. Her shoulders drop and she huffs, throwing back her cover. Mouse is next to her, and she's immediately seething with annoyance. Poking Mouse in the back, the girl doesn't stir. Mouse has wet Rabbit's bed. Why is the little girl sleeping with her, anyway? Mouse always, always sits up with Whitetail.

The wooden bed frame creaks as Rabbit rolls over to the far side of the mattress, trying to escape the soggy puddle at her hip, but ultimately her night dress is clingy and cold. She's forced to rise and confront the situation.

"Mouse!" Rabbit shakes the little girl again. Mouse stirs, her lip twitching, but she still doesn't wake. "Hey!" Rabbit pinches her cheek roughly.

"Ugh?" Mouse rubs her eyes and sits up, oblivious to her clothes. "Rabbit?"

"You wet it!" Rabbit whispers angrily. "Get out of my bed."

Mouse sits up. Looking around the room, at the seven other girls. Everyone is asleep.

"It's dark. I can't." Mouse looks scared. Her little hands grip and pull the top sheet to her chest. "We're not us right now, and I need to stay with you."

"What? Get up. Go back to your room. Go back to Ms." Rabbit yanks at the bedclothes. She can see her breath, and she's beginning to shiver already. Mouse doesn't move, just sits there, her wide eyes pleading. "Seems little Miss Perfect isn't so perfect today." Rabbit glares a silent warning. Mouse lies back down and scrunches her eyes tight.

"Get up, Mouse," Rabbit hisses. "Get up—or I'll call dark spirits and throw you at them as a sacrifice. You're the reason we're awake at this hour. Them taking you will be your punishment." Rabbit has scared herself back up onto the edge of the bed at the mention of ghosts.

Mouse whimpers.

Opening the door of the main bedroom, Rabbit peers out into the long hallway. It's dark and Mouse's pushing timidly at her back is giving her the willies. Spotting Whitetail's room at the other end of the long hall, Rabbit resigns herself to marching over there. Mouse's cold little fingertips press at her back, and Rabbit brushes her off for being too pushy. When the child's fingers reach for her again, her patience is gone entirely.

"You go first then," Rabbit dictates, raising her voice too loudly. Throwing a finger down the hallway toward Whitetail's door, she demands, "Go."

Mouse shakes her head.

"Go!" Rabbit's fury ebbs as Mouse's bottom lip pops out. Rabbit gives the little girl a stiff hug, and she hushes.

The horribly dark corridor looks longer now than by day. Its floorboards, typically shining in the morning sun, are matte in the flat light from the windows that face the river. There are many places for spirits to hide, and that alone makes this walk treacherous in Rabbit's mind. Rabbit clutches Mouse's hand and has to drag her out of the bedroom. She plunks along a stubborn step, then halts again.

"You're our only friend, Rabbit. Please don't send me back. We're not the same as we were. You're our best friend."

Admittedly, Whitetail seemed more withered tonight than Rabbit has ever seen her. But this child is not her problem, and the opportunity to show how imperfect the perfect one is—is irresistible.

"Then do what I say." If only Rook were here, but he's in his own quarters across the courtyard, alone. *Brave of him,* Rabbit thinks. If she were put out there, she'd have climbed into Sarah's pen sooner than sleeping in the little house alone.

Padding down the hall, Rabbit stops at the window to peer across the way at Rook's darkened window, and Mouse bumps into her back. Rabbit turns around to scowl—not too angrily. She doesn't want the girl's crying to kick back up again. Nothing stirs as the two wait, listening. The house is quiet. Rabbit feels her lungs take in more air as she relaxes some.

Quietly she drags squirming Mouse to Whitetail's door. Cracking it open, she peers into the room. Whitetail is not sleeping, and that's expected. At night, in her room, she never sleeps. She talks to the spirits of the Dirt, the thought of which makes Rabbit's hair stand on end. Whitetail says they're harmless, their foremothers—there for the visiting, or a catch-up—but Rabbit's not so sure of their motives because she can't see or hear them. Sitting in summer, they're settled spirits.

Squinting into the darkness, Rabbit's eyes adjust to the room. It looks as usual. Sparse, with a desk, a lantern, and a simple hand-woven colorful carpet with a star on it that Whitetail knotted herself. There are two chairs, one of which Whitetail sits in now.

A funny smell is in the air. Like sour kelp. It doesn't grow in the local rivers. Another plant? Perhaps the night is even younger than she'd understood it to be. Maybe Ms. has just come in from outdoors. The river? No, it's still too early in the season for this scent. Something's off.

"What do you want?" Whitetail says.

It's not like her to say cold things, but she's certainly had a hard day. It's too bad Whitetail never sleeps. She could do with some rest. Give in, the way Mouse had tonight.

Whitetail's voice softens when she says, "You should be in bed."

Mouse gathers in close behind Rabbit, and, grabbing her forearm, holds on for dear life. They two creep closer.

"The sheets of my bed are wet," Rabbit says.

Whitetail looks hollow where she sits. Frail. Her antlers are huge, and it strikes Rabbit that perhaps something's being birthed, erupting from Whitetail's skull. Tearing out of her husk. A new entity, wriggling out like black poison, needing to be purged.

Whitetail leans to one side, recognizing Mouse is there too.

"Ah." Whitetail's voice is quiet and sullen. "Mouse."

Whitetail's arms hang heavily. Her head falls forward as the weight of her horns pulls her face down and to one side. Her chest heaves with apparent disappointment. Over the sheets or something else?

In the silence of the room, Whitetail's stillness makes Rabbit think that Ms. *could* very well have fallen asleep. And sitting up in a chair, no less. Creeping closer with Mouse at her side, Rabbit looks up into Whitetail's blank face. The quiet makes Rabbit's heart beat faster. Time stops.

Whitetail's eyes are black, and her mouth hangs open. Her lip twitches in anger. Inside her open mouth is only more black. Unsure of what to do, Rabbit feels she shouldn't have come in here. She should have listened to Mouse. Whitetail is not herself. Besides, Rabbit's a big girl now. She doesn't need help. She had just wanted to prove to Whitetail that Miss Perfect Mouse isn't so perfect after all. That, in fact, Rabbit herself had acted perfectly in delivering the lost child back to Whitetail's bed.

"It was our doing. We did it. I was scared to open my eyes to find the privy or my pan. Held it too long and fell asleep," Mouse says from behind Rabbit. "I held it. Until I couldn't."

Rabbit narrows her eyes at Whitetail, trying to figure out what's different about her. What's wrong. Looking back at Mouse, it's too dim to tell whether the girl can see something's off too.

"Rabbit?" Mouse whispers, quivering. She sounds scared and small.

"Shh!" As Rabbit hisses, Mouse's hands grow even tighter around her wrist.

Looking back at Whitetail's blank face, Rabbit knows they should not have come in here, and they need to leave.

"She's not us right now," Mouse whispers. "I told you."

"C'mon, I'll change the bedclothes up myself," Rabbit says to Mouse, whose eyes are still locked on Ms.

A black tongue rolls along Whitetail's top lip. "Girls?" Whitetail's demeanor snaps back into action. Like she's either just woken or had an epiphany.

"We're sorry, Ms." Rabbit's reached the door and wants to run down the hall back to bed. "We're going to clean it up."

Whitetail's nose gives a snarling sniff. "Wet. Wet sheets."

Whitetail seems to have lost or forgotten some of their conversation just now.

Silently, Whitetail points to Rabbit. No, she's pointing to the door behind Rabbit. "Downstairs," Whitetail directs.

Obliging, Rabbit must steady herself as she reaches the top stair. Linens are kept in a chest in the living room, the only room big enough to hold it.

It's so dark that Rabbit's even more scared of falling down the fifteen steps than meeting a ghost. Usually, Whitetail would light a lantern for a night walk such as this. Mouse pushes at Rabbit's back again, and Rabbit resists some. Mouse has gotten them into this. Behind Mouse, Whitetail looks impossibly tall. Her looming silhouette drives Rabbit on. Rabbit begins plunking down the steps heavily, one by one. Whitetail follows with deep thuds, as though she's suddenly made of lead.

Rabbit looks back to see Mouse try to grab ahold of Whitetail's hand, but the woman won't take it. Her hands are limp. Normally Mouse is irresistible to Ms.

Something is wrong. Very wrong. In fact, Ms. seems not really to be Ms. at all . . .

Rabbit hurries the rest of the way down the stairs and clings to the newel post, looking toward the living room and the chest. There's a *bang* beside her that makes her heart stop. Mouse has taken a spill down the last two steps and is on her knees on the hallway floor.

Whitetail bumps down the stairs after Mouse. Standing over her, says, "Get up."

Mouse stands, wiping the loose strands from her braid from her tired eyes. Rabbit looks back at Whitetail's face. It looks more tormented than Rabbit's ever seen it. It's so overcome with sadness and anger, it seems not even hers anymore.

Rabbit eyes the big chest again and makes a move in its direction.

"No. Go sit," Whitetail hisses, pointing a long finger. Instead of pointing to the living room where the chest sits, she's pointing down the hall at the kitchen table.

"Really, I can take care of it," Rabbit speaks up about changing the sheets. It's unclear why they'll need to go to the kitchen.

"That way," Whitetail instructs. "Sit."

In the kitchen, Rabbit takes a seat. Her wet clothes are drying, and the intensifying smell of Mouse's urine is making her feel sick. Instead of sitting at the table, Mouse stands hiding behind Rabbit's back, ducking to watch Whitetail move around the kitchen. Rabbit winces, cranes her neck, and elbows Mouse again, plagued with irritation that the girl has gotten them into some kind of trouble.

As Whitetail walks past what remains of the kitchen fire, there's a crackle, and an ember pops out onto the hearth. As it blazes with new access to air, Whitetail gasps.

"No," Whitetail growls, as she rushes to the ember, the size of an acorn. She stomps it out with her bare foot. Smoke from her burning flesh poofs into the air, and Rabbit can't help but squirm.

Rabbit blinks in disbelief. She's never known Whitetail to be sensitive to pain, but this was gruesome. Whitetail stares at the char on the ground with disdain and doesn't return the black coal to the fireplace. Instead, she goes to the cold room and retrieves bread. Taking up a knife, she turns to watch Mouse and Rabbit a moment before carving off a single thick slab.

Whitetail places the slice of bread carefully on a plate. Turning with her dark, hollow eyes, she says, "I know you're hungry, Rabbit."

Having not eaten dinner, Rabbit's mouth waters and her stomach growls.

Whitetail moves erratically as she lifts the plate. She shivers once, stooping like she's hurt, before righting herself again. Taking the bread up, she inspects it, then carries it over to Rabbit.

"You're more than you think you are," Whitetail says to Rabbit, her voice sounding unfamiliar, low and repulsive. "I did love you. And want to protect you. Once. But my child, what kind of mother would I be if I let you inherit our greatest potential and then watched you squander it." Her face is all shadows. Her shoulders slump. As Whitetail holds the plate with bread aloft, Rabbit can see she's forgotten to set down the knife she used to cut the bread. It's long and sharp. The one Whitetail uses to butcher fish. Rabbit hopes Whitetail doesn't cut herself by mistake. She's pained by the woman's inexplicably cruel statement. Her mouth freezes in Whitetail's gaze. Rabbit can't decide if Whitetail's grown terribly big, or if she herself has shrunk small.

Mouse gasps at her back. "Rabbit?" Rabbit feels Mouse's head duck, pressing between her shoulder blades. "We've always loved you," she whispers.

We? Why always linked? Why always "we" and "us"? Rabbit has long known that Whitetail and Mouse are somehow inexplicably linked, but right now, their oneness feels like salt in her wound. *Loved you once?* As Mouse puts something in Rabbit's hand, Rabbit can't stand to open it.

"Don't forget." Mouse holds up a lone tiny index finger as though she'll scold Rabbit, but she simply eyes Rabbit's fist—or what she's just placed in it.

Rabbit's knees are shaking with heartache. She presses her tongue behind her teeth, ready to shush Mouse, but she's too frozen by hurt to make the noise. Whitetail loved her once? All their years together with Whitetail's nurturing. It'd been imagined?

"Hear me, Rabbit?" Mouse whispers more urgently.

Tears cloud Rabbit's eyes as she drops her gaze to her lap in shame. As Whitetail sets the bread in front of her, she croaks, "Eat up."

Rabbit stares at the plate and can't bring herself to look up until the silence in the room drives it up there.

Whitetail looks hungrily over Rabbit's shoulder at Mouse.

"Let's change the sheets. C'mon," Whitetail says softly to Mouse. As she takes a step toward the kitchen door in the direction of the living room, she reaches out a long, blackened hand for Mouse. Mouse shakes her head in argument, choosing to stay glued to Rabbit's back. Rabbit's too depleted to shake the child off again. She's never felt so numb. So deceived.

Rabbit gently pushes the plate of bread away from herself. She feels sick. Too sick to eat. She can't figure. Has Whitetail learned that she made mud? And worse, made Rook do the same? Was it because she cursed the Beard to winterland, inviting dangerous consequences that might hurt her family someway? Always wrong. Always mistakes. She couldn't trust herself anymore.

"Come on now, Mouse," Whitetail urges even more softly, her hand still waiting for Mouse's.

Rabbit looks at Whitetail again. And then back at Mouse. Perfect little Mouse with her grass hair and perfect eyes, and her perfect behavior. Mouse's eyes are pleading with Rabbit, though Rabbit's not sure why.

"We love you," Mouse says. Her tiny hand on Rabbit's shoulder makes her feel angry. Rabbit wipes it off.

That's not what Whitetail said. She said, "I loved you once." As in, previously.

"Mouse?" Across the room, Whitetail's voice is sterner.

"We love you, Rabbit. Always loved you, Rabbit," Mouse mouths almost inaudibly. The panic in her eyes is confounding.

Rabbit glares at Mouse, feeling immune to the child's bottom lip this time. Rabbit wants to drive the foolish thing away. Make her go, leave her alone. She wants to never see anyone again. She herself is a foolish, ugly creature, who not even a mother could love.

"We'll wave," Mouse whispers at her back before drawing away. Mouse takes slow, small steps toward Whitetail, and, reaching up, hesitates when taking her outstretched hand. Whitetail's face changes, and she looks broken by anger.

Whitetail lets out a slow cry. Her mouth sets in a grimace, but her eyes stay blank and unreadable. Rabbit startles as Whitetail darts forward in Mouse's direction.

Rabbit's heart kicks up a notch and it takes a minute to register: Whitetail's abandoned waiting for Mouse to take her hand. Instead, she's got Mouse yanked up by the braid. Mouse gasps.

"You come when I say," Whitetail barks.

The little girl's toes are dangling an inch above the floor.

Mouse yelps.

Tears stream down Mouse's face, and Rabbit's legs bolt upright. Stunned, Rabbit's heart is racing. She wants to do the right thing, intervene, but how can she confront the only woman whose opinion matters? Rabbit's just decided she can't trust her own intuition. Her own understanding—of anything.

Mouse's hands pry at her braid, at Whitetail's grip on it.

"Let her go!" The authority in Rabbit's voice catches her off guard. Whitetail has never, and would never, hurt them—but here, Rabbit's stunned. It had cost more of Rabbit's spirit than was comfortable to quit fighting the Beard yesterday when he grabbed her neck. She can't sit by and have Mouse limply be a victim, spend any grain of her spirit to endure abuse from a woman they suddenly don't know.

Whitetail takes note that Rabbit's not eating. Her eyes grow glassy with fury.

"Sit down!" Whitetail shrieks in a monster's voice.

Rabbit's knees buckle, and she sits. Her mouth is dry. *Where are the others? Where is Rook?* She'd give anything to stand in his shadow right now.

"You're eating, remember? Can't any of you follow the simplest of instructions? Nobody ever, ever listens to me," Whitetail says to Rabbit as Mouse's feet reach the ground. Mouse bucks, kicking Whitetail, who's undeterred as she turns and drags Mouse out of the room. There's a scuffle as they move down the hall, and Rabbit knows Mouse is being hauled away by the ankle. There's a noise of resistance. Perhaps it's the little girl's nails dragging.

Rabbit stays glued to her chair as a horrendous pain rises in her chest. She's never felt so conflicted. She needs to do what she's told. And Whitetail would never hurt anyone. Rabbit herself is mistaken because she's silly and evil.

The scuffle in the hallway picks up in fury, and Rabbit gulps as the back door slams.

As Rabbit opens her hand, a smell plumes from her palm. It's Mouse. The smell of her, her hair, her skin. It's still on her hand from when she dragged her down the hall to Whitetail's room. The smell makes her feel sick. She gnashes her teeth, inspecting what's been placed in her palm. It's a ring. It has a small achromatic stone setting.

Rabbit drops the ring next to the bread on her plate as a cacophony of birds and wildlife erupts from the backyard. Despite the midnight hour, news of an arrived danger sends the birds flying over the roof and off to shelter.

Rabbit sprints for the stairs and her room as there's a lone chilling scream out in back of the house. *It's Sarah the goat,* she tells herself. *Startled by a fox.* Reaching her room, she hopes and prays for sleep.

Chapter 8

A Bang on the Door

Rabbit is in bed when a bang on the door sounds. She's cold. Opening her eyes, she realizes it's because she hasn't got a blanket on. Wiping her eyes, she looks around the room. Everyone's up already. Her heart feels sluggish, like she's not slept at all.

Stretching, she reaches her hand under her pillow, and it hits something hard. Reaching for it, she withdraws Whitetail's cigarette tin. There's something uncharacteristic in its weight. Opening the lid, she sees it's not only filled with pieces of spirit, but also the die, her slate marker—and the ring from Mouse that she'd abandoned on her plate. Feeling the side of her night shorts, she remembers last night. She examines her sheets. Dry. Her bedding has been changed. Or was it a dream? *No.* She can still smell Mouse's hair under her nose. She gets dressed, with shaky hands, in pants and a shirt, remembering to place the cigarette tin in her pocket. Surely Whitetail is looking for it, and perhaps Rabbit's recovery of the tin will help mend whatever bridge broke between the two yesterday. Her chest is filling with an inexplicable growing panic. *Check on Mouse? Make sure she is okay? Go directly to Whitetail? Avoid them both altogether?* Mind spinning, she stubbornly seeks clarity. There's none to be found.

Another bang on the door sounds. Louder this time—more urgent. There's the bump of sprinting footsteps along the downstairs hall to answer it. She's pretty sure it's Rook. The thought of his big, round brown eyes and crooked grin gives her no comfort. Again, she's struck by the fact that she's in different bedclothes than she'd gone to sleep in last night. In fact, these aren't even hers. They're castoffs of Snake's, who's gone to Syracuse. A blessing because she'd always bossed Rabbit and the little ones around. Saying, "When you're eight, I'll be gone." Sixteen was too old for care. Snake and Whitetail had consulted the will of the wilds, and regardless, Snake chose indebted service to some Freemen family over running into the shadows.

First the front door, then screen door, squeaks open downstairs. Rabbit perks at the sound of a man's authoritative voice. It booms through the house, and her heart stops. Has the Beard come back? Her heart kicks up a notch as she thinks of what she did to him yesterday. Bolting for the door, she sprints downstairs, taking them two at a time.

"Ms.?" Rabbit calls out. She'll confess, if that's what Whitetail tells her to do. She cocks her chin, listening in the direction of the kitchen where breakfast should be on, but she smells nothing. Her heart is racing. "Whitetail?"

She doesn't want to look out the front door, but its proximity to the foot of the stairs makes avoiding it impossible. Instead of passing by, Rabbit ducks behind the door where she can't exactly see who's come knocking, but has a clear vantage point of Rook, who's bravely answered the door. His red hand grips the doorknob, and his feet are braced in a defensive stance.

"Yes?" Rook's mouth is tight. His eyes momentarily dart to hers, then away, telling her there's trouble, and she needs to stay quiet. Feeling vulnerable, a blazing heat comes to her cheeks. She fears seeing a Freemen's black eyes and scary, square hood. Freemen are monsters. Entitled to anything, including beating her for not wearing enough clothing on her ankles and neck. Who was to say what might happen if they saw her bare feet.

Rabbit gulps. This is it. They're here for her. This man knows it was her who yelled at the Beard yesterday. Threw the rock. Cast the curse. He's here to kill her, or at the least, cart her off to prison. What she said yesterday to the Beard scares her. What she's done. What Whitetail thinks of her now that she's brought mud.

"Ms. Elizabeth Whittle. She at home?" the man says.

The man hasn't asked for Rabbit at all. She's surprised, but far from relieved. The man's still here looking for someone. The man's voice is commanding and gruff. It's quite possibly the loudest voice Rabbit's ever heard. Looking around, into what she can see of the living room, down what's visible of the hall, there's no sign of the other children. Rabbit listens to the stillness of the house, wondering why she and Rook are the only people at the door. What could possibly be more interesting than this man looking for a stranger at their house?

"No such Elizabeth Whittle lives here," Rook says. He clears his throat curtly, and, casting his eyes down, moves to shut the door. Rook's feet are covered in fresh dirt. He's already been outside this morning without her? Disappointed, she crosses her arms in front of her chest.

The visitor puts out a hand. As he stops the door from closing, his pink fingertips become visible along the door's edge. Then a shiny black boot takes a step inside. It seems like not only has the house stopped breathing, but the birds outside have stopped their songs. As the man's boot settles, Rabbit hears the grit brought into the house grinding into the floorboards.

"Elizabeth Whittle," the man says again. "Runs this place, no? Who's in charge here?" He looks behind him, then scans the hall, the top of the stairs. "Your mistress."

Rook freezes. Craning his neck, he looks straight up at the stranger, whose chest is in his face. The man at the door is a blackcoat, Rabbit can tell. The cuff visible beyond his wrist is a black uniform.

Licking her lips, Rabbit's simultaneously grateful that whoever the man is looking for isn't here and worried about yesterday. The man having come inside is a very bad sign. If the blackcoats were coming to cart her off, wouldn't he know her name? Hopefully, this man will go away quickly and leave them all alone. Peeking from around a corner, she inspects his square face and the authoritative look in his eye. He's commanding, intrusive, hard, and unfriendly. His blackcoat has shiny gold buttons and there's a square, black cap on his head. He's white-pine tall and wearing a flat-line mouth with no whiff of courtesy.

Rook takes a step back. "One minute." He sprints off, running down the hall and out back.

Something about the speed of his steps has Rabbit sprinting, chasing after him too.

"You!" The man calls as he spots her.

Rabbit freezes, turning to look back at the man. His eyes are wide and scanning. Though he's scared to come in here, into this particular house, it's plain to see he's not going away.

"Whatcha want?" Rabbit barks, delivering a scowl. Turning around, she checks to see she's the only one standing there. *Where is everyone?*

"Tell Ms. Whittle to come, now. Round up the children, set them in the living room. *All of them.*"

Rabbit nods and knots her fingers together, anxiety ripping through her forearms. Afraid of what's coming, she questions if it's just her who'll be punished for cursing the Beard. Or if they will all be reprimanded. Or worse, taken away. Turning, she runs back through the far side of the kitchen, around the table, to the hearth. Whitetail isn't there. The hearth is cold; there's no breakfast cooking. She hears Rook in the backyard. He's calling to the others, but she can't make out what he's saying. *Won?* He's telling them he won?

Where is everyone? He won a game they'd all played without her? Stopping to look back down the hall, she sees the blackcoat stomping in her direction. Feet racing, she darts out the back door, vaulting down the steps to land in the muck. Trotting out into the backyard, she spots the other children. But their game, holding hands in a ring, doesn't look happy. In fact, when all their eyes meet hers, she sees nothing but fear.

A twig cracks to her right, and she spots a blackcoat. He's heading, crouched, toward Pea, his hands slightly raised like he's ready to catch a moth. Another branch cracks on her left, and it's clear there are more men, all of them in matching blackcoats. The yard is surrounded. The men are encroaching quickly.

But Rook had won? *Won?*

Not won. *Run!* He was telling the children to run!

These men are here to take the children? The way two men are poised to tackle Rook chills her to the bone.

"Whitetail!" Rabbit screams for help. Spinning, she looks up to the darkened second-story window. Where is she? The person in charge of Andrews. Their caretaker. The most powerful person Rabbit knows, capable of casting off all of these men with her choice words. Whitetail could level these men, direct the children, get that garden seeded, and cook breakfast, all without one hair slipping from her braid. Where on earth could she be?

A thought to last night's bad dream has Rabbit doing a double take at the upstairs windows that remain dark, still with no sign of Whitetail. The men around her look up at the windows, too, and one man nods to another, who walks toward the back steps, then ascends and marches into the kitchen.

Eyes darting to Rook's, Rabbit can tell by his face that, somehow, some way or other, Rabbit's let him down again. She wasn't supposed to call out for the only adult in the house for help? She turns to stare at the other kids, all assembled around the big rock in the backyard. They're standing, encircling the rock like reverent mourners. Rook had told them to run. Why are they just standing there? The others turn to look at her too. And the inexplicable sadness their mouths wear speaks again to a loss. Not a game, though. It's something she can't comprehend.

One by one, the children's eyes flit to hers, and she feels dread. At what she hears: sniffling. But why tears?

Rabbit takes a few steps toward the rock, desperate to understand the situation. The children's circle is tight, and even as Rabbit grabs their hands, Pheasant and Rat won't break their grasp. Between them, Rabbit gets a view of the big rock. Mouse is lying on top of it. She's lying there, sleeping. But her eyes are open. The look in her eyes, vacant. She's so pale. She's—

Rabbit sprints, pushing toward the rock, toward the girl she'd envied and loathed. The one so perfect. The one she didn't care a scrap about. *Mouse!* Last night wasn't a dream.

"Wha—!" Sobs escape her trembling lips. "What has Whitetail done?"

A man nearby utters, "Father Almighty." He turns to his neighbor. "Careful now, when you take her."

The children's hands don't break for Rabbit when she leans in. Like a terrible game of reorder, she pushes and pushes, but the children won't let her through. Heartache overwhelming her, she falls to her knees in the dirt before something moves in her periphery.

The men. A blackcoat grabs Pea's slender wrist, and for a moment, she holds fast to Rat and Goose at her sides, trying to keep the men from Mouse's body. Another man grabs Pheasant, hoisting her up by her underarms, then Rat by the shoulders. The ring of children is overpowered, and quickly they are cast off like clumps of dandelion seeds. A man stands over Mouse's body, looking down on it with disdain.

"On your knees!" the blackcoat holding Goose's wrists barks, and all the men push the kids down on the ground. "Bind their wrists," he says, throwing an extra set of irons to his neighbor for Goose, who's banging on the man's stomach and legs with furious fists. As the blackcoat wrangles wild Goose, Rabbit's hands are shaking so badly they've become inoperable, and her feet inexplicably stay glued in the dead grass under her feet. Rabbit's nauseous with indecision. She needs someone to tell her what to do. How to be of the most service to the group. She picks up a rock and scans for Rook. She spots him, spots his eyes where he's standing statue-still next to the skeletal berry bushes. As Rabbit opens her mouth to speak, Rook turns to take off sprinting for the underbrush that leads down to the river. And like a vole, he's gone. She is abandoned. Left to fight alone.

A man pinches her shoulder and pushes her down when she's not ready to catch herself. Her knees fail, leaving her falling flat on her face. Immediately, she feels a heat on the bridge of her nose, and she knows it's bleeding. The blackcoat binds her wrists with a quick *clink* of cold irons before yanking her back up by the arms, leaving her shoulders to take her weight. Like that, she's upright again, and looking into the foreign darkness of the kitchen. There's a stir, and the blackcoats standing near the kitchen door stumble down the steps, one almost toppling backward, losing footing before they all pool out in a rush. They look over their shoulders in surprise before they straighten and regain a sense of authority.

Someone's coming outside.

"Ms. Elizabeth Whittle?" a blackcoat barks, straightening his jacket with a rough tug. His stance widens as his eyes trail upward from the bottom of the step to the dark of the kitchen. "You're under arrest for . . . for"—he half coughs with confusion. He's seen something that's unnerved him? —"murders by magic," he finally finishes.

A floorboard creaks as Whitetail comes into the light, then she pauses.

Thank summer, Rabbit thinks. Whitetail's come to tell these men to stop being ridiculous. To get off her land or she'll send them choking to the river, or worse!

"Come on, then," the blackcoat says again, more easily. Ushering a wild animal.

As Whitetail takes in her surroundings, her gaze meets Rabbit's before she closes her eyes. She takes a long breath, then opens her eyes again, training them on the horizon. When Whitetail takes a step forward, Rabbit's shoulders drop. *Why isn't she protesting? Reasoning or pleading? How can she not say anything?* Aching disappointment rises in Rabbit, and she feels deceived. *Whitetail's saying goodbye to the house.* Panic rises in Rabbit's gut. How can Whitetail be so ready to leave her home and let the children be taken by these blackcoats?

Walking out, she's dressed for her death. The red vestment looks stunning in the morning light, so bright against spring's bleak morning colors. Her black wrap hangs swirling around her shoulders. She'd made the shawl by hand. Her hair is knotted in an elaborate twist across the top of her head and sits in a nest between her antlers. This was the elaborate costume she planned to wear to summerland. Face stoic. As she descends, bowing her face to eye the stairs, she slowly looks back up, bringing her full rack of antlers out into the morning light.

"Ho!" one of the men says, urgently. Taking a step back, he looks at the man next to him. The man's eyes blink in confusion, and both shift their stance, perhaps readying to run away.

The blackcoat nearest Mouse, the one evaluating her level of dead, looks back once at Whitetail, then twice, and winds up nearly spilling over the big rock and Mouse's dead body.

The wind shifts, and the children turn on their knees to see her too. See the one who would always take care of them, their keeper—who was as formidable as approaching thunderclouds and just as breathtaking—surrendering.

Whitetail descends the stairs, one bare foot at a time, and when she reaches the lawn, she towers over the blackcoat waiting for her. Turning, she gracefully takes a knee and waits, wrists together behind her back. The blackcoat smirks at his neighbor.

"Cart them off," the blackcoat says, putting irons on Whitetail's wrists.

Chapter 9

Meeting Sr.

The room is big. Bigger than the ten strides she'd be able to take across the kitchen at Andrews anyway. Despite the room's openness—tall ceilings, high walls, and evening light filtering through the tall windows—it feels constricting here. The building is a strange style. Black, shiny bricks and metal window fastenings. Looking at her reflection in the windowpanes, she sees nothing but a dark smear. That's how she feels. Blurry and out of place. Rabbit's never been in a building like this before. She's put it together. This is a place called "the station." She heard one of the blackcoats say it when they pushed her into the back of a cart.

The door opens, and the face of a new man leans in. He's the fourth to come within the hour. Leaning back, she sighs with disappointment. She's already told her story three times and doesn't know whether she has the stamina to go another round. Walking in, he has a bunch of papers under his arm. He sits down opposite her. Oh summer, if only he could help.

She's told the truth already. Most of it, anyway. She hasn't told the part about cursing the Beard. Or making mud. No one has asked her about that yet. They asked her about Whitetail's antlers, about the Beard's visit, what time he had come, and had he been alone with Ms. She told the blackcoats that Beard had attacked Whitetail. That she'd had to fight him back with the pan. That there had been blood running down the back of his neck as he was leaving. How it showed on his shirt collar before he collapsed. How Whitetail had been fighting for her spirit.

How the driver had to drag Beard's limp body away.

But not who'd thrown the rock. Or cursed.

Rook had thrown rocks at a limping man, yes. But she and she alone had cursed the man to winter. She believes she cast the curse that killed him.

A second man pokes his head in the doorway. He has a white beard, a fancy plum-colored coat, and wire-rimmed glasses. He walks in to stand behind the blackcoat with the papers. Idling a moment to glance at her black feet dangling below the table, the man with the white beard sits down beside the first man. The blackcoat looks to the elder who's staring at her. Even though it's the blackcoat who wears the suit, the black jacket of authority, it's clear he's waiting for the older man to lead in the talking. The man with the white beard doesn't, though; he just waits, watching her.

It's the blackcoat who finally speaks. "Abigail. That's your real name, isn't it?" He opens a folder he's carried in and lays it on the table. Inside, there appear to be old papers scrawled with writing. He points to the writing at the top of the page.

Sure, she could read it. Though her parents hadn't read, Snake's father had. Snake taught Rabbit, starting with names on packets of seeds. Market purchases Whitetail couldn't harvest locally, like Cucurbita.

"Abigail Charlotte?"

There is an echo in her memory, but it isn't fully formed. That name exists in a different lifetime. With his utterance, she's flooded with memories. The blind reverence on the other orphans' faces on the day Mouse was anointed. How Rabbit held on to Rook's hand when they all walked outside. The mud had been frozen in January. And instead of waiting for springtime's thaw to allow for tracks to be trod the way Whitetail had told she'd once done for the other orphans, Whitetail directed the newly arrived to simply walk through the snow. After studying the tracks, and a few nights' consultation with the wilds, Whitetail announced the strange newcomer as Mouse.

Rabbit would sit here arguing that Abigail was the name of a stranger had she not remembered Whitetail revealing that, after the fire, men in black had given her and the others civilized names. Hers was Abigail. But in a second ceremony by the orphanage's big rock, Whitetail returned their original names, symbolizing their new life in covenant.

"I'm Rabbit," she says flatly.

The officer looks at the man with the white beard.

Rabbit smells something she's never encountered before. Airy and floral, it's filling the room. Rabbit believes it's coming from the man with the white beard. He looks familiar, though she knows for certain they've never met. His nose whistles as he lets out a deep breath. She can't tell if he's confused or disappointed as he studies her face.

The white beard lowers his gaze.

Both men's wooden chairs creak as their weights shift.

The officer holds out a picture. He shows her there are names written on the back in a crooked script, different from the shapes in the books Snake showed her. Curlier. The officer flips the picture over and lets the old man inspect the back. Then he flips it right side up again and leaves it on the desk between them. The old man's eyes flit from the picture up to Rabbit's face and back again. Even upside down, Rabbit can see it's the picture of her and the other orphans. She's but a toddler, dwarfed by a towering Ms., who is holding her hand. Scowling, she looks up at the two men.

"Says here 'Abigail Charlotte Alone,'" the officer says, this time adding a new name at the end. He points to the picture. *Alone?* Ms. once explained that a man at the market let her keep an account. He'd asked her name. She'd said, "Whitetail." When he'd asked, "Whitetail what?", she'd said, "Whitetail Alone."

All the children laughed at her tale. "Alone" was what the man had written down. *Is this the same as that?* The room is silent a moment, and Rabbit senses danger, like a taraxacum seed feathering past her nose. Her cheeks feel hot, and her eyes drop to the floor.

Always look them in the eye, Rook would say, playing war in the woods. Today, it's harder than usual.

The man with the beard skids the photo in her direction.

Picking it up, she looks it over, one hand gripping the table's edge for grounding. The table's surface is scratched with little gouges. She feels them under her fingertips. Rabbit thinks of little Mouse. Of her fingers and broken bloody fingernails. How limp her body looked where it lay on the boulder. The big rock's quartz twinkling in the morning sun like diamonds.

"Do you know who the man sitting beside me is?" The blackcoat is speaking too loudly, as though Rabbit is having a hard time understanding what he's saying.

Rabbit shakes her head only lightly. She's suspicious of the man with the white beard. Of his seeming authority. How accommodating should she be? Mesmerized by the old man's perfume, she can't fathom the richness of his coat, tailored, like the Beard's. The vest beneath his coat is shiny. His beard is trimmed perfectly into a point and his mustache, curled. He's handsome, with many lines around his eyes, and his brow, now sympathetic looking, is strikingly warm.

"This is Mr. Andrews."

"Andrews, like Andrews House?" Rabbit tucks her legs back tight under the seat of her chair, then swings them up quickly and under her bottom to sit cross-legged. The men exchange glances.

The old man crosses his arms and leans back in his chair, his weight making the chair's back squeak. Voices rush by in the hallway outside, and Rabbit rubs her tired eyes. She's so hungry she could eat turnips.

Mr. Andrews's gaze is heavy. Evaluating. And as his mouth turns up at a corner, she thinks he's knowing of the big things. Like the railway and the Dirty, and the Freemen.

As Mr. Andrews takes off the rimmed glasses, his big brown eyes shine. He leans in and she looks him straight in the eye, her knees shivering, tucking tighter in her cross-legged position. A moment ago, he seemed pleasant, but now, glasses off, she's less sure.

"Yes. Mr. Andrews," the blackcoat continues loudly, "owns Andrews Orphanage. The house you've been living in these past eight years." The officer pauses. "This man's been buying your meals. Your clothing too. He owns Roscoe. And the ten thousand acres of Blackmoor that surround it."

Rabbit watches the blackcoat's Adam's apple bob. It's grotesque.

"He'd like a word with you about the last few days."

Her eyes tear with self-loathing. *They want clarification on who was responsible for the mud?*

The blackcoat looks at Mr. Andrews. "Go ahead," he says.

"Abigail," Mr. Andrews says.

"Rabbit," she corrects.

"Right. Do you remember the man that was killed at Andrews, Rabbit?"

Reaching into his breast pocket, he pulls out another photo. He holds his thumb over half of it when he extends it. It takes a minute for her to recognize who's sitting in the fancy parlor, but when she examines the eyes a little closer, she recognizes it's the Beard. Only at the time of the picture being taken, he'd been . . . beardless. "He came to visit you and the other children yesterday."

"The Beard. Yes. I said that already, two blackcoats ago." Rabbit wrinkles her nose and looks at the old man. Hands gripping the sides of her seat, she bobs up and down once, trying to make her legs more comfortable but not wanting to let them hang under the table.

Mr. Andrews Sr.'s smile is gone. "The B—what?"

"It's how the children identified him," the blackcoat clarifies.

Crossing his arms, Sr. leans back in his chair. "Why do you think you're here, Rabbit?"

She shrugs, even though she knows it's for one or both of two reasons: she cursed the Beard to winter, killing him, and Mouse died at Andrews last night.

"You were there when he visited yesterday? Saw him get hurt?"

"Yes."

"What happened?"

Rabbit stiffens, feeling uncooperative.

"I can't help you and your friends if you don't talk to me," Sr. says.

Her eyebrows involuntarily dart up in surprise. If he's any relation to the Beard, she doubts this man could ever be of any help.

"You want to see your friends again, don't you?"

A thought to Mouse, dead, and the others being ironed and escorted from their own home brings tears to her eyes.

"Where are they?" How come she's not with them?

"You can be together after you tell me what's gone on."

What to say? Where to start? "Whitetail was in the kitchen and sent us away. But we didn't mind her instructions, ate all the bread, came back before sundown, and saw her—"

"Who's we?"

"Me 'n' Rook. The others, too, even though we told them to stay at the Beaverkill while we scouted. They never listen."

"Rook?" Andrews Sr. looks confused.

"The boy," the blackcoat adds. "Still on the run, missing."

"Then?" Mr. Andrews Sr. asks, wrinkling his brow in concentration.

"She, Whitetail, wrestled Bea—Mr. Andrews in the kitchen, and then when she lost bad, and he was hurting her—her eyes went black and—" Even if she was hurt and disappointed by Whitetail, was she really going to spill her guts like a pike to these men? Who to be loyal to? *Truth,* she thinks. *Whitetail says, "Always truth."*

"I really need to know more so I can help your friends," Sr. says.

"She hit him with the pan." She'd be more loyal to her mother if Whitetail weren't ugly and mean, and a murderer. *Why did she kill Mouse? Why?*

"When Beard came outside, he was hopping mad and walking funny, like a snake, sideways-like, from the pan. He was a madman! Gone mad-like."

Mr. Andrews's hand shoots to his mouth. "You said her eyes turned black?" A suspicious look overtakes his face.

She forges on, "And then, when Mr. saw me, he got even more mad. And—" Eyes filling with tears and shame, she knows the ultimate confession, should she give it, would land her in jail with Whitetail. She thinks of Rook on the run. "He choked me until I passed out." *Then I cursed him to winter.*

The blackcoat's face reddens as he fights back an irritated interjection.

Sr. delivers the officer a scolding glance to stay quiet.

"You shared a room with . . . the wee girl." Mr. Andrews Sr. looks searchingly at the officer again. His use of "wee"—adoring, warm, loving—makes her spin with indecision about him. This kind, heartfelt man is a Freemen? The father of the Beard, no less? She can't stand the subject, and as her stomach rolls over with hunger and fury, she feels the need to run away, if only she had the strength.

"Unidentified," the officer clarifies. "Kidnapped maybe? Stolen, or lost. They called her Mouse." The blackcoat nods at Rabbit. "No idea who she really is."

"What happened to her?" Sr. asks.

As Rabbit chokes back tears, she wants to go to sleep. Not recall the memory of Mouse's face or her pleading eyes as she looked back over her shoulder in search of help that Rabbit never offered.

"Ms. killed her last night. I thought it was Sarah, our goat, screaming. But—"

"My dear child," Mr. Andrews says in a quiet voice, wavering with apparent shock. "What have I done? Dirty women, under my nose. I've harbored one of the biggest threats to the modern world as we know it. The resurgence of Dirty women. She. On my land." He simply blinks, turning to look at the blackcoat. "I've paid for them to teach this new generation the evil of the Dirt." He points at Rabbit. "That's why my son is dead? Penance for my blindness?"

Sr. holds up the picture of the Beard with a shaking hand. Putting the picture back in his breast pocket, his face changes from sorrow to fury.

Rabbit gulps. This is indeed a dangerous place. This man seems to think there's evil in the Dirt? Rabbit loves the Dirt, just like Whitetail told her to. *Any man who tells you magic is evil is a man who's scared of you. That's how they keep you. They tell you that lie. They tell it, over and over and over, until you believe it. But it isn't true.*

Mr. Andrews puts his hand to his chest and delivers another look of dismay to the officer next to him. He winces, crinkling his brow.

There's silence in the room, and all Rabbit can hear is rain ticking on the windows beside her.

Sr. tilts his head in thought, his brow wrinkles, then his eyes widen with some apparent conclusion. A lost thread found.

"But—black eyes, you said her eyes turned black?" He looks at her searchingly. "Black?"

"Her eyes were dark. Blacker than the river bottom in winter. Hate filled. Animal." Rabbit's cheeks burn with confusion because she's apparently said something Sr. hungrily wanted to hear. The blackcoat's complexion pales as he clues into Sr.'s conclusion. Putting an alarmed hand on his mouth, he bows his head in dismay.

"If you know of the Dirt, surely you know the name Morgan."

"I don't."

Sr.'s brow crinkles a moment, and he stiffly wipes each wing of his mustache with pause. Leaning close, he says, "You'd know her as . . . Hyena?"

"Sure," Rabbit says quietly, guarding her face from her emotions. "She lives in Whitetail's belly." There. She spits that truth out too.

The doubtful way the men look at one another, mouths open, makes her feel small.

"Whitetail swallowed her. The night of the Roscoe fire. The one that killed our parents. Because she's a rifter, she hates light. And heat. She can be one with the dim, even to the point of a weightless wraith. An almost ghost. Whitetail saved her and keeps her safe. She's stuck in there now."

Sr. pales. "Alive," he whispers, almost inaudibly. "Can it be?" he says to no one. Smoothing his beard with a hand, he takes a long look and almost smiles at her, but it's not happiness. Sr. crosses his arms, leaning back in his chair.

His look of victory is so confusing, Rabbit slaps her face into her crossed arms on the table and weeps, chest heaving with sadness. She's answered enough questions and is ready to join the other children.

"Where is everyone?" She sniffs into the table. "The other orphans. My sisters had no part in this, you can let them all go. They don't even know why they got irons." She imagines them cold, in the dark, and hungry.

"They're on their way to Liberty in Albany." The blackcoat's chair squeaks as he shifts in his seat.

"They're good children. They can come home," she cries.

"What home—"

Sr. cuts the blackcoat off. "I think you're a good girl. Are you a good girl, Rabbit?" Mr. Andrews asks.

"No," she says angrily. *Not as good as the others, that's for sure.* She'd not finished Sixty-Three with Rook. Brought mud. Delivered the curse to the Beard. A final blow to an evil, but dying, man was bad. Unloved by Whitetail. Failed to help Mouse. She was bad and brought bad things. Her prison and punishment would need to be eternal.

Sr.'s voice softens. "I'm . . . I'm so sorry, Rabbit, for how blindly permissive of my son I've been. I—I—overestimated him." Rabbit doubts Sr.'s statement is true, but it's like nothing she's ever encountered. Like honey. Her heart thumps harder. Rabbit looks up from the table, wiping her face with the back of her hand.

"I'd like to make it up to you. I'd like more than anything to help your friends." His smile shows he is amused by her. "I want you to come with me, to my home in Syracuse. While we work on getting your friends out of Liberty, you'll have a safe, warm place to sleep. More food than you could ever eat. I can show you things you've only dreamed of. You'll have a voice. It's the least I can do for what you've endured in my negligence."

"I have a voice," Rabbit snaps.

"I mean, girl, that if you speak while you're at *my* side, everyone will want to listen. None of your friends are guilty of magic, but fact is, they're in cages labeled illegals by association to your mistress. You'll need to speak the truth about what's transpired at Andrews in court to get them out. Tell them what you told me." Sr. uncrosses, then re-crosses his arms. "Explain how innocent your friends are. Tell them, Whitetail's a killer."

A court? "Tell?"

"You don't want all your friends to rot and die in Liberty, do you?" His voice isn't unkind, but it is patronizing.

Liberty. The penitentiary where murderers hunted and ghosts haunted? The prospect was terrifying, but as of last night, no one, not anything, could make her feel as unsafe as Whitetail had. Never as unsafe. And never as scared.

"You don't want them to stay there, do you? Or for you to have to go there with them?" Taking a pocket watch out of his vest, he eyes it. Then replaces it. "You don't want to be behind bars. You want to help your friends, right? Be with them and free?"

She nods, yes.

"I really did believe she was a smart girl," he says to the blackcoat.

"I want to help my friends." This seems a dangerous confession.

"Smart, pretty girl," he assures her. "Now"—he stands, turning to look down at the blackcoat—"let's find this girl some shoes."

Chapter 10

Liberty

The carriage pulls up, and Whitetail is asked to step out of the back bin by a different deputy than shoved her roughly in. She looks him straight in the eye, but he avoids hers. Thankfully, no one touches her. It's the antlers, she supposes. *Everyone's afraid of me. What I am, and what they think I've done. Murdered a child.*

Stepping her black feet into heavily tracked mud, they sink to the ankles, and she feels a fleeting joy. Even in here, in this bricked and mortared place, she can feel the wilds, Dirt, an electric breeze that grounds her. Her lungs fill with peace before the smell hits—horse piss—and her stomach turns. The walls surrounding the property are black like coal and tall as a spruce.

High wooden doors stand before her, ornate and lacquered. Grand even. But they don't open for her. Instead, a man points, not speaking, and she's directed through a smaller door, right of the main doors. Four men walk with her. Two out front, two in back. She walks carefully, her chin up. Her mother always told her: *Always look them in the eye.* Whitetail knows Hyena would like to obliterate these men in one go if she were to relax, even for a moment. Hyena's angry that they've been brought here. And angry that Whitetail vowed never to speak to her again. But what does Hyena expect with what she's done?

It isn't unenjoyable, watching Hyena squirm. Whitetail would like to say "I told you so." That Hyena is, in fact, not trustworthy, and should never be freed. Not if a body count is to be staved off. Perhaps it's Whitetail's own fault, Mouse's death. After all, she'd been the one to fall asleep, for the first time in her life, when she should have been watching. The victim of kelp tea. She hadn't even been aware that her sister had brewed it. She was supposed to be vigilant. It was her vow to the parents as a keeper.

Her antlers barely fit through the door as she enters. It takes a moment to finagle them through. A guard snickers at her, and Hyena's so outraged, she forces a growl out of Whitetail's lips. The guard straightens and grips a bully stick at his hip.

She's brought in past the guard, then out into a main yard. Its grass is spotty with icy, wet snow and is heavily trodden. Mud spots.

They reach a big set of doors. The writing over the door's archway shows letters she doesn't know how to read. Still, she knows this is prison. Inside, the lighting is dim, and the walls are black. She's escorted into a little office with the tiniest window she's ever seen. It opens out into a hallway.

The man in front of her stops and looks in the window at the man waiting behind it.

"Warden," he says to the man in the window before looking over his shoulder. "I got a five-point for you."

Warden, the man behind the window, is lean and balding and looks startled when he sees her. His high collar towers above a fall-grass-colored suit. He looks worn.

"You sure she's not meant for the zoo?" His eyes lock with hers, then turn to the guard gripping her arm.

"No, sir," the guard says through the window as he looks at some papers pinched in his hands. He hands them over. "This here's a multiple murderess." Her escort holds onto his s's playfully.

Murderess. The title makes her heart break. Thinking of little Mouse takes her breath away. The little girl's round nostrils. The curve of her earlobes. The tiny fingers, fingernails with their shell-like sheen.

Whitetail refuses to let these men see her cry. Like she holds Hyena, she holds her grief. The guard looks over his shoulder at her again. "This here is Warden Davidson. Your new master." He looks at the warden. "They say upstate she ran free through them woods, but here, she'll be getting a leash." The guard jests yanking an imaginary noose at his throat and sticking out his tongue with a gurgle.

"She'll get that soon enough," Warden answers. After leafing through papers, he files them.

If she hangs, will these men watch? Their smiling eyes will be the last she sees?

"Sit." A deputy behind her summons some nerve and knocks her in the back. The corners of her mouth turn down, but she sits without looking back at him. Bowing her head, she rubs her neck with both hands, her wrists bound. It hurts enough to bring tears. The weight she carries on her neck, in her heart, it's taking its toll.

"No tears. Understand?" The warden seems to have read her mind. He turns, twirling his mustache, to look at the deputy beside her. "This is the part where they all cry, tell you they 'never did it.' Never fucked for money. Never stole." He turns back to her. "Not you though, hey?"

The man behind her snickers. "Guilty as sin, I'd say."

"Indeed." Warden smirks.

After taking her record, a woman is summoned.

"Warden," she greets Davidson. Middle-aged and stout, she looks vacantly at the room until she spots Whitetail. The woman's demeanor is telling. She's broken and kept. Her aura speaks to Whitetail, no magic required.

The woman's gaping mouth snaps closed before her face turns back to stoicism. "Over 'ere!" the round woman demands in a lilt Whitetail doesn't recognize. They all have a chuckle as Whitetail stares.

"Come," she says, pointing to the doorway. It has a metal rule up its side. Whitetail walks to the doorway and waits.

"Back against it now. There you go." The woman is holding a piece of chalk and as she raises her hand, she realizes she can't reach the topmost of Whitetail's antlers to measure her height.

"Ah?" She looks searchingly at the warden. "Sir?"

"No, Ms. P. Just to the top of her head, not—whatever those are."

"What are they?" a guard asks.

The men all shrug.

Reaching over Whitetail's head, the woman's hand contorts. She stands on her tiptoes, a bird ready to fly, and struggles in a way that makes it clear to Whitetail she's scared to touch any part of her. Ms. P gulps and startles when one of the men yells a jeering, "Ah! Go on, P!"

Whitetail turns to look down at her. As Whitetail holds out her hand, the stout woman drops the piece of chalk in it with a frown. Whitetail marks her own height on the wall carefully, and, after locking eyes with the woman, hands the chalk back.

Ms. P refuses it, and all the men in the room howl with laughter. Grabbing the woman's hand up by the wrist, Whitetail tries to return the chalk. The woman tries to pull away, and the men laugh harder than before. The woman looks to the men for help, but it's clear: she's like Whitetail. They'll leave her to be eaten or killed before they go near her. No need to stick your neck out on behalf of a female colleague.

Whitetail drops the chalk into Ms. P's palm. The woman looks at it, then glares, confounded, at the men laughing. As she shifts her stance, Whitetail knows that this woman is remembering who she should actually be afraid of around here. She frowns.

"And?" Warden barks.

The woman struggles to look over Whitetail's head to the chalk mark.

Whitetail curtseys to let her read.

"Six-seven," Ms. P says.

Warden jots it down on his yellow paper, tilting his head and raising an eyebrow, impressed.

As Whitetail rises, Ms. P's demeanor changes. She looks crestfallen, as though she's come to some conclusion. An admittance that she, with all her experience and knowledge, still has things to learn. The two women stare at each other a moment until the woman's eyes glass over.

"Ms. P?" The warden breaks Whitetail's connection to her.

Ms. P blinks in wonder.

The warden clears his throat, regaining command of the room. "Inmates may have one visitor a month, if you make it a month," he says to no one. "Sign this."

He hands over a slip of paper; it says something Whitetail can't read.

She sets the pen down.

Warden irritably snatches up the paper and reads, "I hereby authorize the warden and his assistants to receive, open, read, deliver, destroy, retain, or return any letters addressed to me."

Letters? She lifts the pen and signs it with an *X.* No one would be writing to her even if she could read. She is limited to reading only hair. All she knows is the spoken history of the Dirty texts and whatever she'd overheard Snake, who knew from her father, teach the children.

Oh, how she longs for her cigarette tin. She left it under Rabbit's pillow after rousing from a sleep as deep as an overwintered bear's. Between the Beard's departure and a dead child on the premises, she knew she had to deliver the tin to the most capable of hands. Oh, to know where Rabbit is. Where the children are. She prays to the wilds they're safe.

Ms. P won't stop staring at Whitetail.

Warden notices, and with a look of sincere annoyance, he takes off his glasses. "Ms. P?" he says sternly.

"I'll take her now," she says quietly, turning on her heels and bustling in the direction of the door.

"Not alone. I have orders for four guards to be stationed on her at all times." His eyes bulge.

Four guards flank her. "You might follow me—I mean *us,* Miss . . ." Ms. P says.

"Whitetail."

"Whitetail. Of course." A greater understanding registers. "Right. This way."

Chapter 11

The Train Again

Rabbit spent the entire night in a room like a cage at the station. Sleep didn't come to her despite her exhaustion. She lay awake, her hand on the cigarette tin in her pocket, protecting the children all night long, hoping they were warm and safe. She wanted so badly to open the tin, to see what she could see, but she dared not. A blackcoat sat staring at her all the while. And when that man got tired, another man—same coat, same square hat, same suspicious gaze—slid into his place. The fact that the tin had been under her pillow yesterday morning was curious. Whitetail had changed her bedclothes, had changed her night shorts, and had also given her the tin? After she killed Mouse?

On the train platform, she sees the huge steam engine. The metal snake. The smell of coal smoke is so intense, she can barely breathe. It's as black as the bricks at the station. Oily looking. Its engine is loud, but not as loud as the people talking as they walk around her. A man bumps her elbow, and as she turns to kick him in the back of the leg, the blackcoat that's behind her ushers her forward with a shove. She's tempted to kick him, too, but she sees Sr.'s eyes on her and she's unsure.

When they reach a train car, all turn to look at the door. She can't fathom what the train car looks like inside. More metal?

Rabbit watches a tall man next to the door extend a hand toward her, and she recoils. Another man in a blackcoat wanting to shove her around? No, his pause tells her he's attempting to assist her as she steps up onto a stool, then into the railcar.

"A pretty girl like you should smile more!" the tall man says, forcing her frown.

Andrews Sr. moves past her, turns, and extends a hand to her.

"Up." He winks. Sr. wants to ease her nerves that this whole trip isn't terrifying, that everything isn't wrong and scary, but it isn't working. She's never been on a train. Never even seen one this close. Just their smoke. She's only doing this to save her family. Though testifying means betraying Whitetail to help the other children, her anger over what Whitetail did to Mouse—what she said in the kitchen, "I did love you. Once," past tense—well, her pain of rejection refuses to settle, no matter how riddled with homesickness she feels right now. Whitetail is a keeper. Keepers are supposed to keep people safe, not hurt them.

Instead of accepting Sr.'s assistance, she cocks her jaw stubbornly to one side and hops up the steps and into the railcar with ease. She won't need a man's assistance with this, now or ever.

Inside, the train car is furnished like a parlor room, but much more ornate than the front room at Andrews House. Instead of one couch and one table, there are so many wooden tables and plush couches; there're enough for all the orphans at Andrews to sit, no one on the floor!

Beautiful chairs with curved backs and elegantly arching legs are stationed about the car. The fabric's colors, gold and red, are shiny with tighter weaves than any she's ever seen. Engraved wooden paneling adorns the walls and ceiling, carved with birds and flowers, vines and cattle. The floor is covered wall-to-wall in a burgundy rug woven with gold flowers and green curly leaves. The room's fantastical, and all at once, Rabbit feels so homesick, her bones ache. Nervously, she wiggles her loose tooth.

"Have a seat over there, Abigail," Mr. Andrews says. His use of Rabbit has frustratingly switched back to Abigail now that she's agreed to travel with him to Syracuse.

Rabbit walks over to a seat by the window as another gentleman steps up into the car. He's rushed and disheveled. Immediately, he takes off the hat he's wearing and hangs it on a hook on the wall. Mr. Andrews doesn't seem thrilled to see him and stiffly acknowledges the man as he sits down at the biggest table in the room. The train's whistle sounds outside, and Rabbit's heart pumps fast. Two days ago, she was kneeling in the dirt with Rook, and here she is today on a steam engine. This railway has scarred the land and decimated the woods. She's so overwhelmed, her joints ache, and she thinks she might be sick.

Looking out the window to her right, she sees people on the platform take off running for their doors. The big metal serpent is about to leave. The train lurches, and her heart stops. Her feet are vibrating, and her hips buzz like she's sitting on thunder.

Heart kicking back to life, she can't help but feel a certain elation. A curiosity quenched. Even the whistle sounds different now than when it echoes off the hills.

"Abigail, this is Mr. Hughes," Sr. says as he lifts a cut crystal glass from a cupboard and pours two drinks. Walking across the room, he sets both glasses on the table, then slides one over to Mr.

Hughes. Sr. loosens his tie and sits down. There's no drink for Rabbit, even though she's terribly thirsty.

"Tell me," Sr. says to Hughes.

"Well, from what I can figure, Johnathan was, in fact ..." Hughes pauses to clear his throat. ". . . enamored with Ms. Whittle. He'd bought a ring. It's missing, however."

Sr. looks pained.

"They say that the antlers are new."

"Who says? She really has . . ." As he forks his hands above his head to simulate Whitetail's antlers, Rabbit can see the disbelief in Sr.'s eyes. He looks at Rabbit, but she feigns distraction. A tree is gliding slowly past her window.

"As you can see from the *Times* article from '86, she once was a looker. Perhaps John didn't know what he was courting. That the sisters, carnivores, had lain waiting for Father knows how long. Regardless, the antlers prove a deep deviance from the truce."

"Can a private not be dispatched to just dispose of the Dirty woman quickly? The longer the witch sits in a cell, the more time she'll have to cause pain, and the scandal. My wife lives with the same name as my son. My business relationships aside, I'll not have Johnathan tarnish my wife's reputation with his silly judgment." Sr.'s eyebrows shoot up, and his voice softens as he's lost in thought. "I can't let her down."

Hughes tilts his head with concern. "The courts advise a full public hearing. We'll need the charade to seal public opinion. It's what serves us in the long game of overturning the truce: if Freemen want to speak opinions over what's acceptable, they'll have to prove that a lax governing has spawned deep deviance."

Sr. looks unsure.

Hughes looks at Rabbit, then at Sr. "The courts have you and your wife's good name in mind." Hughes swallows hard. "You and your wife will be pleased with this outcome."

Sr.'s loyalty to his wife and his want to protect her proves he's kind, but silly. She's stronger than she likely knows. Still, Hughes has left something unsaid. He wants Whitetail to be more than a murderer.

"For this to work," Sr. says, "the sentencing has to be specific. We can't have the truce overturned only to have the charade of a reconciliation after the fact. The marble must be destroyed with the witch. We can't have squeaky wheels after they've only just been greased. We can't bury the body, then put it in a coffin."

Hughes seems to know what Sr.'s getting at, but Rabbit might as well be listening to dove chatter. The sounds are familiar but indecipherable.

"The list of charges will be so long and so horrendous, there'll be no sympathizers. The verdict and public opinion will align. With the witch in prison, more have come forward with what they were previously too afraid to report. We're waitin' on a full body count. Charges are still coming in and being investigated. Aside from the obvious Dirty murder of a child, we have five more men in two different instances killed, two with potions, and a woman claims the children were brainwashed into stealing her goat for satanic ceremonies."

Rabbit's stomach turns over, and she feels a fight tighten her fists. "That's a rotten lie," she blurts. Why make up lies? The truth is already terrible enough. "Ms. summons advice from the wilds to help people." She looks hard at the two men.

"The way she cared to help your little Mouse?" Sr. asks, his face reddening.

The memory of Mouse's little body on the big rock, the children gathered around, forces tears out of her eyes and renders her speechless.

"No, it's right. The devil is in that woman. She's deviant through and through," Sr. says, setting her straight.

"No one stole a goat," Rabbit argues. "Those McNealys asked Whitetail for help with their crops in exchange for the goat. Nothing flourished in their garden this past summer, but that's because they didn't heed Ms.'s advice. Whitetail told the McNealys to drink more water to get better crops. The McNealys didn't, and that's their doing. We children didn't steal Sarah, she was payment. She's lived with us for months, and the only ceremony Ms. ever had was to thank Dirt for the milk she gave." Who will care for Sarah now? Rabbit hopes she's gnawed through her pen and is roaming free.

Hughes shakes his head, irritated with her noise. He continues speaking to Mr. Andrews like he's been bothered by a gnat. "The girls are charged with Dirty magic. They'll be baptized, hopefully not hang—that would cost our image." Hughes eyes Rabbit. "But they'll be disbanded and sent to four corners of the country. The boy, yet to be recovered, is to be charged for collusion. Wanted posters have gone up. Some want to paint him as a Dirty sympathizer, but given the circumstances—he has his whole life ahead of him—I think we can all agree, boys are allowed to make mistakes. He'll be a cautionary tale for what dabbling in the Dirt brings; it led to his involvement in Johnathan's death. He'll be sent to work in the mines before he's eligible for the army."

"What!" Rabbit cries out, and her legs shoot up. *Armies mean war!* "You said I would be helping them." The other children are the only reason she's here. "The girls sent to four corners and the boy to the army!" These are not positive prospects.

"You are helping. We were never avoiding charges, we're avoiding sentencing to death," Sr. clarifies, waving a hand at her to sit down. "We have much work to do, Abigail." The car bumps and lurches as the train picks up more speed. Rabbit's mouth goes dry as her eyes scan the mountains. *Oh, Rook, can you see me being taken away?*

"Have they found the young girl's origin yet? She very well may have been a nobody, but clearly, she didn't come from nowhere, and if she's of society, it could only help us. Are we positive she isn't a Roscoe orphan?" Sr. asks.

Hughes shakes his head. "Our records show ten children were orphaned by the Roscoe fire, not eleven. Ten children were being financed at Andrews."

"One left to work for me, Tilley. That leaves nine," Sr. says. He turns to Rabbit. "At what point did this new mouth to feed show up on your doorstep?"

Hughes also turns to look at her. "Tell me, Abigail, when and how did Mouse come to live at Andrews?"

Rabbit considers it. Whitetail's face seemed like someone else's that night. She'd licked her top lip hungrily as she held up the die and invited no partner at Sixty-Three.

"Mouse arrived the night of the big storm. January. Dead of winter, Ms. called it. Whitetail had been suffering with pains in her belly that day. Headaches. Before Hyena got quite so big as now. It was late, just Ms. and Rook and Snake and me—alone in the kitchen. She stood up and got her game. But played alone, being bold." *Or stupid.* "Said it was too complicated. Too dangerous to involve any of us." Whitetail didn't want to share what she was cursing for. It was a secret.

"Sixty-Three?" Sr. whispers. "But with what goal?"

"Witchcraft," Hughes says, covering his mouth in disgust.

Sr. gives Hughes a scolding glance. "What was she asking the wilds for?" Sr. asks, returning his attention to Rabbit.

"I don't know." Whitetail's ways aren't questioned. "She never said. It was important, though."

"How could you tell?" He leans forward.

"Because she sat the two days prior, rubbing her belly, staring at the hearth trying to figure the exact right question to ask the wilds, I think. She's known for a long time she was dying. There was a problem needing solving before she died."

"Did she finish the game?"

"Yes. She finished it." Eleven rolls. Rabbit's surprised that Sr. knows enough about Sixty-Three to understand it must be finished. As she scrunches her face in thought, all Rabbit can recall is Mouse's knock at the door. Not the roll.

The look in Sr.'s eye is so serious, it scares her.

Rabbit remembers the way Whitetail's eyebrows had jumped with surprise. She remembers Whitetail moving her marker. But before she or any of the children could speak to announce the roll, there was a quiet knock at the door. Rabbit remembers barely hearing it. Thirty-three? No, it was further along. Fifty-six. *Incarnation.*

"After her last roll, Mouse was at the door. No clothes, barely a track in the snow, like she'd tunneled through it, not over it. A light came with her."

"A light?"

"A goodness. Too good, even. And her knock was so quiet, I—I think I felt it in my chest before I even heard it. Like a grouse taking flight." Wiggling her tooth, all Rabbit can remember is the surprised look on Snake's face. Then . . . the knock.

"Conjured a girl to your doorstep?" Sr. slowly rises from his chair.

"Damn it, child!" Hughes slaps a hand down on the table, making Rabbit's heart stop.

Rabbit's suddenly breathless. Her hands search for each other and knot in her lap.

Hughes's chest is heaving even though he hasn't been on a walk. He delivers an anxious look to Sr.

Some of Sr.'s neatly greased hair has fallen into his flushed face. Wobbling with the motion of the train, Sr. leans his knuckles on the table. His mouth pursed in thought. For a few moments, the only sound is the train's heavy pulse. Trees fly past Rabbit's window again.

Sr. scowls, then he sourly mutters over his shoulder to Hughes, "Have Sanderson's kept dispatch the faders."

Who's kept? Rabbit's hearing is so good she can find a snake during the cicadas' call. Even with the train's din, with Sr.'s turned head, she can hear what Sr. is thinking she doesn't.

Hughes looks rattled. "But—surely the faraday walls—"

Sr. furiously shakes his head, and Hughes's voice falls off.

"We need this witch's cell guarded day and night by unshakable faders. If she can infect my son, think of what she could do to simple guards, hired muscle? Have faders stationed until her sentencing. Who knows what damage has been done.

What close calls we've already had. What she's capable of. If she called this . . . so-called light, conjured a whole Dirty girl once, she could do it again. We have no choice. It's the price of control."

Hughes blinks with confusion. Leaning closer to Sr., he side-eyes Rabbit. "But, sir, even through . . . associates, we never acknowledge natur—" He stops, seemingly unable to finish the sentence. His eyebrows raise. "If it ever came back to us, the scandal, the peoples' support . . ." He delivers a look of warning. "Conversing with spirits puts us in a moral fog. If it ever came out—"

"It won't."

Rabbit has never heard of faders. *Guard Ms.?*

"Do it." Sr. pauses, his eyes darting. "Do it now." He stomps a foot. With a thick hand, he wipes the white hair out of his eyes and back into place.

Hughes nods in agreement, scowling. Getting tentatively up from his chair, he turns, walking toward a door at the car's end. Opening the door, a breeze of outside air rushes in. Hughes slips out of view.

The train is moving faster now, every second faster than the one before, and Rabbit feels soon it will take off the ground and fly. She's never felt so scared, and her cheeks flush with heat as she tightens her eyes.

The train's whistle wails.

M s. P and the guards lead Whitetail down the hall, away from the warden's little window and through a series of smaller corridors. Ms. P periodically moves past her to lead the way with a stomping mission-driven march, then falls, circling behind in Whitetail's wake, as she shepherds her down into the bowels of this place. It's very dark, and the deeper they travel into the building, the fewer windows there are. The ceilings are so low in places, Whitetail might bump an antler if she doesn't duck. As they tread the quiet of the hallways, Ms. P's knocking heels, the men's footfalls behind her, are answered by distant human echoes. Eventually the guards halt outside a doorway. Whitetail's directed into a tiled room, and she knows what the large white tubs are.

"There," Ms. P says. She motions to a bathtub. It's porcelain and curved. The water in it is gray and smells different from the water from the spring at Andrews House or the river.

"In you get." Ms. P's face is stern.

Whitetail wants to argue that she bathed only last moon, but Ms. P's eyes have already sparked with a challenge at Whitetail's hesitation. She says, "It's standard. Everyone goes in, even the livestock. Here, before it's as cold as the river." She offers to help Whitetail disrobe.

Whitetail can't say that cold water would have suited her better. Best not to argue. When Ms. P touches the buttons on the front of Whitetail's suit, Hyena rolls over violently in her chest. Whitetail holds out a hand, warning Ms. P to wait.

Something in how tightly Ms. P's hair is pulled back. The highly buffed dry skin of her forehead scoured with soap. The tight clasp of her hands hooking together, poised at her front in dismay, tell she's in search of control. Perhaps in her world this is the only place she has any. Grooming herself, poising herself like a noble, puritan statue. She purses her lips.

With one more look at her reflection in the water, Whitetail disrobes. Undressing is slow and sorrowful. Piece by piece, she takes off the ensemble she wished to be buried in after her voyage to summer. *Silly*, she thinks, understanding she'd have been killed immediately rather than the public spectacle that would come now. When she's naked, she turns to face Ms. P, who looks her over, shocked, maybe appalled. This woman wants to not like her.

"I say . . . who beat you?"

Looking down at her own ribs, her hips and her breasts, she sees them mottled with bruises. Her belly is big, large enough to be nine months with child. *Who beat me?* Whitetail can't say it's the man who she's accused of killing because it's not him. Hyena's done this.

"Lord, strike me down, there's a child in there," Ms. P argues coldly. She winces and pales, sucking in a quick breath. As she slaps a cold hand on Whitetail's belly and presses roughly, Whitetail reaches for Ms. P's wrist.

"I assure you, there's not."

Ms. P feels the boulder sitting beneath Whitetail's navel and recoils, yanking her hand away like she's been burned. She scowls in confusion. Whitetail can see that Ms. P's unaccustomed to admitting wrong. Witnessing this error is upsetting to Ms. P. She looks Whitetail's nude frame up and down, regaining authority in this awful place.

"I wonder what you are." Ms. P raises an eyebrow. "Do you even know?" Her concerned expression softens to a look of haughty sympathy.

"My mother's daughter. Born out of the ground." She had no father of practical importance.

Ms. P's smile falls, and she shakes her head, pinching her eyes closed. "The *Lord* Father had formed out of the ground all the wild animals and all the birds in the sky. He brought them to the man to see what he would name them, and whatever the man called each living creature, that was its name." When she opens her eyes, they're glassy with conviction. "You, however, have no name. If you were born of God, your kind would have a name."

But she wasn't born of any god. She was born of the Dirt. And surely no man had named her.

"Not born of Father means born of sin. You're Dirty, I'd say. Through and through." Ms. P glances at the water. "Get in."

Dipping one foot and then another into the tub, Whitetail can feel Ms. P's eyes on her. She knows it's risky. This woman prides herself on serving the Freemen, obligingly hurting women with their bidding, but Whitetail has to ask about the children. They're all she can think about and what she misses. They're her home.

Lowering her hips and then her ribs into the tepid water, she keeps her eyes down. In this position, head bowed, she sees the opportunity to ask the mighty Ms. P for mercy.

"Do you have any word of my children?"

"Your children. Thank heavens, they're not. They've been saved. Saved from the likes of your sinful incarnation. From your murderous hands. They'll be baptized and allowed to stand trial." Ms. P hands Whitetail a small brick. "Wash up." The brick is ash-colored and smells of something putrid. Putting it between her palms, she dunks it under the water and rubs. Raising it above water, there is too much lather.

Whitetail's chest hurts with Ms. P's speaking of the children. *Baptized?* They'd already been given nature's rite. Nothing would take that from them, so what would a foolish ceremony mean? It was the question of how many of her children were here that she needed answering. Whether they were upset. Were they caring for each other the way she'd always taught them? Rook? And dear Rabbit? What Rabbit must think of her, a monster, now is devastating. Heat and sting come to her eyes. She tries to fight the impulse, but hot tears stream down her cold cheeks, deceiving her.

"What will become of them?" Her voice is level. Her body is bulletproof; she'll persevere through anything if it means protecting her family. Opening her up one day, they'd see survival marks like tree rings. Her body is still standing, if a little less of her spirit.

"Don't worry. They'll have a day in court, same as you." She pauses, handing Whitetail a rag with which to wash. It's gray and rough, tattered at its edges. Whitetail turns her face away, but not beyond Ms. P's vantage point.

"Oh, tears?" Ms. P spots Whitetail's face. "Why bother? Enough of those. They can't help you, dear. In the light of the Lord, not one sparrow falls to the ground apart from God's notice, and neither does one of his follower's tears. But yours, heathen, well, they're just spilling in the dark." Ms. P shrugs.

"I'm not dear to you," Whitetail whispers as she gazes up into Ms. P's cold face. Her prefix, Ms., means she is unmarried. Perhaps widowed. Spotting the woman's anger, a trout in the shadows, her dominating and condescending temperament, Whitetail pegs it. "You're alone."

She can see it now. Though she knows quite well that a husband does not a happy woman make, Ms. P reeks of loneliness. "No family. No friend. Where you stand, above me, above all the women in this place. You're tall. A giant, even. In here. But out there . . ." Whitetail looks at the windowless walls. "But out there, you're invisible. And in either place, you've got no one."

Ms. P slaps Whitetail so hard and fast across the face, she doesn't see it coming.

"How dare—I stand with two, the warden and God." She points a finger to the ceiling and Whitetail can't tell which figure she's pointing to. "With Him, I am never alone. I'm devoted to my work. I work for Him. If the Almighty directs, I take to task. Women like you are morally depraved and in need of special, closer forms of control and confinement than even the sinners upstairs. A man who takes a child from God is depraved. A woman, a monster." Her voice falls off.

There it is again. Marriage, God, prison . . . Ms. P has two of the three and still stands here utterly alone. Ms. P looks indignant, an ugly curl rising in her top lip.

"Your being brought to justice will be the world's salvation. First a cage for you, then you'll be strung," Ms. P hisses. "You're proof of sin, and the cause for all women to gather their intuitions before the worst comes. Yes, I am above you, dear. A class all my own, perhaps. If that's the position God's elevated me to, I'll count myself a lucky woman, guided by men under the grace of God Almighty."

"When you treat no one as your equal, you'll always be alone," Whitetail whispers.

Ms. P delivers a disgusted look to Whitetail's feet. "When someone finally stands as tall as me, I'll look them in the eye."

Whitetail looks over the edge of the bathtub at the hem of Ms. P's long dress. At the shoes tucked beneath. Her prison mistress attire. The high heels she's wearing.

"Now get dressed in this," Ms. P says eventually, handing Whitetail a coarse cotton undergarment, a blouse, and a black denim skirt.

Of course it would be a skirt.

"You'll have an hour to settle into your cell over in the ribs before supper."

Whitetail looks at her quizzically.

"The building across the way where your room is. It's not a kind place, you'll find. But with any luck, you won't be here long."

Whitetail already knows she won't.

Ms. P freezes, studying the bathwater. Ripples course across the surface, cascading erratically. Turning, she looks up at the ceiling as Whitetail hears a coming thunder. Like a thousand hooves, asynchronous, coming closer.

"Ah, faders. A wise decision from our Supreme," Ms. P says.

Goose pimples envelop Whitetail's back and breasts, but it's not the tepid water that's brought them. Deceased Freemen forefaders—or faders, old Dirt called them—are the spirits of Freemen founders of government and authors of the Blackbook, penned at the same time as the Dirty texts. John Freemen himself is one such spirit. The summoning of these faders means escalation. Not just a political strategy to keep her under a most ugly and powerful guard, but an admission: they fear her enough to corrupt themselves. To call upon one of the ugliest parts of their past to guard her. Something that, before now, would have drawn attention to crumbling foundations, somehow now promises the comfort of control. To their brethren. To the masses.

Control over the narrative. And over her.

Chapter 13

The Tin

When they said Mr. Andrews Sr.'s house, Rabbit assumed it would look like *her* Andrews House in the mountains. Wooden siding, blackened porch, only two layers of windows, and the strangle vine. Instead, the building they're approaching is made of black stones that look an awful lot like the ones they just left at the train station in Syracuse.

Rabbit dislikes the auto she is riding in even more than the train. The auto is bumpy and loud, and it forces her to sit too close to Sr. Sr. and Hughes speak over her head. The auto goes around corners too fast, and quickly she feels sick to her stomach.

As they ride up a long road, dirt changes to black gravel and Rabbit recognizes this is a driveway. Peering out, she gets a better look at Sr.'s house. Six pillars on the front and four on the side. A tower that looks made for a lonely queen and three levels of windows. Multitudes of chimneys. And as they pull up out front, lots and lots of people are waiting. Strangers. Her gut rolls over. All she can think of is Rook. How could he have deserted her?

Sr. climbs out of the car first. Then Hughes, who's been muttering nonstop in Sr.'s ear the whole ride. When Rabbit steps out of the auto, it's like she's climbing out of the belly of a tired bear. Looking up at the faces, all orderly, lined up and surrounding them, she notes they are smiling at Sr. when he looks at them. They seem friendly, but their smiles don't stick. They become unfastened when they notice her. She brings a dark cloud of different experience with her, she supposes. She's lived all these years in the forest, in the Dirt.

Perhaps the Beard lived here when he was her age.

"Welcome to Westwood House," Sr. says, turning to look at a tall woman. "Marianne, this is Abigail." The tall woman with knotted shiny black hair steps forward, approaching hesitantly. She's dressed in a gray coat with tight sleeves that extend all the way down to her wrists. There are far too many buttons down the sides of her sleeves. The white apron she wears on top of her thick jacket doesn't have a single crease or stain on it, and it isn't sliced up the middle the way Whitetail always wore hers. Her garments are so long, they make her look like she's floating.

Whitetail would've been able to make four girls' pants from this much fabric.

Marianne gives a curt nod. Rabbit's hands are twisting together with her nerves. The woman's thick, heavy brows look stern, though not altogether unkind. It's hard to tell her age. She's not a girl like Rabbit and not as wise as Whitetail. She's middle-ish like bark that's lost all its green.

"Ms. Marianne will take care of you during your stay. What you need, she'll get," Sr. says, throwing up a matter-of-fact hand. In the distance, a wobbly man emerges around the corner of the building and halts, giving her a flat stare. His gaping mouth and sunken cheeks are irksome.

Sr. notices her distractedness.

"Ah, that's Mr. Martin. My highest guard. He keeps the grounds secure." Three more gangly men emerge behind Mr. Martin. In unison, they turn to look in her direction, eyes widening, having homed in on some foreign matter: *her*. Looking in the other direction, to the rear end of the building, she sees there're others dressed identically to the first strange men. Unlike the lineup of staff, these men in the fringes can't pretend they're happy she's here. Something awful guards Sr.'s home. The men all wear yucky expressions on their blank faces; they jerk and quiver and see without really seeing.

"And . . ." Sr. says, drawing her attention back to Marianne and her neighbors. He guides her by the shoulders and points her in the direction of the woman standing on Marianne's left. "You know Tilley."

It takes Rabbit a minute to recognize the face and name together. This person was a slender reed back when Rabbit last saw her. Her shoulders are square, and her wild black hair is pulled back so tight it makes her almost unrecognizable.

"Snake?" Rabbit gasps, running over to the familiar stranger and wrapping her cold hands around her sister's waist. "We worried about you," she says, never having been so relieved to see such an irritable person.

Snake scowls before she pries Rabbit off and gives an apologetic look to Ms. Marianne. Snake is pretending not to know her, but the scowl tells: it's her. Snake has never been a happy girl, and her work here apparently hasn't changed that.

"Sir, we must get to work," Hughes says. As Sr. walks away, Hughes in tow, Rabbit isn't introduced to anyone else. As the men disappear through the house's great double doors, all the staff disperses except Marianne and Snake, and the strange men. Rabbit feels inspected by them all. To the men in the shadows, she's a mystery that needs to be regulated. To Snake and Marianne, a challenge to be won.

The wind blows, and, uncomfortable, Rabbit looks down at Snake's apron, blowing in the wind. She notes Snake is wearing shoes, and she can't help but let her jaw drop. When she looks up wide-eyed at Snake, she's met with narrowed eyes. What a long three months it has been.

"Come with me, Miss," Marianne says. With a quick snatch, Marianne has Rabbit's arm in her hand and she's pulling, almost dragging Rabbit across the gravel. They cross the threshold of a different door than Sr. went through. Snake follows behind.

Looking back, Rabbit sees this Snake—reborn "Tilley"—is someone with as much anger as the girl she'd once known, but far less fire.

"Go turn down beds, Tilley. The Adamses and McCarthys will be staying tonight," Marianne says.

Rabbit wonders whyever a bed would need to be turned any which way, and which way in this city was considered down. *South*, she decides. But the head or the foot of the bed? After a last glance at Rabbit, Tilley departs, veering off down a long hallway, traveling in a different direction than the one Marianne is leading Rabbit down. Rabbit's hand feels for her pocket, for the tin, wishing she could stay with Snake, or at least keep track of where the only familiar face is going. If she were Whitetail, she could open the tin, see Snake turning all the beds. Confirm down as south. But for now, she'll just keep it safe.

"Hurry up," Marianne says as they cross a kitchen and walk farther on to another hallway. "You'll need washing up. Mr. Andrews has company tonight, and you're to sit with them."

Marianne sucks her teeth and mumbles the word "lousy," though Rabbit's never heard that word before. Marianne seems angry, and Rabbit recognizes she's been made a chore for this woman. Why? She'd been bathing in the river on her own for years. Could be trusted to clean her own hair too.

Just as Rabbit runs to catch up to Marianne's pace, Marianne walks even faster to stay out in front, not letting Rabbit stand by her side. *Always walk with them, never behind.* But Rabbit's legs are only so long.

Rabbit falls behind now. Marianne takes up Rabbit's wrist again in a pinching-painful grip.

Rabbit whimpers, her suspicions confirmed; Marianne's polite smile in the driveway moments ago was only for Sr., not for Rabbit.

They come to a room that opens out onto a courtyard where lines of laundry hang. Rabbit can smell the garments drying, sour on the air.

Marianne turns, knuckles on her hips and disdain in her eyes. "Look-it here, I'll not have any running in this house. You'll do as I say and wash up. Then you'll stay in your room until supper. I'll take you outside once a day. You'll work for me when I say. Twice a day you'll be called out for food. After the company leaves tomorrow morning, you'll eat in the kitchen with us help."

Rabbit nods, wondering where else there is to eat other than the kitchen. It is a curious statement. Marianne is cutting her down, but Rabbit can't figure from where. She hasn't asked to come here, nor does she need someone looking after her.

Marianne's face looks young. She can't be much older than Snake, but both look worn and older than their years.

Marianne bends down toward Rabbit, face in hers, and lowers her voice. "And I catch you doing any Dirty business, I'll have you burned alongside your friends so fast, the mister won't even smell the smoke!"

Rabbit shudders. There it is again, her family in danger. But *burned?* Her eyes flood with tears at the thought of the others. Her loved ones being burned up. *Is that what will happen?* She tries not to move, or let any tears roll down her cheeks. She doesn't want Marianne to see her upset. Being burned at the stake is not allowed. It makes it too hard for the Grimm to sort those bound for summer from those damned to winter. And it was outlawed with the signing of the contract.

It's okay to cry. Rook would have put a hand on her back.

She longs to talk to Snake. About what happened. Mouse. About the blackcoats. Ms. Her nose is running. It's registered that she's transferred from cool outside air to warm. She wipes her nose with the back of her hand.

"Ugh. Filthy," Marianne growls. "Into the bath for you. Come along."

As Marianne walks ahead into a stone-walled room, she points to a wooden tub. Rabbit frowns at the gray water and notes the smell. This pool is filled with the same scent as the clothing hanging outside. Grime of previous uses makes it so putrid that if it were spring, it would have attracted wasps. Her nose wrinkles.

Ms. Marianne seems to be waiting for something.

"You *do* know how to wash, even though you haven't?"

"'Course I do." She isn't some wild animal. Marianne's eyes shoot to the tub, and Rabbit's heart falls. This is not the cool, clear water of the river she is used to.

"Well, go on then. They've ordered you clothes." She turns to walk away, then stops. "What are you waiting for, child?"

Rabbit lets her toes, black with dirt, grip the stone of the floor. "Nothing."

"Nothing?" Her eyebrows rise. "You may be classless, but you'll show me respect. I'll have you call me Ms. Marianne or Ms. from now on."

"Yes, Ms."

"Use that nailbrush. I won't have a child in my care carrying filth throughout this house." Marianne leaves, shaking her head.

Upending her shirt, she feels a chill. Rabbit stands in only her pants. She's bathed a thousand times outdoors. January through December. Has never been shy. What keeps her so reserved now? When Rabbit reluctantly drops her pants, Tilley appears in the doorway.

Rabbit's heart rises, but she knows hugging is unwanted. "I forgot you'd be here. But I'm glad to see you," Rabbit whispers. "We worried."

As Snake picks up Rabbit's pants, her mouth twists with disappointment. Rabbit feels a wave of sadness for Tilley. Here she is waiting on Rabbit as though she's someone, which she absolutely isn't. *Or is she?* As Rabbit considers Marianne's curious statement about eating with the company, for just tonight, she's unsure.

That meant not eating with Tilley, whose miserable company, the familiarity of it, she craved.

As Rabbit steps into the tub, the water meets her knees. The cloudy water feels warm on her skin. Warm as June, and it makes her nauseous. This is not the way to clean. Clean is with the trout, with the butterflies drinking on shore in summer, and with the icicles in the trees in winter. Clear, always cold, water.

Tilley offers her a rag with a huff. "Scrub."

"It's poison," Rabbit says, wrinkling her nose.

"It's not. It's lye, the cleanest you'll ever be. At least until you take confession."

"Conf—what?" Rabbit gags as she unfurls the rag, then balls it up, wringing out all its gray water. Tilley crosses her arms with silent fury as Rabbit holds her breath and rubs the cloth across the back of her neck and under her chin. Had Tilley converted? The Freemen's religion? Rabbit crouches and rubs her legs and thighs. She shivers as she stands again, wiping her arms and belly. Rabbit washes her hands. And the dirt from under her fingernails with the nailbrush. Her toenails still have dirt. She hopes it will be overlooked so she can keep it. The smell of the water is overwhelming, and as her stomach rolls over, she heaves involuntarily.

"Poison," she chokes out in a whisper, trying not to gag.

"Poisoned is what you've already been. Your brain." Snake roughly slaps the side of Rabbit's head.

"Hardly," Rabbit says.

Snake rounds on the tub with a smirk, crossing her arms again. "You still think that any of that stuff about the Dirt being good is even true, you foolish creature? Even with all that's happened?"

Rabbit stands speechless. Dirt, not good? But that would mean—it couldn't be true.

Snake smirks. "You've got so much to learn about the real world, Abigail." Walking across the room, Tilley inspects Rabbit's pants, possibly taking pride in their craftsmanship. They are Tilley's hand-me-downs after all. Running her fingers along the seams, she frowns, as though lost in thought. As she spins to look at Rabbit, she says, "That new girl, what did you all name her? Mouse? She's really gone?"

Snake left almost immediately after Mouse's arrival, and never even directly acknowledged the girl before leaving. Rabbit knows Snake to be a jealous creature, but her disdain for Mouse seems more complicated than resentment. Darker than spite. Mouse had somehow driven Snake away.

"Whitetail killed her. I don't know why. I'm only here so I can help the others."

Snake's face turns sour and her eyes narrow. "You fool," she says, looking sick. She waves a dismissive hand at Rabbit before she turns to leave. As she gets to the door, something falls, clanging. It tumbles across the floor.

Rabbit gasps. *The tin.* She'd left it in her pants pocket. As Tilley stoops to snatch it, Rabbit's frozen with panic.

"Snake?" Eyes pleading, Rabbit runs out of the tub, splashing water on the floor. Tilley puts the tin behind her back. She cocks her shoulder back defensively as Rabbit lunges for the cigarette tin. "Give it—please."

When Marianne turns the corner and enters the room, she's carrying a bundle of pressed clothes under an arm. Rabbit freezes as Tilley tucks the tin behind the waist of her apron.

"Tilley?" Marianne looks at both girls suspiciously. "Have the beds all been turned?"

"Almost, ma'am. I'll take these to wash, ma'am." She holds out the pants and shows Marianne the blackened knees.

"Or rather the oven," Marianne directs.

Snake leaves as Marianne turns, her round eyes spotting naked Rabbit and then the puddle underneath her on the floor. "What is this?" she shrieks.

Putting the pile of pressed clothes on a chair, Marianne reaches for Rabbit. "Back, back!" Marianne pushes her back into the tub. "You put your filth on my floor, and I'll tan you."

Rabbit can't speak. Turning around to look at the door, Snake is gone. So is the tin. Marianne is fussing, but Rabbit can't hear what she's saying. A cold wind blows as she waits to dry, her arms crossed in front of her. There's nothing else to hold on to.

Chapter 14

The Wolves

*S*hoes. She never thought she'd wind up in shoes. Though wearing them isn't against any principle of Dirt, far as she can tell, they symbolize repression. *It's amazing what the spirit can cope with to preserve the body. My spirit is a mighty oak that just won't fall.* Her strength of spirit is not guarding her against anything so constricting as these shoes. Her feet are crammed into what Ms. Marianne called "spring heels." Spring-ish, these shoes are not. They are heavy, hard, and hot. Too tight. She feels unable to walk as she normally does, but Marianne's eyes on her as she follows the woman down to the dining room are forcing her to try.

"Because of your fussing, you're late," Marianne whispers at the back of Rabbit's head as they walk into the dining hall. Rabbit shrugging and pulling her neck at the high collar of the yellow dress she's wearing. Marianne practically forced it over her head. The fabric it's made of is hard and rough. The sleeves too poufy. The skirt it features is ruffled, and wearing it, she's simultaneously feeling silly and uncomfortable.

Rabbit's wooden heels knock loudly as they tread off carpet and onto the marble floors, alerting everyone seated at the long dinner table to her arrival. All eyes turn to land on her, so she slows her pace, making Marianne put a firm hand on her back to give her a shove. At one end of the long table sits Sr. and five people she doesn't know. Three women and two more men.

Rabbit's struck by the cut flowers standing in vases around the room. They're also depicted in paintings on the walls. They appear embroidered in the upholstery pattern too. The buds are colorful, but Rabbit's excitement ebbs, then falls away entirely as a hideous artificial perfume strikes her nose. Despite their bright palette, the flowers are as fake as the smile Marianne is giving to Sr. right now.

Rabbit's heart heaves in her chest as she sees where she's supposed to sit, next to a woman aside Sr. Feeling bluer and more homesick than ever, she plunks in the chair, and a man in a gray coat surprises her by pushing it toward the table before walking away to stand in a corner. Rabbit misses Rook, always stealing her seat from under her, not pushing her in tight. She misses the sweetgrass they used to sit in. The river and its bugs. All of it . . .

But Whitetail too? At the very least, Rabbit misses her own ignorance that the only mother she's ever known is an imperfect person. She pushes Snake's question of the goodness of the Dirt from her mind.

"Well, hello, Abigail. We finally meet," the woman next to Rabbit says with a smile. Her teeth are so white they look unreal. Her auburn hair is long but tied up in a curious bird's nest shape. She's beautiful but also powerful; it's apparent like the cramer moth. She looks to Sr. with her chin high. He looks pleased, so she in turn smiles even more broadly before returning her gaze to Rabbit.

"Hello." Rabbit would never correct this woman for calling her the wrong name. The woman's eyes are honest, big and brown. Her smile is reassuring and her voice calming.

"I'm Mrs. Andrews."

"Oh," Rabbit manages. *But she seems so young.* The two other couples at the table titter with laughter.

Rabbit shrinks inside. She can't help but feel that this woman should not be belonging to anyone. Least of all to elderly Sr. She seems so charming, beautiful like a spring plum, while Sr. is more like a dried prune.

"And this is Mr. and Mrs. McCarthy." Mrs. Andrews points to a woman in a purple dress the color of aster. "And Mr. and Mrs. Adams." Mrs. Adams has white hair. Mr. Adams has the same coat as Mr. McCarthy, Sr. too. The men are all dressed in matching black shirts with an emblem of four dots on their biceps.

"Abigail, how is your stay so far? Are you settling in?" Mrs. Adams asks.

"Not really." Lost in thought, Rabbit winds up staring at the ceiling. It looks like it's made of gold. What river would have been wide enough to pan so much?

"Oh, the poor dear!" The other woman, Mrs. McCarthy, dabs her cheek with a handkerchief as her eyes dart from Rabbit to the man next to her, then back again. *Are there deer here?* Rabbit's hopes are high before it clicks, the woman has said it *about* Rabbit, not directly to Rabbit about a rangale.

These people, everything feels so exaggerated. Their faces, their expressions. Their clothes. The house with its rooms, too many to count. Drapes and cushions made of fabrics Rabbit's never seen the likes of before. Rabbit thinks, based on Tilley's words, that she should feel safe here. But it feels rough, it's *heavy.* A prison.

"Well, you're safe now," Mr. Adams says. His face looks older than his years. Dark hollows sink under his eyes. He has a bushy mustache and a dark complexion. His face is disturbingly mottled with acne scars. No, blisters. Deep pocks. Almost nightmarish.

Mr. McCarthy has no scabs or scars.

As Rabbit turns her attention to Mrs. Adams, she's unassured. Then she sees what's behind the woman's high-backed chair: a flag. It is enormous and hangs over a stone hearth. Rabbit's seen it before. No, something very much like it. Crimson red, it features the silhouette of a broad-winged great horned owl in white at its center, but unlike the 'Librium flag she's grown up knowing, this owl's wings are raised, not lowered. Around the owl sit four solid black dots. The four corners of the earth. Rabbit sighs so deep it's almost a yawn. The flag announces these people as allies of the Dirt? Is it proof she is cooperating with the good guys? The owl's wing positioning makes her mouth twist with indecision.

"She is very pretty, Mrs. Andrews. An orphan . . ." Mrs. Adams turns to wink at Mrs. Andrews, whose smile falls as she watches Rabbit.

"Shush, Ramona."

Mr. Adams's wife blushes.

"Sorry, she's all chatterbox, I'm afraid," Mr. Adams says, giving his wife a second scolding glance.

There's a sadness in Mrs. Andrews, Rabbit can feel it.

Mrs. Andrews shakes her head politely at Mrs. Adams, but Rabbit's not sure why.

Mr. Adams takes a somber tone. "Of course, they couldn't be put up for adoption." Wrinkling his nose, he gazes around the room.

Mr. McCarthy interrupts. "There will never be another Johnathan, Mrs. Andrews. The loss of a child." He looks at the tablecloth. "John was salt of the earth and pride of—" Mr.

McCarthy stops speaking as he looks at Mrs. Andrews. Her eyes plead with Sr. to make the all comments stop.

Mrs. McCarthy looks down at her plate. Mr. McCarthy's attempt to soothe the subject of children, come and gone, is unsuccessful.

Fresh dread over the fact that she cursed the Beard wells up in Rabbit's chest. The room fills with silence and Rabbit wonders if living in this place, with the memories of a child lost, is painful for Mrs. Andrews. Though she spent most of their time together despising Mouse, Rabbit misses her so much right now, it feels like it might break her forever.

"What news of Elizabeth Whittle?" Mr. Adams asks Sr.

"She's locked up in Liberty. Walls of pure faraday. We're getting ready to pull the trigger on the trial," Sr. says curtly.

"Oh, what did that Dirty woman do to you, Mrs. Andrews? Oh, my! Such a tragedy!" Mrs. Adams holds her chest as though her heart might tumble out onto her plate. "Is it true?" Looking now at Rabbit. "She has real antlers?"

"Yes." Rabbit knows what they're thinking and doesn't like it. That she's ready to tell them all the bad. But what bad there had been at Andrews House happened so fast and only this week.

Jittery with the feeling of Whitetail's betrayal, she can't say anything more. And what Snake said about Dirt. Good or bad. It has rattled her.

"And your parents?" Mrs. Adams presses a hand to her mouth, though she doesn't cough.

Rabbit perks up on the subject of her parents. "They died in the fire." Whitetail always claimed the fire wasn't an accident.

But that the railway men, the Andrewses, labeled it an accident. *Labeled like jars of plum?* Rabbit isn't sure.

"It's just too bad."

"Shh!" Mr. Adams shushes his wife again. Mr. McCarthy's brow wrinkles at the mention of the fire and Rabbit's dead parents. He looks at his wife, and then at Rabbit, a thoughtful expression in his eyes.

Someone lays a piece of fabric across Rabbit's lap and her mouth opens a little with confusion until she sees all the adults at the table accept their fabric and leave it where it lies.

A small staff brings in a platter and some dishes, and a familiar scent hits her nose. Lamb. *But it's not even summer moon!* Unlike the hunks of meat she's used to, this meat is carved in medallions still hanging onto bone. Rabbit smells mint and recognizes it's the green stuff in a little bowl set next to her. She thinks of the huge bushes of it in the garden and the rest of it that she liked to run through by the big rock. The mint here is mush and smells like maybe there is sugar added. What a way to spoil good mint. But it's a feast, and she's ravenous.

"I'm so sorry for what you've been through, Abigail. For how you were treated up there," says the woman with white hair, Mrs. Adams. "All those years." She shakes her head in dismay, eyeing Rabbit like she's a baby bunny needing a mother. It's bothersome. Rabbit wants no sympathy.

"You seem a dear," the woman adds.

"No, a Rabbit." She scrunches her toes inside her shoes. Poking her finger in the bowl of green, she scoops up a big fingerful of the mint. And as she sticks her finger in her mouth, she tastes the most beautiful taste she's ever experienced. Some of it runs down her chin.

"Oh," someone says, as though they've met a pool of tadpoles by the river's edge.

"You mean she seems feral," Mr. Adams says, disapprovingly.

"I'm sure you're hungry, Abigail. But in this house, little girls mind their manners," Mrs. Andrews says. "And pay respect to who feeds us." She looks at Sr.

Rabbit freezes. "I'm sorry, I forgot to ask the Dirt." Dirt offered the food. She would always ask before eating.

Mr. Adams's amused face turns dark with disgust and the women at the table, Mrs. Adams especially, wrinkle their brows. Sr.'s face turns a rosy hue.

"She doesn't know any better. Give her time," Mrs. Andrews says as she looks around the room. "To the Dirt? Not in this house, miss!" Mrs. Andrews says sharply to Rabbit. "As long as you're here, you'll give thanks to Father first, and then Mr. Andrews second. He bought you this meal."

The statement isn't unkind, but it hits Rabbit hard. Sitting here at the dining table, it's striking how unlike home this is. Now all the adults bow their heads and fold their hands on the edge of the table. The quiet lasts so long it's as though everyone is frozen.

But she can't pray to the Dirt or Sr. for this food. She's wearing shoes and indoors. Under the table, she shakes off her summer heels and they pad lightly onto the floor. If she could have hooked a finger into her socks without Ms. Marianne, watching from across the room, noticing, she would have them off too. Her heart aches with homesickness and guilt for not being able to properly pray with her family. She looks at her lap so she doesn't choke with tears. It's awful being here in Sr.'s house. She's here for one reason, the children, her sisters and brother, but now, in this company, with this meal, it feels utterly disloyal. To her kin, to the Dirt.

"Go ahead and eat now, Abigail." Mrs. Andrews watches her carefully.

Rabbit nods but can't bring herself to touch the strange shiny cutlery. She's used to just a spoon.

Mr. Adams continues, "You should know, Abigail, that this family are well-known in your parts, the Catskills. They call Mr. Andrews Sr. here, 'the man who saved paradise.' You owe him and his fathers many thanks." Mr. Adams nods to Sr. as he cuts into his lamb, sawing some off the bone.

Rabbit sees there is an open sore on the back side of Adams's hand. It's small but weepy. Like sores from poison oak.

"They say a lot of things," Mr. McCarthy utters, smiling lightly as he brings a forked chunk of meat halfway to his mouth. He eyes Adams and then Mrs. Andrews before he lets out a puff of air, making it very clear, even to Rabbit, that his opinion has slipped out.

"I'm sure you're aware by now, I'm pushing to move the nation in a progressive direction. To do this, we'll have to make amends with the past," McCarthy admits.

Mrs. Adams sets her knife and fork down on the side of her plate and chews. The air in the room grows thick.

"Luckily, you're not sitting at the head of this table right now, and Sanderson is still Alpha," Mr. Adams says, nodding reassuringly to Sr., who looks surprised at the turn in conversation. Mr. Adams adds, "Just what are you insinuating, Charles?"

"Spit it out." Sr. looks rigid.

"Perhaps save it for the drawing room after dinner, gentlemen?" Mrs. Andrews smiles at Mrs. McCarthy, then at Rabbit. Mrs. Andrews puts down her fork. Reaching for her glass, she takes a sip of wine. "And how are your gardens coming along, Mrs. Ada—"

"Say it, McCarthy," Sr. says, slamming a clenched fist down on the table, making the glassware and everyone jump.

Mr. McCarthy looks around the room before raising his chin a notch higher. His eyes turn to Sr. "You stole the land out from under them." He gestures to Rabbit. "Reparations should be made. Sanderson should be advised as much."

Mr. Adams's chin rises in defiance as he delivers a look of reverence to Sr.

McCarthy's chest heaves, and his face reddens. He speaks to his plate now. "You didn't save paradise, Andrews. You stole it. All those rules and restrictions set up, you stormed through with more of your father's rail ties, ready to build . . . You've run all over it as though none of it was ever theirs and fed it all to your bank account." He swallows hard. "You stole it from those poor people when no one was looking, like a thief. Those left, they were paid to leave. Or were burned alive."

"They were discovered to be Dirt!" Sr.'s breath catches in his throat. "You voted to contain Hyena," Sr. says indignantly. His bottom teeth are showing. "It was a matter of public safety."

"To contain the thief, sure, but not incinerate the entire town," McCarthy says.

"May I remind you, some of the entire town is sitting at this very table?" Andrews's eyes dart to Rabbit's.

"Dangerous steps have been made. People sentenced before a trial. We've become—" McCarthy's eyes dart to Adams in confrontation. "I dare say, if we witnessed our very steps taken in the name of Dirt, we'd condemn the perpetrators to an eternity of the strap in After. I'm willing to concede, we've made a mistake. Hyena's reemergence could be the opportunity—a moment to open conversation and confront polarization."

"What's polarized? My husband is a very practical man," Mrs. Andrews interrupts. "He swept out trash. It's gone. Restrictions were made to keep the riffraff at bay. Rivers clean, and the land forested. Hyena was the last straw. The Dirty colony was growing too large to be ignored. Don't forget that this country was founded on the principles of progressive thought over magical rot." Mrs. Andrews's voice is cutting as her eyes dart around the room.

"If any of those Dirty people were still alive down there, they'd be fighting you, and you know it. You yanked the carpet out from under them after Hyena's theft. That culture was all but destroyed. Strategically. Collateral damage in a hunt for one woman, yes. But also, she was a moment of convenience to destroy Roscoe."

"That town—" Sr. argues.

Rabbit can't think what Hyena might have stolen that would be so precious.

"You killed it. A near cultural cleansing occurred the day you all waltzed onto that land. The people are watching. After three generations of Andrewses holding that seat, what's been accomplished is polarization. Hell, if Father Freemen's lack of heir, if the endowment had fallen to anyone but your grandfather . . ." McCarthy scoffs, shaking his head.

All turn to look at Rabbit and it's clear her presence is what has sparked this conversation.

After a look at his blushing wife, Mr. McCarthy lowers his voice, but he's visibly shaking. "It's taken Stephanie here to show me the dark side of this. She grew up near there. Her family. I've seen it. They've moved on, but because they've had to. Not allowed so much as a hunt . . . Americans united in the goal of making things safe—it has devolved into a, a—castration. We need to fess up to it. Admit we were afraid—"

"*Ugh!*" Sr. throws down his napkin. "Who's afraid? What's left of that people could be sad, looking at a place that's not theirs any longer, or they could have some greater perspective. It's because of me they'll have bread and butter on their table. I gave dollar enough for that. Gave them more than took. Relocation put money in everyone's pocket. You know as well as anyone that control by design is necessary for peace."

"I can see how you'd want to believe it, but from my perspective, the endeavor was stacked in your family's favor," Mr. McCarthy snaps. "Not the country's. Truth will come out."

"Don't you even bring up fifty-eight. A level playing field still exists. We started as equals at the start. We've all played out this reality, and this is the way it should be."

"Stephanie," Mr. McCarthy says, tenderly holding out a hand, "we should be going, dear." And with that, he gets up to leave. A corpse of a guard is waiting across the room. Spotting him, Mr. McCarthy adds, "To our room. We'll retire and will be leaving in the morning."

Sr. slams a hand down on the table again, making Rabbit jump.

"Damn it, Charles! It needed an infrastructure to sustain and regulate itself! That's something *your piece-of-dirt wife* here has no head for. Honestly, man." Sr. huffs, eyeing Mrs. McCarthy.

"You'll have no say what her head is good for. I heard you polished the headstones in the graveyard to make them prettier before you re-marked the cemetery in your name!"

"You have a problem with my name, you best remove that patch from your jacket and take your chances with the wolves."

"You're mistaken; the wolves are here," McCarthy says, eyeing Adams.

"It's what helps me sleep at night," Sr. says.

Mrs. McCarthy rises to stand beside her husband. The pair leaves silently, but not before Mr. McCarthy stops to salute the almost 'Librium flag.

Rabbit is shocked. She has never seen grown men fight. The words they used, the palpable tension in the room.

Mr. Adams looks at her, her untouched lamb, with a double take, and his face sours. "Is it not to your liking?" His eyes dart from her plate to her open mouth.

She snaps her mouth shut.

"Not enough fur left on the corpse? Or is it the fact it's cooked?" He snickers, and his wife frowns disapprovingly. Something Rabbit's said about the Dirt, what happened with the McCarthys, has affected Mr. Adams. Made him turn on her.

Picking up the chop with her fingers, Rabbit moves to take a bite when Mrs. Andrews clears her throat and looks down at her own cutlery, halfway to her mouth.

"Why, I'm afraid I've lost my appetite," Mrs. Adams says.

Ashamed and out of place, Rabbit licks her fingers and wraps them in the fabric in her lap, though her hands aren't cold. Her hunger's gone. She wants to please Mrs. Andrews but isn't sure how. Sitting still seems like the best plan.

Mrs. Andrews watches her a moment before she places her fabric on the tabletop. "Won't you excuse us, Sr. I think Abigail and I shall retire to my parlor to get more acquainted." Rising, Marianne retrieves a cane Rabbit hadn't noticed hanging on a stand nearby and marches briskly to hand it to Mrs. Andrews.

"Tea?" Marianne offers, as Mrs. Andrews agrees with a smile.

The wooden cane is shiny and smooth, composed of a high-contrasting marbling of colors. It has a small white stone at the top. After a graceful step, Mrs. Andrews nods a thanks to the room, then casts an expectant glance at Rabbit.

"I do believe we have a lot to learn from each other."

Chapter 15

Confessions

Walking into the rosy-colored parlor behind Mrs. Andrews, Rabbit wiggles her tooth, feeling nervous. Already she's developed the habit of checking her pocket, but this time when she puts her hands to her hip, the tin isn't there. This dress has no pockets. A streak of anxiety runs through her as she fears she'll never get the tin back. Never get her family back. The strangeness here at Westwood House is painful.

There's the chatter of birds. Rabbit locates them in a cage in the corner. As she watches them hop lightly and nuzzle, their sweet sound warms her heart until Mrs. Andrews lifts a heavy, dark fabric and covers the cage with a square, black hood.

"Shhh," Mrs. Andrews says. The birds' songs, their cheerful conversations become stifled by the black fabric and are blotted out entirely. The birds were the only thing distracting Rabbit from the paintings on the walls. Seeing them now, more cut flowers, her breath grows shallow.

"Come, sit." Mrs. Andrews waves a hand at a settee as she walks across the room. "Would you like some tea?" Her eyes flit to the tray Marianne left nearby with a beautiful setting, all frills and gold rims. Mrs. Andrews's expression is compassionate. Not like Mrs. Adams or Mrs. McCarthy at dinner just now. It's heartfelt, not pitying. Mrs. Andrews's inhumanly long white fingers gesture to a green chair across the room with a high-pillowed back. Same as in all the other rooms, the furniture in the salon faces inward instead of outward like at home for good window-watching. So very curious.

"Thank you." Wearily, Rabbit can't figure out why people eat and drink so often here. Wiping her tired eyes and cheek with the sleeve of her dress, she hopes Mrs. Andrews won't remember how she behaved at dinner. Though she's happy to have left the dining room, those men fighting and Mrs. McCarthy's stares, she's not fully comfortable in this small room one-on-one with such an intimidating woman. Rabbit's yet to move a muscle, and yet she knows she's doing it wrong. Standing wrong. Put her ankles together? Hands at her sides or behind her back? Why does she care what this woman thinks of her? One thing is certain: Rabbit fears one more disappointed look from Mrs. Andrews might turn her to stone.

Rabbit looks at Mrs. Andrews's cane more closely. The marble, set in a crevice on the cane's top, looks like it's being held by a bird's talons.

"Beautiful, isn't it?" Mrs. Andrews says of the marble.

"Yes. Very. What is it?" Rabbit's cheeks feel hot.

"A gift from my husband from the day we met. It reminds me that loyalty to my husband is loyalty to myself. It holds many secrets." She narrows her eyes at the marble. "I wanted a chance to talk. Without all those bulls in the room." Mrs. Andrews pours some tea into two cups, then pours milk, and drops a lump of something white in each.

Rabbit wants Snake. Even her brutal company would be a gift right now. She wants the cigarette tin back. And out of this place, because dinner and tea have nothing to do with setting the other children free.

Carrying the cup of tea over on a plate, Mrs. Andrews sets it on a table in front of Rabbit. It smells delicious, very sweet. Not like the dandelion tea at home.

"Do you like black tea?" Mrs. Andrews asks.

Rabbit half nods, unsure.

Turning, Mrs. Andrews walks back toward the tea tray for her own cup. As Rabbit reaches for her teacup handle, fine like a wing bone, she's worried she'll break it.

Mrs. Andrews's smile drops.

"Careful there! That tea is very hot. I'd hate for you to burn that precious tongue," she says, her face at once turning sweet again.

Rabbit looks at the cup. Curls of steam trail off it. She's grateful for the warning, but Mrs. Andrews's sentiment had curious undertones. Not altogether sincere. Rabbit wants to get to the point without being rude. "Um. My sisters. The others?"

"You'll testify at the trial, yes? You'll be called on by what's called the prosecution," Mrs. Andrews explains.

Rabbit can't respond. Too many words she doesn't know.

Lifting her own cup of tea on a plate, Mrs. Andrews carries it over to the couch where she perches gently on the edge. She leans her cane next to her. The teacup on her plate is in fine, steady hands, and Rabbit's curious about the necessity of the cane. The woman's strides and movements speak of no disability. The cane is certainly just for show.

Rabbit slides back in her chair an inch and watches Mrs. Andrews's strange hands. They don't have the sunspots Whitetail's have.

"Are you nervous, my dear?" Mrs. Andrews looks at Rabbit's tea, then back into Rabbit's eyes.

"Yes."

"Don't be. All you'll need to do is tell the court how awful and scary Elizabeth Whittle is and it will help lift all the blame off the children." Mrs. Andrews's eyes are earnest, sharp and clear.

"But they really didn't do anything. Except come home early when Rook asked them to wait by the river while we scouted."

"Mmm." Mrs. Andrews picks up her tea and blows on it gently before placing it back down. "That's exactly what you'll say." Leaning over, she reaches for Rabbit's cup. Raising the cup to her red-stained lips, she gently blows on Rabbit's tea, as if Rabbit were Mouse waiting for her hot porridge to cool. Rabbit always wanted Whitetail to blow on her porridge, too, but couldn't ask because she'd be told she was able enough to blow on her own cereal.

Mrs. Andrews sets the tea back down on Rabbit's tiny plate. When she smiles, Rabbit gulps, noticing her teeth. White in the front, black in the back. Rabbit's never in her life imagined anyone ever blowing on anything of hers to save her stupid tongue, especially this strange creature.

"Would you like to see one of my scrapbooks?" Mrs. Andrews asks.

"Scraps?" As far as Rabbit knows, those were leftover pieces of meat for stew. If not nice enough for stew, a welcome treat for the bears. Rabbit didn't care to see Mrs. Andrews's scraps much but didn't want to disappoint the woman.

Perhaps sensing Rabbit's skepticism, Mrs. Andrews elaborates.

"I collect articles that interest me in books. Papers. The news. The press investigates and reports the truth. I have some old Dirty history." She lightly taps the spine of a black-and-gold book. "And a new one for Elizabeth Whittle." She grabs her cane and walks across the room to a shelf. "And another that will follow the trial you'll star in."

"Star?" Rabbit's so homesick that another word from her lips might start her crying. Her chest shudders.

Reaching for a book with a red spine, Mrs. Andrews looks back over her shoulder. "Well, you're my star." She smiles. "A star witness is what you're called."

"Oh," Rabbit says as she watches Mrs. Andrews retrieve the biggest book she's ever seen.

Pulling it off the shelf, Mrs. Andrews carries it over to Rabbit and places it heavily in her lap. It smells of paper and dust. Mrs. Andrews sits gently down beside her. Rabbit had learned to read some thanks to Snake's learning from her father—a learned man. Before Snake left, she'd offered to help Whitetail learn to read, too, but Ms. claimed that reading stars was enough for her.

"The Roscoe fire is how you ten all came to live with the witch. They refer to her here by her real name, of course: Whittle."

Again, the use of "real" is irksome, but Rabbit's too distracted by hunger for more information about her past, or Whitetail's past, to argue the truth. The first page of the book is a slip of type-written paper. Rabbit scans. *Roscoe Ten: Ten orphans to be given a home.* Great fire. Homestead raised in memory of the ancestors of the forest and their city lost. Orphans to be presided over by housemistress Elizabeth Whittle, sole adult survivor of the blaze.

Mrs. Andrews smiles knowingly as she taps Elizabeth Whittle's name on the page. "She also used the surnames Waters and White at times. When she was scheming and stealing. Stealing children, apparently."

Rabbit feels Mrs. Andrews's eyes on her, looking for a reaction. Rabbit doesn't give one. She can't. She may as well be a scarecrow.

With that, Mrs. Andrews raises her teacup and takes a noiseless sip. "We found a paper trail. An Elizabeth White signed a slip for a tab back in a Liberty general store a year ago, before a child was stolen from out front of the very same store."

"Stealing children," Rabbit says flatly, seeking out the root of misinformation. In all her time at Andrews House, she'd never seen a child brought in whose parents weren't a victim of the fire. *Except Mouse.*

"This is a drawing of the suspect." Mrs. Andrews turns to the next page, which shows a drawing of a woman in a bonnet. It has no resemblance to Whitetail. It shows a much rounder face, slightly different angled eyes, and a piggish nose. Whoever drew this picture recorded a chillingly blank expression that Rabbit had never seen Whitetail wear.

Mrs. Andrews points to the lines of text printed below the drawing: *Woman wanted for stealing child: Rose Rene of West Shokan, aged eight years.*

Rabbit shivers. *Stolen? West Shokan?* That was two days' travel, maybe more, from Andrews. Whitetail never left the children unattended for more than a few hours. Mouse was at most six years old, not eight like her.

Besides, Mouse had plodded naked onto the porch in the

middle of a snowstorm. Rabbit had seen it with her own two eyes. Rabbit remembers Whitetail opening the back door. How Mouse stood as tall as Rabbit's shoulder.

Flipping to the next page, she sees four photographs. *Four Roscoe Youth Die by Indeterminable Ailment.* James Koll, brothers Robert Jones and John Jones, and Jack Voles. Rabbit recognizes the boys immediately. It's the four youth who stole from Whitetail's garden last summer. Rabbit and Rook had been sent to retrieve squash from the garden and bring it back to Whitetail. Rook had scoffed at Rabbit's proposal to run to the river to cool off, committing instead to his chore. Rabbit had felt irritable as she crouched to break off a fruit from its stem, and with an inexplicable need to stand up and look west, she spotted four men. Boys, really. They were exiting through the tall grass with a chicken under one arm, a tomato plant in the other, and a whole mess of half-ripe apples in the last two's shirts.

She squealed when she saw them. *Thieves!*

Rook ran back to the house to tell. Whitetail hollered from the porch. She'd gotten so mad, she cursed them up and down for stealing food from children. Rabbit remembers one of the boy's mothers coming to the door a week later. Crying at first. Then screaming and pointing a long finger.

"August 19, 1893. All wracked with unknown disease. The last of which, Mr. Voles, expired fitfully at midnight," Mrs. Andrews reads aloud. "A rumored curse."

"But Whitetail's curse didn't *kill* them." Rabbit grinds out her doubt. A woman who killed a child in her care was capable of murder. That was a certainty. But Whitetail guessed that these men, barely sixteen, were mostly still boys and had likely eaten poisonous wrack grass thinking it was sweet onion. "Their death was the will of the wilds. No more," Rabbit states flatly. "She may have cursed them, but she didn't—" A thought to her curse on the Beard has her shaking. She can't say any more.

Looking up at Mrs. Andrews, Rabbit seeks reason in the woman's face, but all she finds is a cloud of questions.

"What are you thinking?" Mrs. Andrews finally asks.

"That this is bad. Tragic, even. But not all true. Bad things happen. But it's not all Whitetail's fault. Magical doesn't mean evil . . . just because it's magic." Why would Mrs. Andrews want to believe lies so badly? How could the papers, the ones Mrs. Andrews claim "spoke truth," be so misleading and salacious?

"I know what you want to believe—what you've been raised to believe—but misinformation is damaging. With magic comes evil every time." Stoically, Mrs. Andrews stands and moves across the room, sitting in her original position on the settee. "Not only is it so inconsistent, it hurts more than it's ever helped. It's been placed in the most inherently sinful of hands. Just think, the power of revenge, to covet and steal, to lazily sit back and reap rewards from a few words. The toss of a die. Some stones. Whether they're words spoken in a moment of sincere longing or flippant impulse, it's still sin. To curse. Raise the dead! And revenge?" She huffs. "The power to kill someone, Rabbit. It's not a power at all, is it? It's crime. It's dangerous because it's so difficult to govern."

"But Whitetail prayed every day to the wilds and used Sixty-Three while governed by the great presence itself." What other government does mankind need?

"The wilds." Mrs. Andrews shakes her head. "The Blackbook states in parable fifty-six, Sarah picked the magical apple when her father told her not to. Magical sin. It follows women like a plague. Whitetail carries that plague. The wilds breed the wicked. Regulation is the way out of the wood."

Rabbit's unsure of what parable fifty-six in the Blackbook is, but she knows Sarah's parable fifty-eight in the Dirty texts. In the same fashion Whitetail had been taught, Ms. would tell bedtime stories, parables rich in meaning, from the Dirty scripts. Rabbit has heard the oral histories so many times, she knows them like the phases of the moon. Fifty-eight tells of Sarah being beaten on the ground by her father for picking a forbidden apple as a gift for her mother, Eve. Sarah's punished fingers gripped stones. When broken Sarah brought the stones back to her mother instead of the apple, Eve despaired. Eve cast the stones into the dust, knelt, prayed to the Dirt, and tallied a line with the sixty-three ways in which she was still in love with her husband despite his ignorance over believing an apple was more significant than his daughter. After a night and a day, the wind responded with a symbol on each of Eve's sixty-three notches that would ever after serve as guiding idioms with which to dialogue directly with the wilds in times of crisis. It was the birth of Sixty-Three.

"Her father was wrong for beating her; the apple was hers as much as anyone's. You can't own nature. Just thank it for what you get." The third rule of consent: *Don't become confused over what's yours.* Sarah's father got confused. He was wrong to say that apple was not for her as much as him. "Why would nature create something we're not supposed to have? If the wilds gave her the skill to ask the Dirt for help, speak to nature directly, why would that need governing?"

"Man's changed his mind. So has nature. Time decides which parts of us melt away. Muscles in our heads, ears, in our arms, they're disappearing because we don't need them. We've suppressed magic almost long enough—but it will take more time and legislature to eliminate it entirely. Elizabeth Whittle is a rare breed. Like a poisonous seed, she's burrowed deep, and like a fever, she's fallen one, and others." She gestures at Rabbit. "I for one was born free of the Dirt, and therefore I'm not a Dirty sinner. To save ourselves, we must change ourselves. Else we devolve into murderous wild animals."

"Born without Dirt? But that's impossible. All girls are born with endless fields of magic. Didn't anybody tell you? Dog said we're all children of the same Eve . . . a chip off the same block as her. Girls don't come unmagical, they just forget. Or get told lies."

Mrs. Andrews freezes, and her bottom lip hangs speechless. After a hard gulp, she reaches a cold hand for Rabbit's.

"When I was young, only eight years old, I was in love with a boy." She leans in, tilting her head like she's got a secret. "He was strong, kind, and a devout Freemen. Jacob Maloy. I used to run up behind him and say, 'Knock-knock!' And he used to tease me over a crooked tooth." She places a finger on her top lip. "He used to call me names. But he liked me. Really liked me. And, oh! I cursed that crooked tooth," she says with a light smile. "I cursed it every day. As all children do, I lost that tooth. More teeth. Lost all my teeth, one by one.

"Over the course of a year, they all fell out. On my plate after porridge. On my pillow after a night's dreaming. I swallowed four . . . But unlike other children who lose their teeth, my second set of teeth never emerged.

"Without teeth, I lost my appetite. My smile. My every happiness was gone. I couldn't play with my older sisters for the torment they'd put me through. Wouldn't see friends, or let Jacob Maloy see me. I'd hide when he'd call and soon became a distant memory. Strangers wouldn't have known I existed. I hid and was hidden by my mother. I was a wraith.

"My mother was an old bird. Her knowledge of the Dirt was not strong; if she had any at all, she was devout in not using it. And when I sinfully asked her about any Dirty help, she said, 'No, Floyd Louise. The shame you'd bring me would be my death.' She handed me the Freemen Blackbook and told me to pray. For forgiveness for whatever evil deed had brought spoil to my mouth. At ten, she handed me the book. At twelve too.

"My oldest sister married. I didn't attend her wedding party. My second eldest's either. I spent my days locked away, my arms wrapped around the good book, desperate for the Lord's forgiveness while my mouth became a black, putrid hole. I'd never be wed. I'd never work outside my own home. Never survive. I hated myself. I told my mother, 'I'd rather die than live this way'—I hadn't been outside in years."

Rabbit gulps.

"I reminded my mother that after her death, I'd be left hungry and unloved, with no keeper. Still, my mother argued, 'Bring Dirt into my house and it's a handful of Dirt on my grave.' My mother cried.

"One day, a woman came by the yard. I could see her from the window. She—she knew I was there. She was the answer to all my prayers. A Dirty visitor. She heard my torment like the devil seeks sin. Wild and unkempt. From the deep wood. I snuck out back to the yard."

Mrs. Andrews's gaze shifts from Rabbit to the floor. She frowns, her eyes pained. Her shoulders drop.

"I was weak. Unmagical, I assisted as representative of the wilds when we played Sixty-Three. On my eleventh roll, I rolled *Confrontation*." Mrs. Andrews cocks her jaw bitterly to one side. "She said my body would heal; it would call up every tooth after I 'made peace with my shadow.' You know what that means?"

Rabbit shakes her head, still trying to grapple with the fact that Mrs. Andrews is without magic altogether and, like Rook, can only assist in Sixty-Three. No magic in her bones. Just willingness to participate.

"Peace with my shadow, ha! She said I was to leave my home every day for a month. And every day, I was to smile at a stranger.

"Some cowered when they saw me. Some ran away, calling me a monster. And I was a monster. I'd been starving in the dark for years; I looked a wretch."

Mrs. Andrews's eyebrows raise, her gaze back up to Rabbit now. "But it worked. Every day I smiled—every day a tooth grew in my mouth. On the sixteenth day, I went out into the sun feeling freer and more like myself than I'd ever felt. I went to town. I went to the market. I ate an apple in the sun. On the street, lo and behold, I found Jacob, standing there, grown yet, and as handsome as ever. He didn't see me. I went to him—up from behind like old times." She smiles, but then it falls. "'Knock-knock,'" she barely whispers.

She places a hand on her mouth, almost kissing her fingertips. "I'll never forget the look on his face." She winces with the memory. "He knocked them all out with one thrown fist. He thought I was a monster."

Rabbit's stomach lurches.

"And rightly so for how sinful I'd been." Turning, Mrs. Andrews lowers her eyes on Rabbit. "My mother was dead before I made it home," she says wistfully before raising a brow.

"Eve's apple was the plague. Sarah's father knew best. Magic is evil. My mother knew best."

Rabbit tries not to scowl. "Your husband knows best?" She's been bold, neck-deep in the river, but she's too upset to stop herself.

"That's right!" Mrs. Andrews acts pleased, even though Rabbit knows she's gone too far.

Looking down, Rabbit spots the group photo. The one of all the children and Ms. standing on the porch at Andrews. Whitetail is on one side, the Beard on the other, with all the orphans lined up in between.

"You haven't touched your tea."

Rabbit's eyes stay glued to the picture. Her hands are shaking so bad she couldn't reach for the tea even if she wanted to oblige. She's stuck, unsure what to do. She'd like to run to the privy for privacy. To get away from Mrs. Andrews. *The Beard's proud chin.* The style of hat he always wore. The way he held his eyes, a cat watching the garden from the porch, self-important and lofty.

Rabbit's eyes flit to the opposite page. Mr. Johnathan Andrews's obituary. It shows a drawing of a great-antlered monstrosity of a woman with black eyes. The headline over the dreadful drawing reads: *Magic Murderess Charged in Heir's Death. Six victims include children and Andrews rail heir, authorities say.*

Below lists thievery and more aliases. Mrs. Andrews retrieves a handkerchief from her sleeve. Her face crumples in pain. She sniffs, blotting her eyes. Mrs. Andrews's breath casts a putrid smell on the air. Thinking of the woman's teeth—fake teeth, white in the front, black in the back—Rabbit holds her breath.

Rabbit shifts her weight, looking at Mrs. Andrews, then at the drawing again. *Is that how Whitetail looks now?* Could the antlers have gotten so large so fast? It has been but a few days since she's seen this woman with her own eyes.

"Monstrous, isn't she? Horns are proof of consorting with the devil. Deviation. Proof of the evil."

"Antlers, not horns."

"I'm so happy you've come to us and that you're safe, Abigail." Mrs. Andrews speaks over her. "She stole my son from me with her Dirty magic. Misled and hurt your friends. She'll pay. She'll not only pay, but hopefully show America, once and for all, that magic needs more regulation." She looks down at the head of the cane she's holding, caressing its high polish with her thumb.

As Rabbit's eyes dart to the drawing in her lap again, they fill with tears. She hates how the antlers look. What they remind her of: Mouse's screaming . . . A flame of fear rises in Rabbit's belly. *Consorting with the devil?* Had she been living with a thief and a con woman?

The drawing of Whitetail implies that she is no more than an animal. An evil one at that. Rabbit feels utter disappointment in

Ms.—and a creeping despair. Had she been gullible, like Tilley said? Mouse had loved an insincere fake? Rabbit herself had been so desperate to please the woman. Had she been fooled, and now sat here, justly feeling foolish? Maybe a girl as gullible and stupid as herself, taking a mad woman's word as truth, deserves a cage smaller than her siblings.

What is the truth?

Magic isn't evil! Akin to the difference of opinion on Sarah's parable, there is a discrepancy in these so-called truthful pages. Rabbit wants to hurt Mrs. Andrews for all the horrible things she's just said. For making Rabbit feel the ways she feels right now. Rabbit stands, shaking her head, trying to summon an argument in defense of all her own truths.

Mrs. Andrews shudders as she reaches for Rabbit's shoulder with a comforting hand. Tears overflow Mrs. Andrews's eyes, and she dabs them with her handkerchief. "You're safe now. But those children can't be allowed to grow into murderous, Dirty semblances of the woman who raised them. And spread the plague." Her weary eyes grow round. "They need to be saved."

"How can we save them?" Irked by the touch of Mrs. Andrews's hand, Rabbit's voice is so quiet she can't decide if she's imagined herself speaking. She's anticipating Mrs. Andrews's answer having more discrepancies.

"You simply tell the truth about what happened."

Rabbit nods. Regardless of how she feels about the Andrews family, the truth would be simple enough.

"The whole truth," Mrs. Andrews adds. "You'll start by swearing on the Freemen Blackbook that you disavow the Dirt forever. Your friends will have to do the same."

Disavow Dirt forever? But that would mutilate her magic; it would stunt, or even cease her and her sisters' growth. It would cut her own life expectancy by half in the process. It would mean no magic being handed down to her daughter, should she have one, the inheritance lost. *It's amazing what the spirit can cope with to preserve the body. My spirit is a mighty oak that just won't fall.* But. But. This would be her whole spirit spent for survival. It would leave nothing for summerland. That wouldn't be better than tea with the Grimm?

Rabbit's arms twitch as adrenaline shoots through her veins. She can concede that Ms. Elizabeth Waters. Whittle. Whitetail is not a perfect woman. In fact, that she is even a wicked woman who maybe kidnapped, told lies, and cast hexes that killed. She did kill Mouse, after all. But—disavowing the Dirt would mean becoming an entirely different person.

Panic rakes through her chest. All she wants is for the children to be safe, but at this cost? A price that would make them all strangers to themselves and each other? Would it be worth it?

Chest heaving, Rabbit's reeling. She knows she must leave this place. The easiest way would be to get swept out like a spider. It would be impossible to break into a jail. To save the other children. She would need a police escort. A way into prison.

What better way than to be labeled a murderess herself?

"I cursed your son. I killed him," she says, narrowing her eyes.

Mrs. Andrews's gaze looks stung and mean. "What?"

"It isn't magic that hurts people, it's people going against the will of the wilds. Defying the four consents," Rabbit yells.

"My son . . ." Mrs. Andrews's voice slips out ragged. Her glare is insufferable. Bolting to her feet, she reaches for her cane, and, lifting it by its pointy bottom, she raises the stone setting up like she's ready to beat Rabbit's face, a filthy rug. Her eyes brim with tears.

Rabbit flinches, pinching her eyes and lips shut, fearing for all her teeth. One strike from the head of the cane and they'd be gone. All Rabbit can hear is the beating of her own heart, and after a silence, muscles aching and hands tingling, she dares to open an eye.

Pain washes over Mrs. Andrews's face, and it collapses a moment before she stoically lowers the cane and roughly snatches the book from Rabbit's lap.

As Mrs. Andrews slides the book into its spot on the shelf, she hangs her head a moment.

Her back heaves. She growls, "Go to your room!"

Rabbit runs. Tearing out of the room, her feet are seemingly under someone else's command. Down the hall, up the stairs, she sprints into her room.

Let them come, she decides. *Let the blackcoats haul me away.*

At least then she could be with the others. At least she would still be herself.

Considering her location, she expects blackcoats will come imminently. And she will wait for them in the room she's been given.

But as evening turns into night, Rabbit realizes she's been sitting on the end of her bed for hours, listening for the sound of boots in the hall. No one's come for her. No blackcoats stomping in to slap irons on her wrists and haul her away. Not Mrs. Andrews come to beat her. *Murderer!* Not even Tilley, to smile at Rabbit's predicament. Rabbit, overwhelmed, lays her head down for a moment. And falls asleep.

Until a gentle knock at the door wakes her.

Chapter 16

The Rocks You Got

Groggily Rabbit opens her eyes, head reeling with dread, guilt, and homesickness. Looking at the door, she sees it's not blackcoats come to take her away, but Ms. Marianne. She's standing in the doorway, and when she spots Rabbit waking, she briskly comes in. The light outside her window is gone, and Rabbit's stomach churns. The lone bite of lamb she had for dinner isn't sitting well.

"Time for bed." Marianne's voice is as unfriendly as usual. She walks over with a night shift clasped between her hands, and she wears a look of business on her face.

Rabbit thinks she must have misheard; there is no way she'll be permitted to stay here tonight. Doesn't want to if she could. She'd like to be cast into the city to be swallowed up by machines, or quietly disposed of, dropped into a grave in the courtyard if the blackcoats aren't coming to take her to Liberty to be with the others. She can't stay. Not in this big, awful bed. In this terrible house. With them knowing that she killed their son. With the looming prospect of having to disavow her Dirtiness with a disingenuous hand on the Blackbook.

Marianne hands over the shift. Reluctantly, unbelievingly, Rabbit takes it. "I won't need it," Rabbit says.

"Well, I can assure you, you'll not be sleeping in *that*." Marianne delivers a look of warning before she proceeds to help Rabbit out of the fancy yellow dress she'd worn to dinner earlier.

As Marianne unties the ribbon at the back of Rabbit's neck with cold, unfriendly fingers, Rabbit pulls her arms out through the sleeves, feeling more vulnerable than ever. She's heartbroken and confused, uncomfortable and unconnected. Bones aching and head cloudy, all she wants is a safe space to sleep to regain perspective. A reset.

And Rook.

"But I'm not staying," she reiterates.

The blackcoats are surely coming. Surely! Why would the Andrewses keep her here after what she admitted in the salon earlier?

"Check with Mrs. Andrews. The blackcoats are coming for me. Should be here any minute." As she utters "blackcoats," she feels sick.

"Stupid girl, it's Mrs. Andrews who sent me up here. And this is the blackcoats' commander's house. If they were coming, they'd a-been here."

Rabbit can't fathom why she'd be kept now that she'd admitted to cursing the Beard. For what purpose? To slowly and methodically be tortured? The fact that Mrs. Andrews would let her stay and speak out about Whitetail, but not send her off for cursing Beard, is curious. Confounding, even. What would come after the trial? After her magic was sworn away? If she is to become enslaved here forever, she certainly wouldn't be so graciously offered a night shift by Marianne to wear to bed right now, would she?

"Put it on," Marianne says.

Rabbit can't argue. Marianne is right. If they were carting

her off to Liberty, she would have been gone already. Her ploy to get sent to prison with the other children has failed. Is she trapped here?

As Marianne carefully folds the yellow dress and sets it down on a nearby chair, Rabbit hesitantly puts on the shift. Rabbit's thoughts race to the conversation at dinner. The talk of stolen paradise, allegiances, the railway, and Roscoe. The talk had all been eye-opening and terrifying. Had Sr. *stolen* paradise, as McCarthy claimed? Hyena had stolen? That's sure what it sounded like. The flag in the dining room—it wasn't 'Librium?

All is not as it seems.

How could the flag for 'Librium be owned by both sides of the oldest battle in history?

Mr. Adams's face had been truly terrifying. Rabbit shivers, remembering its hollows, like walnut skin. The blisters on his hand. The way the others, even his wife, didn't seem to see it. The back of his neck. His awful teeth. It was the same as all the men wandering by the gate, but much worse. She has to ask.

"Into bed," Marianne says. Marianne had been in the dining room earlier and heard the same conversation that Rabbit had. Perhaps she can clarify just what everyone was upset about—and what disease plagues Mr. Adams. His wife was so beautiful. Mr. Adams is either a much, much nicer person in private, or he didn't always look like and act like a monster to have gotten Mrs. Adams to marry him.

"Marianne?" Though she works for the Freemen, Rabbit knows Marianne's a woman. Deep down somewhere in her bones, she sees more than she's allowed to admit.

"Yes?" Marianne roughly takes up Rabbit's folded dress in her arms. Marianne looks worn, too, though Rabbit isn't sure why.

"Mr. Adams. His face, the way it looked. What is wrong with him? His face was hollow. Haunting, even. It wasn't natural How come?"

"Wrong with Adams? My girl, that's a high officer of the Freemen, servant to the Supreme you're speaking of."

Rabbit's heart stops. *The Supreme?* The Freemen leader. Was that Mr. Andrews Sr.?

Rabbit squirms with discomfort. Whitetail always claimed the Supreme was the most vile, damaging figure in modern times. How can it be Rabbit is sitting here, about to sleep under the Supreme's roof? And be expected to speak for his cause? It seems impossible.

And the head of Mrs. Andrews's cane? According to Whitetail, the stone in her cane was just as likely as not to be the Necrology. *Oh Rook, if only you were near.*

"What's a high officer?" she pries. Mr. Adams had spoken with great authority; obviously, he is a well-respected man. McCarthy, too, though he'd made Sr. angry.

"Well, that's a high-up in the Freemen party. He oversees the Andrewses' needs. Protects them too. He's a soldier. He'll fight for the Freemen, for the Supreme, to the death."

"Fight who?" Whose side did Rabbit consider herself on?

"The people who don't agree with Freemen, I suppose. Mr. Adams has been by Mr. Andrews's side since, well, longer than I've been here, and that's going on twenty years. He may not be blood, but might as well be. Was like an uncle to young Johnathan."

Rabbit still isn't quick to recognize the Beard by that name.

"Do all high officers have that on their faces? Those marks? The blisters on his hands. His neck. The black eyes. It's like he's haunted!" Rabbit exclaims, almost tearing up. "How come Mr. McCarthy doesn't look like tha—"

"Shh!" Marianne rounds, darting close to the bed. She's raised a hand like she might slap Rabbit. As she glances to the door, she quickly drops to a knee at Rabbit's bedside. Her face is very close to Rabbit's, and it's furious.

"Mr. Adams may very well be haunted. All the guards on this property too. But that's not something we speak of. It's the fashion of Freemen, you see. Mention of Adams being a strangler will get you killed. It's something they all pretend not to see. I see, and you see, but we never mention it. McCarthy has no scars. Maybe he's not haunted, as you say. But un-haunted, that's a dangerous place to be when you sup at the Supreme's table. Swaying allegiance, absence of, or healing scars and all that. Either way, as for McCarthy, as long as he serves the Supreme, does his part, he'll stay in that seat with all the entitlement his position allows. And he knows as much. And the Supreme knows, in this day and age, you keep your scarred friends close, and virtuous unscarred, those who may betray you, closer." Marianne looks searchingly at Rabbit. "Just because you're a star witness in this trial doesn't mean you can't accidentally disappear, same as fifty-eight."

"Fifty-eight?" It'd come up at dinner too. "Do you mean *Reckoning*?" Rabbit's brain is stubborn. She can't fathom what Marianne means by "disappear." Fifty-eight existed on every board she'd ever played on. It was the notch that she and Rook had argued over. The one that, by all rights of the wilderness and her opinion, should be *flame, fire.*

"Yeah. Disappeared, you fool. Privates, blackcoats, and soldiers. They roam like pawns until they kill. Stranglers is what they become. They adopt the dead stare of their victims. Adams's appearance isn't something you'll speak of. McCarthy's healing scars, either."

Not something to speak of? Rabbit sits silently aghast.

"I'll say this. Strangle your moral compass for as long as Adams, you'll wind up haunted too. You can't kill that many women and not wear it on your face. Some stranglers occasionally grimace or cry, but all wear the frozen face of their murdered. Wear the dead's expressions, the last expressions of those women, and adopt the dead, black eyes of their victim."

"Dirty hater. But the flag?" She had to confirm its meaning. She's been raised to revere it as a Dirty symbol. "I saw McCarthy salute it with my own two eyes. Pure of heart and reverent to 'Libriu—"

Marianne cups a hand over Rabbit's mouth.

"Don't you dare say it. That flag," Marianne whispers, "forget what it used to mean. What you were taught in the woods. It represents control and the current established Freemen party now."

Marianne lifts her hand away, but Rabbit keeps her mouth shut.

To the Dirty, the four consents correspond to each dot on the 'Librium flag: *The first consent: If it's not yours, don't touch it. Second consent: If it's yours, defend it. Third consent: Don't become confused over what's yours. Fourth consent: If you're confused over what's yours? Ask!*

"Power belongs to the wilds!" Rabbit whispers furiously. "The four dots mean balance at all four corners of the earth."

Marianne shakes her head. "Not in their eyes. And to the world, they are a most powerful government. They'll stop at nothing to get control of Hyena. Burn her at Pitch Point—the first burning in over a century—and amend laws to scare anyone else coming out of the forest. They'll stop at nothing to control their narrative. But before they kill Hyena, they'll use your Whitetail, your family, as an excuse—all rights of women will be taken in return for Freemen keeping them safer. To keep them safe, the Freemen will seek quiet. The Dirty will accept being quieted. Or die."

She remembers the hungry look on Sr.'s face when she explained where Hyena is. And alive.

"They want Whitetail—to get to Hyena?" Rabbit's hands go numb. She knew Whitetail wanted Hyena's residence to stay secret, but there were so many secrets at Andrews. How was Rabbit to know that secret was specifically precious? That that secret was perhaps of even more concern to Sr. than even his own son's death? Mr. McCarthy's statements earlier become only a little clearer.

Rabbit feels her brow pinch. "Seek quiet?" She needs to be sure. She knows what she thinks it means. Whitetail spoke of quiet—the silencing of all magic.

"You've grown up in the dark, girl. In the dark." Marianne shakes her head pitifully. "These are the times we live in. And it's best you get in line, before you're burnt up like your Ms. and all the other Dirty women that will face your so-called Grimm. Freemen hold control.

"Until you arrived, the name Hyena hadn't been uttered here in years. Years and years. It's rumored she'd met Supreme in New Amsterdam, a right pretty tart. Come out of the shadows as he visited his city quarters in the belly of the Blackbox, the Father church. Hyena tickled Andrews's gizzard so hard in his apartment, the old bear fell asleep. By the time she slapped him across the face to wake him up, she'd swallowed that stone from his safe. Then disappeared before his very eyes. Some say the restless spirits of Sr.'s sisters had whispered Hyena the combination some way." Marianne sucked her teeth in dismay. "Can't see how, though." Her brow furrowed. "It took Sr.'s father eighty years to conceive his male heir. His older sisters, twenty of 'em, are under lock and key under blackhood guard—may those babes be sitting on His knee, and quietly."

What's in the head of Mrs. Andrews's cane is not the Necrology?

"They thought they set her on fire, that Necrology she stole gone with her, and, thank winter, before she used it to expose the list of murdered. If she'd had it her way, we'd all be dead, having sacrificed our bodies to hold on to our spirits. Now that they know Hyena's in your Ms., rumored with the stone, at that . . . on the verge of calling for war? Gonna holler for truth too? Demand reconciliation for a people they don't want anyone remembering. Well, it'll be hard for Freemen to stay on moral high ground if someone points out how much blood is on their hands. Best to quickly get them washed and keep on pretending."

Hyena stole the Necrology? And threatened to use it to reveal the names of the Dirty dead and start a war? Rabbit only knew of one fire. According to Whitetail, the marble is indestructible. If

Whitetail had the stone the whole time, why didn't she say so? Why keep it secret? It takes Rabbit a moment to wrap her head around the probability that Whitetail knew the marble was in her, in Hyena, all along.

"What damage could the truth do?"

"Wouldn't they like to know. The shift in the world's opinion of the Dirty has already happened. The growing list of wrongly dead is—will always be—troubling, but as it's the way it's always been, no one remembers any different. By now, it must be an ocean's depth to endanger Freemen supremacy. Your Miss's deeds and her publicized trial will further divide what's already a chasm. There is no safe harbor for Dirt anymore. People are scared, sure, of Dirty, but even more so of the Freemen. So scared, they'll overturn the law against burnings at Pitch Point to ensure there's no rebellion. Fire at Pitch Point, that's the only way they'll get rid of Hyena, you know. Only way to destroy that deep Dirt is by fire. That's what scared everyone into submission the last time."

Rabbit questions just how Dirty she really is. Deep Dirt have the ability to tap into original Dirt. Oldest magic there is. "Do you still have Dirt in you, Marianne?"

Marianne shakes her head. "Survival was better than endearing myself to what's harmful, anyway. I never had much. My mum knew the dangers, I come from old birds, so what magic I inherited was more grains of sand than the boulders you got. They cursed their Dirt away, trying to un-level the ritual."

Rabbit's heart is in her feet. "Un-level the ritual?" Sure enough, the last five notches were always tricky, or so Whitetail claimed.

Rabbit has no idea what old birds are. What does aligning with Freemen offer a woman? Offer Marianne? Why would women like Marianne join them? Marianne stays here in this awful place even though she *knows* it's unbalanced? Why would someone like her purposefully stand in men's shadows and walk through a world where men demand that the Dirt bear them fruit?

"Why do you stay here?" Rabbit asks. "Knowing all this?"

"I've learned, women like me, staying here and working like this, *is* what keeps 'Librium."

Rabbit gasps. "But it doesn't. It's unbalanced." Rabbit can't go on. She can tell by Marianne's face, she's not listening, or she already knows. Marianne stares at the window, lost in thought. The light is black outside. Nightfall is upon them. There's no seeing through the glass. Marianne's not looking at the night, she's looking at her reflection. Getting up from Rabbit's bedside, she walks to the door.

"I stay for protection, I suppose," Marianne says quietly. "And what little Dirty that exist out there will join me or be condemned."

"To what?"

"The Grimm." Marianne leaves, quietly closing the door.

Though death isn't something Rabbit fears, she has work to do before summer. She'll not stay in shadows to make others more comfortable. Sitting in bed, she feels sick that she's lost the tin. The children's very souls are in jeopardy. How to warn them that Freemen will expect them to disavow their magic with a hand on the Blackbook to gain freedom? She is surrounded by so much confusion and evil. *It's amazing what the spirit can cope with to preserve the body. My spirit is a mighty oak that just won't fall.* Despite Whitetail's willingness to sacrifice her spirit for her body's survival, Rabbit can't help but think she herself would prefer to cut off her own foot to escape this place and the prospect of any spiritual sacrifice. She hates this place with her bones. What it stands for. What it keeps telling her about how she was raised. Which is the right path? Believe a murderess's opinion that every Dirty woman will have her day, she just has to wait? Or do what Marianne has done—what some women need do—denounce the Dirt to survive? She'd been told 'Librium meant peace.

Quietly, Rabbit throws back her bedclothes and stands in the dark of her room, listening. Peeking out of the window, she has an expansive view of the courtyard below and of the servants' quarters. Tilley's room is there too. Oh, how she needs to ask for the tin back, but the expanse of the courtyard is too far to call across without the whole house waking.

Looking out at the sill, Rabbit opens the window and peers out into the black. Below are gardens with trees and shrubs, which would have been soft to land in if it weren't March. Jumping into them from this height would mean a broken head or worse. Closing the window, she latches it quietly.

Tiptoeing to the bedroom door, she turns the knob. It lets out a whisper of a squeak, but as she peers out through the crack, there's no one there. The hallway is long and dark, and all she can think is how much she'd like Mouse's hand to hold onto right now.

She treads softly into the hallway. Her feet hurt a little. From the shoes that she was made to wear? She recognizes her new disadvantage: she'll not be able to run as fast as usual when she hits rocks and grass outside. She meets the grand staircase and idles. It is massive but carpeted. No noise from her footsteps.

Stepping down a few stairs, she sees someone in the corner of her eye and instantly her heart starts smashing. It's only her reflection in some windows. She hasn't been told she has to stay. She's just been told where to go. What would happen if she left here? If she ran away? Would people chase her? The answer is clear when she remembers Rook's predicament.

Walking farther down the stairs, she peeks over the rail. Gripping it in her hand, the railing's the size of a five-year-old birch, thick and cold. A long shadow appears, like a fish underwater, across the patterned marble of the grand entry below.

Rabbit waits, watching it, trying to figure who it is and how closely they're paying attention. There's another long shadow that slides in next to the first. Slowly it glides forward with silent steps. The shadow sways its head in focus, and she knows it's the guards—the stranglers, as Marianne called them. She watches the way they move their heads in her direction and feels chilled by how inhuman they seem. How vacant of emotion. There's the sound of sniffing, and as her heart kicks up, she realizes the three men in the foyer have identified that she's out there, somewhere. No magic, just animal sense. They can smell her. Is it the Dirt or just being female that gives her away?

As one of the shadows wobbles along the floor, Rabbit hears someone approaching from the other wing of the house. Coming to join the others? No, they turn abruptly, and their footsteps are audible on the stairs, their shadow growing taller as they ripple up the bottommost steps. A strangler's awful face comes into view with its gray, vacant eyes and horrible grimace.

Rabbit pulls her head back into the shadows.

The footsteps stop, and there's the sound of a long draw of air. She hopes she's not been seen. Frozen with indecision, she can't decide if she should stay put or run back to her room.

The sniffing stops and there's no noise. *They're all listening.*

Biting her bottom lip, she doesn't breathe.

"Maaa-rtin?" The thing on the stairs says with a low growl. The utterance sends her feet moving, and as she bolts up the stairs, she hits a wall with a bump.

No, not a wall, it's Mr. Martin. He was standing right behind her. Somehow, she knows she looks guilty. Bumping into Mr. Martin has driven one of her teeth into her bottom lip. She tastes blood. Sucking in her bottom lip, she tongues the fresh cut that lies there.

Martin's face is already looking in her direction with empty eyes. The corners of his mouth, oversized and turned down, hang over his weak jaw. His pale skin looks almost transparent in the dim light.

"Need something?" he utters.

She smells the sweet scent of decay on his breath.

"No."

He stoops down, his face to hers. "Then I suggest you get back to bed." He points a long, skeletal finger over her shoulder, then freezes suddenly. He sniffs the air, and she feels like she is being appraised by a curious dog. Is it the shampoo they made her put in her hair?

"Blood," he says.

He's smelled her lip?

"I—I mean. I do need something. I need Tilley."

Martin leans forward, ushering her backward. "What for?" His eyes are dark and unseeing, but a twitch in his brow shows his curiosity.

"Women's things." It isn't untrue.

He gasps, perhaps intrigued by mystery.

"I don't want to soil the bedclothes," she says suddenly, brazenly. Tilley had gotten her blood before she left Andrews. She'd play that card now.

His hands clench. He sniffs the air once, and his top lip curls. Grumbling a low growl, he looks her over, socked feet up to bloody lip.

"I can get her. I need the priv anyhow," Rabbit offers.

He fills his chest with a long whiff of the air.

"No," he says, pushing her shoulder back. She spins on the step as she's forced back up the stairs by his looming presence in tow.

As he follows her back to the room she'd been assigned, she suddenly can't breathe. She stands in the doorway, blocking it. Mr. Martin leans over, seemingly ready to grab her, and she winces. He's only reaching for the doorknob at her hip, but it has scared her. Now as he's shutting the door, she eagerly steps back to let him, wanting him to leave her alone. His presence is unbearably threatening.

When the door's closed and she's left in the stillness of her dark room, she listens for Mr. Martin's departing footsteps. But she only hears three audible paces.

When a shadow moves under her door, then stops, she knows he's guarding her room.

All she hears is the sound of her own breathing as reality hits her. Instead of blackcoats escorting her away tonight like she'd been anticipating, they'd be locking her in here.

Chapter 17

Meet the Doctor

Faders are stationed outside Whitetail's locked cell gate. They're dark, hooded shadows that watch to guard against her connection to the Dirt in any way. Earth of any kind. They're here to keep her disconnected. Unmagical. Their stares would be avoidable if she closed her eyes, but avoiding confrontation isn't her way. Besides, their baritone voices are impossible not to hear. Their verbal assaults have a cumulative effect. Though she'd like to say their efforts are wasted on her, being called an "unnatural deviant" for the short time she's been here is already making her stomach roil with acid.

The cell is hot, damp, and small, built of black faraday stone that reeks of feces and reverberates running fader commentary. There's a small, stained hay mattress on a chipped wooden frame in a corner. She thinks she will prefer the floor to sit on tonight. Fewer insects.

"Bitch," a fader says, his voice rising, his face tilting with the delivery. They never tire and never frustrate; they're a machine of delusional poison that runs on any audience.

She has a small palm-sized window that faces out onto a stubby, small building. There is a fenced yard behind it, and periodically she believes she can see a child's face, a pale thumbprint on slate in one of the windows. Alas, she's not sure.

There's a woman down the hall who has been screaming since Whitetail arrived. Her grunts and gasps trickling down the hall are growing more desperate by the minute. As she lets out a gasp and scream, two faders leave Whitetail's cell, waft down the hall in their ugly, twitching, sniveling way to shush the woman.

There's a knocking down the hall and Whitetail recognizes Ms. P's shoes. She knows she got under the woman's skin earlier. Whatever sting of a flea bite she's delivered is surely itching by now. Time would tell if Ms. P would start scratching or cling to her Almighty for patience.

The woman down the hall shrieks once again. Ms. P's knocking heels halt. "A hard labor is penance for sin, Dorothy. Let me know when that sweet angel baby arrives so they can be saved."

Whitetail had thought as much. The woman down the hall is in labor. She doubts it's a baby she's carried in here. More likely it was a guard, or even the warden. Bars keep the world safe from these women. And bars keep women for men. Her thoughts are lost in sadness a moment before a bang on her bars has her looking up at the dreadful Ms. P. She didn't deliver the sperm to Dorothy, perhaps, but turned a blind eye?

"Dr. Simmons will see you now." Ms. P looks at her with sharp eyes.

Ms. P leads her back down to the basement. Walking back past the tubs, still full of gray water, they take a new, darker corridor and arrive at a door. Ms. P knocks and idles a moment. After a mumble sounds from inside the room, Ms. P opens the door and announces, "Doctor."

"Ah!" As Dr. Simmons turns to spot Whitetail in the hall, his light-colored, heavy-lidded eyes widen. "Come in, please." He has a round face and greased hair parted on one side. He has no hint of facial hair; his face is smooth and plain as dough.

Inside, the room is lit with so many bright lights it seems like a sunny day. There is a small desk in one corner; a metal table and many metal boxes line the black walls. As Dr. Simmons pulls a handle on a metal box, papers slide out. As he withdraws a folder and opens it, he looks over his shoulder at Ms. P.

"That will be all for now."

Ms. P briskly walks past Whitetail, who's still standing in the doorway, and leaves, shutting the door behind her.

The top of Simmons's head is level with Whitetail's chin. As he strains his neck to look up at her, his eyes narrow and his mouth opens. His eyes travel down her front to her belly, and his mouth closes with contemplation. Turning, he begins to organize the papers at the desk, licking his thumb and setting them out one by one before turning to arrange some instruments Whitetail's never seen the likes of before.

"Sit," he finally says, extending his hand in the direction of the metal table after realizing he's left her standing. "It's been requested we give you a full physical to make sure there's no magical weaponry before trial. My supervisor will be with us shortly."

He pauses, but not because he's waiting for her to respond. His eyes are set on selecting an instrument from the tray. Poking two buds from the instrument into his ears, he extends a plate dangling on a cord connecting the ear buds, and, reaching down her smock, places it on her back. His intrusiveness isn't surprising, but it's still unwanted. Whitetail's never experienced anything like this before. She leans away, but he holds it firmly to her skin. It's cold, but not painful. His breath, pluming over her shoulders, smells of mint and some foreign medicinal tincture.

"I'm most curious about your antlers." His voice is soft and nasal.

She's not sure. She hopes they've come as proof of her nearing summer, but the wilds have mysterious ways. When she doesn't speak, Simmons removes the plate from her back. Lifting up her smock in front, he puts the plate on her belly. Hyena delivers a blow to her gut, and it makes her flinch. Her belly moves. Fish in a bag. Simmons licks his lips when he spots it.

"How about this: When did they arrive? I understand they're new."

"Two moons ago," Whitetail answers flatly, remembering Snake's exit from the orphanage.

"What happened two moons ago?" As he circles, inspecting her, she lifts her chin.

"I asked the wilds for help," Whitetail says. "They delivered on my request. But these came too. I think they're proof I'm near summer."

"Ah." Simmons takes a step back. "A side effect of Sixty-Three. My supervisor claims ignorant, deviant use of magic is what brings atrocities."

Whitetail doesn't say anything.

"But I wonder otherwise," he adds, scratching his chin. "You've had headaches?" As he says it, another man enters the room without knocking. He's breathless and carrying a big Blackbook.

It has a red ribbon tongue hanging out one side. "This is Dr. Root, head physician here at Liberty."

Whitetail doesn't acknowledge him but looks him over.

Dr. Root is tall with curly black hair flecked with gray. His gaunt face, white with stubble, shows he's decades older than Simmons. Giant dark eyebrows hang over his emotionless eyes. He isn't as excited to look her over. In fact, he stands back from her with the book braced against his chest like a shield.

"Delusions?" Simmons is back to inquiring about her antlers.

Whitetail watches Root. "No."

"Enough of your theories, Simmons," Root says. "They're clearly grown from the seed of magic. They're proof of deviance."

"If you could entertain my theory for just one more moment, I'd like to get a specimen to examine under lightscope. After that, I'll leave you to your deed."

"Simmons, your newfangled approach to science doesn't leave me much faith in our generations to come. If men like you don't listen to the words of the older and wiser, we'll be in the throes of fiery damnation here on Earth long before we stand, noses to the corners in After."

Simmons smiles, his glossy bottom lip twitching, before he turns to his tray and selects a small knife. Barely big enough to cut a fishing line, it's not threatening, but the way Simmons is gripping it as he approaches her makes her mouth purse.

"It won't hurt even a bit. They're like fingernails—like cutting. . . hair." He brushes the tip of his finger across his thumbnail.

She has no idea what he's looking to do. His posture speaks of kindness, but there's an eager look in his eyes. She's reminded of

Johnathan Andrews Jr. in the kitchen. He moves around back of her. When she turns her head to spot him, he moves in the other direction, her blind spot. He stands there, his hands behind his back. Eyes on Root.

"The fact that you think she can even feel pain shows how mad you've become, Simmons," Root says, speaking past her before directing his attention to her. "You know what this book is?"

"The Blackbook," she says, turning again to look at Simmons, suspiciously standing behind her, and back to Root, in front of her. Of course she knows the book. It's the text the Freemen reference and divine their whole purpose from. Old as the Dirty texts, a copy was recovered from the back of John Freemen's father's closet and used to spark a movement in his family's name. The book is man-made, no input from the wilds—Freemen religion.

"That's right. Do you know what the Blackbook says about tampering with the will of the wilds and conjuring?"

"A lot of manure and daydreams," Whitetail says. To these men, her daily routine of conversing with the wilds and the Dirt is meddlesome and deviant. In her mind, their ignoring the wilds is disrespectful.

"Simmons, I'm warning you," Root says. "The concept that there is no separation of magic and science is poison."

Simmons is smirking at Root when she turns to look at him. "Keratin, Root. The lightscope will show this to be true. You'll see."

Root shrugs and eyes her. The banter between the men is stupefying.

"The Blackbook states—" Root reaches back over his shoulder and pulls on a hood she hadn't realized was hanging on his back.

It has four panels and covers his face, neck, and shoulders, save two eyeholes that feature mounted pieces of tinted glass. Opening the book to the page the ribbon has marked, he reads, in a more muffled voice, "'Dowsing in the wilds and loving the Dirt is a hallmark of the evil enchantress. She who is the Dirtiest, who delves deepest into the heart of the earth, will come up bearing the horns of pure evil, the light from which is capable of giving its owner power beyond the natural realm.'"

He snaps the book closed as a crisp *snip* sounds behind her. The light in the room shifts to blinding, making her squint at Root, standing in her shadow. It's like the sun has just risen at her back.

"*Agh!*" There's a scream from behind her. "*Ah—ah—aaaaaaack!*" Simmons screams again. Turning around, Whitetail spots Simmons; his hand holding the small knife shakes open. The knife rattles and falls, clanging across the floor. In the other hand, Simmons is holding something pinched between forefinger and thumb. It's as tiny as a pine needle, but it's clear; it's the very tip of one of her antlers. Simmons cowers, staggering as he turns away from her. He falls on his knees as the brightness of the light peaks, then, ebbing, flows like blood from a cut scabbing over.

"Simmons." Dr. Root's disappointed voice is still muffled by his mask. Simmons doesn't move for a moment. Instead, he paws at his eyes, streaming with tears.

"Wrong, I was so wrong—" Simmons's shrill voice breaks off, and it's clear from his blinking that he can't see well. He is still, however, pinching the fragment of antler.

"A delineation between the scientific and magical realms? My

God, man, time to go back to the black." Dr. Root walks to the door and opens it. "Guard!" He throws back his hood as he calls down the hall. "Guard!"

A man appears in the doorway. "Call on Ms. P. Take Simmons to the infirmary. He'll need to pray on the book for his sins of disbelief if he expects to ever get his sight back."

As Simmons screams and guards lead him down the hall, it's apparent that what's happened just now has settled a dispute between the two men.

"Now," Root says, holding out the Blackbook. "Let's show Dr. Simmons how it's done, shall we? Before we move ahead with your Dirty debilitation, this is our first medical intervention." He raises the book closer to her. "Else damnation, penance. Let us pray John Freemen accept your soul in the After. And allow you to sit on his knee quietly for eternity."

Chapter 18

Milk

Rabbit stays close to Marianne through the early morning as she orders staff through cleaning rounds, and she even helps the staff with "women's work" where she can, trying to avoid any stranglers along her way. The shoes she's wearing are so uncomfortable, she's almost sick to her stomach. When she spots Mr. Martin walking away from her down a hall, he pauses and looks over his shoulder at her. It's not the wooden soles of her shoes that have given her away, it's something else she's left on the air. Last night proved it. Mr. Martin's a cat on the porch watching her, a bird just out of reach. His awareness of her is no coincidence. It's instinct. It's animal. He, they—stranglers—know where she is at all times.

He watches her a moment as she helps to dust a vase before proceeding down a different corridor. The cut on her bottom lip is sore. Sucking it, she tries not to reopen the wound.

Helping to clean the Adamses' room, Rabbit's struck by the fact that they've left before breakfast and that the bed doesn't seem to have been slept in, only sat on. Whitetail had a bed that she never slept in too. She would pace at night, intermittently sitting by the window, lost in communications with the spirits, her eyes open. But the sheer number of cigarette butts in the guest room's ashtray tells that someone restlessly, perhaps even feverishly, stayed awake all night.

When Marianne heads to the kitchen for a break, Rabbit follows without conversation. Marianne knows how to navigate a system she doesn't fully agree with, and though Marianne's back to her cold-as-ice persona, Rabbit knows that by her side, she'll be out of trouble.

And that where Marianne is, Snake will be sure to follow.

The cigarette tin with the children's hair. Her slate marker. They are all she's been able to think about since her talk with Marianne last night.

When Snake finally enters the kitchen, Rabbit widens her eyes, asking Snake for her attention, but her pleading eyes do nothing. Snake doesn't give her any notice, and instead of joining her and Marianne at the counter to cut flowers, she chooses to sit at the lower kitchen table to polish silver, her back to the room.

A door bangs. As it sounds, Marianne shoots quizzically off in the direction of the courtyard. Staff has come and gone all morning, but none so loudly as this. Rounding the corner, she's out of view only a moment before she jumps back a step.

"*Ack!*" It looks as though shock has driven all the air from her chest.

"Look what I found in the root cellar," a man's voice says. "Look at it, older than John Freemen the first."

"Milk! Oh, Ms. Marianne—" Snake says urgently, her face pained, though she's not yet made it across the room to see what the man found. As Rabbit follows closely behind, she's met with Snake's back. Marianne retreats into the room while the man walks in holding a white cat. Its fur is heavily matted, the edges of its ears scabby, black crusts clot its eyes, and it appears to be dead. No, barely breathing. It hangs limp in the man's arms as he holds the poor thing far away from his body, not unlike the way Snake held Rabbit's soiled, tattered clothing yesterday.

"What's wrong with it?" Rabbit asks. It is clearly an old cat, but it isn't age it's dying of. Rabbit can feel it in her toes.

"Go back to work," Snake demands, turning to Rabbit with a scowl.

Snake's eyes dart over to the man's, then back to Marianne's. The cat's belly looks distended with a tumor or mass of some kind. Its eyes close peacefully.

"Please, put her down. Please. Don't hold her like that. You're being so cruel," Snake says to the man holding the cat as she reaches up to take it.

"She's sufferin', Till," the man says. He looks at Marianne. "Gotta put 'er down."

Marianne looks at Snake disapprovingly. "You promised me you'd get rid of that old dirty cat! Hiding her, were you? Look at the thing! Why you putting her through that?"

"Please. Oh, Milk." Heartbreak and desperation sound in Snake's voice. Tears brim in her eyes as she attempts to snatch the old cat from the man, but he holds it behind him, and he's wide as a doorway, so he easily evades Snake's arms. The cat stays out of her reach, and the man pivots whenever Snake's hands get close.

Unnoticed, Rabbit easily reaches out to stroke the cat. Milk's fur is cold.

"Don't touch her!" Snake snaps, pushing Rabbit back a step with an elbow. Rabbit can see Snake has started to cry. As she circles the man in vain, he stops to hold out a hand to keep Snake at bay.

Rabbit touches Milk again, massaging its broad forehead and cold ears, the pulse in the cat's neck a passing dragonfly. She is fading. *Summerland.* That's where all animals go because they're sinless.

"Let me be with her then. A little time. She'll be gone soon," Snake cries.

"There's peace in the dirt. You got dirt?" Rabbit asks. Greening gardens, manicured lawns, and budding flower beds she'd seen. No forest, though. No bald ground. They could dig up dirt, but she didn't feel a bald spot on the lawn would suit Mrs. Andrews.

Snake blinks. She huffs with her brow furrowed. Both Snake and Marianne close their open mouths and freeze, looking at the man. His eyes have widened at Rabbit, then Marianne suspiciously. Rabbit realizes she's offered up something this man can't allow. And implicated the other women just by uttering it in their presence.

"Ignore that, she's new. And foolish." Marianne looks furious.

"I'll have a word with Sr. about this."

"Not necessary, he's well aware of the situation. This is Abigail. The orphan."

The man's eyebrows raise, and he takes a step back. With a nod, he tells he's just understood who she is. He takes a step back from her and stares unpleasantly. Although he's scared, he's not opposed to a fight.

"Let me have time to say goodbye to her. To hold her." Snake's muffled voice is soft. She buries her face into the cat's side, drying her tears on its fur.

"Not in here. Off you go. Out," Marianne barks, throwing a finger at the door. "Take the mangy thing out. Say goodbye a minute." She turns to the man. "Then bring her back to Mr. John, who'll put her down. Have your goodbye. But her pain's been going on weeks or more. It's not right."

Mr. John nods. "Come find me when you're ready. I'll put it down," he says, "though it'll be gone before long, anyway. It's ate its last meal days ago, I'd say."

"All the more reason to put it out of its misery, then—before it makes a mess." Marianne's face is stern. She ignores Snake's sniffing.

Snake's eyes stay on Rabbit's a moment before she burrows her face once more in the cat's neck. Marianne shrugs, back to work on her flowers. "Don't be long. Mrs. wants that silver polished."

"I'll be in the south garden, Till. I'll start digging," Mr. John says.

"Call off the guards for me?" Snake's eyes are pleading again.

"Why?" Mr. John takes a suspicious step back into the room.

"I—I just want some bloody peace. I don't want them staring at me. Would you want them staring at you while trying to say goodbye to something you love?"

Mr. John concedes, but tilts his head, raising an eyebrow in warning before he turns to leave. With Mr. John's departing footsteps, Snake idles only a moment before she heads for the door too. Stopping in the doorframe, Snake looks back over her shoulder.

"Thank you, Marianne," Snake says. Her voice is soft. Momentarily she looks at Rabbit; she bites her lip, perhaps about to speak, but leaves with the cat.

Rabbit stays put, feet antsy. She shifts her weight side to side. She wants to comfort Snake. Loss is the worst pain there is. Rabbit's chest fills with heat, and her eyes fog with tears as she thinks of Mouse. Of her family.

"Off you go too," Marianne says, not looking up from her task as she snips another flower stem. "'Bout time you see what the real world looks like."

Chapter 19

Her Crown

A guard, not Ms. P, has come to Whitetail's cell pre-dawn. He's called her out and walked her down the hall. Some urgent direction from above to transport must have come in the night because she's been ushered by the guard and a parade of faders down to the infirmary again. Two men in black hoods motion to a wooden chair in the middle of the familiar room. Restraints, hanging like loose tongues, adorn the chair. A blackhood tells her to sit.

This morning, she can tell, she's an animal in a cage. Not an inmate, or even a human. They'd already poked and prodded her yesterday. Asked her to disavow the Dirt, which she adamantly refused. Was prayed over by Dr. Root, who later measured her with rulers and calipers too. Stolen a piece of her antler, even. Among the ranks of murderers and thieves, she has to be the most well-documented person in here.

"It's safer if a woman touches her." It's Dr. Root again. The man next to him shrugs his shoulders.

Ms. P walks briskly in, smoothing her hair like she's just wakened. Looking surprised to see Whitetail, she walks toward a blackhood and stands by his side.

"Dr. Root, pardon my tardiness. It's quite early, sir."

"Urgent deeds necessitate timely measures, Ms. P."

A corner of Ms. P's mouth turns up, then down. She doesn't know why she's here either.

"Ms. P, the straps, please."

Ms. P steps forward. Her eyes catch Whitetail's, and there's no apology in them. The meek smile she'd worn in here is gone, and she's altered to a stoic creature. Obediently she cuffs leather straps on Whitetail's wrists and fastens them each with buckles. Whitetail can't move her arms.

"Legs too . . ." Dr. Root's voice falls off with unreadable emotion.

Ms. P does as she's told and cuffs Whitetail's ankles. Mouth dry, she feels Hyena roll over in her belly as adrenaline ricochets through her veins.

The doctor hands Ms. P a pair of scissors. After she looks them over, she hesitantly meets Whitetail's eyes.

A man in the back clears his throat. "Cut all the hair."

Whitetail knows from yesterday that it's Simmons speaking from under a hood at the back of the room. Whitetail can't see his face, can't tell what's transpired, what damage was done by his chipping her horn yesterday.

"Sir?" Ms. P asks. Her posture's stunned.

"That's right. Quickly now."

As Ms. P rounds behind Whitetail, she sniffles nervously.

Whitetail wants to tell Ms. P it's all right, cutting her hair. Braided, short, or balding, Whitetail cares little about her hair. It was never what made her beautiful in her mother's eyes. Her children's eyes are the only ones she cares about now, and to them, she's already a monster. She hangs her head and closes her eyes.

Mighty oak. Her spirit for her body's survival.

Ms. P cuts her long hair quickly, in chunks. She trims close and carefully all over. Then, judging by the clang of the scissors put down nearby, and brushing noises, Ms. P sweeps the hair away.

When Whitetail opens her eyes, all the men are standing around her in the room. Flanking her. The warden has joined with another man who has a black box dangling from his neck. The warden's balding head glistens with light from overhead, and his mouth sits in a flat line. He clears his throat, looking at the Blackbook that's still on the table, with its red tongue still hanging out. Then he looks at the hood he's carried in.

"You sure it's safe?" the warden asks Simmons, looking to Root.

"Yes." Root's voice is even colder than yesterday. As he rounds on Whitetail, noting her antlers' new growth overnight, his distance is close and constant. A bee to a flower. Spectating, he's invasive. A moon in her orbit.

The warden rocks back on his heels. "They're incredible. This is unprecedented." He nods to the man he's brought in, who shakes his head with enthusiasm. Like he's just so excited he's here and she's real.

"Indeed," says Simmons from farther back in the room. His voice falters with either pain or fear.

"Go ahead," the warden says to the man holding the black box around his neck as he joins her left flank.

Clicking a button, the man with the box makes it flash.

Wincing, Whitetail recognizes it's a camera. Her picture is being taken. She's only ever seen one camera before, at Andrews on the day she and the children moved in. Johnathan Andrews Jr. had brought the camera man. It was the only time she'd ever had her picture taken until now. The camera's pulses go off so quickly, she can't tell how many snaps are taken.

"Uh." She lets out an unsure utterance as the lights and stares become overwhelming.

The warden widens his stance as he watches Root tentatively stride her way. Nervously the warden scrubs his chin. "She dies, this is on you, Root. You'll answer to the Supreme." The warden puts on a hood.

"Yes, Warden," Root says, conviction in his tone. "This isn't a job for the faint of faith. I kill her, you know what's spewing outta there." He points to her stomach. "I'm looking to protect my boy at home, not make him confront tragedy." Root looks at Simmons, who says nothing beneath his hood. "Besides," Root adds, "if the Supreme has called the order, who are we to say no?"

"I say it's a good day for good to conquer evil," one of the other men in the room says from beneath his hood.

"In the name of science, let's begin." Dr. Root won't look her in the eye as he puts on his hood; instead, he gives one last glance to the others in the room and slips on heavy black rubber gloves. "One more shot for posterity," he says. The hooded men all line up to get a last picture taken at her sides.

Posterity. Root's statement makes her heart burst into a fresh sprint. It's unclear what's going to take place today.

"Gentlemen, you're about to go down in history."

All but the doctor line up in front of her. What an audience she has. She thinks of the children gathered in the kitchen. The way they'd ask her questions for hours. Loved her stories. Tears spill down her cheeks.

"Ready?" Root says over her head to the others. "I'll have you step outside, Ms. P. This isn't for the delicate. Please shut the door behind you."

Ms. P sports an accommodating smile before her brow lowers in a furrow.

Simmons walks across the room, retrieves something, and holds it out.

Eyeing her right, she sees it's a pan with something on it. It's a saw. Like a river fish on the run catching the light. As Root grabs it, it casts unreadable falling stars across the wall. Whitetail's never had to beg for anything in her life. And now? Dr. Root takes her roughly by the left antler. More tears brim in her eyes and flood her cheeks. Her spirit must be strong.

I am a mighty oak that will not fall. But the condition of her body . . . Enduring this might cost what little pulse she has left.

Hyena thrusts violently into her chest and throat; it feels like she'll burst directly through Whitetail's skin. Hyena darts into her brain, and Whitetail screams with pain.

"The delineation between science and magic is precisely what makes magic curable," Simmons utters quietly. He's been convinced since yesterday.

When Whitetail comes to, the doctors and surrounding men are sliding off their gloves and hoods, their task finished. One man gasps as another groans with some happy surprise. As one of the men opens the front of his shirt to show his neighbor a bad sunburn on his chest, Whitetail surmises it was acquired through his clothes. It's already starting to blister. Her head is swimming with a splitting pain. Her neck aches, and fire encompasses her skull. Root's face is beet red, and he's sweating profusely.

"Ms. P?" one of the men yells too loudly down the hall.

When Whitetail opens her eyes again, Ms. P is standing in the doorway. The dutiful gaze she gives the doctors falls to wide-eyed disbelief when she sees Whitetail. She blinks, and her bottom lip falters with a tremble before she stands an inch taller, recovering her businesslike demeanor.

"There, there," Ms. P says, as though Whitetail has simply nodded off. "Looks like you did just fine." Her eyes search for the doctor's. "Just fine."

"Back to her cell. We're done," Root says breathlessly.

Simmons wanders closer. His face is burned red, and the pupils of his eyes are white. He reaches a tentative hand out to touch something at her side.

"No!" Root barks when he notices. Surrounding faders scream in alarm, and the room shakes. All the men in the room turn to spot Simmons. Ms. P practically falls on the floor with shock from the noise as she tries to unfasten Whitetail's ankle. Quickly, Root rolls something up in a towel and tucks it under an arm and out of sight.

"You mustn't touch them," Root scolds. Simmons is blinking like he's waking from a trance. His trembling ceases.

Root takes a step closer and lowers his voice. "Are you prepared to tell your Supreme leader that *you've* become the first man in history infected by magic?"

Whitetail feels cooling wet on her shoulders. She's drenched in blood. Whitetail lets out a whimper as she thinks of Rabbit. Hyena pulses, panting, under her ribs.

"Let's get you cleaned up." Ms. P glances around the room before she unbuckles Whitetail's wrists and remaining ankle, the leather wet with her perspiration. Then Ms. P helps her out of the chair. As Whitetail stands, she staggers with stiff hips, off-balance. She was out for some time. Her heart halts as she catches sight of her shadow across the room. *It's gone.* Her crown is gone. She can see the ends of her antlers as Root rolls them up in a black cloth, a collection of coveted kindling that used to be part of her. Amputated, they look foreign. She can see their ends as he carries them away. Faders surround and escort him out of the room like an emperor's guard.

Blood clouds Whitetail's vision as she lifts her chin, her head lighter than before. As she stands on wobbly legs, she realizes her feet have fallen asleep. A step forward, and fresh warm blood trickles down from her forehead in a slow stream. It floods over the bridge of her nose, the top of her lip, and over her chin. Wiping her face with the back of her arm, she looks at the men turning off the hot bright lights that seem to have burnt Whitetail's retinas. She sees blinding spots.

They are ignoring her.

The warden turns to leave with the cameraman behind Root and the faders. "They'll travel by fader troop straight to Westwood. The dead are the only kind who can't be tempted by them," the warden says on the way out, eyeing Simmons, who seems lost.

"Oh, there. Now that that's done, you look almost human. Do you feel better? There, there," Ms. P says as a guard unlocks her cell and stands aside. Ms. P's voice, although meant to be soothing, is haughty and chipper. It takes all of Whitetail's courage to stay upright. Whitetail can't exactly make Ms. P out. Her vision is blurry, and she can't stand opening her eyes for the blinding light that seems to be all around, even though it's dark.

Whitetail practically falls onto the black stone floor of her cell upon entering. The guard locks the door behind her, and she can just make him out, a mere shadow from where she lies. The stone floor is cold and damp. Grounding, even.

The guard slams the door to her cell closed with a *clang* that might as well be a knife in Whitetail's ear. He breathes heavily at Ms. P's side before stepping back, not gone but in the shadows amongst faders murmuring noises of approval.

"You should be grateful they performed this procedure," Ms. P says to Whitetail. "Removing the sin may give you a shot at redemption before you die." With a smile, Ms. P folds her hands in front of her and takes a step toward the bars before she recognizes the guard is still standing nearby, staring at Whitetail.

"I don't know how you do it, Ms. P. Manage these lot. Every day, they become more and more like animals. It might be a paying job you got, but it's a selfless spirit you give it." The guard delivers another look of disgust to Whitetail where she lies.

"Ah! Selflessness." Ms. P drinks in his compliment. "So the Blackbook goes, 'For this very reason, make every effort to supplement your faith with virtue, and virtue with knowledge, and knowledge with self-control, and self-control with steadfastness, and steadfastness with godliness, and godliness with brotherly affection, and brotherly affection with love.' Love! Selflessness *is* godliness, sir."

She turns to look down on Whitetail. "Greed is a testament as to why girls like you wind up in here. Your determination to ask for more. To take more. Take everything without earning it. You want to break rules." She huffs, pleased with herself.

"The children?" Whitetail mumbles.

"Ha!" Ms. P hacks a laugh. "All you gave them was sin. Yes, yes, you'd like to see them. I know. But the wicked do not profit. What did you ever give? What have you ever sacrificed? What have you offered when someone else was in need?"

Reaching up to her head, Whitetail feels how swollen her scalp is. How foreign the open cuts feel to her cold fingertips. Brushing her head with tentative fingers, a tendril of her hair falls out in her hand. She opens her palm, turning the hair over limply. There's nothing left but this. If it cost her the last bit of her soul, she'd spend it now to see the children. Just once more.

"That's right. Nothing. You've never given a thing."

Rolling painfully up onto her knees, Whitetail's head is a thundercloud. Crawling on her knees toward the cell bars, she sees Ms. P's smile drop.

"Just to see them again . . ." Holding out the shock of hair, her last, Whitetail offers it up. Ms. P frowns. Ms. P grabs the gift and turns it over in her hands once. Her mouth falls open. Her eyes dart in search of something invisible before she freezes.

There's nothing but the noise of condensation dripping from the walls and a gagging wretch from someone's cell farther down the corridor.

A fader startles Ms. P with a hiss of disdain for the offering. Visibly rattled, Ms. P snaps her fingers closed around the hair as she blinks away the gloss in her eyes.

"Lock the door," Ms. P says to the guard. "I have an appointment with the incinerator."

Chapter 20

By the River

Walking outside, Rabbit follows Snake. In the distance, she sees Mr. John already has a shovel in his hand. He points at a coming strangler, eyes trained on the girls, and waves him off. Ahead is the stone wall that keeps the stranglers on their course around the perimeter of the building night and day. Through the main garden, past the courtyard, and out under an archway to a bank by a river they travel. The great circular driveway arcs in the distance. Rabbit can see from here that the stranglers are circling back and forth in front of the main gate. The one through which Rabbit first entered this place. It feels so good to be outside. She takes in a deep breath, and once again, she thinks of escape. *But not without the tin.*

A large tree stands on a bank, and Rabbit's sure it's where Snake is headed. Having almost reached it, Snake turns around, not surprised that Rabbit has followed. But the disappointment on her face, her posture as she holds the cat show indecision. She grips the cat close to her chest, looking resentful.

"You don't want me to help? Why'd you look over your shoulder just now in the kitchen?" Rabbit hadn't made it up. Snake wanted her to come out here. The look she'd delivered from the kitchen door wasn't her imagination. There isn't time to waste. Mr. John's going to dig that grave in no time.

"You think you can help, but you can't." Fresh tears fill Snake's eyes. "Nothing can help in this place." She looks up at the sky and stomps her foot. "If you think you have power, you're blind. This is Freemen times. And you're nothing but a puppet. You're owned. Leashed. You still think Whitetail is a good and wise woman? I say you're wrong. Elizabeth Whittle is mad, and she'll burn with all her madness till she's dead. You can't make me feel better. You can't help Milk," she says angrily. The statement is so big and bitter, and yet, it has a seed of disbelief in its delivery. Snake's conviction is fleeting. Rabbit can see it.

"There's no good to be had of magic, Abigail. Never was. Just hurtful curses." Snake's gaze is scornful. Her shoulders slump, and her chest caves. Falling to her knees, she looks up at Rabbit with desperation in her eyes. "Playing in the dirt only brings graves. I'm about to drop her in one." She looks at the cat. "We play with mud here today, we might as well have Mr. John dig three."

"Because they'll hurt us. The Freemen?"

"Because magic only brings death—damnation."

"How can it be bad if we've got it in our bones, Snake?" Rabbit's voice is stern, though she feels a creep of doubt. Could Snake be right? With the deaths at Andrews House, what Mrs. Andrews said. What the men at the dinner table said. Marianne had said. Evidence is building to support the Blackbook's claim that a world without magic, with women walking in men's shadows, could be a safer one.

"Because . . . look at history. Mad Dog saw it for herself," Snake says. "That's why she signed the September Contract. If you support life and nature above all else, you can't spread death. Mad Dog saved countless lives by disallowing magic."

"She did it to stop the murders of women strung up as witches. Women beaten in their own homes behind closed doors. She did it out of desperation, not noble chivalry or some greater good."

"She did it to cleanse us. A higher, sinless path will lead us to Father. She knew if we stopped offering down our powers as inheritance, we'd be cured of it in time."

Cured? Of magic? "What Father? There is only the wilds, and their demands aren't ones we can read like a book. They're by mysterious, spontaneous design. You can't ignore how the wilds built you."

Snake shakes her head. "You've been in the woods too long."

Rabbit wants to beg for the tin. Though she has no idea how to read the hair, she's desperate for a chance to see her siblings. Check if they're safe right now. Where they are. How she can get to them or help them.

The doubtful look on Snake's face ignites a fresh argument in Rabbit. "As a woman, you're born Dirty whether you like it or not. And yes, your magic is imperfect. But it's yours to control. You're telling me you're willing to surrender all power of yourself to a Freemen? To make everyone more comfortable? You'd deny your daughter her rightful magic for her own good?" She looks to the garden and Snake does too.

"And if you don't believe there is good in magic, power in women's own decisions, then you will never see the future that should be," Rabbit argues.

"Even if I hadn't already denounced it, I'd not be risking my neck trying it. Even for her."

Snake reads her shock. "For summer's sake, look where I live, you fool."

Rabbit solemnly inspects the cat. "Then let *me* do it. I could try to ask the Dirt for help."

Snake scoffs.

"For the tin back," Rabbit continues, and Snake's face hardens.

Cradling the cat on its back, Snake rubs Milk's downy tummy. Rabbit joins her using soft, long strokes. Rabbit can tell the cat is in pain. She can feel it in her bones now. In her heart too.

What notch would she strive for? Twelve, *Rejuvenation*? No, this cat is far too sick for that to work. She racks her brain for the best-case scenario for the cat. The cat retching, spitting up a bloody ball of poison, all the disease spilling out on the ground would be best. *Purge* is an uncommon notch to land on, but it has the clearest consequence.

Rabbit looks at the cat, thinking it through. "Let's see if we can get it purged."

Running a cold finger across the scab on her bottom lip, she considers the worst that could come of her trying. The cat would die. But it is dying anyway. Worst-case scenario, this cat's spirit would run to summer.

Snake watches her a moment. "Okay. If you'll agree to do it, I'll give you the stupid tin back. But you'll have to do it alone. I love Milk, but I'm not going to winter to save her." Snake's use of winter doesn't go unnoticed. Her lack of conviction in the Blackbook, the lengths she'd go to save the cat—it's so muddy.

Rabbit pauses, thinking it through. Helping Milk, playing Sixty-Three alone, could be a bold move. Or a stupid one.

"For the tin," Rabbit says as she holds out a hand to touch Milk's fur. It's cool in the afternoon fog.

Snake reaches into her pocket and hands over the tin.

Taking the tin in one hand, Rabbit gently pats the cat's head with the other. She'll need the die. She braces herself. *If the hair inside the tin is moving, if she can see it like Whitetail sees it, she will know her connection to the Dirt is real. And that she can do this.* Gripping the tin, she opens it, and her chest falls. The swaths of hair are lying as still, dry, and haphazard as ever. Mouse's, Rabbit notes, has turned silver gray and brittle, all spirit gone. The bundle of hair crumbles and is taken by the wind.

"They're all still there. I never even opened it," Snake clarifies defensively.

The die and her marker are still in there, too, thank summer. And the ring Mouse had put in Rabbit's hand before Whitetail killed her.

Rabbit retrieves her small piece of slate, feeling unsure. Why, oh, why can't she read the hair? Watch it move like Whitetail had—or hear it whisper? Does it speak to her inept magical ability?

Eyeing the house, Rabbit knows she can't work here on the open lawn. It's too exposed, with grass heavily embedded in the dirt. Looking around, she spots a ravine to her right. It's small but has a bank big enough to offer cover. Sidestepping down the hill, she moves, ducking sideways out of view of the house. Edging her way down to the murky creek, Rabbit finds mud and squats. Drawing a spiral, she skips the sixty-three notches—no time.

"Hurry. Lay her down." Rabbit points to the earth next to her drawing. Her heart is racing.

"No, I'd like to hold her." Snake looks back at the house with a quick glance before jumping into the ravine after Rabbit.

"We need a marker for you." Destiny will need representation on the board. "You still got the chrysalis Ms. gave you?"

"'Course not." Snake's irritation is growing. As she scrubs Milk's neck, the cat's fur is falling out in her hands. Recognizing the tuft of undercoat in her grasp, she tenderly rolls it into a small ball.

"Here." Snake sets it down. Ideally, and for the spell to work, the cat would be connected to the dirt in some way. Touching the dirt, standing on dirt, or eating the dirt. It looks like even a breath would blow the puffball away, but quickly the cat hair becomes soiled by enough mud to weigh it down. This will do.

"It won't take a big man like John long to dig a tiny grave," Snake says. "Please." Snake shudders, her whisper-voice cracking. "Oh, Milk." The corners of her mouth turn down. She looks back over her shoulder even though there's no view of the house from here.

"For summer's sake, keep calm," Rabbit instructs.

Setting her stone on notch one, Rabbit says a prayer to the Dirt before she begins, "O wilds, the power in you—"

"—shall come through me." Snake, who's jumped up to peek at the house, rushes Rabbit through the last four words.

Rabbit reaches out and gently strokes the cat. "And what should be, will be."

Pinching her eyes closed, she lets the words sink in. It isn't far to go to get to *Purge* on twenty-two. But that means there are only a few combinations of small numbers to be made. She rolls and gets a five. Moving her marker to notch five, she eyes the cat. Milk's breathing is so shallow now that the rise and fall of her chest is indistinguishable. Her mouth opens some as the cat relaxes. Eyes closed, its tongue is slipping out of one side of its mouth like a ribbon.

Rabbit rolls again. This time, six. She moves Milk's ball of fur.

"Till?" Mr. John calls out from up near the house. Rabbit hears him grumble about the cat. "Ready?"

Snake freezes. Her face pales and she pinches her eyes shut.

Rabbit pops up to peek over the ravine's edge in time to see Mr. John walk past, not seeing them, and begin to round the corner of the building.

"Hey! Tilley!" He pauses to look behind him once, irate, then walks on, disappearing around the corner of the building. The man's voice is getting farther away. He is walking the full perimeter of the house. It's a large building, but it's still no time.

When Rabbit looks down at Snake, her eyes are scolding with horror.

"Your shoes!" Snake hisses.

Rabbit rushes to take off her shoes and peel off her socks. Flexing her toes, she digs them into the freezing mud and closes her eyes, hoping she hasn't messed this up already. Snake's face is hopelessly worn. Her shoulders drop.

The next series of rolls comes in a frenzy of determination, and by cast nineteen, Rabbit's slate has long passed *Purge* back at twenty-two. She's sitting all the way up on fifty-two, *Saw*. She rolls for destiny's marker, Milk's fur. Fifty, *Goose*.

"So stupid," Snake says to no one, tears glassing her eyes as she looks at the sky. Puffing a breath, she nods, shaking her head at the ground.

"Might as well finish it. Not like there's any more mud we need being made." Her put-out jaw makes Rabbit want to scream. Milk is lifeless in Snake's arms. Though Rabbit would rather not finish this game at all, throw the die into the far side of the ravine, she can't fathom what any more mud would mean for those she loves.

"I—" Rabbit wants to explain her good intentions.

"Just do it." Snake sighs, petting the dead cat.

Picking up the die, Rabbit cradles it in her palm, then tosses it to the dirt. Moving her piece of slate, she lands on fifty-six: *Incarnation. One last roll.* She eyes the cat fur. Rolling a six, she moves the cat hair to *Incarnation* too. The ball of cat fur blows a few inches along the ground before Rabbit can apologize.

"*Ugh,*" Snake snarls, her face collapsing. Milk is dead. "What even—"

Rabbit had been so sure this time that she could do it. Roll the correct amount that would bring her bidding. She'd focused. Believed. And still—she failed? Was it the socks she forgot to remove?

"I knew it." Snake's eyes stream with tears as she looks around. "It's all bad. All of it." Her mouth twists. "Told you magic is damnation. You killed her."

"Ti-lleeeey?" Mr. John's voice comes from her right on the wind, echoing far off, and filled with deep suspicion.

The pain in Snake's eyes is plain to see. Mr. John's voice seems to have caught Marianne's attention inside.

"Get in here now, Abigail Alone!" Marianne yells, her voice peaking with anxiety. "Tilley, if you've lost that child, you might as well climb into that cage alongside the horned witch! You escaped her clutches once before, girl. Don't think you'll be so lucky again."

"Coming, Mr. John," Snake barks, her sharp eyes trained on Rabbit. Mud stains the cuff of her shirt. A look of despair overtakes her face. Snake pulls her cuff down to cover it, but it doesn't really disguise what's there. Tears flood her red eyes. Her mouth hangs crooked with disappointment.

Snake's chest heaves. "Look what you've done. All lies. You fool," she whispers. "Look what you've done. I might as well have Mr. John put me down now. Dig my grave next to Milk's." As Snake's face pales to a lighter shade, Rabbit can see that something is very wrong. A blue vein is showing in Tilley's forehead. Not stress. This is not sorrow. This is from hate. It's ugly. The fresh sag under her typically sharp eyes fills with a dark hue. Her pink lips crack. A sore Rabbit hadn't noticed before breaks open on Snake's wrist.

"Fall as you run to him crying," Rabbit suggests. "After that— you're burying a cat. They won't question mud on your dress."

Snake stands and glowers at Rabbit, fixing herself to conceal the mud.

"Freemen own you, puppet. And you'll run to them now, all your magic hidden away. You'll do what they say. Now you've learned, you have no power here. Or there," she says, pointing at the ground. "None at all. You're just some stupid, mixed-up, evil girl who's about to stop asking any more questions. And you'll put yourself second to everyone before you know it."

Rabbit looks at the mud on the ball of cat fur. It has dried. Another wind blows, and the ball rolls all the way into the creek.

The sluggish current takes it away downstream. Rabbit doesn't stop it. Milk's spirit is gone.

Snake stomps out the board with her shoe, the cat still in her arms, then kicks, flicking dirt up into Rabbit's eyes and marking her face. "Wear that inside, you fool. I dare you." She points in the direction of the house.

Walking up the bank, Snake heads for the garden and Mr. John. Rabbit picks up her shoes and socks and trudges toward the house. This is a horrible place. How could magic not be in her? As she rounds the corner of the building, she looks up to a window and stops. Mrs. Andrews is watching her. Her cold, perfect stare strikes fear in Rabbit's belly. Could Mrs. Andrews see the mud on her face from this distance?

As Rabbit walks inside, Marianne turns to scowl at her face, at the shoes and socks she carries in her dirty hands. "I say," Marianne practically gasps. "Get washed. Clean up, you scab. Put yourself together! Mr. Andrews is leaving shortly, and you're going with him."

"Where?" She won't go without asking the questions. Not like Snake says she will.

"What do you mean where?" Marianne snaps. "Bite your tongue. Clean up. He's taking you somewhere, that's all you need to know."

And you'll go to them, puppet.

Chapter 21

The Judge

Rabbit's more at ease this time riding in the car. And good thing, too, because it's a long ride to wherever she and Sr. are going. Like a good girl, she hasn't asked. As they drive past fields and occasional buildings, a fresh loneliness creeps into her chest. Disappointed at what happened with Snake this morning, she's spiraling like dust on a draft. Sr. is so quiet. So is the driver of the car. There are no advisors here droning in Sr.'s ear. No wife, no servants, just him and Rabbit. She might as well be invisible because he hasn't spoken a word to her since he met her in the Westwood foyer with a nod, when he popped on a square, black hat and black trench and said, "Shall we?"

It's raining, but even that's no comfort to her. When they arrive at a tall, brown building, the car slows to a halt. The driver parks, then opens Sr.'s door. The building they've come to is constructed of big, squared-off rocks, and it has a round column with a peaked roof at one end. Like a tower where a maiden might need rescuing in one of Snake's old fairy books. It's beautiful, though, almost a castle, and its gardens circle it like a moat. The gardens almost convince her this is a good place.

Stepping out of the car, trailing up the path to the front door behind Sr., she notes the gardens, dry and dead from a hard winter, are planted with flowers that don't naturally occur together. Daffodil next to cacti, it is disorganized. Someone has reorganized natural order out here. It makes her nervous about who and what's confused inside the building.

Standing on the porch, Sr. knocks once lightly at the door, and it immediately opens. There's a woman standing there, and she's dressed all in gray just like Marianne, Snake, and the other servants at Westwood House.

She curtseys. "Hail, Freemen."

Sr. simply nods at the woman before he walks through the door without any further invitation. His stride is the same gait the Beard always had. Though he is more likable than the Beard, Sr.'s bold mannerisms are confounding to Rabbit. Sr. walks through every door like he owns it. If he's the Supreme, maybe he does? How many homes does he own? Can someone own? How much land, and all Blackmoor on top of that too? Walking in, there's a second younger woman standing in the hall waiting to be of service.

"Hail, Freemen. He's expecting you, Mr. Andrews. Can she take your coat?" The first servant gestures to the second. The second woman has very red cheeks like someone's slapped her.

"Your cheeks are so very red," Rabbit blurts.

When the woman averts her eyes, Rabbit recognizes that she is merely a child dressed like an adult, perhaps a year or two older than Rabbit. The girl looks at the woman who's answered the door, then at the floor.

"Beauty for the Freemen," the first woman answers for the second as she nods knowingly at Sr. "Just as the contract states."

"Which contract?" Rabbit feels stunned.

"Why, the September Contract." The older woman delivers a close-lipped smile.

All the lightness Rabbit felt at the prospect of ridding herself of the oppressive coat evaporates, leaving her heavy with confusion. She knows every word of the contract. The terms: Dirty women were to surrender the Wood and the Necrology to the Freemen so they would not forget their past wrongs while they prospered. Asked Dirty to work and play quietly.

There was no mention of red cheeks.

Rabbit is silent and can't help frowning as the young servant takes her coat and drops it over Sr.'s and carries it away.

"Please follow me." The older woman's eyes flit to Rabbit for only a moment, then look at her shoes before turning on her heels to tread down a long hallway. It's sickeningly grand, like Westwood House, only instead of wooden walls this house has red wallpaper. Whitetail always said "red was for the brave." But this wallpaper doesn't seem brave; it feels staged. Like the coat. Unnatural like the red on the young woman's cheeks as she follows behind them after apparently having delivered the coats.

The older woman knocks on a door before touching the knob. A muffled voice sounds from inside. *Male. Curt.* The woman opens the door, walks into the bright room, and then stands aside, holding the door to let them in. Rabbit walks into the room hidden in Sr.'s shadow. The young woman waits outside in the hall.

"Ah! Hail, Supreme," an old man with white hair says. Standing up from his broad wooden desk, he walks around it, trailing his fingertips across the desk's sheen before shaking Sr.'s hand.

"Andrews, always an honor to have you." The man is the same age as Sr. and wearing the same black shirt with the four-stones emblem at its bicep that Adams and McCarthy had worn.

"I'm—so sorry about Johnathan," the man says. "Surely he's in After, sitting on Father's knee as we speak." His caterpillar eyebrows raise as he delivers a genuine smile.

"Thank you. Loss of a child, our heartbreak is . . . profound. It's hard, as you know all too well," Sr. responds. "But in your case, you've been fortunate enough to still possess an heir. Your seat, the brotherhood Dodd, is safe." His voice is filled with longing.

The man with white hair's brows fall. "Oh, no. It's more complicated than you could ever know." Leaning in, he pauses, struggling for composure. "Little Jeremiah has decided they're *Jane.*" He over enunciates the name and shakes his head.

"What? No!" Sr. says.

The man with white hair nods regretfully. "And claiming thoughts of Dirt, no less."

Sr.'s hand flies to his mouth in dismay. "He's not . . . still custodian of the Box." His brow crinkles.

Rabbit has no idea what the big deal is. Whitetail had made it clear that Rook had seeds of Dirt to sow. Perhaps Jeremiah had more than just seeds. If it were true, how could Jeremiah deny her most magical self?

"Indeed. Let go and stripped of his arm patch. All the more reason to get straight to business." His attention shifts. "This must be her, your star witness," the man says as he rocks on his heels, smiling a moment. There's a silence before he turns to walk back to his seat. He opens a palm toward two chairs in front of his desk.

"Sit, please."

Recognizing the older woman is still in the room watching Rabbit, the man with the white hair says, "That will be all."

Quickly and silently the woman leaves the room, shutting the door behind her.

"Abigail, this is Judge Dodd, the smartest man I know." Sr.'s voice is boisterous as he sits. He clears his throat and looks at Rabbit. "He's head of the courts. He and the judges in his office decide if your mistress's actions go against the agreement."

Rabbit slides all the way back in her chair, puts her hands on her knees, and waits.

"It's nice to finally meet you," Dodd says, prideful, looking at Rabbit.

His eyes aren't as kind as his voice. "I'll be the lead presiding in the court in a few weeks' time—when you testify. Someone's got to make sure the trial is conducted with no ruckus. That the outcome is fair. I wanted to have you come in so we could spend some time going over what you'll need to say when called upon to testify."

He's going to make sure the trial is fair? The trial is still an abstract idea. Words at war. Destiny in the balance; how this would help the children, she is still trying to figure it out. She doesn't like the idea of her words influencing anyone's destiny or committing anyone to their swearing on the Blackbook.

"Do you know what testimony is?"

"Mrs. Andrews says it's the story of what happened. You want me to explain what happened at Andrews House. How Mr. Andrews Jr. . . . and Mouse, died."

"And the others too. We want the truth, you hear? About all wrongs done by Dirt." He eyes her over his glasses.

At present, she isn't sure just how much she believes in the goodness of Dirt. She feels knee-deep in the river, unsure if she wants to swim or walk back to shore. Whether Dirt is innately good or evil aside, Whitetail killed Mouse. An indefensible deed. *But align with the Andrewses?*

"Just the truth," Rabbit says. Looking at the judge's desk, she sees the 'Librium flag with its victorious-looking owl.

The men's eyes connect, and then Dodd tilts his head. "That's absolutely correct. The truth is what will save us, Abigail. What will keep the truce. And you, girl, are the only one who knows the truth, who can speak the truth as to what happened. To John Andrews, to the girl—"

"Mouse."

"To the neighbors," Dodd continues, going through the list again the way Pheasant would nervously recite facts, names of mayflies, to stay grounded. "Only you, your lived experience can tell of how sinister and disastrous magic can be. Yours will be a cautionary tale."

Sr. nods, leaning forward in his chair. He shifts the hat, the small brim of which he's been pinching, from one knee to the other. Abandoning it, he grips the arms of his chair. He seems pleased with the way this meeting is going.

"There are possibly more eyes on this trial than any in history. The world will be watching you. Because the nation's gotten complacent, magic's making a huge comeback. And we can't have that. No, after over two hundred years of peace, we've had a 'free magic' banner in downtown Ohio, and a shoeless march through Washington. Magic is going to get ignorant people hurt."

Rabbit remembers what she told Mrs. Andrews, that it was her who cursed the Beard, and how Mrs. Andrews made it no matter at all. How could her curse not matter, while Whitetail's matters so very much? Neither Mrs. Andrews nor this man have mentioned Hyena yet.

Curious about what Marianne said the night before, Rabbit's waiting for mention of the Necrology.

"I need you to understand," Dodd says, clearing his throat and dropping his gaze to his desktop, "what will happen if you . . ." He pauses, looking at Sr. "If you don't tell the truth."

"I don't need to lie." The volume of her voice clearly catches Dodd off guard.

"Do you know what will happen if you don't tell the truth? If you speak of nature and nonsense? Magic and cursing?"

"If I lie there'll be injustice. We're looking for 'Librium."

Dodd's eyes widen. "Injustice is what's already taken place, my dear. And it's not 'Librium we're looking for. It's called control. Before the Dirt dooms us all, we need to get it contained. Again." His eyes drift across the room to a frame on the wall next to the flag. It's small but stationed prominently. His gaze stays trained on the frame as he continues. "What Elizabeth Whittle has done, what she represents—if it's painted in any other light than deviant sin, it will be catastrophic to our fair nation. Catastrophic . . ."

Rabbit doesn't know that word.

The frame on the wall is ornate, and it houses something that looks old. A painting with chipped lacquer and browning edges.

It shows a line of squares in a meandering trail. Symbols mark the trail. It takes Rabbit several blinks to recognize it, but it seems it's a very, very old iteration of Sixty-Three. Surprising that it would be here in this Freemen's office.

"Your former mistress is not the first Dirty woman I've had to hold accountable. And my fathers before me did the same. There've always been challengers. Those who want to upend order unfairly. Who believe they can redefine reality in the world to suit themselves, but, Lord save us, do you know what happens when a woman convinces herself Dirtiness is fair and good?" He winces.

Rabbit shakes her head.

"A ruined economy, a threat to natural order and hierarchy just to start. Worse, it will mean, well, war. The biggest war. Would Dirty women willingly present themselves as lambs for the slaughter because they'd rather hold on to a filthy habit in the name of an archaic grudge? It's their suicide." Holding up the flag by its post, he waves it, lost in thought a moment.

There's a long silence. Rabbit's shocked. "But—"

"Shh!" Sr.'s cheeks flush.

She bites her tongue.

"It's okay," Dodd assures Sr. "Speak, child. But what? I need to know you understand the stakes here before I let you in my courtroom."

"But . . . the flag. Why do you hold it if you don't believe in the potential for 'Librium?" She knows what Marianne said. She wants this man to explain it from his point of view. Getting up from her chair, she walks toward the flag. "If you believe, and you're the most powerful man, why do you claim there will be war? The owl screams for no war. But balance. Humility. Peace."

Now it's Dodd's turn to flush. Not with embarrassment like Sr., though. He's angry. "This owl's wings are spread in celebration of balance and control. Peace *is* what Freemen seek. This war for control, if it came, wouldn't just require more laws. It would require Dirty, living and dead, to put it all to bed for good. That requires cooperation that will just never come. Do you intend to speak to the dead and tell them to calm down and let the past go? Can you? No."

At the prospect of ghosts, goose bumps rise on Rabbit's neck. To keep from panicking, she wiggles her loose tooth. Averting her eyes from the flag, a symbol she no longer recognizes, she's left staring at the old framed Sixty-Three board. Has its meaning also been muddied?

It takes Dodd a moment to compose himself. "You should know, I am but a servant. The flag, the *Freemen* flag, may scream for no war through controlled order, the order of men leading women into the future and securing this at all four corners of the globe, but it's impossible to attain balance until Dirty let old slights against them go and agree to stop acting out from their manipulative and magical nature."

"Slights?" Rabbit says, training her eyes on the Sixty-Three board. Something's not right with it. Quickly she scans the symbols that look different from than those on Whitetail's board. The symbol at the end looks right. The beginning too. But there are sixty-four symbols here. She narrows her eyes, tracing back from sixty-four. These symbols have all been furthered one place, sixty-three at sixty-four, sixty-one sitting at sixty-two . . . Her eyes trace for the outlier.

"Women's anger. In our pilgrimage for peace, I'll not let anyone stand in the way of this future because they're holding a grudge." His fists slam down on the table and Rabbit jumps, her eyes landing on fifty-eight. There's a new symbol there. A small flame. A spark.

"For your sake, Ms. Alone, and the other children's, you better speak to our cause next week in front of me and my brothers, or Father help you, your soul will face Death. He'll drag you down. And it will be an eternity of Father's belt in the After. I'll do whatever it takes to save our great nation and avoid any damnation you'll bring," Dodd says.

Death? Rabbit's so scared, yet there's nowhere to run.

Sr. stands, cueing Rabbit it's time to leave. Rabbit does an about-face, working to keep the surprise she feels in her heart off her face.

"My God, Andrews. Tell me this isn't a mistake. Putting all our trust in a little girl." Dodd's voice is filled with disdain.

"If it comes from her, the world will listen." Sr. looks down at her, his hat pivoting between his hands again. "When she stands next to me, the world will believe it."

Chapter 22

Animals in the Yard

Now that she has no antlers, she's permitted to eat in the mess hall with the other women. It's too dim in here for the number of windows that line the walls. Tall and slender, the windows show a lawn outside that the residents of this building seem to never tread upon. The city beyond is bigger and busier than any she's ever seen, though she'd never want to set foot in it. Smoke hovers over hundreds of rooftops, and she's confounded by the question of how so many people could live so close together in such a small area with no trees. By stars, isn't close enough to smell another's shit too close? Albany looks too busy for her liking. How she yearns for her rivers. Her hills.

Staring into her bowl of coffee, she thinks of the children again and feels a painful longing. Perhaps in practicing what she preaches she's let them down. Was she right to put so much faith in Rabbit by giving her the tin? And to keep Hyena locked away? What the children must think of her now.

Loss leaches at her bones. The thought that the children might be frightened sickens her. Their separation was always coming, but this was a violent stake splitting her brood. So fast it left her mourning. She sniffs but doesn't dare cry.

Footsteps approach, and she knows better than to make eye

contact. Many women get beaten here. Sometimes by Ms. P's strap, but usually by men.

Two women stand up from their bench across from her and nudge their bowls of coffee toward her. They lay their bread beside the bowls, and with that, they are gone. Wiping the fronts of their dresses and fixing their bonnets, they walk away to their work in the kitchen: washing. Some women have begun treating her like a peasant queen from some other universe, and she can't really understand it. Do they pity her, perhaps? But their eyes plead with reverence. Her crown is gone, and she holds no power here except strength of spirit. Her horns had prompted one woman to mumble "white stag" as she walked past.

Even with her crown missing, she's treated as an other. Ms. P believes in a Lord above all, one spirit, a grand designer, but Whitetail knows she herself is the very same spirit as the wilds. And that the wilds are a force built by all spirits, including each and every woman here. Ms. P is one with the governing wilds, just as all these women are. These women don't question her guilt. She is guilty, after all. They see her. They really see her. Not as a wife. A servant. Or something measurable in looks or social status. She's herself here. They accept her. And that's the greatest respect they can show.

As she sits on her bench, she looks from the coffee to the women walking away. She catches others in her periphery stealing glances at her. At her hair. Her head. She's not been given a bonnet the way everyone else has. The stumps left by the doctor's saws are left for the world to see. But the women's looks are not sympathetic, they're encouraging. Respectful. She wonders just how she's earned any of it.

Is it that each woman who enters this place has experienced their very own uncrowning? They relate to her disgrace? They too have been wounded by those prideful and superior people who believe, without evidence, that they had any choice in their guilt? Perhaps guilt is irrelevant to her species, and in this place, they aren't a class of flawed so much as a congregation of the incomprehensible.

A guard notices the gifts of bread and the women's backward glances and rings a bell.

Ms. P marches into the room, her eyes keen and the corners of her mouth turned down. She barks, "Breakfast is over." After a stern look to the guard, he bangs the bell a few more times to get everyone moving.

Time to go back to her cell. Unlike most of the other women, she's not allowed a job. No laundry. No seamstress work. No gardening for the warden. She'll have to wait for the others to leave before she'll even be allowed to stand and be personally exported back to her cell by Ms. P.

"That's it, off you go, girls. Off you go." Ms. P slaps her belt once quickly across the palm of her hand with a flagellating *whack*. Whitetail flinches. As the room stands and begins to clear, Whitetail can see that all the women have left their bread behind.

Left it for her.

The women who walk directly past her nod silently, covertly acknowledging her as they pass. Their heads bow as they leave. Others glance back over their shoulders at her before they waft out the door.

"It will be the will of the wilds," a woman whispers. She glances furtively at the guard, at Ms. P. She's not supposed to be speaking.

"Do you have something to say?" Ms. P's eyes are piercing.

The woman tucks her chin, her bonnet covering her eyes as she exits the room with a swift march.

"See that they all make it where they're headed," Ms. P says to the guard. Without a word, he turns on his heels and marches with quick steps out into the corridor after the women.

Ms. P sets her sights on Whitetail, sitting, waiting to be allowed to stand up. Ms. P's typically lead-heavy stare is even weightier than usual. As Ms. P's eyes narrow in her direction before she walks across the room to stand before Whitetail, she shifts from foot to foot a few times before she finally settles into a wide static stance. She's looking down, but her chin is held high.

"I've thought it through." One hand tucks the leather belt she's holding under one arm before it reaches into her pocket, slowly withdrawing something. It's dark and twisted into a small ring. It takes Whitetail a minute to recognize it.

It's the hair she offered.

"If I am to live by my principles, then I am to have mercy on a selfless soul. Selflessness is godliness." Her voice is judgmental. "I know what you think this means to you." She pinches the hair between thumb and forefinger and raises it like a candle. "Though it's a heathen's offering, I know enough about your kind to understand that, although it's a heathen's offering, it is heartfelt." She eyes the hair, then twists it, winding it over a finger like a ring. It doesn't have even a trace of the blood it had been delivered with.

Ms. P has washed it. Like she washed Whitetail in the tub.

"They're not yours. I stick by my verdict on that. Not by blood or maternal bond. I doubt even by kinship . . ." Ms. P's voice falls off. Her brow is sweating, and her cheeks are blushing. All at once she's flustered and even drops her eyes to the floor. "But you owe them moral guidance—the children."

Whitetail feels Ms. P's frustration as she's changing her mind. She's conflicted by her creeping sympathies for a monster-murderer-wretch, the nearly unredeemable in her Father's view. By sticking to her principles, she's allowing something she doesn't want but hopes to regain power by allowing.

The guard is returning. His heavy steps announcing his approach like the trot of a loyal dog.

Ms. P tucks the loop of hair back into her pocket.

Reaching the doorway, the guard's posture straightens. Suspiciously, he enters the room and looks searchingly at Ms. P, at Whitetail.

"You're wanted in the yard. It's almost one o'clock. Animals need to go outside so they can get their cages cleaned."

Ms. P makes a low noise in acknowledgment. Wheels spinning. "I was just explaining to the child-killer that I'll have you bring her up to her cell *after* she's done clearing the bread from all these tables. Every crumb.

"But you always escort the—" He looks shaken, either by the break in routine or by the prospect of being left alone with Whitetail without the bars between them.

"She's not the first murderer you'll escort. Or the last. And it seems the right punishment for whatever's going on here," Ms. P says to Whitetail, looking at the excess scraps near her coffee bowl. And when you've picked everything up, you'll dump it in the trash by the window."

"But—" the guard says.

Ms. P's face grows stern. "I must go, the animals are in the yard." She eyes Whitetail and then the windows with an uncomfortable-looking crook in her jaw. Her hand is in her pocket, the one holding the hair. Whitetail imagines it being turned over again and again, a thorn that's been burrowing deeper and deeper.

Ms. P quickly leaves the room, her footsteps disappearing down the corridor.

"You got hands, use 'em," the guard barks.

Whitetail stands up, stretching her back and locking her knees to keep her erect.

Staggering to the first table, she gathers the chunks of bread into a pile before walking across the room to dump them in an oversized bucket. There's an open window meant to dissipate the reek of sour food above the trash bucket. It brings welcome fresh air. And a sound. A whistle.

Walking back to the table, Whitetail uses the side of her hands to sweep the lingering crumbs and bring them carefully back to the bucket. The guard's gaze is heavy. This time, at the open window, she hears the unmistakable noise of children playing. There's a child's voice, not altogether unhappy, but reserved. And then there's another whistle from outside. She can see there are children in the yard.

Heart in her throat, she quickly scans for her children but doesn't linger. She can't see them. Walking to the next table, she does as before. Piling bread more quickly now, she gathers up a smaller handful. More trips will mean more visits to the window, more chances to see them. She hurries back to the trash.

Now at the window she can see a woman there in the yard. Her brown dress is an unattractive stump around which all the children are playing. She blows a whistle a long toot, and the last of the children file out of the building and sprint into the yard. All at once she sees Pea running. Her red hair has been cut below her chin and she's dressed like the rest, in a black dress. Whitetail must summon all her self-restraint not to scream to her daughter.

The guard behind her clears his throat, snapping Whitetail back to the task at hand. A quick glance to the guard shows he's not going to let her linger. In fact, he wants her back in her cell as quickly as possible. His gaze is steady, and he's worried by her movement. Back at the second table, she gingerly but quickly sweeps more crumbs into her hand and goes back to the trash, to the window.

This time Whitetail's heart soars. She knows each and every one of her children. As Whitetail draws in a tight breath, tears filling her eyes, the guard barks, "Hey! You got no business lookin' out there." He takes a step toward her, but it's too late—she sees them all, clinging together like burrs: Pea, Pheasant, Rat, Bear, Goose, Dove, and Mole, all huddled together, bodies connected by linked arms and hands on shoulders. Rabbit and Rook are missing. Her stomach rolls over with dread of the unknown. Inexplicably the children turn into the wind and look up. They look strong, wiser than ever before. She can't tell if they see her, but it doesn't really matter. They are sticking together, and this is most important for their survival.

Staggering, she admits that she's dug a very big hole for herself. What she's given of her spirit to preserve her body for the sake of these children may cost her the ultimate price. She's sacrificed most all her spirit to protect these little people from Hyena and intended to devote what remained of her hair and antlers, gone now, to see things through. Seeing the kids right now, together, it was all worth it. If this is the only summer she'll ever see, she'll enjoy it while the lone moment lasts.

Chapter 23

Alone with the Tin

Looking out her bedroom window, Rabbit watches for Snake, but she's nowhere to be seen. Rabbit hasn't seen her since yesterday by the river. Maybe down in the cellar helping the cook? Rabbit longs for the orphanage. For the porch. For the kitchen floor where she'd sit and listen to Whitetail for hours, lost in her parables about Dirty women and a future free in the woods. She misses Mouse. Rook too.

She needs to know where he is. Her obsession as to why he abandoned her on the lawn, surrounded by blackcoats, was all-consuming. Had he stayed, he would have been sent to Holesome Prison and maybe even be dead by now as a traitor. Is he alone? Dead? Where is he sleeping? If he is alive, she knows he's eating. A boy with snare skills like his would never be hungry in this season.

But why had he left her alone? To be taken by police, to be brought here to this confusing place where she is made to wear a skirt. And shoes! To live with Snake who is so incessantly unkind. Oh, if only her asking the Dirt for help wasn't always putting her in deep mud. Had all of this come of the mud she'd made that day in the forest with Rook? How she misses him.

How could he leave her? How could he?

The rain begins to pour harder outside, tick-tacking in gusts across her window. When she turns the latch, swinging the window open to watch the sky, a fine mist of water blows on her face, dusting over her shoulders and through the room. The wind gusts again, and this time she steps aside, letting it blow the edge of her blanket up in a wave and a sprinkle of water down onto the floor, dulling the room's shiny wooden floorboards. Closing the window, she sits cross-legged on the floor.

Taking the cigarette tin out of her pocket, she presses it between her cold, wet palms. If she cast a token-free curse on the Beard the day she sent him to winter, she should be able to read the hair here today.

She feels the cold damp of the floor soak through her skirt to the back of her thighs. The tin feels surprisingly warm as she clasps it, as though it has a heart beating inside it, same as Mouse had. The hearts of her family? Pieces of their spirits, like Whitetail believed? She presses the tin again, questioning whether it's just her own body heat radiating back to her. Oh, how she needs some power here. Some hope. Proof her magic is good. An answer as to Rook's whereabouts.

Hot tears roll down her cheeks. Knocking on the tin three times, she hopes the hair will show her something today. Anything. She commits all her energy to the task of reading it. She's so desperate to find Rook, she can barely breathe.

The expanse of this room is too open to comfortably open the tin. If she were to lose the tin again, she would never forgive herself. Sliding under the bed, she conceals herself. On her tummy, propped on her elbows, she tries to relax and take big, calm breaths.

O Mother, the power in you shall come through me. And what should be, will be. Show me where he is.

Opening the tin, she blows on the swaths of hair the way Whitetail always had when she wanted the children's attention. A shiver travels up her back. Lining up all the others first—Pea, Goose, Rat, Pheasant, even herself—she lays them tenderly on the floor in a row. Lastly, Rabbit takes out Rook's hair. She tenderly draws the leather strap wrapping the hair through her fingers. She rolls the shock over, twisting it back and forth between her thumb and forefinger before bringing it to her nose and taking in its smell. Her heart sinks. The hair doesn't even smell like him. It smells like rain. And like smoke.

But not just any smoke, it smells like the A&O. *Curious.*

"Where? Where are you?" she says aloud. It is an impossibly important question. Looking at the hair in her hand, she holds it in her palm and watches the extended curl shrink and coil. She closes her eyes.

Pinching some of the hair, she opens her eyes and counts three hairs that have come away from the bundle. Three, *Goat. The consumer.* Tracing her fingers through the dust under her, she begins marking a tally. Closing her eyes, she runs her hands through the hair again and pinches one. A single notch is marked on her tally bringing her to four, *Elemental.* The dust on the floor is thin. She'll need to really pay attention and try not to lose track. Pulling away five hairs, she notches her tally. *Hummingbird. Rook's moving. Traveling.* Another comb adds three to her tally. *But anywhere in particular? Or is he just on the run?* She takes a deep breath and looks at Rook's black hair. Combing it this time, she gets a two. She adds it to her tallies. She combs a four, a nine, a two, a two, a two.

Thirty-three*, the Flag. He has a destination.*

One last roll and she'll have her answer. Gripping the hair, she closes her eyes and hopes. She prays. She presses her legs and bare feet into the dust, the only dirt she's got, and, combing her fingers through the shock one last time, she opens her eyes and looks down. It's a four.

She draws her last notch on her tally and takes stock. Thirty-seven total. *Approach.*

Approach where?

Here? The hair being soaked with the smell of the A&O makes sense. He's traveling here. To her!

Heart exploding with hopefulness, she feels it must be true. It simply has to be. Lifting Rook's hair, she kisses it before putting it and the others' hair back in the tin and smudging out her drawing with her belly.

But if he's coming to take me, where will we go? How would they escape with stranglers guarding? She'll have to be ready. She'll have to be ready to run when he comes. Will they make a move to save the others in Liberty? She isn't sure. But oh, how light she feels, how electric. Her heart aches with the thought that Rook is on the way. She believes he is. She knows she's done it this time. The wilds have helped her, thank summer! *Of course Rook is coming,* she thinks. *Of course he is.* He'd never really, actually leave her alone to be taken in by the enemy. Judge Dodd's words about his mission for peace flit through her thoughts like leaves in fall. He is the enemy, right?

Scurrying to gather the rest of the bundles of hair, she stuffs almost all of them into the tin. Reaching for an outlier that lies farther off, she grabs it and slides out from under the bed with it gripped in her fist. Looking out the window, she surveys the nearby trees in hopes of spotting Rook, but sees nothing. Of course, no one would see him coming.

Unfurling her hand to reveal the last gathered shock of hair, she sees it's Snake's. Her smile falls. Bringing the hair to her chest, she's torn.

She'll have to leave her contrary sister behind, abandon her to this place.

Instead of eating with the Andrewses, like other nights, tonight she sits in the dining room alone. Rabbit sits, lost in thought. Looking over her shoulder, she spots the door that leads into the hallway that stretches to the main foyer. Rook will know better than to come through the front door. Rabbit considers the window in the room. It's a height Rook couldn't reach, save a frond of ivy or some trellis for assistance. She gets up, looks out the window to check. There is none. When Marianne walks back into the room, clearing her throat with disapproval that Rabbit is away from the table, Rabbit quickly plunks back in her seat and eats her soup.

She thinks of the kitchen. It is downstairs, but windowless. Racking her brain, she thinks of what is on the second floor, and with a window. There is either the library or Mrs. Andrews's bedroom on that side of the house. Nowhere near Rabbit's bedroom. Her bedroom, the main sitting room, and a smoking room are on the east side of the building. If only she could get a better idea of the building's layout and possible entrances.

"May I go to the library after dinner?" she asks Marianne.

"I say, you haven't grown any less bold since your arrival. Or smarter. Of course not, you'll bathe and be off to bed."

"I'm tired now." Rabbit's shoulders slump in defeat.

"You, too, ah?"

Rabbit's brow furrows in question.

"Tilley's declined dinner as well, not coming out of her room for so much as a cup of tea. Insisting on burying that cat in the rain earlier this week has brought her the cold. You better hope for your sake she's better by morning or else—"

She does feel bold. "Else what?" Rabbit keeps her face stone still. If she's needed by the Andrewses to be their star, she's certainly out of Marianne's reach. After such a great loss, isn't Snake due a mourning period? Rabbit couldn't take Snake's fury earlier as sincere. Heartache brings out the worst in people.

"Or else you'll take up her tomorrow's workload. Now, up."

Rabbit shrugs. She doesn't plan on being here tomorrow.

Chapter 24

Marble

Marianne keeps a close eye on Rabbit, walking her to her room, watching her get changed into a nightie, and shutting her in. When Rabbit hears the door lock, her heart falls. But Rook will know how to get in here and out with Rabbit when he comes later tonight. Knotting her gown in the back, she makes the dress become biped knickers. She can't have Rook seeing her like this, in a dress.

She opens her window and gazes out awhile. Spotting the stranglers walking the perimeter of the building, she wonders just how Rook will make it past them. Taking one of the red shoes from the corner, she picks it up and chucks it hard in the direction of a guard. It lands by a hedge. The guard she wanted to bait keeps walking militantly round, but two more stranglers dart out of seemingly nowhere. They pick up the shoe and smell it. Synchronously, they turn their quivering heads to look up at her window. They know it is hers immediately.

Rook making it past them seems Impossible.

Not wanting to draw any more attention to her room, she shuts the window and watches the horizon. Eventually, the sky grows black, and all she can see is her reflection in the windowpane. She turns her light off to help her see, but dark is all around.

Rook will know where to run, how to get there. Where? He is so very wise. Sitting on her bed, she lies back and tells her muscles to relax. She needs to rest up if tonight's going to be a runner.

She wakes with her muscles tensed, jaw tight to the sound of stomping feet. For a split second she is transported back in time to the morning blackcoats took over Andrews House. The morning she discovered Whitetail had given her the tin and saw Mouse dead on the rock outside. The morning Rook ran away. But blinking up into the sunlit room, she confirms she isn't at Andrews, she's in Syracuse, and someone is walking down the hall toward her bedroom door. She'd fallen asleep!

Rook!

She bolts upright and runs for the door as she again notes that sunlight is streaming through her window. He is running late? How will Rook ever save her in daylight? She jiggles the locked knob just as the door unlocks. When it opens, it's Marianne's face, not Rook's, poking into the room. Marianne's expression is a mix of fear and disdain.

"No time for dressing," she says. "Downstairs to Mrs. Andrews's salon right away."

As Rabbit steps into the hall, Marianne marches behind her. "Quickly, now. Hurry. Teams of blackcoats and more just arrived."

Oh summer! What if Rook's been captured? What if he's down there in the salon now, being held by blackcoats! What then? He'll be locked up with the others. No, he'll be locked up somewhere else. As a boy, he'd be sent to Holesome Prison, not Liberty.

Walking into the salon, Rabbit spots Sr. and Mrs. Andrews. He's standing off to the side, talking to four blackcoats, Mr. Martin, and a gaggle of stranglers. Mrs. Andrews, seated on her chaise, looks tired and unmistakably shaken. Although she's dressed in day clothes, there's a shawl over her shoulders speaking of crisis.

Snapping her fingers, Mrs. Andrews cues Marianne toward a chest. Marianne walks over to it and withdraws a blanket, and, bringing it over to Mrs. Andrews, she lays it across her lap.

"No, I heard him before I saw him. I was restless in bed, and as I lay, a shadow crossed the moon, or so I thought. I guess it was him scaling the drainpipe outside."

Rabbit's ears perk. *He. What boy? Which boy? Her boy?*

Sr. points to the window. "My bedroom is below Floyd's." He stares at the ceiling. "But I didn't register it was a person until I heard a light noise overhead, like a bump. Someone coming in. For a moment, I thought it was my wife, awake. And that it was quite early for her to be up. My wife never wakes before dawn. I went up to check on her. Walking in, I saw the window open, a boy with the cane in his hand. He lifted the cane, snapped it over a knee, and threw the marble head up in the air, catching it like a prize before he jumped back out the window as if he could fly." Sr. looks back and forth at Mr. Martin and the blackcoat, holding up what Rabbit recognizes are the remnants of Mrs. Andrews's cane. Sure enough, the head's been snapped clean off.

Mrs. Andrews is speechless. A trembling hand noisily lifts a teacup to her mouth, and her cracked, dry lips take in some liquid.

The blackcoat glares at Mr. Martin. "A single boy alone is nimbler than all twenty of your guard?" He raises an eyebrow. "Sir, your home is not safe."

Mr. Martin grimaces before defensively letting out a hiss. The blackcoat visibly gulps. Rabbit's never known anyone, anything nimbler than Rook.

Sr.'s gaze slowly hardens.

"We ran our route last night, sir," Mr. Martin says, his voice raspy. Even Rabbit knows this is true. Nothing deterred these creatures from their task in guarding this horrible place. She'd been watching them.

When Mrs. Andrews spots Rabbit in the room, the silky stare she'd been giving the visiting blackcoats hardens.

"Abigail, the head of Mrs. Andrews's cane was stolen by a stranger last night," Sr. says, the first to speak.

Rabbit's mouth drops open, but nothing comes out. She was so sure it would be her missing from this house this morning, not the head of the cane. Rook came, but not for her. It made some sense; he'd always been fascinated with the Necrology. But he came all the way into the lion's den for the wrong marble. What now?

Sr. closes his eyes. "That stone has been with the Freemen for centuries. It's—" He looks to his wife. "It's priceless. Imperative that we get it back." He lets out a shudder.

"Supreme." The blackcoat pales, shaking his head with concern. "This—this is an act of terrorism. A last straw. Savages coming into this of all houses—" Mrs. Andrews clears her throat with an awful cough. The blackcoat raises his voice a little, as it seems Mrs. Andrews is about to speak over him. His eyes look at Sr., Mr. Martin, and back to Sr. again. "If I am understanding . . . the situation. Properly," he says, now with carefully guarded words. "The Necrology is missing."

Rabbit furrows her brow in confusion, and her jaw drops. *The Necrology in the head of the cane? But Marianne said Hyena stole it years back.* Mrs. Andrews's eyes flash in Rabbit's direction. All heads in the room turn as Mrs. Andrews rises. Taking a step toward Rabbit, she stumbles. The blanket Marianne had gotten her falls to the floor. Half-losing her footing, Mrs. Andrews grabs Rabbit heavily by the shoulders. Whether her grip is for stability or intimidation, it's unclear. She pauses, licking her lips.

"As you can see, without my cane, I'm unsteady. Not myself." She sways a moment, her grip tightening, but she doesn't falter. "Tell me. Tell me what you know. About the boy. About the Necrology." Mrs. Andrews searches Rabbit's face. Putting a hot hand on Rabbit's cheek, she wipes back imagined hairs in a show of concern. The room is so quiet, Rabbit can hear her own heartbeat.

"Mrs.?" Rabbit has no idea what to reveal. What to say.

Mrs. Andrews's proximity is too close. Rabbit's never noticed the black veins in Mrs. Andrews's eyes. Her breath is atrocious. Her tongue looks very red when she licks her cracking lips, as though she's bitten it. Again Mrs. Andrews wavers, seemingly having lost some of her youth and stamina overnight. Something's wrong with her. Very wrong.

"Your eyes are filled with worry," Mrs. Andrews says. "But— you're not worried. At least not about the head of my cane." She tilts her head, and Rabbit tries to relax and clear her brain, hoping she hasn't somehow, someway let Rook down. Rook's coming for the wrong stone has her head spinning.

"I know there are many stones; the Necrology is one of them. I don't know any boys," she squeaks. Before her conversation with Marianne the other night, she'd believed, like Rook, that the marble lived in the head of this woman's cane. Apparently, it's the lie this blackcoat believes too. Sr.'s not correcting him. Whitetail had let the children believe the propaganda for a reason. Marianne said the Freemen were always washing their hands to stay on moral high ground.

"You won't be garnering much sympathy for your friends from a judge who thinks you're a liar." Her grasp tightens. "Secrets and lies will bury you. If you know something, it's best to speak up now."

Mrs. Andrews's face is so uncomfortably close, Rabbit's voice comes out as a whisper. "I don't know who, or why your stone . . ."

Mrs. Andrews unfurls, standing up before looking to her husband. Sr. takes a step in Rabbit's direction and grips his wife's arm to support her. All crinkle their brows.

Rabbit shakes her head before looking back over her shoulder to Marianne for help, but Marianne's eyes are on the floor. The awkward silence in the room makes Rabbit hold her breath. The look on the blackcoat's face is worried. Sr. hangs his head, averting his eyes.

"The little thieving rat," the blackcoat says quietly. "If he's stolen the Necrology, he's looking for war."

"Well, *he* won't be starting any war with that thing, will he?" Mrs. Andrews's irritation is visible as she makes eyes at Sr. over the moot point. "It would take a powerful Dirty to wield it."

Though it's not the Necrology, Rabbit can tell the marble being missing is painful for Mrs. Andrews. Physically painful.

The blackcoat clears his throat. "We'll post more men on the roof. And with how many coats we already have stationed out there looking for the Dirty boy, eyes in every market, bridge, and station—we'll catch him. If the thief tries to trade it, he'll be caught."

Rabbit can't tell if the Andrewses are reassured.

Mrs. Andrews seems frozen.

Rabbit knows Rook isn't a murderer. Or a thief, not usually, for that matter. Rabbit tries to take a step back out of Mrs. Andrews's grasp, but the woman holds her tight.

"The Dirty boy," Mrs. Andrews whispers, her top lip curling with a smile. "Forget guards on the house." She turns to her husband and the guards and lets out a breath. "You won't catch him. He got what he came for, he'll not be back."

"What?" the blackcoat says, a wrinkle of confusion in his brow.

The group of men stares, looking searchingly at Sr. for affirmation. He's clearly not following Mrs. Andrews either.

"The boy and the thief are one and the same," Mrs. Andrews adds, her voice low. Her smile makes Rabbit want to squirm.

"The orphan. The boy we're still looking for." Sr. gasps, making the connection.

The officer glances at the Andrewses before adjusting his stance and taking two straight-legged stomps over to where Rabbit's waiting. "Why would your friend come all the way up here? What's he planning, hey? What do you know?"

"I don't know, sir." She doesn't have to play dumb—she's dumbfounded. The fact that Rook had come, but not for her, stings. She wants to blurt the truth—*Rook stole something else, the Necrology is in Hyena*—but she's unable to weigh the consequences of what it would bring.

Sr. steps in. "Leave it alone. He'll not be able to resist the trial. The burning. I can make sure of that. We'll have it back in three weeks, latest." Sr. looks down at her, narrowing his eyes.

"Three weeks?" Mrs. Andrews's voice is a hollow shell.

"We'll grab him at the courthouse, if we've not caught up with him sooner." Sr.'s posture stiffens as he touches his ring. It's big and gold and set with a green gem. "We'll beat it out of him in Albany."

The corners of Mrs. Andrews's mouth turn down. "Find it, please."

"Go," Sr. says to the blackcoats.

"Yes, Supreme," the blackcoat says as he and his men leave the room.

Chapter 25

Don't Forget Milk

Although the prospect of what the judge described the other day—*war*—and what Marianne said about the deaths that would occur if the truth came out, if the Necrology came out, is terrifying, it's the prospect of the other children sacrificing their magic for freedom and Whitetail keeping Hyena knowing she'll burn and possibly be sent to winter that is more than Rabbit can bear. While it's amazing what the spirit can cope with to preserve the body, these sacrifices seem unfathomable. Even more terrifying than the thought of herself being set on fire. Who to turn to for help? She is utterly alone. Rook's stealing the random stone and not her still has her confounded.

Walking downstairs, Rabbit immediately heads to the kitchen in search of Snake and Marianne. The kitchen staff are bustling, and Marianne looks busy. Turning, Marianne puts a bowl on a tray. Lifting it, she carries it over to the cook and waits.

"That's what she's earned for getting all worked up. Maybe she got sick off that damned cat. I mean really, crying off in the damp. She's sick, and here I am having to take on her jobs. As if I don't have enough on my plate as it is! Sick? She's still crying over that mangy cat!" Waiting with a tray behind the cook, Marianne spots Rabbit coming into the room.

"You're just in time, I say." The cook ladles a portion of soup into the bowl on Marianne's tray. "Here," she says. "Take this down to Tilley's room. She's got a flu, not been out all day. Tell her, if she doesn't at least mend the clothes I left on the chair in her room, she best not ever come out a'tall."

"Yes, ma'am," Rabbit says quietly, taking the tray.

"And hurry back. You got Tilley down in the damp." She hisses, "It'll be on you to turn all the beds down and prep the dining this afternoon."

As Rabbit reaches the hallway, she looks down the stairs toward Snake's room and is reminded of descending the stairs with Mouse the night she died. The strange way Whitetail had acted. Unlike herself.

Holding the tray high, she steps lightly down a stair when she hears a noise. A mew so small, she almost doesn't stop to investigate it. But when it sounds again, Rabbit carefully turns around. The hallway behind her extends out to the courtyard. The rain is still pouring, so it's difficult to see what's come. There's no one standing there. As Rabbit turns to resume her walk down the stairs, the noise sounds again, and as she spins more quickly this time, she accidentally sloshes soup—and spots the source of the noise.

"Oh," she whispers. A kitten is tiptoeing timidly through the door toward her. Marianne is still yammering loudly in the kitchen, and the cook is banging pots and pans. They apparently haven't heard the cat, and for that Rabbit's grateful. Her heart pounds with excitement. The kitten is small, a few months old, and it's white. White, *just like Milk.*

Setting down the tray, sloshing more soup, Rabbit hurries down the hall toward the cat and scoops it up. It's cold, shivering, and as Rabbit cradles it close to her chest, the kitten squirms before letting out a high-pitched cry.

"*Ssp-ssp-ssp!* You have to hush," Rabbit says to the cat, spinning to make sure Marianne is still busy in the kitchen.

Marianne walks by the kitchen door destined for somewhere closer to the hallway, and Rabbit knows if she gets caught with this cat, especially after the other day, she might be okay, but the kitten would not be. Putting the kitten in her skirt pocket next to the tin, she trots quickly back to the tray. Lifting it carefully, Rabbit descends the stairs, spilling soup, navigating the dim and the squirming kitten. Turning down a gloomy corridor, she spots a door at the end of the hall. The only one closed. She knocks on it three times, then waits.

There is no answer.

"Snake," Rabbit whispers. The kitten is quiet but busy, turning over and climbing around in her pocket. Perhaps it's more comfortable now that it's out of the rain. Rabbit knocks again, and when there's no answer, she balances the tray carefully with one hand while touching the doorknob with the other. Tentatively she turns it, and, opening the door, her long shadow precedes her into the room.

"Snake?" She wants to say how sorry she is for not saving Milk. For being silly and bumbling. But all she can get out is, "I have soup. And a surprise."

"Leave me." Snake's voice is raspy. The small, sad room is sparsely furnished and tidy.

"You're ill? Or just upset with the grieving?" How to say she's sorry to this disagreeable, never-forgiving creature? The garments Marianne mentioned, still needing mending, sit on a chair nearby. Pins and fabric shears lie untouched.

"Leave."

"I can't. Not until I say what I've got to say." Rabbit sets the tray down on the table next to Snake's bed. The room has no window, so the only light in the room is what is cast in from the open door, but Rabbit can see Snake is lying in her small bed, covered with a thin blanket. Unsure of how to start, Rabbit offers, "I'm in charge of turndowns today. I'll bring you another blanket."

"No."

As Rabbit sits down on the end of the bed, she takes the kitten from her pocket and pets it. Exposed to the cold again, it livens up, and Rabbit must keep swapping it hand over hand to contain it.

Tilley's feet recoil with Rabbit's proximity.

"I'm sorry for yesterday. I'm sorry about Milk," Rabbit finally says. "But we misunderstood her illness." Her voice rises. "She was just in labor!"

"What?"

"Labor. The bumps in her belly. She must have given birth in the night!" Rabbit says as the cat mews loudly.

Snake sits up. "What is that?"

"It's Milk's daughter. It's her kin. Look. All white, just like her mama." Rabbit's chest fills with hope that she can win Snake over as an ally, if not a friend. She's so alone.

The cat's claws scrape at the backs of her hands as it struggles to be freed from her grasp, but it doesn't hurt; the pain is sobering.

"Mr. John buried Milk yesterday. I watched him with my own two eyes. She didn't give birth in the night, you fool. This is a mean trick."

Rabbit can't help but drop her smile when she sees Snake's face come into the light cast from the hall. It's pale and hollow looking. There are dark circles under her eyes, and she's skin and bones. Her skin is wrinkled and her hair, thinning. There's a rash on her arm. Was it poison oak or ivy that brought these blisters? A nuisance of a plant that grows on the premises? Perhaps in the location where Mr. John buried the cat.

"Buried?" Rabbit's stomach rolls over, knowing it is true. The last time Rabbit saw Milk, the cat seemed undoubtedly dead. The kitten wobbles in Snake's direction along the bedclothes. As Snake leans out of bed, she picks up Marianne's fabric shears. Returning to her sanctuary, she recoils, pointing the shears at the kitten as it comes close.

Rabbit reaches for the kitten and, protectively gathering it up, moves it back to her lap. Even though she's not sure where the kitten came from at this point, she can't let Snake harm an innocent animal.

"I watched him bury her. Besides, this cat is—" Dropping the shears, she takes the kitten roughly from Rabbit's hands and carefully inspects it. Snake's brows fall, then rise again as she turns the cat over in her hands, itemizing paws, ears, and mouth while it mews. "It's . . ." She winces. She seems to know this cat now, but she can't speak.

"It's?" Rabbit wants to be on the same page as Snake, but she isn't. She has no idea whose cat it is.

"It's not her baby." Snake's voice breaks as she makes another connection. Some conclusion Rabbit can't make.

"If it's not her baby, then the wilds knew that you needed her. This kitten is a gift," Rabbit says.

"Get out," Snake whispers as she pets the cat. Again, Rabbit is struck by how emaciated and haggard Snake looks. Rabbit spots blue veins under Snake's bony wrists.

"I'll get you help. Are you feeling worse?" Snake's curious aliment seems to be progressing. Despite Marianne's irritation with Snake, Rabbit is sure the woman would want to know things have deteriorated this much.

"Get out!" Tears are streaming down Snake's face now as she lovingly pets the cat. Coughing with exhaustion, she uses her blanket to buff the cat dry before lifting it to her cheek.

Rabbit doesn't want to leave the room to turn down beds. Her only family is ill, and all she wants is to make things better and strike a connection. "I can help—"

"You can't!" Snake yells, picking up the spoon off the tray. She flings it at Rabbit, knocking her on the side of the face.

Rabbit's cheekbone throbs. "Ow! Snake!"

"My name is Tilley! And you can't. You can't help. You can't make things better. You only do damage." Snake holds the cat up for Rabbit to see. "You don't see what this is?" Snake's delirious panic is so scary that Rabbit's off the end of the bed and back on her feet. "What Mouse was?" Gripping her cheek, Rabbit searches for the spoon, wanting to be helpful, but then gives up.

Rabbit can only shake her head.

"Get out, you evil witch!" Snake cries.

Chapter 26

Dirty Sympathizer

Since Whitetail saw the children yesterday, her steps have been lighter. Her pain has been less. She feels months younger. Even been able to ignore the whispers of the faders taunting from outside her cage. She feels reinforced with power enough to hold Hyena until the end. Part with any whiff of her spirit she still has in order to protect them all.

When Ms. P arrives with the male guard to escort her to breakfast, she even feels a little hungry. As the guard opens the gate, Ms. P opens her mouth to speak, but she's interrupted by coming footsteps. A second guard arrives outside Whitetail's cell.

"Warden says to come now."

"Warden?" Ms. P says. "I'll be along as soon as I drop this sow off at her pasture."

"No. Now. Both of you." The black leather of his boots squeaks as he turns to nod respectfully to the surrounding faders. Taking a step toward Ms. P, he reveals he's brought shackles. He hands them to her. They're two spheres connected by a heavy chain.

Ms. P says, "This one?" She looks skeptical. "Allowed outside?"

The guard says nothing. He just waits.

After Whitetail steps out of the cell, Ms. P opens one of the spheres, revealing a bar for Whitetail's fingers to wrap under like a drawer pull.

"Must be something going on." Ms. P slams the sphere closed on Whitetail's fingers and moves on to the other hand. "They don't want you hexin' or cursing, I guess."

Once Whitetail's hands and ankles are shackled together, unable to touch dirt, Ms. P says, "Come along." The weight of the shackles is so burdensome, Whitetail can barely move.

She hasn't trod the walkways up to the warden's office since the day she got here. It seems as though the passageway has gotten smaller, even though without her antlers, she should have more room. Her scalp stings, and her skull throbs with the antlers' absence. Soft spots of weeping tissue and loosening sutures are all that remain. Walking behind Ms. P, Whitetail is a shin bone taller and easily watches over the woman's head. Ms. P's fast on the stairs up, a dog eager to please its master. Up, up they travel until there are no more stairs. Arriving at a landing, the warden's already standing there with two guards. While one guard steps aside, the other opens the door, and Whitetail's almost blinded by white light. It's the roof.

Dr. Simmons arrives carrying a box. He hands it to the warden.

"Step out here," the warden says, holding the box in front of him. As he walks out onto the roof, followed by Ms. P, a guard knocks Whitetail in the back with a stick.

"That's right, everyone," Warden says. As Whitetail emerges, she takes a deep breath of fresh air. She blinks, trying to drink in the sky and the horizon, but her eyes are stubborn to adjust.

Simmons stands off to one side as he watches a guard block the door behind them.

Ms. P stands near Dr. Simmons, the next ranking authority. Dr. Simmons's irises are still milky, making it hard to tell which direction he's looking. There's a crinkle on his brow, though, that speaks of worry.

The wind blows the warden's hair up and back. The cold feels so good to Whitetail's bones. Even Hyena stops moving, frozen in awe at getting to be outside.

"The good Freemen of this country, the Supreme, trust me to mind this complex." The warden must raise his voice over the whistling wind. "To keep the guard. To reinforce the symbol of what we represent in this day and age." He looks around to survey the land. Whitetail's eyes have stopped tearing enough to see the city in the distance. Black smoke. Automation. Usually she'd despise it, but today it's a welcome sight.

"It's a privilege to serve you all the way I do. But today, I'm a bitter man." The warden rounds to face them, his back to the city. He crosses his arms and widens his stance.

Ms. P's weight shifts as the tension grows. What mystery has brought them all together on the roof today?

"It's been an exciting week." Warden's speaking directly to her. Whitetail can't bring herself to look at Simmons's expression. Whether there's dark guilt or indifference there, she can't stand to check.

"Here." Warden hands a guard the cardboard box Simmons has brought. When he's confused and doesn't immediately accept it, the warden pushes it into the man's chest. The warden's face is buried fire. "Go ahead, open it."

All eyes are on the guard. Whatever's in the box seems very light. Turning it with his fingertips, the guard brings himself to lift a flap.

The warden's eyes stay trained on Simmons. Ms. P and the surrounding guards all have their eyes on the box. Opening the box's last flap, the man pulls out some fabric. It's brown and roughly balled, a thick weight. Bringing it out into the light, the guard's hand is marked. The fabric is stained with a streak of black. He freezes, looking unsure.

"The prison is a few bodies short this morning." The warden's eyes scan the three guards, Whitetail, Ms. P, and the doctor.

As the guard turns the fabric over once in his hands, Whitetail realizes the black on it is blood. All at once, Whitetail recognizes the brown fabric. It's a dress. Worn yesterday by the woman in the yard with the children. *The brown stump around which all the children were playing.*

Shocked, the guard drops the dress back into the box and gulps, looking at the warden. Whitetail avoids eye contact with Ms. P.

But the warden is looking at Ms. P.

Ms. P's mouth forms a hard line as her eyes widen at Whitetail before looking away. Simmons's Adam's apple bobs. Ms. P clears her throat and raises her chin a hair. The guards freeze where they stand.

"You." When he says it, both Simmons and Ms. P's eyes pop back up to the warden. "Ms. P, would you care to humor me a moment? Come over here. A smart woman like yourself could help me figure this quandary." As she walks toward him, her hands are clasped at her chest. Her prideful smile shows she's drinking in respect. A man needs her. And for her opinion, no less.

"Tell me what you see there." He points to a large gate and

fencing system of black pikes and tarred razor wire.

"Why, I see the big yard, sir." Her brow crinkles with confusion.

"What's that beyond it?" His voice is calm, his tone, measured.

Ms. P's posture sinks a little. "Why it's the garden gates, sir." These are not questions the warden needs clarification on. This is an interrogation. Ms. P's expression tells she's just made the connection too.

"That's right. And beyond the garden gates?"

"The main corridor passage, the guard's box, and the principal gates, sir."

"Who has access to the principal gates?"

"Only principal employees, sir."

"Simmons, can you tell me why we're paying special attention to those principal gates today?"

"The Dirty children escaped last night." Simmons's voice is hard. "Someone unlocked their door."

Whitetail's heart booms in her chest.

The warden turns to look at the box the guard's still holding. "That person no longer works here, thank goodness. But this particular Dirty sympathizer couldn't have done it alone. A key to the principal gates would have been necessary to let the children leave the premises. You see, there's still a snake in our house." The warden is calm as he walks toward her. All eyes drift to Whitetail, the only inmate here.

"And if there's one thing I loathe, it's snakes. We have two principal employees with us here on this roof. The only two besides me who were on duty last night," the warden says. He glances at the guards.

Ms. P looks indignant a moment before her head tilts in search of reason from the warden. Simmons looks surprised. After dealing with the brown stump in whatever way he was commanded, he clearly thought he'd avoided suspicion.

"Over there." The warden points to the edge of the building. "Stand over there."

Simmons and Ms. P sluggishly move, shuffling toward the edge of the building, looking over their shoulders in Whitetail and the warden's direction.

"Who's the snake?" the warden says. His stance shifts, and his hands are gripped at his groin. "Who's the Dirty sympathizer?"

Ms. P looks aghast. Looking back over her shoulder, over the edge of the building, she immediately drops to her knees, looking at up the warden.

"Please, sir, I never spoke to the yard mistress yesterday. Was never even near the gate. Or near the children's quarters. There's nothing I don't sacrifice for this job. I hold the Freemen above all else. I've given up everything for this post. I'd never throw it all away for a pack of Dirty mongrels possessed by Dirt."

"Simmons." When the warden says the doctor's name, he jumps, his focus shifting from Ms. P back to the warden. "You were the only other principal on staff last night. Tell me, man . . . that this woman hasn't infected you like she infected John Andrews." The warden points at Whitetail.

Simmons's round face swells with amusement before his mouth falls with seriousness.

"Science proves it's exponentially more likely magical tendencies will reinfect a female denier than infect a devout man."

He pauses, looking down at Ms. P, still on her knees. "You see what the monster's done to my eyes. If I'd had it my way, we would have amputated a whole lot more than just her horns last week. I, for one, am praying for strength from the Almighty while we seek swift justice and brutally painful consequences." He takes a step forward as his voice grows softer.

"I do have a confession to make here and now." He takes another step away from the edge of the building. "I hate to say it. I confronted Ms. P last month about a slip into Dirty territory . . . Unfortunately, it would seem she didn't heed my warning and has fallen into disloyalty."

"What?" Ms. P bolts up. "Disloyal? I have given up *everything* to support you." Her eyes are on the warden. "To support the Freemen. I've no husband, and no children. My devotion to this place has been my life, my only passion next to the good Lord. This post is all that I am. The Supreme is second to you and the Father, Warden. If you are going to stand here and tell me that I'm a—I'm a . . . well, it means . . . I'm . . ."

The warden shakes his head.

Simmons is visibly sweating. As he walks across the roof, he motions to a guard. "Faders have reported, well . . . see for yourself. Check her pockets," Simmons says to one of the guards, who moves in Ms. P's direction.

"My—what!" Tears well in her eyes. "Stop!" As the guard comes closer, Ms. P looks at Whitetail. Her lip trembles a moment before her hand slips into her pocket, and she pulls out the chunk of Whitetail's hair. "If I've lost the respect of men, then—"

Whitetail's intuition was correct, Ms. P still hadn't incinerated the gift of her hair. Despite her keeping it, Whitetail believes Ms. P. She wouldn't have let those children go. Simmons is pointing a thick digit at Ms. P's quivering.

"No!" Whitetail's voice slips out in a whisper. The guard behind her grabs her bicep, not that it's necessary with the weight of the lead on her arms and legs.

"Then I—I'm—I'm nothing." Ms. P's face crumples as she speaks to Whitetail. "The mud you've made . . . the damage. The mud."

Ms. P closes her eyes, spins, and her black dress swirls before the guard is at her side. He swipes for her but is unable to snatch her before she jumps. She falls noiselessly over the edge of the roof as one of the guards lets out a grunt. The warden takes a step back, Simmons's milky eyes are round, and the sound of the wind is resoundingly angry. Everyone freezes.

"Gonna miss those pies." The warden breaks the silence and smirks. He nods at all the guards. "There's a clean-up you need to deal with." Turning to Simmons, he says, "See that she gets put back in her cage." He doesn't look at Whitetail before walking out through the door and out of sight. The guards follow him.

Tears fill Whitetail's eyes as she looks at Simmons. Though Ms. P was wicked, she was principled to a fault. She wouldn't have let the children go. It would have gone against her very self-understanding.

"A man who can't stand by his actions is a vile coward," Whitetail says. She's grateful to Simmons for setting the children free, but what he'd just done to Ms. P was unconscionably cruel and cowardly. Perhaps the truth would have gotten Simmons killed like the woman in the brown dress, but pointing a finger at Ms. P was weak. What had spurred Simmons to free the children last night?

Simmons's milky eyes shift their direction. As he looks at her, he shakily falls to his knees. His hands reach up and grip her shackles. She wants to shake him off, but the leads keep her still.

"I'm sorry. I'm so sorry. Since the light, since I saw it—the Dirty truth—I've thought of nothing else. My God, those children being locked up . . . It haunted me."

Whitetail closes her eyes, not wanting to see this gruesome apology.

"You're a two-faced coward," she says.

He turns to look at the edge of the roof as he stands back up. Smoothing his greasy hair with one stubby hand, he wipes spittle away from his mouth with the other, composing himself. He roughly yanks down his suit vest and straightens his jacket.

After a sniffle, Simmons nods. "Two-faced is right. And neither one pretty."

Chapter 27

Proof

Rabbit's alone. More alone than she's ever been, and perhaps more confused. Mrs. Andrews is upstairs in bed. Sr.'s gone out to meet with advisors. They board the train tomorrow. The trial is coming, and she's trying not to think about seeing Whitetail face-to-face. Marianne said she needs to check on Snake, who is "deteriorating quickly." Snake had called her an evil witch yesterday. What if she is?

It's daytime, so most all the stranglers are outside the building. Circling endlessly, they're guarding the house with their horrible stares, unblinking with constant vigilance.

Opening the door to the library, Rabbit peers into the dark. The room is empty and looks the same as the last time she was here, though there's something shrouded on a desk in the corner. Mrs. Andrews said the black-and-gold scrapbook on the top shelf contains the history of the Dirty. She needs to see it.

Walking across the room, she finds Mrs. Andrews's ladder and moves it to the corner of the room where shelves soar as high as the ceiling. Eyeing the top shelf, she reaches for Mrs. Andrews's scrapbooks, all lined up like sleeping crows. She's already looked at the one with the red binding. *Reports about the* real *Whitetail. The sinister, monstrous murderer.* The tale told to the masses, anyway.

Rabbit's interested in the book sitting next to it, the one with the gold spine.

Pulling the book out, it falls with an unexpected weight off the ledge, and she almost drops it. It smells of mildew. Its black linen covering is worn, the corners of it frayed and broken, butterflying with age. Stepping down from the stool with the book, she cradles it against her chest as she crosses the room, sitting on the settee, the same one as last time. No point in leaving the room. With Mrs. Andrews under the weather, presumably in her room, this is as safe a space as any. A book as big as this under her arm would surely draw unwanted attention in the hall.

Cracking the book's spine, she turns to the first page. Instead of a newspaper clipping like in Whitetail's book, there's a sheet of paper. Written in scribbles of black ink, it looks familiar. It's a simple statement. Like the one she had to sign at the police station in Roscoe. At the bottom, it has a line, and on top of that, a signature. Tituba. *The last Dirty to be publicly persecuted in Salem after all the rest. Before Mad Dog's truce.* Tituba was understood to prophesy the future, the good and bad.

The next page makes her knees weak. She gulps. She can tell by the age-stained edges and the smell of the paper, it's very old. The image shows a central figure kneeling before another figure, a beast who's laying in the mud. The beast has a stone in its monster's paw, a sharp looking claw topping each toe. And a huge, distended mouth filled with awful teeth. Blood runs out of its mouth and down its chest, pooling around its body. Lines radiate from the stone in the figure's hand, and it's marked with a flame, like on Judge Dodd's Sixty-Three—or

Sixty-Four—board. *Flame.* There's a drawing of a spiral next to the kneeling figure.

In the background, there's a series of figures standing on a rock ledge. One person is on fire. There's a monster with great wings holding a flint. The figure on fire looks female, and her forearm seems to be branded with a 'Librium cross. Around the burning woman is a circle of people in the Freemen dress with square, black hoods. They're not idling or spectating the woman on fire, though—they're actively fighting other figures for an unknown cause. Restless spirits with horrible faces and red bones crawl out of the forest floor in the background and swirl through the air above. In the sky, four sticks levitate on one side of the burning figure and four more on the other. One bigger stick hovers above the winged figure with the flint, and it's unclear if her arms are reaching for it, or if she's throwing it. Inspecting the bottom edge of the print, Rabbit reads the title: *Tituba's Prophecy: Chrysalis. A New Age.* While Rabbit, like all the children, knows of Tituba's prophecy, this doesn't seem like a simple beast waking up from a long nap. It looks a lot more like the beast dies, and amidst chaos.

Rabbit can't bear the sight of the image. She'll never forget it.

Turning to the next page, she sees more statements. All similar format, different women's signatures.

Leafing through all the pages to the last, she sees they're all written by the same hand. There are twenty-four in total. After that is a signed document with an official-looking seal. The four circles around it make it look very much like the 'Librium flag. Glancing at the bottom of the page, it takes a bit, but Rabbit recognizes the Xs near the bottom. Rook had once told Rabbit and Pea to open

cuts on their fingers, swear their forever sisterhood, and then trace
Xs side by side on the big rock as a covenant—a contract of love,
forever. The Xs on the bottom of this page sit together but with
writing next to them. She doesn't know dates well, but she does
know what happened in 1693. Disbelieving, her eyes shoot back
up to the document. It appears to be the original contract:

Salem Convention 5th of September, 1693

IN ATTENDANCE:
Freemen representative, Mr. John Freemen
Judges, Brothers Dodd
Dirty representative, ~~Mrs. Mary Hull~~ Mad Dog

REPRESENTATIVES OF BOTH PARTIES DO HEREBY AGREE TO:
*1. The ban of all Dirty magic by all cunning women including
   teachings and history.*
*2. The ceasing of all violence against Dirty women by Freemen
   for circumstance of their sex.*

TERMS:
*1. The surrender of the Wood and the Marble to the Freemen so
   they may not forget past wrongs against the Dirty while Dirt
   prospers. Dirt shall work and play quietly.*
*2. A plebiscite will convene if ever evidence surfaces of this
   contract being broken.*

X. <u>Mad Dog, Dirty</u>　　　*X. <u>John Freemen, Supreme General</u>*

Rabbit can't help but scowl. This is supposed to be an agreement between the Dirty and the Freemen to cease witchcraft in order to save lives. There's nothing to do with neck covering, shoes, or red cheeks here. Or killing unpracticing Dirty for their inherent magic.

More than ever, Rabbit recognizes the importance of Whitetail's words when she said "there will be no innocents in this war." Both sides have broken their promises and spread lies. In her mind, so much of the agreement goes against the will of the wilds and serves one party, Freemen, more than the other. But what then of Hyena's stealing? Her family's lies? Killing the Beard?

On the next page, there's a copy of a telegram. Western Union. The same type of telegram that used to come to Whitetail to give notice of the Beard's impending visits.

Western Union Telegram, 3rd of April, 1886
Dear Stranger,

May I introduce myself and pay my respects to the lost Dirty terrorist, Hyena, and her family at this difficult time. However, their quieted voice will prove a blessed and necessary silence of a problematic people. The Necrology, formerly of my deceased father's possession, was stolen by your sister and is understood to have met her same demise. The stolen, now lost, marble puts stress on our relationship. In good faith, please sign over your land rights, and no further measures need be taken to right the wrong.

Hail,

Freemen Supreme General, John Andrews III.

Rabbit turns to the last page of the book and spots one very small cutout. Printed on press paper with burnt edges, it's a copy of a page from the *Blackmoor Monthly,* dated 1st of April, 1886. *The day before the fire.*

> *BIRTHS, MARRIAGES, DEATHS, 1st of April, 1886*
>
> *Blackmoor—Rabbit ALONE. Born 4th of March, 1886. Information has been received of the birth of a daughter to Hyena Alone by A&O heir J. Freemen, the third. ALONE, now residing in Blackmoor, New York, U.S. America, and until recently, Roscoe, near this town.*

Hyena's daughter? And she was half Freemen? *A sister to the Beard?*

Rabbit blinks with disbelief. A wave of nausea has her rubbing her forehead in search of grounding. Hyena had printed this message as a thorn in the Freemen's side? Or as a publication of Rabbit's birthright?

Heart in her stomach, she sits staring, dazed with a shattering realization. She's not just an orphan of a liquor store clerk like Pheasant—she's Hyena's daughter. She has a mother with whom Whitetail never let her converse? Who, in return, never relayed one message of love? And Whitetail, direct kin?

Tears fill her eyes, and she feels she'll be sick. Running to a trash bin by Mrs. Andrews's desk, she kneels, simultaneously poised to retch and ready to pray to the Dirt for help. She needs clarity. So much of what Whitetail raised her to believe had information omitted. Truths missing. Even the Dirty texts as she'd learned them had omissions, like Tituba's prophecy of 'Librium.

Had she been raised on half-truths by a "deviant," as Mrs. Andrews had called her? Whitetail had been sick with lies?

A sharp headache hits her, and she gulps, taking deep breaths. All she can smell is the nauseating floral scent that hangs heavy around her. Who is right in all of this? Mrs. Andrews, who says Dirty only make trouble and that there is no history of violence against women, just the consequences they've invited after accessing their inherent sin? Or Whitetail, who swears there are sixty-three parables in Dirty texts and that Rabbit's an orphan whose parents died in the fire? Why did Whitetail lie? Kill Mouse? Hold the Necrology?

Again, loneliness has her spinning, and she thinks, *With the Necrology, I could call up the truth from the wrongly dead foremothers.* But the marble is behind bars with a murderer. If only the beast was locatable. Even a chip . . .

Eyes drifting to the draped shape sitting on Mrs. Andrews's desk, she feels compelled to peek at it, at whatever it is. Walking slowly across the room, Rabbit takes a deep breath. The corner of the black silk covering the irregularly shaped object feels cool to the touch. Lifting the corner of the fabric, Rabbit understands it's some beast's antlers, perhaps meant for mounting. A neighbor for all other antlers and amputated crowns? A new addition for the dining hall walls?

Pulling back the fabric, she inspects the antlers' gray, craggy surfaces—and recognizes them. Tears well in her eyes. Taking a step back, she trips. Thumping flat onto her back, she smashes her head on a chair's arm, her teeth cracking together. She tastes blood. She has bitten her tongue, and her loose tooth pains. Testing it, it wiggles. Covering her face with her hands, she begins to cry. A loud thump sounds out in the hall beyond the closed door. The front door closing? There are approaching footsteps.

Scrambling to cover the antlers, Rabbit pulls the black cloth back over them and spins, looking at the door. It's too late, the voices in the hall are close, and there's no time to emerge from the room unnoticed. There's the chest across the room. Rabbit remembers Mrs. Andrews asking Marianne for a blanket from the large steamer chest the morning Rook stole the head of her cane.

Opening the chest's hatch, Rabbit falls to her knees again, this time closing herself inside the small space. She takes a last heaving breath before she hears the doorknob turn. She freezes, looking down at what's poking her in the chest. It's Mrs. Andrews's scrapbook. She's brought it in with her.

"The children have escaped," Sr. says, his voice loud.

Chapter 28

Divining Rods

Closing herself in the chest would have been a great idea if only Rabbit hadn't panicked and brought the scrapbook in here with her. Crouched, she digs her knees into the bottom of the chest, praying to summer that she won't be discovered. The room is visible through a very fine slit.

"The children have escaped," Sr. repeats. As the door to the room closes, Sr. is all business, and his steps are quick while Mrs. Andrews is slower to follow.

"What?" Mrs. Andrews's voice is low.

Rabbit's heart leaps. *Escaped to safety?*

Sr. walks straight toward the beverage cart. Turning over two gold goblets, he selects a bottle from the rack, and, pulling it up by the neck, he pours both tumblers.

"I know, I've sent the dogs out," he says. "They were never leverage in the bigger picture, but this proves how diligent our nation will have to be to keep safe from those so intent on breaking the rules. Copies of their photographs are in every station, market, and blackhood's pocket. A hefty ransom is being offered. Paid for by Liberty's Warden, Davidson, no less, for his incompetence."

At once, gulping with relief, Rabbit's quickly won over by rigid fear. *Dogs.*

"Sit down, Floyd," Sr. says over his shoulder to his wife. "I have a surprise."

She hesitates, a look of dismay on her face before she obeys, new hope sparking in her eyes "The ovum . . . you found it?" she says, her eyes round. She's carrying the Blackbook under her frail right arm. Her reassembled headless cane is in her right hand, but like a drowning woman looking to a boulder for buoyancy, it appears not to be helping her.

"Oh. No," he sputters dismissively. "We'll have to be patient. I have every man looking."

"I've been reading up." She lobs the Blackbook onto the low central table. "Perhaps serpentis ovum isn't unique. Some say the Necrology isn't in just one rock; perhaps in the same way, a new marble is locatable in an overbearing man somewhere out there." Mrs. Andrews's eyes dart from the cane to her husband.

So indeed, it wasn't the Necrology that Rook had stolen. Serpentis ovum? Rabbit knows those words from the Dirty texts. There is a parable about a man creating a monster and making it call him master with an enchantment stone that granted loyalty when bestowed. Should Rook give the stone to another, he would unknowingly become their master. He is not indebted to Mrs. Andrews, however, because he stole it instead of receiving it as a gift from her. Right now, it still "belongs" to Floyd Andrews. Mrs. Andrews said when they first met that the marble was a gift from her husband. At the end of the parable, the monster eats its master. Curious that Sr. had given this to Mrs. Andrews. Rabbit hopes Rook doesn't give the marble to anyone and become eaten, but is okay with the prospect of Mrs. Andrews, should she get the marble back, eating Andrews Sr.

The parable of indebtedness has always terrified Rook, but Whitetail explained that it had been the monster's century of sleep, abiding by his master's intuition, not him waking up and eating the master, that made the story scary. Whitetail assured Rook that the tale was a cautionary one, meant to listen to for wake-up calls.

Mrs. Andrews is wearing a heavy shawl hanging over her shoulders, and her posture is compressed. Her cheeks are slightly sunken, and her eyes are dark. Whatever is affecting her health is getting worse. Looking behind her at the rose sofa, she sits down gently, graceful as a wounded bird.

"No, pet. I have confidence my men will recover it. All my feelers are out for the boy. To what end he'd expected to use the marble—if it had been the Necrology—is still a mystery. But worry not. We'll get it back."

Her face falls.

"In the meantime . . ." he says, turning. Showing he's put on gloves, he lifts both tumblers and extends one to her. "A different type of prize." He nods, raising his glass in a boisterous gesture. Mrs. Andrews mimics him with sadness in her mouth, and they toast.

"Your mantel is a little lean, no? In need of a centerpiece." He smiles at her before taking a big swig of his drink.

Her brow furrows with confusion.

Rabbit's legs are cramping, and she's regretting such a small space to wait in. If she's stuck in this chest for any length of time, she fears she may never walk again. She's starting to feel sick, and her stomach is growling.

Turning, he swiftly yanks the sheet off the cart, revealing the antlers.

Mrs. Andrews's eyes widen as she recognizes what the antlers are—and where they've come from. They draw her to standing and pull her three unsteady steps closer. There's a gleam in her eyes that's unmistakably hungry.

"They can't go out for mounting; we'll have someone trusted come in. We can't have them leaving the premises. Root said their structure is actually fibrous, like a concentration of hairs." He looks up to the wall above the fireplace, lost in thought.

"You've done it," Mrs. Andrews whispers. "And brought them to me." She lets out a breath as though she'd been holding it a long, long time. As her top lip curls in a smile, Rabbit can see how stained her black-spotted teeth are becoming.

"The beholden will always be in debt," she says lightly in thanks.

She flashes him a broad smile, showing even more of her mouth. The rear of Mrs. Andrews's teeth looks black as pitch.

"I can't have them in the main sitting room or the dining, too offensive and unappetizing, but I'm having them mounted for you, dear. We'll hang them here."

Mrs. Andrews's face falls, questioning. "But, Johnathan. I—I—"

"You?" he cuts her off. "Floyd, for my sake, just spit it out."

"I think they may not be what they seem. I know Dr. Root says they're just a perversion, driven from the Dirty scalp, but I believe . . ." Turning to her bookcase, she looks up high in her scrapbook collection for something specific. "I just want to show you—have you heard of the divining rods?"

Tracing the shelf with a skeletal finger, she spots a gap. Mrs. Andrews is looking for the scrapbook Rabbit's holding.

Rabbit's hands start shaking and her mouth goes dry. Cold sweat breaks out on the back of her neck.

Looking around, Mrs. Andrews rifles through some papers before scanning the shelf again, looking perplexed before stilling herself.

"Oh, for Freemen's sake, what is it, woman?" Sr. blusters with annoyance.

"It's—it's nothing," she says, turning to offer him a tight-lipped smile. "Over the mantel would be tremendous, thank you." Her smile drops.

Sr.'s expression stays serious, and he pours himself another drink.

"We're going to have to really see this through. Work for further voter registration. Campaign hard. You know what I learned this morning?"

Mrs. Andrews shakes her head.

"That Charles McCarthy has announced his intention to run for Alpha."

Mrs. Andrews's face is dark. "No. His intentions can't be in our favor . . . Sanderson has another term."

Sr. animatedly nods his head. "Bastard posted it in the press today."

"What?" Mrs. Andrews looks awestruck. She looks at the Blackbook accusingly, as though she's let her guard down. "I've been so consumed."

Sr. pauses, inspecting the antlers. "Freemen have directly advised the Alpha office in this country since before the contract. Here he is, my former blackcoat high officer running against us.

Suggesting that Alpha Dog is out of fashion too. More than half of the population of this country would be a lot of votes for him to sway to his messaging," he says reassuringly.

Mrs. Andrews lets out a light laugh. "Tell Sanderson not to be concerned about old McCarthy. With women's right to half a say each, it's not likely the Dirty alone could cast enough votes to change tides. They'd need to turn Dirt-curious and sympathizers their way, too, to bring McCarthy in. Father! Most of the Dirty don't even know there's an election coming, they're so deep in the wood! Majority have already pledged allegiance to Freemen."

Sr. shrugs. "He intends to amplify Dirty voices. Raise awareness. Change the laws against cursing. He cites overturning outdated laws and a corrupt government as his platform."

"Ha! You're telling me that Charles McCarthy, ex-Freemen officer, murderer of many a Dirty, wants to win the next election in the race for Alpha Dog by rallying Dirty and their sympathizers for change?" She tilts her head with reasoning. "It would be entertaining if it had a leg to stand on. Just have him killed."

"I already gave the order. But right now he's apparently being guarded by the bloody Dirt!" Sr. spits.

Mrs. Andrews stands, wavering but erect. Walking across the room, she looks in her husband's eyes and takes his hand. He raises her bony fingers to his chest but looks distracted.

"Hail, Freemen," she whispers lightly. "It is men like you who keep us safe. Who keep me safe."

"McCarthy will never be able to campaign to the masses from the shadows. And on such a pitiful, grotesque idealism. It's irritating more than threatening."

"You're disappointed in him. He's shown his true colors. Pour your faith into the Freemen as a whole—one man, one body. You are too strong not to succeed because of losing but a toenail," she says with a smile.

"Yes," Sr. says. Lifting a hand to Mrs. Andrews's cheek, he strokes it. "You like them, don't you?" Looking to his left, his eyes trail over the antlers.

"You have no idea." She kisses him lightly on the cheek.

"We'll find a trusted taxidermist to do the mounting."

There's a knock at the door, and the pair turn.

"Yes?" Sr. says curtly.

Marianne pokes her head in. "Hello, Mr. and Mrs., venison is served in the dining hall."

"Thank you," Mrs. Andrews says. "We'll be right there." Mrs. Andrews turns to Sr. "Come, we have a long day of travel tomorrow. The trial is upon us. It's time we eat and you rest. And I think. And be grateful that you are so strong."

"Remember, no mention of the children to Abigail."

"'Course not," Mrs. Andrews agrees.

As the pair leave, Mrs. Andrews turns to look back over her shoulder at the antlers. Smiling at her husband, she winks.

Marianne reaches for the doorknob and closes the door behind them.

Rabbit's left in the quiet of the salon with nothing but the sound of her own heartbeat in her ears. As she waits to make sure the coast is clear, she's again struck by the curious choice Whitetail has made to keep Hyena and the Necrology contained. But why? Why keep someone contained? Loved ones in the dark? Bury the truth?

A wave of fresh sadness hits her as she considers her mother having been so close to her all these years, yet so far away. Oh, would they ever speak face-to-face? Would she see Whitetail at court? Why had she kept the most magical stone buried? Rabbit looks across the room to the antlers, recalling Sr.'s comment about them being like hair. She presses the tin in her pocket to her leg like a hug.

Even though she isn't sure how she feels about Whitetail or her mother, she's so pleased that the children have escaped. It means she's got less to bargain for. And someone to aim to reunite with out there in the world. But still, her loved ones have run into the throes of danger, and she can't help but rethink her want for them to be out of prison. At least in prison they were locked together and presumably fed. Now who was to say what would happen if they were separated or found? She blinks her eyes closed and gives a quick prayer to summer that they stay safe.

Slowly opening the chest, Rabbit stretches her sore back and extends her legs. Her knees ache with the prolonged pressure they've endured. Standing up, she hoists the book and tiptoes across the room. She slides the scrapbook back into its place, next to all the sleeping crows and their dark secrets.

Chapter 29

Time to Go

The icy wind keeps threatening to take her hat, and Rabbit wants to let it. The hat is small and tall with braiding. It's covering her hair, pulled back so tight it's hurting her scalp. Marianne has forced her into a dress. It's long and black with a large skirt. Bows and ties knot the top's front. There's a trailing sash at the back that hangs like a horse's tail. Standing next to Sr. and some of the house staff on the front steps of the mansion, she's waiting for Mrs. Andrews to emerge.

Rabbit's sick. She was unable to eat this morning. Didn't eat last night either. But it's not lack of food that has her wrecked. It's that she can't stay here where she's being told what she's to say, what to wear, and how to act: civilized. But she can't leave either; the trial is tomorrow. And even though the children are safe, she's still the star and perplexed by what she thinks of Whitetail.

Looking back over her shoulder, she searches for Marianne, for anyone to come and say goodbye to her. Attest to the fact that she'd ever been here at all. She emerges from the house carrying a small bag.

"Clothing Mrs. Andrews has selected for tomorrow." Extending the bag, Marianne passes it to Rabbit, leaving her eyes trained on the ground. "Take it, now."

"Thank you, Marianne." Where will she go after tomorrow? Not Andrews House, not back here to Westwood House. If only there was someone to cling to for comfort, or an excuse to prolong her getting in the black bear, Andrews's car. But there's no one. She won't be missed. And likely no one will want to remember her. *Not even Snake?*

As the car pulls around to where she waits on the steps, the driver steps out and opens the door to the cab. Rabbit looks over her shoulder one last time, at the dark windows above. The room where she'd waited for Rook—the boy who came, but not for her. And to the courtyard where Snake still lurks in her cave, ruined by grief or some other plight. Rabbit just can't understand.

Scrambling for connection, family, all Rabbit's got is her father suddenly standing beside her.

"In the car now, Abigail," Sr. says from behind her. "We'll not be late for the train. Though it is mine, and waiting for me, I suppose. *Humph.*" He looks back over his shoulder in earnest. Mrs. Andrews is taking a long time getting her coat on. Watching Sr.'s expectant eyes narrow with disappointment as he waits for Mrs. Andrews, Rabbit wonders if he wore this very expression upon reading notice of her birth. Whether Rabbit's wearing a similar expression now as she contemplates her parentage. If Sr. sees any of her mother in her. Eyes? Jaw?

The concept of Hyena as her mother is one that won't settle. Heartache for her family, the children, is all she can think of. If only Pea were here to talk to about it.

"Where is she?" Sr. mutters as he takes a step back inside. What Mrs. Andrews must think of her husband. Of Rabbit. The prospect of a mother alive out there is overshadowed by questions about Whitetail's motives.

The butler extends a hand to help Rabbit climb into the car that she's perfectly able to climb into on her own. She eyes him and takes his hand with a sigh. *Leashed, as Snake warned.* In this case, it is simply the path of least resistance. Cared for but caged. Alone and held apart. Powerless. As she lifts a foot to climb into the cab, there's a noise.

"Rabbit!" A small, rough voice calls from the courtyard. As Rabbit turns, searching for the sound, a dark figure emerges from behind the gate, running in her direction. At first, she thinks it's a strangler, but it's not, it's a woman. Old, withered, and sickly. The knowing in her eyes is confusing. She clearly said Rabbit's name, but they've never met. The old woman's holding a white kitten in her arms, and her eyes are wide. Not just any white kitten—Milk's baby girl.

"Snake?" Rabbit staggers; she can't believe her eyes. Snake's face is sallow, and the weight she's lost makes her look like a wraith. Clothes hang where she once had breasts; even the cuffs of her dress look too big on what's left of her fine wrists. The dark circles under her eyes have grown deep, and there are only a few strands of hair left on her head. She's caught whatever horrible disease Mr. Adams has? Rabbit puts her foot back on the ground and, turning, lets go of the butler's hand.

"Rabbit." Snake reaches out a waving arm, motioning for her to wait.

The butler yanks Rabbit's shoulder toward him protectively as he looks across the drive to strangler officers idling nearby. They look nervous, moving closer until Snake is upon Rabbit, at which point the stranglers halt.

"Snake?" Rabbit calls.

"I was lying," Snake says. "I was lying when I told you you're evil. It was a lie, and I have proof." She lifts the kitten up, nuzzling it. Cracks in her lips turn bloody and weepy. Her hands are skeletal and pruned. The bridge of her nose has turned black. Her sunken and cloudy eyes search Rabbit's for connection.

Rabbit can't speak, she's so choked with emotion. What has Snake become?

"Proof? What's happened to you? What's happened?" It looks like Snake is destined for death soon. Has she turned foul with grief? How can this be?

"The truth makes you sick if you don't let it out. It makes a hole and comes out on its own. Put a person in any place which is not their own choosing—a woman in a role which is not hers by choice—it makes *you* sick. Not them. I buried my beliefs and spoke someone else's. Here I am, admitting I was wrong. Hopefully, before it's too late."

She extends her skeletal hand, wincing, summoning energy to speak further. She lifts the cat.

"Whitetail always said time was a spiral," Snake says. "And that it doesn't have one vein, it has many. You rolled *Incarnation,* same as Whitetail. Whitetail brought Mouse. This isn't Milk's baby girl! Mouse wasn't Mouse!"

Rabbit struggles for air. Snake is speaking too fast. Whitetail had rolled *Incarnation*? The same as Rabbit when she tried to save Milk. But who, what, was Mouse?

"Guards!" the butler screams. The stranglers across the drive pick their pace up; they're running.

"She *is* Milk!" Snake says, holding up the kitten. "Another Milk."

Rabbit's stunned. That means. *Mouse was . . . Whitetail? Another Whitetail?*

"Guards!" The butler cranes his neck, looking to bring in more forces. Sr. walks out the front door looking confused. Spotting Snake, he bolts in her direction.

"Restrain her," he says. Mr. Martin grabs Snake, knocking the kitten from her arms. It tumbles to the ground and darts under a hedge.

"Milk," she cries, fighting restraint.

Wrestling free of the men, Snake lunges at Sr., grabbing him by the neck. "No more damage," she growls.

"Whoa," a strangler says as he hunkers low, adjusting his stance. "Wait now." His wraith's voice is stern.

The stranglers encircle Snake, and Sr. sputters with a momentary reprieve for air.

"No," Snake says, pointing at the stranglers; she's withdrawn fabric shears from somewhere inside the deep front pocket of her apron. *The sewing that Marianne asked her to do.*

In an instant, the shears are at Sr.'s throat.

Sr.'s face is growing purple with Snake's forearm up under his chin. Rabbit's brain is too overloaded to track the scene.

"I'm saying no. *I'm* saying quiet. You're the one that needs to stop. Stop hurting. Stop controlling. Stop speaking. We've been listening to you for centuries. It's your turn to listen," Snake whispers.

The stranglers nervously exchange glances, and the scene grows quiet, everyone at a standstill.

Rabbit thinks of Judge Dodd, the court she'll be speaking in front of tomorrow. *The truth.* What Marianne told her, back when she'd asked about the truth and the damage it would do.

Andrews Sr.'s destruction here today would mean a dent in a bigger beast's armor. It could mean the eventual liberation of magical women, or the onslaught of the greatest war ever fought, bringing death to innocents.

Snake's face crumples with panic as she rounds to see Rabbit, whipping Sr. around by the throat as she turns. Her wounds are healing. Her nose, the sunken black hole, is frosted over with a layer of flesh. It's scarred from blisters but healing. She'd become haunted like Adams? Whatever plagued her seems to be resolving itself.

"*Grr—ssss,*" Sr. says, gagging. "*Ggg!*" His eyes are darting, pleading to the guards for help.

A look to his men says Sr.'s scared. Snake digs the scissors into the man's neck. With the strain of her holding him, the tip of the shears digs into Sr.'s flesh, and a ruby bead of blood shows through the white whiskers on his neck. His knees are bent, lowering to his captor's height. Though she's a great deal smaller than him, her desperate fury seems to offer her superhuman strength. She keeps him close to her heaving chest. Her eyes are wild, and spittle clings to the corner of her gasping mouth.

Snake blinks tears out of her eyes, not as cloudy as before.

"You can't remain Supreme."

"P-plea—" he sputters, resigning.

"No! It's time for you to be quiet," she yells, jabbing the scissors into Sr.'s neck. As the hole in the side of his throat opens, dark blood quickly spills down his shirt front.

"No!" A new voice comes from up the steps, inside the house. "John?"

Rabbit turns to spot Mrs. Andrews, newly arrived on the front step, lurching over a stand-in cane. Stooped low, her hair is graying and her eyes milky. She struggles forward a step.

"Please! Guards!" she cries, flapping out a weak wave of her free hand. It's striking now how similar Mrs. Andrews's and Snake's grotesque conditions have become. The strangler pushing a wheelchair behind Mrs. Andrews cues into the scene, abandons the chair, and sprints for Sr.

Mrs. Andrews screams again, and a flurry of stranglers clambers around the pair.

Mrs. Andrews's escort grabs Snake by the shoulders, shaking her. Unable to lessen Snake's grip on Sr.'s throat, he raises his elbow and lands a punch to her jaw with a *crack*.

Snake lets go, the shears clang onto the ground, and Sr. keels, staggering. Slumping, he winces, his hands clamoring to grip his neck, searching to stop the tide of spilling blood. He collapses. Mr. Martin and the stranglers grab Snake by the wrists. As they tackle her to the ground, one of the stranglers clambers on top of her thrashing torso and bucking legs. He decks her with the full force of his fist across her jaw, sounding a terrible knock.

When Mr. Martin comes away, he howls a horrible honking scream and a red spot appears on his cheek, mirroring Snake's. The other stranglers snicker and twitch around him, looking to a coming blackhood, the last man to arrive, for more direction. Mrs. Andrews covers her face, collapsing into her chair, looking small.

Snake lies still.

Rabbit tastes blood and realizes that at some point she must have reopened the cut on her lip. Shock seizes her legs and makes them shake. Mr. Andrews Sr., the Supreme, is dead.

One of her sisters, Snake, is gone.

A strangler recovers the kitten from the bushes. As he brings it close to his face, dangling by the scruff of its neck, it mews. Tossing it, it flails awkwardly onto the ground next to Snake's stone-blue face before he stomps on its head with the heel of his boot.

Chapter 30

You Need Me

Rabbit's been a good girl these last two weeks, staying in her room, heartsick for Snake and consumed by what her sister had revealed before she died. If Whitetail really had successfully reincarnated herself as little Mouse in her own lifeline, then why would she turn around and kill herself? Had the will of the wilds considered Whitetail's request bold? Or stupid? Rabbit saw Whitetail drag away Mouse with her own two eyes. Whitetail is guilty.

But why?

Rabbit's consulted the cigarette tin of hair various times for guidance, but without a shock of Whitetail's hair, it is painfully uninformative. Snake's hair has grown as dry and brittle as ash. And Mouse's is not even dust.

Snake's absence from Westwood House has made the days since her death even more painful. The trial was on hold given what one man in the driveway below Rabbit's bedroom window called the "national tragedy." Strange men and women have been circulating in and out of halls and rooms for days now, and the spring of those wanting to pay respects to the dead Supreme seemingly runs eternal. Stranglers had taken Milk's and Snake's bodies out to a field and burned them. Unjust. And proof the

Freemen didn't obey their very own laws on burning. Rabbit can still see the black spot in the field where the un-grand pyre lasted for two days. Burnt dry grass remains. It haunts Rabbit from her bedroom window. She hopes with all her spirit that the Grimm saw through all the soot to Snake's good soul when she got to his door. Summerland.

The last time Rabbit saw Mrs. Andrews, she had been screaming, had collapsed, thrown herself out of her wheelchair onto her deceased, but cleaned and re-dressed husband.

Marianne said the trial would wait long enough for Mrs. Andrews to be permitted to mourn and accept mourners for the body's visitation. To allow time for a funeral. Mr. Andrews Sr.'s funeral is today. Rabbit wasn't invited.

Though a full A&O train's length of cars departed from Westwood earlier for the Supreme's daylong funeral, only five cars have come back with the black bear. When a man brings out Mrs. Andrews's chair from the auto's trunk, he opens a door to the backseat and Mrs. Andrews slides out. The strangler pushes her, her chair's wheels bumping and skidding, rolling across the gravel. A crowd of older men with white hair follows her inside in a formal-looking procession. The men are dressed in Freemen suits fancier than Rabbit's ever seen before. The fabric they wear is shiny. At the shoulder and wrists, their jackets are heavily tailored. They have square hats, and though the expressions they wear are sorrowful, their eyes dart at one another, bees on flowers. They're nervous. Why?

The man at the back of the procession is carrying a square, black box. It's smooth, and from the way the man is carrying it, Rabbit can tell, precious. Curiosity overcomes her.

Rabbit opens her door to the hallway. What is in the black box the man carried inside just now? Why all the formality?

Mr. Martin isn't there outside her door when she opens it, but as she takes a step into the hallway, Rabbit can see his shadow slinking up the stairs in her direction. She'll not be able to sneak down to see what the men and Mrs. Andrews are doing with the black box. Looking across the corridor, she spots the servant stairs and makes a dash for them. If she can get far enough away from Martin, the distance will make it harder for him to find her. Descending the stairs, she makes it to the first floor, but, entering the east wing, she spots Marianne and another maid whispering and is driven in the opposite direction, down a dead-end hallway. Below a table with a vase of cut flowers, Rabbit spots a grate. The ducting surely leads throughout the house. She opens the grate and looks inside.

From inside the wall, Rabbit can see in two directions. She can see into the main sitting room, where a fire is roaring and the men are filtering in and out into the hallway where Marianne is scrambling nervously for reasons unknown to Rabbit.

Mr. Martin has yet to come down the stairs looking for her, but it won't be long before he figures out she's not in her room.

In the living room, a strangler rolls Mrs. Andrews up to the hearth and spins her to sit in front of everyone. The man from the back of the procession sets the strange box he's carried in down next to her.

"Freemen," she says, her voice hoarse. Her red-rimmed eyes drift slowly around the room. The gentlemen are all seated, and attentively they watch her. The flames at her back are high, and even though Mrs. Andrews is a withered shell of what she was when Rabbit first met her, she holds a fierce power.

Looking back over her shoulder, Rabbit sees Martin's quivering shadow before she spots him. He rushes down the stairs and in her direction. But when he sees no one there, he turns around and walks in the other direction at a quickening pace. It won't be long before he recognizes where she's hiding. She hopes she can make it back up to her room before she's caught.

A man in a black coat stands and walks over to the box; he places a hand on top of it.

"John Andrews Sr. is dead, as are his brothers and only son. We've never been in this position before. An heirless Supreme without brothers or nephews. We have a decision before us today. By election, we'll choose the new Supreme. A post that will endow the most deserving in the room for the rest of their lives. Their son too. Who here is ready to stand on the shoulders of their brethren and forge, leading onward all Freemen in their father's tradition? Say I."

After a quiet moment of the men looking around the room at one another, a man stands and opens his mouth to speak.

"I," Mrs. Andrews says.

All the men's brows crinkle at once, and immediately the man who was about to volunteer for Supreme takes a step back. Someone clears his throat, and another man lets out a honk of laughter.

"I say, Mrs. Andrews, you are aware that this post is a man's post."

"Scripture says no such thing. It says 'heir apparent,' not male heir. I am the wife of deceased Supreme John Andrews, devout Blackbook devotee, and therefore, as his living heir, shall wear the lace." As she smirks with the challenge, the men all look at each other with dismay.

Lace is a term Rabbit recognizes. It's the Freemen's crown used in Freemen coronation. Heir apparent isn't a term Rabbit knows, but if birth gives right to status, Rabbit is Sr.'s blood, or so the papers in the scrapbook told. The thought of Hyena also being blood makes her swallow hard. Half Freemen, half rifter—which half is most confounding?

"Now, Mrs. Andrews," a man says sternly. "You, more than anyone, can understand that, historically, Supreme has been held by a man, and for the sake of the party, we should keep in line with a leader whom the Freemen can adamantly support."

"Yes."

"That that person, well, he'll need to be male. There's never been proof that swearing off magic would eliminate it from a woman's bones permanently. It's not realistic."

"I am not Dirty."

"We're not seriously discussing this," he says.

"With the Necrology already stolen, we can't afford to consider it. It's time for a firm hand," another man says dismissively. As he stands and turns to leave, he realizes that the box is still there in the room. *It contains something he can't leave without?* Shifting on his feet, the man seems undecided on whether he's willing to leave without it. And, perhaps, the Supreme title.

Looking around at the other seated men, two of them stand to support him, but no one leads the charge, so no one leaves.

Mrs. Andrews cocks her jaw to one side as her eyes graze the room again. Grabbing her headless cane from the back of her chair, she bangs it three times on the floor.

Looking back over her shoulder again, Rabbit can see Marianne hoofing it, springing down the hallway past the heating grate and into the sitting room.

"Yes, Mrs. Andrews," Marianne says, her chest heaving as she opens the door. Clearly, the arrival of these men has taxed Marianne with unanticipated duties. This visit wasn't planned.

"Wheel them in now." Mrs. Andrews's face is cold pride.

"Yes, Mrs."

The room sits in silence. Most of the men watch Marianne close the door. She races down the hallway past the grate, her gray skirt flapping briskly as she steps. She walks past the main hall and down toward Mrs. Andrews's salon.

When Marianne pops back into view, she's rolling a cart in front of her. It still has a black cloth covering what it carries. Rabbit knows what's underneath—it's Whitetail's antlers.

As Marianne walks past the stairs, Mr. Martin is standing on the bottom step. He looks in the sitting room's direction but doesn't move; he just stands there, watching Marianne roll the cart into the sitting room.

The men waiting in the room are whispering. Their hands flip back and forth through inaudible discussions, and their faces wear fearful expressions.

"Ah." Mrs. Andrews's voice is light, and it brings all the men's attention back to her. Marianne rolls the cart over to Mrs. Andrews and leaves it within reach by her side.

"Thank you," she says to Marianne. Marianne turns to walk away. "Uh, Marianne?" Mrs. Andrews isn't ready to let Marianne leave.

"Yes, ma'am."

"How many years ago now did you give up your inheritance to the Dirt?"

"Oh, I never had much to begin with, Mrs. My mother's mother didn't leave me much. I come from old birds, mind you. None, really. My mother's never spoke of the Dirt—my grandmother only once in my memory and she'd said it spitting! Fact is, my foremothers are who helped cast the curse to erase fifty-eight, *Flame*. They knew uprising wasn't worth it and that it'd come time for a new age. Move on. Cast fifty-eight off, don't you know. Redefined Sixty-Four for the new age. Without them . . ." Marianne's voice falls off and her lip trembles. "Well, the Dirty would be marching because their footing would be level."

Rabbit's breath catches in her throat. There it is again. *Erasing fifty-eight.*

Mrs. Andrews smiles. "That's valiant of them."

Marianne nods, looking a little relieved with the admission.

"But how long?" Mrs. Andrews presses. "How long would you say?"

"I came to work for you and the master twenty years ago now."

Mrs. Andrews nods.

"So, no witchcraft in twenty years. Not one Dirty slip? Do you ever worry it will come back?"

Marianne shakes her head furiously.

"Never?" Mrs. Andrews raises an eyebrow.

Marianne backtracks. "Well if it did, I'd pray on the Blackbook and get it gone really fast. That's a certainty, Mrs. Andrews." She looks meekly around the room.

"If I offered you the ability to ensure the Dirt never comes back to you, never, would you take it?"

Marianne looks aghast. She stays silent.

"What would you say?"

"I'd say yes, Mrs." Marianne looks at the ground, her hands clinging together at her front.

"Yes!" Mrs. Andrews looks around the room. "A voluntary denial of Dirt."

"Old news. We have that already in the contract. The Dirty have signed!" a man says angrily, looking at his neighbor. The direction of the discussion and Mrs. Andrews's look of accomplishment have sparked agitation in the room. "It's already a law of the land!" he says.

"You're not seeing what I see before me." Mrs. Andrews looks at Marianne. She rolls her chair an inch closer to the men.

"You weep for my son, my husband, and you curse the Dirty. You have that luxury. You weren't born with evil in your veins that necessitated a cap over your instincts. You have the luxury of not knowing what I know: that magic isn't something that you deny. The Blackbook doesn't keep it at bay for long. It. Always. Comes. Back." She hammers her cane with each utterance. "Your laws, thus far, have been pointless. A bandage to stem an un-clotting flow." Marianne looks outed. Her cheeks flush.

Rabbit feels awestruck. Heart in her ears, she hears the words of wisdom spilling out of Mrs. Andrews's mouth. Behind her in the hall she hears Mr. Martin's footsteps fall closer in her direction.

Mrs. Andrews throws the cover off the antlers. Grabbing Marianne's hand, Mrs. Andrews has to work to keep ahold of it. Marianne's side-eyeing the antlers like a tragedy. Mrs. Andrews forcibly places an antler in Marianne's hand. Marianne's mouth hangs open with dismay; her left arm braces the right as she's left holding the heavy antler.

"Say it," Mrs. Andrews says. She looks around the room at the men.

"What, Mrs.? Say what?" Marianne's eyes are wide and frightened as she looks around the room.

Mrs. Andrews curls a finger in her direction, cueing Marianne to lean in. As Marianne stoops, top lip sweating, Mrs. Andrews reaches up and roughly yanks out a chunk of Marianne's hair.

Marianne cowers, sucking in a chest full of air.

"That you disavow the Dirt. Forever," Mrs. Andrews hisses.

"I already have." Marianne weeps. "And every night before bed on the Blackbook. I swear it!" Tears are in her eyes now, and she's shuddering.

"Here and now," Mrs. Andrews directs. "Forever." She glances at the black box before raising her chin an inch higher. Two of the men gasp, and the rest swivel their heads back and forth at one another, whispering with fury.

"I—I—" Marianne says.

Everyone in the room leans in closer to her.

"I disavow the Dirt."

"There!" Mrs. Andrews says, taking the antler back and putting it on the table. Marianne staggers a moment as Mrs. Andrews holds up the shock of hair in Marianne's direction. Instead of being drawn to her as the will of the wilds typically designs, it floats, drifting like a magnetic opposite away from Marianne and into the fire where it sparkles, then burns. All the men gasp. Marianne's hands reach for her cheeks.

"My succession here today, while unconventional, would save lives. Freemen lives. Dirty lives. I've come up with a plan that would end the war for good." She points to the table. To the antlers. "I have something you don't."

"Mrs. Andrews," a spokesperson blurts in protest.

"You don't want me because deep down you feel you can't trust me, isn't that right? But you need me," Mrs. Andrews says.

"Ha! But you're a woman."

"Not just any woman. A woman holding the answer to eliminating magic from the face of this earth. A woman with the ability to use magic . . . to preeminently eradicate magic. This." She runs her withered hands across the spines of Whitetail's antlers. "These are the Nine Cunning Wands." She places a finger atop one of the nine spines. "The second happening of the Woodfeast predicted in the Blackbook—that *you* gentlemen don't have the ability to use."

The men in the room blink with understanding as Rabbit gasps. Marianne had just lost her Dirt for good. Forever. And the antlers . . . are wands. Her mind races back to the photo of the woman on fire and the nine wands eerily hovering in the sky. *The branches of Whitetail's antlers. Woodfeast? A second happening of*

what Mother nature held in her jaw during the birth of the world?
All the men in the room stand, their legs bolting them upright.
"I didn't recognize—the Nine. You've found them. You've found
them," one of the men says. They look around, breathless. Fearful
tears sparkle in the corners of a man's eyes as he looks to his
neighbor. Quickly he walks across the room and opens the black
box sitting opposite Whitetail's antlers.

"Tomorrow's trial and burning will set the tone. Public
opinion is with us. This is the first step in the magical cleansing
we've all been waiting for."

The man holding the black box open looks around at the men
in the room. They nod, then, one by one, they clap.

"Hail, Supreme," the man says as he lifts a horrible-looking
square, black hood out of the box.

Rabbit recognizes it. The lace skull.

Bang! A rattle sounds beside Rabbit as Martin's arm reaches
into the duct and grabs her by a leg. Though Rabbit kicks and
squirms, it's too late. She's been found.

"*Mmph!*" Rabbit yelps as Mr. Martin pulls her out and up by
one wrist, he lets her dangle as he delivers a lone swat to her rear.
No idea if her back's been broken, Rabbit's knees buckle when her
feet reach the ground.

"Uh-uh." A stern voice sounds from across the room halting
Mr. Martin's would-be follow-up spank. "No visible marks,
Martin." It's Marianne, her eyes red and puffy. "I'll do it," she says.

Holding out a hand, Mr. Martin delivers Rabbit's wrist to
Marianne's grasp. Marianne doesn't let go as they walk down
the hall, up the stairs, and in the direction of Rabbit's quarters.

Marianne says nothing as they travel. Rabbit has no words either. But when they get to the corridor leading to Rabbit's bedroom, Marianne picks her up and carries her in a hug the rest of the way to the door.

Chapter 31

Biggest Dirty Sin

Whitetail's lying on the floor. It's late afternoon. Her window lost its light at some point, but she hadn't noticed it leaving. She feels herself slipping away, a fly on the river. With a snap, she tries to stay awake, scared she'll die and let Hyena go.

Looking at her hands, she sees they match the walls. Knobby, black, and her knuckles bulge. Her tendons are yanked tight like sinewy cords, looking brittle and strained. The damp has grown more penetrating than before. The loss of all her body fat has her bones aching. She feels limp and lies still, trying to conserve some form of power.

Tomorrow you will die, Hyena announces.

A creep of peace comes into her heart before she's pained with remembering the children. She's longed for relief from this husk, but oh, how she worries what will happen to her brood in the future when the truth about her is revealed to all. When Hyena is revealed. She shudders with heartache, looking to hold on. She's held a war, a revolution, at bay for the sake of the little people she loves. She hopes the children will understand what they meant to her. What they'll always mean. *Everything.* And why she's done what she's done in keeping Hyena. The children's coming evolution . . . coming war, what the will of the wilds has in store, it's terrifying.

And like that, with a thought to the wilds, she's comforted, overcome with peace again. But she'd miss this life, or at least the years she lived in Blackmoor with the children. If only there were someone to hold her now. Though she is old, she longs for the comfort of her mother's arms. If only there were a way to call to her mother now, whisper through the faraday walls to the spirit world.

Hyena rolls over in her with a miserable rumble. Whitetail feels the darkness steal a little bit more of her spirit. Hyena's in her liver now, supping at it like it's a dandelion stalk offering sustenance. It takes her down another peg. Whitetail gasps. The faders guarding her beyond the bars snicker.

Hyena's right. Whitetail will be dying tomorrow, whether it's by flame or her own body's retirement, in which case Hyena will be freed.

Still, she doesn't know if she's ready to talk to Hyena. The way she killed Mouse. There's so much to be bitter about.

"Hyena." It could be her last chance.

Now you speak to me?

"You needed to be more patient, sister. Your freedom was always coming. Always coming. At the right time. In good time. You needn't have killed Mouse." She waits in the silence, the stone walls echoing her own breath. "You should have trusted in me. My plan."

You were keeping me, sister. Stowed and chained. It is unfair to leave me in here. What about what I want?

It stings, all things considered. Whitetail knew full well that holding Mouse down, blowing Hyena into her body was going to be messy, even fatal for Whitetail. And Mouse holding Hyena for possibly another hundred and fifty years was going to feel like an eternity for both of them.

I couldn't let her keep me.

"She was scared when you killed her, you know. A child, afraid. I could still smell it in the air the morning after, when I walked outside, out to where she lies, the blackcoats surrounding her like flies. The other children too. There was terror on the wind. How could you? After all I've sacrificed. And your daughter . . ."

Ha! You served yourself by keeping me. Greedily, you wanted to keep your quiet life. Your children—fell in love with my daughter and kept her for yourself.

"Shhh!" Whitetail cuts her off, unable to stand Hyena's callous reframing of her old life and the children. She'd only ever wanted to keep the war at bay until the Dirty's numbers would allow any chance at all for their success in the fight for 'Librium. Until the beast rose, yawning, stone in its jaw. What mother would volunteer her children for war? Who would knowingly chance the lives of their loved ones?

Playing Sixty-Three had been a conundrum. Sure, she'd known how dangerous it was to play alone. But protecting the children . . . never before had she felt so completely lost in a task as that night she played alone. Her promise to the children that she'd always keep them warm and safe had to be seen to. Like the spirits of the foremothers had willed it, she dared to be bold. How was she to keep the children safe amidst a war, with her dead and them in crisis and being attacked at the very heart of who they were and what they believed?

How could Whitetail not have foreseen Hyena killing Mouse? She was stolen without warning. She's failed the children. The future is coming; the war is upon them, and life is about to get so extremely dangerous.

What will happen tomorrow? What will come in the future now that the children will have to face her legacy?

You didn't fail them. You failed everyone else, Hyena growls.

A fader comes closer to the bars to try to make out the sounds Whitetail's uttering. He knows she's convening with something or someone, and it angers him.

"Noisy, wicked. Speaking to the devil, are you?" the fader says.

Whitetail watches the surrounding faders' eyes glaring at her with skepticism. They look her over, their eyes widening, evaluating her, making sure that she hasn't cut her own wrists with what little is left of her fingernails. She imagines that some women on trial like to cut to the chase.

"I'll never forgive you for what you've done," Whitetail whispers. "For killing Mouse."

Forgiveness? Hyena's tone is cutting. *I'm due the apology. You kept my daughter for yourself. Became the mother I never could be.*

Whitetail gasps. "You never wanted a child. Rabbit was only ever an object to you. You never fed her, bathed her, you barely even held her past your birth-bed. She'd been but a nuisance before she became a pawn. Your publishing her birth announcement was a vulgar attempt at embarrassing Freemen. You've always been so juvenile."

Why can't you trust what I saw in the stars the night she was born? Arm's length, that's what Rabbit needed. To be hardened to reach her potential, not coddled. As her mother, I deserved a say. To mother her my way.

"You mean not at all?"

The faders rush close to the bars, hard of hearing her one-sided conversation.

Whitetail knew, weeks before the fire, just how much she adored the child. Hyena claimed the stars had shown her child left at arm's-length. But baby neglected and alone, stars or not, Whitetail had read the coming fire. It only made her want to protect the child more.

What she's done for Rabbit, for all the children, she's done out of true love.

She tried to govern the children with a cool hand. Now she regrets it. Will she ever have the opportunity to tell the children how proud of them she is? Even their mistakes? Wave, or blow them all a first and last kiss?

You put them and yourself before me and what I stand for. You're my sister.

Whitetail begins to weep. "I'm no vulture. And the children never meant less love for you. Never for a second. Your daughter is like mine; what mother doesn't sacrifice happiness to protect their child? Their family. My love for Mouse was also love for you. You're blind. The wilds—"

Don't speak to me of the wilds. We've both seen it. Rabbit won't be spared in the long run! You've coddled her. Now you've left a soft child with too much responsibility. Blind? Can't you see that in your vow to protect the children, always, you've all but sacrificed your entire spirit? Before these walls, you couldn't hear the wilds at all anymore, could you? You're a wraith with nothing left to transcend to summer with.

Whitetail knows it could be true, and there's no reversing it. She feels pressure. Hyena trembles, boiling with a fresh fervor as she kicks Whitetail's diaphragm down with a swift blow, forcing out a guttural scream.

Why don't you just die already?

Whitetail feels the lining of her throat sear with pain until she chokes. All the air is forced out of her lungs, and they collapse a moment.

Your love for Mouse, love for the children, it did *mean less for me,* Hyena clarifies. *And the Grimm will judge your deeds for himself.*

The biggest Dirty sin there is, is a woman holding another woman down.

Chapter 32

Back Aboard

Back aboard the A&O en route to Albany, the train car sways and budding trees blur past the car's windows. Spring is typically Rabbit's most favorite season, but this year, she wants nothing more than to rewind to a few weeks ago when she made mud.

Vibrations from the tracks speeding below her work their way up, through the bottoms of her feet, through her belly, and rattle her jaw. For the first time in weeks, Rabbit sees the sun. It's peeking out from behind bulging clouds, but it does nothing to ease Rabbit's mind. She's so confounded, she's ready to explode. If only she could trade all she's come to learn of Hyena, Sr., and the antlers for ignorance.

She and Mrs. Andrews are alone, and the car is quiet, save for the *click-clack* that chips at her nerves. Even Hughes is back in another car, demoted in the moon since they'd met. Where Sr. constantly listened to snakes whispering in his ears, Mrs. Andrews seems more comfortable with isolation.

Rabbit sits thinking about life. It all seems so big. So incredibly mysterious. Her life, Snake's, and the other orphans'. Rabbit thinks about Mr. Andrews Sr., the Supreme, dying. Beard dying. Mouse dying. The question remains: Why would Whitetail have reincarnated herself in her own lifeline and then raised her as her own? And why would she murder herself incarnate? It's because of the Necrology, Rabbit's sure of it. There are so many stones in this world, all with their purposes, but the connection between Hyena stealing the Necrology, then Whitetail keeping Hyena and the stone, is one she can't make.

Mrs. Andrews blots under one dry eye with a handkerchief. Rabbit wants to ask what's next. Mrs. Andrews is a woman in a position of much power. As the new Supreme, she could be poised to demand change for the better, but here she is making strides to abolish magic forever. Here and now, nothing stands in her way. Except Rabbit.

"Why will you do it?" Rabbit asks.

Mrs. Andrews raises her brows; she knows exactly what Rabbit is talking about. Looking at the heavy black case next to her, she touches the handle with wrinkled, golem-like fingers.

The antlers are in there. Rabbit can tell from the way Mrs. Andrews keeps looking at it. How concerned she was about its placement when two large men brought the case aboard.

"It's a matter of survival, isn't it?" Her knobby fingers come away from the case's handle. "You may think me a villain for the work I intend to do. But a world without differences is a safer one."

"But it's for each girl to decide. You can't decide for them." Rabbit's tone is recklessly unguarded, but Mrs. Andrews is withered, and there's no cane here with which to whack out all her teeth.

"Oh, but I can. I will. My husband was a man who liked to direct. I've long been a close study." Mrs. Andrews's eyes are hollow, blank, and rimmed with dark circles. Her cheeks are dry, and it's striking that although she's regularly blotted a handkerchief under each eye, there're no tears. She looks more withered by the minute. Her hair is graying before Rabbit's very eyes and the backs of her hands are becoming more vascular. But not a tear.

How could Mrs. Andrews, having lost her other hemisphere, her mate, not be haunted every waking minute by legitimate grief?

"You didn't love him." Rabbit had lost people. People she loved. A thought to Hyena breaks her heart over what could have been. A mother she's never known, and there the whole time. What did Hyena think of her, seeing her day in and day out? Had she seen Rabbit stealing bread from Pheasant's plate when Ms.'s back was turned?

Does Hyena love Whitetail as hard and true as Rabbit does? Did Hyena care for Rabbit?

"You've caught me. Try as I may, I can't cry." She sighs. "How could I love any man after Maloy? And my husband deserved what he got after the black he created, what his advisors tried to cover up. As if I didn't know what he did on his trips to New Amsterdam. His whores were a relief to me. Black Dean, that bishop, should be demoted to a pimp." She sneers. Mumbling, her lips tremble. "Visiting his sisters at the Blackbox, ha!" She tosses the handkerchief on the floor. "We wouldn't be here today if my husband had stayed away from Hyena. If he hadn't been directed by vanity and what he had in his pants," she says wistfully. She looks Rabbit directly in the eyes. "I know who you are."

Rabbit blinks, swallowing hard. She'd wondered whether Mrs. Andrews knew of the affair. Marianne had mentioned the Blackbox. She still has no idea what it is, what a pimp is, or who Sr.'s sisters are. She has aunts on both sides?

"No. There are no tears. The black clothes will have to do." Mrs. Andrews stands, walking shakily to the table nearby to pour herself a drink. Uncorking a bottle, she pours brown liquid into a small cut crystal glass.

"After Maloy, my late husband found me in a gutter. It had been a long winter, and I'd almost entirely soaked through with black despair. John lifted me up, got me a blanket, and said, 'The beholden will always be of service, always be loyal.' And he handed me my beautiful cane, crowned with serpentis ovum. The cane made me beautiful. It made me whole. It cured my heartbreak, my worries, and soothed my conscience. I had confidence that I'd never felt. A dog on a leash, perhaps, to my husband. But it made my life whole. It was breathtaking."

Rabbit's mouth opens, but she can't speak. She's always known that offerings directly from the wilds—like the Necrology, serpentis ovum, the Woodfeast—were life-giving. Apparently, Mrs. Andrews had been hiding, disguised by the ovum for years, yielding youth from its pulse.

"Blindness is easy. But you know what I admitted to myself yesterday? With all those fancy, proud-nosed men sitting around, agreeing with me?"

"No, ma'am," Rabbit whispers.

"That although my leash is gone, after years of being blindfolded, I'll see what I damn well please. Dirty is damage. Before girls wind up hurt the way I was hurt, I'll do everything within my power"—she turns her head to spot the case—"to keep girls from ever touching Dirt again." Looking out the window, she crosses her arms. Rabbit can see her blank expression in the window's reflection.

Tears stream down Rabbit's face, and she's desperate. Helplessness rushes into her hands like a tide. Angrily she wipes her face, recovering with a huff.

"Dirt isn't the reason you lost your teeth. You didn't appreciate what you had, so it got taken away. And when Jacob knocked them out again, it was . . . it . . . ." She's left staring at Mrs. Andrews's back.

"Yes?"

But Rabbit doesn't know how to continue. "Sometimes, when bad stuff like that happens, it's just the will of the wilds. The wilds are always looking for 'Librium."

"So I, the child not even a mother could love, was supposed to lose it all, be left for dead? For the sake of balance? My son, taken for balance? My loss brings your 'Librium?"

Rabbit's not sure, and her heart breaks at the reality of what Mrs. Andrews has just said. Why does balance always cost?

"Maybe. Maybe it's what it took for you to get right here, right now, today. Like the moth who emerges from her chrysalis—you've emerged in a position to do good. You own the A&O. You're the first female Supreme in history. You're the most powerful woman in America. Why not speak out against violence against women's magic? You know firsthand what men's opinions leave in their wake. It's their opinions that put you in the gutter, not magic. Why not rise to assume your place—work for 'Librium?"

Mrs. Andrews shudders, turning toward Rabbit. "*My son!*" she shrieks. Quivering, her body shakes so hard Rabbit worries she'll hear the woman's stone heart rattle in her bones.

"There is no future living with damaging magic. There are no more laws for its governing because there's no law that will prevent it, or an uprising in its defense." She shoots an accusatory finger at Rabbit. "For those who wield Dirt, it's always the same slippery slope down into mud. War in magic's defense or in its suppression, the potential conflict, needs to be snuffed out altogether. To a forest, moths can prove to be omens of the end of days. Let's not hope for those. John Freemen's blessings on who or whatever had the witch keeping the war contained this long . . ." Mrs. Andrews shakes her head. "And his blessings upon your Ms. . . ." Her voice falls off before a cleft joins her brows.

Who or whatever had the witch keeping the war contained? The idea settles in Rabbit again. As a keeper, Whitetail meant to keep her and the other children safe. It's her life's promise. Whitetail swallowed Hyena to keep her safe from the same flames that killed the other children's parents. But also to keep a war at bay. *Why?*

"Flame will kill Hyena and the witch," Mrs. Andrews says. "Contained all these years, she no doubt wants to be free—bring her truth, and her war. With her Dirty prison dying, we'll need to kill Hyena before she's able to escape. And with the pair's ignition, the constant threat of tides to be turned by the Dirty will be extinguished. It's precisely the opening act we'll need to the ultimate cleansing."

Mrs. Andrews throws the entirety of her glass of brandy back before hanging her head. And again, Rabbit's eyes shoot to the big black case.

Chapter 33

Trial

Rabbit has never seen so many people in her life. Crowds stand out front of the courthouse, pushing and jockeying for prime footing on the courthouse's front steps. When they see the Andrewses' caravan of cars approach, they turn their heads and swarm. The courthouse isn't as big as Westwood House, but it's just as grand and made of black stones that are glued together with little mortar. As the six cars that have traveled with them empty of blackcoats and stranglers, the men surround the auto Rabbit and Mrs. Andrews have ridden in.

Hughes opens the auto's door and grabs Rabbit's wrist, dragging her sideways, past men standing tightly together, each of them shouting communications to the others. There are more stranglers peppered throughout the crowds. Rabbit can see them swing in place—angry, tormented, and watchful. So many people are shouting.

"Witch!" someone yells, and Rabbit wonders if these men would prefer she burn beside Whitetail.

"Shut up, she's brave to come forward." Someone else's rebuttal is in her favor.

"Agh! Dirty girl," someone else yells as wet hits Rabbit's cheek. It's a big wad, and it sticks. Realizing someone's spit on her, she trips, stumbling onto one knee, making it thunder with pain. A heat and damp immediately flare under her nose.

Hughes wrenches her up by the arm as though she's light as a leaf and drags her, straining her shoulder socket, out of the advancing crowd's reach as the other guards keep a defensive ring around her and Mrs. Andrews. There's a thud on the ground beside Rabbit's foot, and she sees an apple roll by. Someone's thrown it, but not at her—over her head. Hughes is dragging her so fast she might as well be a kite.

Raising her arm, she wipes the spit off her cheek with the cuff of her coat and struggles to slow her heaving chest.

"Dirty witch!" someone screams, wailing at her again, and Rabbit knows it to be true. She is a witch, capable of incarnation and reading hair. Rabbit looks at Mrs. Andrews, pushed in her wheelchair by Mr. Martin, and therefore defended by a much bigger berth. She looks back over her shoulder, cueing Rabbit that it's not her the people are yelling at. It's someone else. Someone else nearby.

Rabbit can see a furious swirl of people. Whitetail is entering the building, too. A different entrance, though. The crowds don't give Whitetail the same room they've permitted her and Mrs. Andrews to have. Craning her neck, Rabbit yanks against Hughes's bullish progress, straining to see Whitetail, but it's in vain. She's moving too quickly, and everyone around her is too tall, too hostile.

Rounding a corner, Hughes heads for a big metal slab outlined with big knobby rivets and no handle. *A side entrance.* Unlike Whitetail, who's being forced up the court's front steps through the mob, Rabbit is being given the luxury of a less humiliating entrance. She's with Mrs. Andrews. And she's the star. When they reach the side door, Hughes bangs on it three times with his big fist before a small window slides open.

"Supreme," Hughes announces flatly, and the door flies open, the man holding it nodding before he steps aside quickly, eyes averted. Here is the new owner of A&O, Mrs. Andrews, the new Supreme. What could Rabbit do to convince Mrs. Andrews to stand her place and speak? Not for repression, but for all women's right to their nature. Rabbit searches back to Mrs. Andrews, but the woman's eyes are stone-cold and never meet hers.

Walking into the courthouse, Rabbit is brought into a big room. It's filled with more fencing and rails than Whitetail's gardens, only instead of chickens and beans, the pens are filled with chairs and people quickly claiming them. The lights on the ceiling are many. Like stars. Ten or more orbs of light atop big metal rings. They're so high up, it must be giants that light them each morning.

A chair sits at the front of the room, tall-backed, black, hide-covered, and it's grander than any other. There's a bench in front of it, and Rabbit knows that is where the judge will sit. Remembering him the day she visited. Remembering what he said about her testimony. About what would happen if she didn't say the lies. About how telling the truth would bring a war that would kill many women. That Whitetail needed to be shown as an example.

The chair has two flags flanking it, one American, with one star on a white square and red stripes, the other one 'Librium, featuring the four dots that represent the four corners of the earth.

There's a rustle in the back of the room, and the masses fall silent. Those who are seated stand.

"All you considering yourselves Freemen, rise," a man's voice booms, and Rabbit agrees, it's only right that people be standing to greet Whitetail. Everyone rises, including Rabbit. She's shaking all over, her nerves a series of fireflies igniting her joints. All heads turn, leaning and craning, blocking Rabbit's view. It's quiet, so Rabbit can hear heavy footsteps. Some men appear, and then next to them is a tall, broad figure dressed in black. With her wild locks shorn, only a sparse few hairs peek out from under a gray bonnet stained on either side with blood. She knew her antlers would be gone, but it still takes Rabbit a blink to realize it's really her. Whitetail is here. But rather than the strong, commanding, graceful creature that emerged from Andrews House last moon, this woman is hobbling and looks emaciated aside from her distended, bulging belly. Rabbit's stomach drops at the thought that she's become a strangler herself—but something about the way she holds her chin, the way her eyes stay trained on the flag, says otherwise. She's still in there. *Barely.*

"Here, Honorable Judge Dodd." The man calling out gestures a hand to the entering judge. "And Honorable Committee of Brothers Dodd." All heads turn to see the judge, looking small, at the front of the room. Behind him and off to one side, his brothers emerge from behind smaller chairs and sit. Rabbit can see the judge has put on a special headpiece for this occasion. The coif is rolled in bundles and looks more like a hat than the hair it's meant to emulate.

The judge acknowledges no one other than Mrs. Andrews, and even she only gets a quick nod. Judge Dodd sits down, scowling over his low specs to scan the back wall of the room.

Rabbit looks back there, too, and sees painted pictures, framed portraits of many men, each with the same strange hairpiece and fashion of black coat the judge wears. All of them wear the same dutiful scowl as the judge.

A woman briefly reaches out, pressing a comforting hand on Whitetail's shoulder as she passes. Her husband slaps it away, either protectively or with hatred. Rabbit can't see Whitetail's face.

Blackcoats, quivering and hunched, bring Whitetail toward the platform. Toward the judge, their batons poised at the ready. They wait as she ascends the steps as lightly as she always had on Andrews House's porch. And when she gets to the top stair, hissing and jeering from the crowd kicks up. Everyone's getting the full view of the witch. Someone throws a rock they smuggled in, and it knocks Whitetail on the shoulder, spinning her back a stride. She sways, but her face gives no indication of any pain. Rabbit remembers the way she'd thrown the rock at Johnathan Andrews, and nervously, she begins to cry.

The platform Whitetail sits on is as high up as Andrews House's porch roof and is crowded around by blackcoats, privates, one of whom raises a hand to silence the crowds. Judge Dodd whacks a hammer down on his desk to make everyone settle, but it does nothing to quiet the room. Finally, he whacks his hammer down so hard Rabbit thinks he'll crack the desk. A sheen breaks out on his brow with the effort as the mob's volume finally subsides to a level that would let Rabbit hear a cat groom.

Tears fill Rabbit's eyes and acid wells in her stomach as she watches Whitetail sit down, still flanked by men. They will apparently continue to surround her for the duration. Rabbit's legs are stubborn dandelion stems poised through a September wind. Rabbit tries to wave, but Hughes stops her. The commotion catches Whitetail's eye.

Ms.! Rabbit mouths, and Whitetail's eyes glass over and narrow. There's a fresh cleft between the woman's brows. Rabbit's been seen. A flat smile appears on Whitetail's face.

How could she smile at me while I sit here in the company of the Supreme? Rabbit brims with self-hatred. The judge clears his throat and tightens the tie at his neck. His irritation is unmistakable, and he eyes Rabbit sternly.

Rabbit's will to defy his orders crumbles.

Thrown off balance by his attention, Rabbit falls into her chair. People around her laugh as Hughes finally gets her seated. She feels fury. Eyes scanning, she knows she is more powerful than these people. More knowing. They don't even understand the very world they live in, and it shows in their petty amusement.

Mr. Martin walks briskly through the room and marches up to Mrs. Andrews. He bends at the waist to whisper something in her ear. Mrs. Andrews's eyes flit across their seating pen to Rabbit's, and she feels herself start to sweat.

Mrs. Andrews's hair is turning auburn again. *How?* It's notably less white than earlier.

Mrs. Andrews gives Mr. Martin a knowing nod before she lifts her chin in the air, eyes less black. She's been rejuvenated somehow. Her eyes are sharp. Her lips fuller. Even her earlobes have shrunk. Mrs. Andrews stands from her wheelchair with her cane and moves to a seat as though she never had as serious a health problem as she had this morning. She sits on the bench directly beside Rabbit. Mr. Martin rolls the wheelchair away.

The effect of Whitetail's antlers? Them being in Mrs. Andrews's possession is giving the awful hag new life? Their proximity could explain why Mrs. Andrews is looking and feeling the way she does. But—*why now?*

Rabbit scours the room, and very quickly she spots a man she thinks looks familiar. His long face is flushed, and as he wipes his brow, she recognizes him. He's the man who drove the carriage the day Beard came to Andrews House. The day Rabbit threw the stone and killed Mr. Johnathan Andrews Jr. with the curse.

He looks shaken, and when he spots her, his eyes widen with distress. She knows what he thinks. What the room thinks. That she's spent the last eight years living with a witch and that he's seen evidence Rabbit's learned dark magic. That she's been schooled in it—cursing and the like. Rabbit narrows her eyes at him, and as he shrinks even more, he looks to the bailiff across the room who's preoccupied with guarding Whitetail.

Judge Dodd is handling some papers, then he speaks to a man who stands to his left, next to the 'Librium flag.

Feeling Mrs. Andrews's eyes on her, Rabbit stiffens.

Mr. Martin comes to stand at their end of the pew and leans close, speaking in Mrs. Andrews's ear again. He says something apparently reassuring. Mrs. Andrews happily pats her hairline in that way that says she's thinking.

Gazing across the room, back at the ever-more-beautiful Mrs. Andrews, then back again into the crowd, Mr. Martin is on high alert and scanning.

Mrs. Andrews nods once more and Mr. Martin walks away.

Rounding the back of the room, he heads to a row of chairs opposite Rabbit. Mr. Martin zeroes in on someone, and with sharp eyes, he proceeds quickly to the center of the section. Rabbit's eyes search the crowd on the opposite side of the room. She spots a boy sitting there. He's grubby and thin. Looks like he's straight out of Andrews House. Mr. Martin reaches the boy; he grabs the boy's shoulders before the woman on the boy's right turns to whack Mr. Martin on the forearm with her fist. *The boy's mother.* Behind her, a man stands; the boy's father. Mr. Martin looks startled a moment before he backs away apologetically. He'd been mistaken? He was looking for a different grubby young boy?

Hairs stand up on Rabbit's neck. Of course it's not Mrs. Andrews's proximity to the antlers that is rejuvenating her—it's her proximity to the ovum. It's calling. Rook, wherever he might be, has just outed himself as being near.

Rabbit scans the room, trying to look oblivious.

Off in the fringes, she spots a young man. He's attractive and well put together; he looks familiar. There were once freckles on his cheeks. Dirt in his fingernails. His eyes catch hers with a knowing glint, and Rabbit feels fortified, electricity coming into her bones. She looks at her feet.

Rook. His black, wavy hair is combed back; there is a sparse yet definite mustache on his upper lip. His jaw looks fuller and his shoulders broader. He must be a foot taller than the last time she saw him. He's almost unrecognizable, and she can't believe what she's seeing. The ovum's effect has forced serious changes in him. If this were *her* Rook, she would have run to him, but this boy-man is altered, something other than her Rook. He looks like he's the one who's been fed and who's slept at Westwood House, not her. Heart kicking up a notch, she must bite her tongue so as not to call out asking him for directions. *What's the plan?* She needs to be told what to do!

She's elated she's not alone in this place.

"Be seated. Order, the court is now in session," the judge says. Deep creases sit in the corners of Judge Dodd's eyes. Rabbit's still standing, not wanting the proceedings to begin. Hughes pushes Rabbit down hard by the shoulders. Someone nearby snickers, but Rabbit resists, a fish fighting upstream through washed-down grasses. Finally, she gives in.

A woman storms into the room from a side door, mostly unnoticed. Breathless, she leaves it swinging behind her as she wipes a shag of thick, dark hair from her face. She scans the room before her coal eyes land squarely on Rabbit like she recognizes her.

Rabbit's never seen this woman in her life.

About the same age as Mrs. Andrews, but weathered by sun and different experience, the woman's dressed in muddy beggar's clothes that Rabbit envies. She's a sturdy worker's build with a smattering of black freckles across the brown skin of her cheeks. Setting her jaw in a frown, she turns, making it only three paces in the direction of the judge's bench before guards grab her by the arms. The guards deliver a worried look to Dodd before Dodd sees her too.

"No!" she yells.

Pointing a large, thick digit, Judge Dodd yells, "No extra Dirt on my courtroom floor."

The guards haul the woman away by the arms, dragging her

back out the door she came through. As she's almost out of sight, Rabbit hears her call again, "Father . . ."

Dodd's Dirty daughter. *Jane?*

The judge's forehead glistens with sweat as he composes himself. It's clear: this is a high-pressure moment for his people. The room's grown balmy with its compacted attendees. Those previously standing, sit, and benches squeak with the shuffling of their hips. Everyone prepares for the big moment. History. The time they'll tell their kin and grandkin about. Rabbit remembers how Whitetail used to tell stories by the stove in the kitchen. She understands the excitement these people feel. They're hoping for a good story.

Rabbit can't breathe. With Rook across the room, an ally, she feels the need to speak up now. Before this whole thing even starts. But what to say? The judge is already fixed on his verdict. And the public, according to Mrs. Andrews, is hungry to hear it. Rabbit has no explanation that could sway these people other than asking for mercy.

"Miss Elizabeth Whittle, you're charged with one count fraud for your squandering funds from the orphanage known as Andrews House. Child neglect. Child abuse. Five counts second-degree murder: the murders of James Koll, Robert and John Jones, and Jack Voles, and Johnathan Andrews Jr. And finally, one count first-degree murder of a child, recovered, and as of now, still unnamed. I ask you, woman, what is your plea?" His jowls shake.

"Not guilty." As Whitetail says it, she flinches—jeers and clapping erupt from the rows of seated spectators in the room.

"Order!" Irate, the judge bangs his gavel. He seems caught off guard by the show of enthusiasm from the masses.

Whitetail says nothing, just bows her head.

Rabbit's eyes scan the entirety of the room, not letting her eyes rest on Rook. She can't read his expression. The attendees quiet, and eventually the room falls silent.

A splitting anxiety rakes through Rabbit's body as she considers all the ways in which Whitetail is guilty—killing Mouse?—but also, isn't guilty, of murdering the men or stealing from the Beard. Rabbit covers her face, throws it down in her lap a moment, crying silently, as conflicted as ever. *Is the person at the front of the room a mother or a monster?*

Whitetail's selflessness couldn't be what made her Mother. Her love for the children either. Teachings? *Maybe.* No, it might be Rabbit's security in how well she's come to know herself that is Whitetail's biggest gift. Whitetail's patience while Rabbit worked to figure herself out without pressure to lean this way or that, unconditional support, that's what made her Mother.

But. A *murderess?*

Rabbit remembers Mouse's little hands dragging across the floor as Whitetail hauled her away by the ankle. Rabbit remembers the black in Whitetail's eyes that night. The way she stomped out the ember on the hearth. The way she gasped when she saw the ember. The way she'd ground it out, fevered, with her dirty, bare foot. Like she feared it. *Whitetail's not scared of anything.*

But Hyena is. She's scared of fire.

On the train yesterday, Mrs. Andrews had been frank, speaking openly about her goal here today. Her want was to stifle the potential war that would make Whitetail a martyr and launch any revolution of equality. Prevent Whitetail from becoming a martyr—moral high-road symbol of a last stand—and instead, taint her story and reconstruct her memory as a case study of how and of why magic needs to be removed from this country. They were starting with Whitetail and Hyena on fire but would be coming for the rest of them.

Mrs. Andrews wants to kill Hyena just as much as, if not more than, Whitetail.

Hyena has been contained all these years. She, no doubt, wants to be free.

What would have happened if Rabbit hadn't made the mud that day with Rook in the woods? If Whitetail had died at home, the children at her side, dressed in her red suit? *What would have become of Hyena then? What does a war for 'Librium look like?*

Rabbit remembers the night in the kitchen and the ember on the hearth. *Hyena.* All at once, Rabbit has a hunch, and an answer to so many questions. Hyena killed Mouse. After Hyena killed the Beard.

Chapter 34

The Truth

Judge Dodd clears his throat. "Miss Whittle, can you explain the events that took place at Andrews House on the eve of March sixteenth? Johnathan Andrews's murder?"

Whitetail shakes her head. Her eyes roll a little with fatigue or delirium.

Rabbit's heart swells with guilt over the rock she'd thrown. She feels Mrs. Andrews's eyes on her.

"No? Moving on, can you explain how a child's body came to lie dead on a rock out back of Andrews House the next morning?"

Whitetail does not answer.

The judge looks at her, impatience showing in his tightening jaw. "Are you not head and sole matron of Andrews House and the chief of all goings-on there? If you can't tell me what's gone on, who can?"

She sits, still not answering.

"My Afterward, woman, if you didn't kill them, who in our Father's name did?" he grumbles. Whitetail holds a hand up to her chest, perhaps in heartache. Rabbit sees Whitetail's hands aren't the hands that used to milk Sarah the goat or shuck peas. The skin on her hands looks so dark and her fingers fine. Her hand pats her chest a few beats before eventually working its way up to her throat where she waits, looking tortured. Not trying to speak, but to actively hold a voice at bay. Pained by something, Whitetail grips her belly and winces.

Rabbit slaps a hand over her mouth to keep quiet.

The judge's face is red. He's looking for damning and gruesome testimony, and all he's getting is fog. Though her not answering is not helping Whitetail, it's not serving the judge either in his cause to deliver a big, bad story to everyone listening. Fodder for Mrs. Andrews's new legislature.

With half-hearted exasperation, he sighs. "Perhaps it would be most productive for the established star witness to come forward at this time. After all, they're the only one here with a firsthand account of the incidents in question." In a show of impartiality, Judge Dodd looks down at his page as though he's never met her and doesn't know her name. "Abigail Alone," he says, looking in her direction. "Come up here, please."

Rabbit stands and walks toward the front of the room. The room is quiet save a few squeaking pews and the rustle of anticipation.

Rabbit knows Whitetail incarnated Mouse. That she'd boldly or stupidly asked the wilds for guidance the night of the snowstorm. But now the question "what for?" was also answered. *Mouse was a way to contain Hyena, would-be war, after Whitetail's death.*

Did Whitetail simply let her guard down? Or had her plan to move Hyena to Mouse gone to winter? *Either way, damn Whitetail for not accusing Hyena here and now,* Rabbit thinks. *Damn her for not trying to save herself here today. For not speaking the whole truth.*

A sickening wave of grief makes her reel with clarity; Whitetail had entrusted Rabbit to look after Mouse so often—*always special care.* It had been a monumental task. So much had been at stake.

Whitetail really had believed in Rabbit. Had bestowed such faith.

Looking at Whitetail, Rabbit can see she's all but gone, having long held on past her appointment with the Grimm. Her innocence means nothing.

Whitetail would rather be burned alive than let loose a war? Not only die, but risk the fate of eternal winter?

How can Mrs. Andrews and Whitetail want the very same thing? Who is right?

All heads in the room turn to look at Rabbit, and she feels small. Rabbit makes a point of not looking at Rook, not wanting to reveal him. Mrs. Andrews's cheeks are flush and rosy like the night they first met. Her eyes are round, encouraging, and Rabbit knows she's gotten her full strength back.

As Rabbit walks to the front of the room, a blackcoat holds open a gate like she's being corralled into a pen in front of the judge. She stands, hands folded in front of her, looking at the judge, legs quivering. What can she say? What can she do to make things better?

If Whitetail's determined to keep Hyena under wraps for some higher cause, it can't be Rabbit who defies her. Her heart breaks at the reality; she must respect Whitetail's dying wish.

The moment is here. Rabbit's supposed to tell all the bad things Whitetail did. It's what the room wants. What the judge wants too. What the Supreme wants. With the orphans safe, what does Rabbit stand to lose? Whitetail would rather be burned at the stake, accept an undeservedly cruel afterlife, than speak here today? And Mrs. Andrews had gone so far as to thank winter for who or what kept Whitetail from expelling Hyena so far. What *had* kept Whitetail from letting loose a revolution? Who had she been protecting?

Looking at Whitetail's weak smile, her downcast eyes, Rabbit knows the answer. *Herself.* The orphans. All of them. Rabbit gasps at the prospect that she should fear her birth mother.

Whitetail had been protecting her family.

"Raise your right hand, put the other on your heart." A blackcoat stands in front of Rabbit, towering so tall he's eclipsed one of the room's bright lights, and he's holding out the thick Blackbook. "Before your testimony, do you swear on the Blackbook that you'll tell all truths, and only those, by disavowing magic, every magic, here today and evermore?"

Rabbit opens her mouth but chokes, unsure what to say. Looking at Whitetail, Rabbit sees she's withering before her very eyes and that her time left on earth is not long. An agreement to the blackcoat's statement is the only gift she can offer Whitetail in this moment, but she feels she can't do it. Tears cloud her eyes. If only she hadn't made mud that day. She'd inherited much strength of spirit from Whitetail during the years at Andrews. She needs to summon it to her bones. *It's amazing what the spirit can cope with to preserve the body. My spirit is a mighty oak that just won't fall.* With the thought of physical preservation, she can feel some of her spirit disappearing. Without her spirit, her body is . . . is . . . well, nothing.

"I won't," says Rabbit, loyal to none. "I can't." Physical compliance here today would cost her very soul. The oak wouldn't just fall, it would disappear. Everything and more of what precisely connects her to the wilds. To her mother, Whitetail. She can't disavow the most precious gift the woman had ever given her.

Recalling the judge's comments on the consequences of a woman's loyalty and her singing the praises of Dirt: a ruined economy, a threat to natural order and hierarchy. *War.* Rabbit knows she won't have long to stand here. But this moment is her only chance at a confession of love and admiration to Whitetail. She'll not lose it. A world in which she'd agree to swearing off all love for her faith only to contribute to statements damning her mother to be set on fire wasn't one her body needed to exist in anyway. *My body before my faith,* Dodd had warned her. This was suicide.

There are gasps in the room. Someone snickers before the attendees erupt.

"Order!" the judge yells.

As she turns to face the room, she spots Mrs. Andrews. Her eyes, hungry. Scanning for Rook's, Rabbit can't find him.

"I dug my feet in the Dirt. I made mud."

"Order!" the judge yells again, his voice barely audible above the chatter in the room.

Rabbit raises her voice over the judge's warning. "It was me. I made mud. I was angry that it seemed I couldn't have what I wanted the way I wanted it cursing at Sixty-Three." She chokes a painful gulp. "That the wilds weren't bending to my bidding, so I quit halfway through"—her chest heaves—"the askin'. Mud made." When Rabbit looks at Whitetail, tears fill her eyes and cloud her vision. "I broke my promise to you."

The Dodd brothers lean forward in their seats and motion to blackcoats on the sides.

"Coats!" the judge yells, banging his gavel.

"I'm sorry," Rabbit says to Whitetail. Tears run down her cheeks, and she lets them fall.

Whitetail shudders, her expression blank with nothing but a ripple of knowing compassion.

"I'm not good like you needed me to be. I'm sorry, Mother." She'd never said the word aloud before. "You're my mama, Whitetail." Spittle lands on her chin and she's heaving with grief. Whatever Hyena is to Rabbit, she isn't a mother. Not one whom she needs, anyway.

As two blackcoats take Rabbit roughly up by the arms, she thrashes to be free of them.

"If you want to burn a Dirty woman for making mud while working to save people she loves, do it. But in her case"—Rabbit points a finger at Whitetail—"know that you'll be ridding the world of a little bit of summer . . ." She loses her voice; emotion steals her words as she's being dragged away.

"Take her out. Lock her up. Stoning to happen at a later day. My God—it's a time-necessitating moral fortitude. Evil is everywhere," the judge barks as Rabbit is dragged off, the toes of the shoes she's wearing trailing behind her on the ground. One, then the other, falls off.

The blackcoat's grip is tight, and she can't wriggle free. Her arms are immobile but not her tongue. Spotting Mrs. Andrews, Rabbit screams, "And I'm the rightful heir to Supre—" A blackcoat's big hand covers her mouth, hard. *And if Mad Dog really was my mother's mother's mother, in line behind Whitetail as would-be Omega.*

Before her, Rabbit can see people in the room stand, the pews they've been sitting in hooting on the floor as they move. People crane to watch her getting dragged toward the back of the building, the entrance through which Whitetail arrived.

The judge continues in a booming voice behind her. "In an effort to save on a colossal waste of your time," he says, banging his hammer, "I'm going to call on my brothers to agree that it's clear this Dirty woman, Miss Elizabeth Whittle, is infested by magic and contaminates everyone whom she encounters. Her incessant using of the Dirt is shockingly perverted, the insistence of which has brought tragedy and death. To prohibit the transfer of her deviance to our atmosphere, wherein it could infect others like a plague, I call to overrule the ban on death by burning so that this woman's potential, any further potential inheritance thereof, can be permanently snuffed out."

He stands as his eyes drift around the room.

"My call for sentencing shall be death by burning." The judge's jowls shake.

"Aye, aye!" the brothers' voices boom, and the room erupts with a frenzied cheer.

Immediately, people are out of their seats, pushing past Rabbit in a race toward the door. Someone's hand is on her, pushing at her back. Someone steps on the back of her leg, and it bends at a painful angle. Still trailing in the blackcoats' grasps, she's defiant. She screams in pain and fury hoping to break free in the chaos. Someone knocks her feet out from under her and Rabbit falls, breaking one arm free from the blackcoat's grip. Her wrist pains with impact on one of the room's thick wooden planks as her face knocks on the ground. When her cheek meets the floor's grit, she's left gazing momentarily under a bench nearby where she spots two pale faces. Figures hiding under a pew. They gaze out at her.

Bear? Pheasant? Rabbit blinks.

Are the other orphans here too?

The blackcoat that's still got her wrist scolds his partner, "Get her up, for Freemen's sake! All hell's breaking loose. Get her up."

A man shouts from somewhere in the room, and it's clear: a fight has broken out. People are yelling. Louder and louder, there's nowhere in the room that isn't a mass of rioting people. A woman screams.

"Up!" the scolded blackcoat barks as he yanks her wrist.

A man running up behind Rabbit practically tackles the blackcoat to get down the aisle and out of the building, distracting him. The blackcoat spins. Grunting with frustration, he recovers.

Rabbit thinks maybe she's dreamed of Pheasant's and Bear's faces as she's hauled back up so fiercely by her wrist that her shoulder threatens to dislocate. As she and the blackcoats reach the courthouse's front steps, Rabbit gasps when she sees the magnitude of the crowds that have assembled. The crowds are holding Freemen flags and cheering, but it's clear from their angry voices that erupt when they see her, these people are happy she's contained.

It would be a beautiful sight, Rabbit thinks, *if they weren't all chanting "burn the witch."* The posse is beginning to move, some turning to walk in another direction. In the distance, Rabbit sees a stage-like ridge of rock where a platform with a pyre stands. Men are shouting at Rabbit. When she looks to her right, she sees a flash of black—Whitetail's frail body hoisted momentarily overhead by large men, then dropped, picked up again, and escorted in the direction of the pyre in the meadow.

"No!" Rabbit screams.

"*Agh!*" the blackcoat on her right yells as he's tackled by something small. It clings to his front. "It bit me!"

Another something jumps onto his front next to the first and begins to wrestle him. On Rabbit's right, she spots Pea's glowing red hair. She's running in her direction through the crowds on the steps. When Pea meets the blackcoat on Rabbit's left, she vaults up his front and climbs onto his face. A woman frantically running by bumps the pair and the blackcoat falls, prying at Pea, clawing at his face and letting go of Rabbit's wrist.

The other blackcoat, consumed with Bear and Pheasant, lets go too.

"Run, Rabbit!" Pheasant says, clamoring all over the staggering blackcoat like a wild animal. "Run to the rock! The meadow! Pitch Point!" Rabbit's never heard Pheasant's voice at full volume before. When she wipes her coarse, kinky hair aside, her hazel eyes shine wild. Pheasant points to the horizon, to a clearing with a stone crest in the distance. Rabbit spots Rook walking in the crowds.

"Run to Rook!"

Chapter 35

And What Do *You* Say?

R abbit's eyes dart, searching for Rook. What little dry grass carpets the patchy ground in the meadow is being trampled by the stomping, charging feet of a population of stranglers, men, and women that's growing with every blink of her eye. She wiggles her tooth with the tip of her tongue as she fights the pain in her brow. *Think. Think.* Rabbit is scowling so hard she's given herself a headache. The wind is cold, and her nose has begun to run.

Peeling her socks off and throwing them down, she sprints, ricocheting off stranglers who are charging toward the platform. When she spots Rook through the tumultuous crowds, tears fill her eyes. Almost relief. He'll know what to do. He'll be able to help, like always. That's what he does. He helps. Always has a plan. But he hadn't really tried to intervene at all with her being dragged through the court hall to a stoning . . .

"Rook!" Rabbit calls.

Whitetail's been escorted into the field and is headed for the platform when she collapses. Limply her arms are hanging, her head dangling on her neck. They hoist her up, turn her over; she twists, and the stranglers recover.

"Rook!"

As Rook takes a step into the growing crowd, hands in his pockets, a crease forms in his brow. His stillness, idling, feet stuck in place, a spectator here, steals what's left of her dwindling breath. The Rook she knew would fight all these stranglers and jeerers until he collapsed dead. He was built for a fight. Who is this person?

When he spots her, his eyes light up with relief. He runs to her. She spots the ridge of rock nearby and drags him by the wrist, sprinting for cover, lest someone recognize her and drag her up on the point too. Surely the blackcoats will rally soon, looking to take stock of their accomplishment here today, and discover her missing. Ducking behind the rock, they take cover.

"Rabbit! Thank summer," he says breathlessly. Grabbing her forearms with firm, sincere hands, he asks, "Are you okay? I saw them drag you away! I—" He turns her arms over, checking to see if she's hurt.

"We have to help. We have to help her!" Rabbit cuts to the chase. *What to do?*

As he looks at her, she sees apology in his eyes. "It's so awful."

She's surprised by his admission. She'd wondered if she'd be dealing with a heart as cold as Mrs. Andrews, but in him, she sees someone with a conscience, just . . . *It's a blindness, an inability to criticize injustice.*

"This is awful," he says again, and she fills with relief. Perhaps Rook hasn't lost all allegiance to the Dirty. Perhaps he is still the boy she knows?

Rabbit grabs the tin from her pocket. Pulling it out, she eyes him. He seems like the old Rook. Like the boy she loves, her other half. They'll need to work together to bring a curse.

"Get down here." She yanks his wrist. "We need to curse for—for—" She's at a loss. Rook's still standing, and it's infuriating.

Looking up at him, she barks, "What are you doing? C'mon! Why aren't you helping?" What *should* she curse for?

"It's done," he says, his eyes narrowing. Though Rook's clearly not immune to pain or tragedy, he seems stagnant. His eyes are glassy, and he looks so sad he might cry. "We can't save her. Don't you see? It's what she wanted. She made this mess." He looks around, bewildered. "It's out of our hands. It's done. In the future, it will be different. I hope."

"The future? What's done? Don't be stupid." As she'd feared, the stone is immobilizing him. "Nothing's done, nothing's finished. You have the ability to help. Help me. Help me cast a curse—" Her eyes flit to Whitetail.

As he shakes his head, sluggishly turning to oversee the scene, she's so furious she wants to slap the sympathy off his face. Something roils inside her, and, standing, she unleashes it. She knocks him in the chest roughly with a bullying fist. He falls against the rock, taken aback.

"You give me that ovum!" she orders, reaching for his pocket. Thrusting her hand in, she tries to locate it.

"Wha—?" His look of surprise quickly turns to one of challenge. Defensively, he twists and shoves her back a step with his shoulder.

"You promised me! You promised you would always be an ally. You—" She's at a loss for words. "You give it!" The prospect that this ally has become a complacent drone is unacceptable to her. Not him. Never him. As he grips her hand, yanking it away, she's left twisting, aiming with her free hand for his other pocket, desperate to separate him from the stone.

"Stupid, you can't just stand by!"

"There's nothing to be done, Rabbit! What the heck do you expect to bring here today? It's the will of the wilds." As he restrains her, she moves to elbow him in the chest, but he ducks, and she winds up knocking his jaw. A fresh look of fury overtakes his face, and suddenly she's scared, but ready. Pushing her shoulders, he knocks her flat on her back, leaving her coughing. But she gets up.

Always look them in the eye. He'd taught her that. In a world that's asked her spirit to sacrifice everything for her body to survive, she's done with all of it. Ready to give it all, right here, right now—she'd rather die fighting him for the stone than let this boy become complacent. Before she'd let this boy, her boy, devolve into a mass of living, breathing indifference.

"You son of a Freemen!" she hisses. Charging him, her legs are shaking, and the pain in her heart is almost more than she can bear. This time when she approaches, he yanks back an elbow and punches her straight across the mouth, knocking her jaw off-kilter, the sound of which rattles, penetrating her brain like a bell's been rung.

"Stop!" he screams, his voice filled with heartache.

She tastes blood, and she likes it. It proves she's held her ground and that a new Rabbit has awakened. Clasping a hand over her mouth, an animal cry of frustration erupts from her chest. Like something sleeping, buried deep in her spirit, just burrowed out and staggered into the cold light of day. Blinking at Rook, she gathers something hard between her cheek and gums. Moving her tongue, she rolls it forward in her mouth and spits it into her palm, covered in blood.

Rook's eyes grow. Chest heaving, he licks his bottom lip. His eyes dart to hers.

He's knocked out her tooth.

As he watches her, surprised, there's guilt in his eyes.

All your mother's histories are in you when you're born. The legacy of all magical inheritance and the list of mothers . . . it is in her palm. Looking at Rook, she feels warm blood at the side of her mouth. Using the back of her hand, she wipes it away. A piece of the Necrology. She's found a chip off the mother rock.

Gripping the tooth in her fist, she says, "That's not who you really are." She eyes his pocket. "You throw that stone away right now, Rook!" The piece off the most powerful stone of all magic must trump his piece of enchanted ovum. She gnashes her teeth before summoning all her breath.

"You're an ally! Always will be. Wake. Up!"

As she commands it, a freezing wind blows at her back, and it looks as though it slaps Rook square in the face.

As Rook takes the ovum out of his pocket, he inspects it a moment before his lips part. Winding an arm, he chucks the ovum far into the brush. He looks injured for only a moment before his look of confusion makes way for one of apology. Plunking down in the Dirt, he takes off his shoes and draws a spiral, quickly notching it with sixty-three slashes.

Rook reaches up for her hand. Taking it in his, he presses it to his cheek, warming it. He kisses the back of her fingers. "I'm sorry."

She kneels on the far side of the spiral and, looking it over, knows it's drawn wrong.

She adds a new notch. *No more "ifs" in balance.* "The spiral of sixty-three needs to be sixty-four," she yells over the growing noise. If Marianne's foremothers, turned old birds, had erased a notch to help Freemen, surely all sixty-four notches on the timeline needed to be reestablished for accuracy.

"It's sixty-four total. Fifty-eight is *Flame.* The rest follow in the familiar order ever after," she explains.

His mouth is a hard line of indecision before he gives her a stiff nod. "Okay, then." His brows knit in concentration. Reaching into his pocket, he withdraws his twist of wood.

"Should we ask the wilds to save her spirit from winter? Hide her from Death?"

Not with this stone. Rabbit remembers Whitetail's question that day on the porch when Rook proposed she hide from the Beard. *What, dear girl, will we do tomorrow when he comes back?* The Grimm, like the Beard, would always be back.

"She'll not hide." Rabbit shakes her head. A rush of frustrated energy flows through her veins like sap in the trees surrounding. Rabbit pinches her eyes closed. It feels too important to be all on her. She looks down at the tooth in her hand. If the sleeping beast has, in fact, been awakened . . . if she is the beast . . . this is her moment. Her Dirty day.

The prophecy said that "revolution" would be born in the beast's jaw. By the fire, Whitetail said that for 'Librium, there'd need to be a reconciliation—power needed to be returned to where it was first stolen from. But that Freemen would never allow it.

Was Tituba's prophecy destiny? Revolution is a possibility—*or an inevitability.* What's in her palm? *Is revolution what she wants?* She doesn't know.

She flounders, agreeing with Rook. All she can focus on is her want for the wilds to spare Whitetail, or at the very least obey her wishes. The woman craved only safety for her family, and summerland. Rabbit can't go directly against her mother's dying wish here today, even if it helps stop Mrs. Andrews.

Tituba's drawing of this scene showed spirits coming out of the forest. *Why?* She sure doesn't want to meet with red-boned wraiths. Why would they be necessary here today?

"'Librium," she concedes, unable to consider Hyena's revolution or Whitetail's preservation. "It's what Whitetail has been striving for all these years. Marianne, Snake, Mouse, even Hyena—they've all given everything for that singular goal, no?" Rabbit's prepared to ask for it to start today. If the change takes a thousand years, she can accept it, long as it starts today. *Unquestionably, roles reversed, Whitetail would be asking for 'Librium.*

"Okay." Rook's eyes scan the board. "Whitetail always said that balance means offering power to where it was first stolen. Where's that?"

Rook's worried look makes Rabbit gulp. She shakes her head. Whitetail stole control from Hyena. Hyena from Freemen. Freemen from the Dirty . . .

Rabbit gives thanks to the Dirt, grinding her fingernails into the frigid soil to the point of them breaking. She curls and flexes her toes in gratitude and desperation. She again thinks of the wraiths crawling out of the woods in Tituba's drawing.

Of course.

"To the dead." The wrongfully dead had their power stolen first. "They need their injustice heard by the living. Whitetail said that's how balance starts. The day the first innocent woman died at the hands of a man calling himself her master, that was the day power got stolen. It's what divided Dirty from Freemen. That's where we return power. To the dead. Let her say her truth. Everyone here will witness it. They'll have to." She is sure of it.

Rook nods. "But who was the first?"

She has no idea. How to summon a nameless erased? Looking at the board, she scans. There's only one figure she knows for certain is capable of summoning ghosts. All of them. A divining rod for specters. If she called him here today, he would summon every ghost. Every last restless spirit.

"The Grimm," she says.

His shoulders fall. "But . . ." He looks around. Looks at Whitetail. "Here? But that's exactly who we don't want here today. She's about to get called for winter, for summer's sake!" Aghast, he rocks back on his haunches.

He still doesn't understand that Hyena's at fault for the murders.

Would Whitetail be sent to winter for conjuring Mouse? Keeping Hyena? A fate like winter would be an awful one for a woman so wholly bound to her principles. Whatever Mouse saw in the stars that last evening in the kitchen before she died had clearly made her worry. *Was it done with malice in the heart?* Whitetail had asked. Rabbit remembers the way Mouse patted Whitetail's hand and shrugged. "The only malice living in Whitetail is murderous Hyena." Rabbit winces with a momentary hatred for her birth mother. Shaking her head, she says, "There's never been any malice in Whitetail's heart. If 'Librium starts with dead Dirt's injustice being heard, that's what we do. We invite them here today."

"Okay. Sixty-four, Grimm . . ." He shifts uncomfortably. "And Tituba's prophecy. If dead Dirt speaking their truth starts a war today?" Rook asks, looking at the tooth in her palm. Whitetail's fireside musings and warnings are coming back to him too.

She shudders. Her adoptive mother's goal, her birth mother's goal. They both would agree on 'Librium.

"It's up to the wilds," she says.

Rabbit looks up to the point as a cacophony of cheers erupts. Someone has run the Freemen flag up an old flagpole, and it's flapping violently. Whitetail is a white spot on a red tapestry. She's slumped and tied to a stake. Mrs. Andrews is circling her, but as she looks back over her shoulder, it's clear she's become distracted by something. Taking a step back from Whitetail, then another, Mrs. Andrews spins to first look around herself, then farther off at the crowds. Rabbit watches Mrs. Andrews's piercing eyes glide down along the ground and trail up toward where she and Rook are hiding; Rabbit knows they're out of time.

Rabbit gulps. "Mr. Grimm. Come. Call the dead Dirt. They have a score to settle—let them be heard here today." She wishes so hard, her toes curl. After putting her tooth, the chip of Necrology, on the ground next to his twist of wood, she rolls the die.

The die shows a six. She moves her tooth, then hands the die over to Rook, and he rolls. He lands a four. Then Rabbit rolls another six. Twelve, *Rejuvenation*. Rook rolls a six, *Revelation*. As the sky darkens, she notes it's starting to snow. The sun is almost set in a red blaze, casting crimson along the bottom of low cloud cover. With a fleeting connection, remembering the red hue of Whitetail's death suit, Rabbit tries to block out the noise and the momentousness of this moment.

"Good focus," Rook says.

The crowd's chanting subsides, and there's a quieting at someone's command.

Rabbit hears a sharp, angry voice. "There!" Mrs. Andrews's shrill voice echoes off rock faces and up into the sky.

A gurgle of confusion ricochets through the masses before complete silence falls.

"I said, stop them!" Mrs. Andrews calls, her shrill voice ripping over the top of the crowds and echoing off the surrounding hills. "Over there! Stop those children. They're Dirtily gambling with your fate as we speak. Stop them, now! Stop them! Fools!"

Rabbit and Rook rapidly play, passing the die back and forth even before they've moved their marker.

On cue, Rabbit peeks out to spot stranglers in the crowd spin and wander in their direction, losing all focus on Whitetail, who's still lingering limply, tied to her post. Rook peeks out, too, gripping the boulder with cold, red fingers. The stranglers march closer like drones, sniffing them out.

Rabbit pinches her eyes shut and concentrates.

Rabbit rolls and progresses to notch fifty-four. *Joker,* roll again. She does so without speaking. The die shows a four.

Rook takes the die up in his fist and shakes it. He tosses a four and places his twist of wood on notch fifty-eight, atop hers. *Flame.*

Rook nods encouragingly. Rabbit bumps one notch. Fifty-nine, *Reckoning.*

Peeking out, Rabbit watches a strangler zero in on them. He halts a moment, staring vacantly, then simply points, locating them, and picks up his pace. The strangler next to him lines up, shoulder to the first's, and points the same. Slowly they are assembling in a ring around the children.

Whitetail's hanging in the cold. She looks so small. Her dark eyes scan the crowd, then drift to the horizon. Whitetail's posture is strikingly unfamiliar now that it's no longer commanding and strong, yet the copy of Tituba's print in Mrs. Andrews's scrapbook showed precisely this. *Only with someone lying on the ground.*

"Hurry," Rook says.

Rabbit quickly rolls, her hands shaking with adrenaline. Five. She progresses to notch sixty-four, *Grimm*. She's done it.

As the final say, it's up to Rook. *Approval from the wilds.*

There are stranglers surrounding them. They swing and jockey, quivering with dutiful poise. There's a break in the stranglers' wall. As they step aside, Mrs. Andrews appears; having shouldered her way to the front, her face is an ember amongst ash. She looks positively radiant holding the antlers, one in each hand like huge fans.

Rook lets the die loose, and when it stops rolling, it shows six.

He moves his marker. "Rabbit." Rook's face is full of wonder. *The Grimm.*

Rabbit gasps. Rook almost smiles before he's distracted. Mrs. Andrews is circling them. Rabbit stands to take it in. *The Grimm, where is he?*

"What have you done?" Mrs. Andrews is hulking overhead with disappointment as she surveys the completed ritual.

Spinning to search for the Grimm's coach, a sharp pain in Rabbit's chest steals her breath, leaving her frozen. As she looks down at Rook for explanation, he staggers to his feet in time to catch her as she helplessly pitches forward.

"*Noo!*" Rook yells, his knees buckling as her weight slams into him. He collapses with the impact before they both fall to the ground, her in his lap.

When Rabbit opens her eyes again, she's lying in his arms. He's shaking her. There's a foreign hand on her front with gray-blue fingernails, and it's gripping a stick. The hand is her hand. As she struggles to take a breath, she realizes she's been stabbed.

A piece of Whitetail's antler is sticking out of her chest.

Pulling her up into his arms, Rook cries hot tears on her neck. Mrs. Andrews is looming overhead, her gaze victorious. Rabbit spots something beyond Mrs. Andrews's skirt. *Mouse?* She's standing in the dark near some brush under a big old oak tree, and her gaze holds its typical understanding. Mouse's chin rises in some acknowledgment before she turns to peer into the woods for something. Someone behind her. Running away, she quickly disappears back into the forest, hands wrapped around her mouth as she calls out at the dark.

Chapter 36

Sixty-Four

L ying in Rook's arms, Rabbit blinks into the night sky. There are small, ash-like flakes falling. So late. Snow in May. The snowflakes don't melt on her cheeks. She's never felt so cold. It's defeat, failure, that stings so much more than the antler in her chest.

Mrs. Andrews's enthusiastic, wild-dog mob cheers exuberantly. For what she's done. To them, she's the do-gooder who's triumphed over evil, stabbed the beast in the chest, showing them her radical progress. Mrs. Andrews looks at Rook and smirks. Kicking her foot through the dirt, destroying evidence of the curse, she throws black mud into Rabbit's face.

Mrs. Andrews rounds the pair with stalking steps. Then, with one hand perched on a bent knee, she gracefully reaches down and yanks, withdrawing the antler. It locks behind Rabbit's rib. When Mrs. Andrews yanks again, Rabbit lurches and there's a snapping sound.

"*Ahh!*" Rabbit's own voice sounds foreign. A searing pain ignites in her chest, like a hot needle in her lungs. Looking at the antler in Mrs. Andrews's hand, Rabbit can see one of the antler's smallest spines has been removed. It's still in her ribcage.

The stranglers clap, a mission accomplished, and they turn one by one on their heels to walk back toward the stage, toward Whitetail.

"Uh, what about the boy?" Mrs. Andrews has a crinkle in her brow as she looks around for support. "The Dirty sympathizer might as well have cast the curse himself. He's filthy."

"Boys are allowed to make mistakes," a strangler gurgles assumingly as he and the surrounding ghouls turn to leave. Mrs. Andrews looks unsatisfied, but turning to spot Whitetail, her big fish still tied to the post on the point, she departs with no noise but the crunching of dead grass under her leather shoes.

A gurgle rumbles from Rabbit's chest above the pain in her back. With each breath, the growling noise grows a little louder. Blood in her lungs.

"I'm—I'm—" she stammers. She wants to say she's sorry, but the words won't form.

"Wait. Have faith in the Dirt," Rook responds, gripping her left hand and placing her recovered tooth into her palm. There's no strength in hers to grip. The last of the stranglers turn and leave. The crowd has gone. Rabbit lies in Rook's arms, watching, eyes trained on the old oak in search of Mouse, but there's no one there. The air is still, heavy and oppressive.

"I'm sorry," Rabbit whispers as Rook holds her tighter.

The blood-red sky is low and it's warmer now, but the snow is falling heavier. Mrs. Andrews is back up front on the point. The crowd cheers, and everyone knows the big moment is upon them. It's time to burn the witch. Rabbit sees people clapping and smiling excitedly, but all she can hear is the slowing thump of her own heart in her ears.

Rabbit feels Rook shaking. His embrace is firm, but she

knows he's crying. As he burrows his wet face in her neck, she prays that when she's gone, he'll keep his word and always fight for girls like her.

"It's—" he says.

Her feet are shaking so badly, they almost tickle. "Rook," she says, needing him to be still. The pain in her back is suffocating. "Please stop." The vibrating sensation is in her legs now. "P-please stop."

"He's coming," Rook says, disbelief in his voice.

All at once, Rabbit realizes it's not Rook who's jittery at her back. It's the earth beneath them.

With all the hollering and excitement in the crowds, it takes several moments for them to look to each other for an explanation of the sound they've just recognized too. As the earth's rumbling increases, strangler heads in the crowd turn and look over their shoulders. At the field at their backs.

A fine crack forms on the ground, and like an arrow pointing at Whitetail, there's a snapping sound, then a quick, vacuous suck of air. As it's drawn down with suction, a frosty vapor plumes. The ground along the opening's edge frosts over, growing white with new ice.

More tendrils of fog emerge from the depths, curling and reaching out of the fresh void. The rumbling of moving rock plates, masses of upturned soil, and the popping of gravel grow to such a painful volume that Rabbit would cover her ears if only she could move her hands. Stones on the ground jump. Remains of dead leaves in the surrounding trees fall from violent vibration. Dust rises.

The stranglers stagger as the crack snakes, slithering toward the rocky point before a cavern tears open with a deafening *crack* in its wake. The crowd of spectators splits, staggering on the un-leveling, overturning earth, and like that, a deep crevice opens directly in front of the stone ridge. It's as wide as the orphanage porch and frosting over with ice. As the crevice widens and settles, there's the underlay of a new sound: the echo of impending hooves.

Whitetail seems oblivious; her head hangs low.

Mrs. Andrews shushes the crowd. Her hand gestures, urging them to stay in place, not to run for the hills from whatever is coming.

Mrs. Andrews growls, her voice overshadowed by the rumbling of hooves. "He's coming. Oh, yes. Death! Father waits with his strap. The beast is coming up here to"—the earthquake settles some to let her finish—"take her to After! Oh, Father's so disappointed, hanging his head in shame too." She finishes by pointing a long finger at Whitetail, but no one's paying attention.

The sound of rumbling earth lowers in decibel with the slowing of the distinct *clickity-clack* of hooves. A pop of black shows itself along the ground as something heavily tops the icy steps and walks out into open air. It's a front-runner of a team, and behind it, harnessed row after row, are black horses. Finally, with a slither, a black sled lurches out of the ground at the rear. The driver, the Grimm, sitting in the coachman's seat, looks around. There's no wind, and the falling snow is catching on the Grimm's black cloak in clusters. Despite it, the air is growing so warm it's hard for Rabbit to breathe.

The coach croaks along mud as it approaches the stage, and the horses make a wide arc, allowing it to settle directly in front of the Point's stairs. When the Grimm stands up from his perch, his glistening wax-black skull face is unemotive. His robes are tailored—angular, sharp—and it's striking that the headdress he wears makes him look as though he has horns. Unlike Whitetail's antlers, the Grimm's helmet features shorter, thicker flutes, like hunter's horns. His back and knees audibly crack, the sound echoing off the hills behind them. Descending the coach steps, his tall boots meet his long coattails at the back. He walks around back to the coach door. Heavily the Grimm's knuckles snap as he opens the coach door with a red-gloved hand. When the hatch glides up, a sour smell floats on the wind and under Rabbit's nose.

Turning to look at Whitetail, he waits like a flame expecting a moth. Rabbit feels so much heaviness in the air, she might as well already be buried.

Standing back, Mrs. Andrews raises her chin defiantly. Her eyes shine as she looks around at the crowd. She's ready to strike her flint.

"Last words?" a blackcoat says with a gruff growl. The flapping of the Freemen flag has taken on a loud snapping rhythm high over his head.

Whitetail is limp and motionless. She says nothing, doesn't move, just hangs her head, the skin and bones of her frame shakily sinking. She'd always been dying, Rabbit reminds herself, though she's so sad for what's come. Whitetail knew her time was soon. Wanted summer. It's what prompted her to play Sixty-Four and ask for Mouse.

"*Agh!*" Someone in the crowd erupts with celebration. "Back to the dirt for the Dirty!" they yell. The maddening, confounding threat, Whitetail, is about to be eliminated. As the blackcoat slides a ceremonial square black hood over Whitetail's face, he says, "For her crimes of Dirty witchcraft in countless murders, we here today condemn via the biting fierceness of Freemen flame the use of the Dirt which is unforgivable, and therefore, this witch shall burn."

Rabbit knows Whitetail's body is here in the cold, the rope binding her to the post, her feet dangling over kindling ready to ignite, but Rabbit prays Whitetail's lost in memory—the times she sat with her mother in a field of warm sweetgrass with a bottle of whisky.

Or of a happier time with the children.

"Rabbit," someone whispers. Feeling a weight on her shoulder, then her arm, she sees the children have come. They gather around her, looking solemn. Pea's glassy eyes blink down at Rabbit where she lies. Goose, Bear, Mole, Rat, and Dove. Pheasant is there too. She lays her hand on Rabbit's chest as her hazel eyes stare into an unknown space a few moments. Blinking, she, like the rest, looks back over her shoulder at the Grimm.

The Grimm folds his arms, waiting, but when a shrill, hollow sound cuts through the quiet, his attention turns to the forest. He unfolds his arms, then glances back at Rabbit and the children.

Then at Whitetail. But then back at Rabbit.

Then back to the forest. Taking a step in the direction of the forest, he looks searchingly.

Mrs. Andrews strikes her flint, and it sparks. Again, and it sparks. The crowds are quiet with reverent attention as she tries a third time to make a flame. But the wind stirs.

Rabbit can hear the Grimm's raspy breath. It's a pulling, heaving noise, drawing, sucking. It draws at the surrounding forest. Trees slowly bend, arching, bowing into the clearing. The wind kicks up with a fresh bluster, pulling all air toward the coach.

A cry sounds. It's so sad that Rabbit feels it'll cost the last of her pulse. Echoing off surrounding rocks, it slowly, surely reveals itself as a lonely, mournful, bloodcurdling howl.

Rabbit's skin crawls, and her stomach heaves. As she succumbs to a weary level of blurriness, there's a far-off answer to the cry from the deepest, darkest part of the forest. *Others.*

The red-boned wraith's black hair is stringy on her scarlet skull. She's glistening with blood. And her stance is unmistakably ready. Who knows just how long she's waited for this. In her bony grasp is a tall post. On top of it flaps the Dirty 'Librium flag, the owl with demure wings. From the surrounding skeletal trees emerge more red wraiths. Vines from beneath them reach up, gather, and knot, snaking like veins from the forest floor, delineating what must have once been cracked ribs, broken shoulders, hobbled legs, and severed necks. On the wind, the sound of crying quickly escalates to a sizzling like a midsummer night's field of cicadas.

Rabbit's chest moves unproductively. There's no air to be found.

The wraiths all look around at one another as though they're waking from a dream, but this isn't where they fell asleep. Together, they let out a piercing battle cry so angry and loud; the sound is even more powerful than the A&O's steam whistle, and it quickly gets the attention of the stranglers. With the noise, Rabbit shudders as the raw burning in her chest settles, sending out what she believes will be her last breath. The breath slips out like a whisper, and she thinks of Whitetail, her mother, and she thinks, *That's it.*

But a chest full of air rushes into her lungs.

Violently, she's left coughing. A new dull throb aches in her lungs as though the antler's fragment is cauterizing a gap—tissue and vein, bone and organ. Her heart heals over the sliver of antler like a tree gall.

Rabbit sits up, fighting for more air. Upright, she fights the urge to run. Looking at the flag once more, the sun behind it, the owl's figure is burned into her retina.

The angry mob buckles its knees as though a crack of thunder has surprised them. Their heads all snap in the direction of the forest to spot what's surrounding them. Rabbit sees the whites of the stranglers' eyes. As they look around, mouths open, they stagger in confusion.

As the Dirt's dead army charges full sprint, there's only the sound of labored breathing and echoing as they race, rushing centrifugally inward. Barreling forward, they seem intent on colliding with the stranglers. As they run, their auras intermittently show peek-a-boo glimpses of limbs: femurs, broken; legs, severed; pumping arms with hands missing their fingers.

For the briefest of moments, the Dirty flag overlaps the Freemen flag behind it, forcing Rabbit's brain to recognize a new symbol entirely. With the owls' wings crisscrossed, their head feathers misaligned, the owl looks like an entirely new symbol: A moth? Then it's gone.

"*Ung?*" A strangler grunts. There's the sound of mass recognition. The look on each strangler's face tells they recognize their attacker. Like looking into mirrors, they're confronted, forced to see themselves simultaneously as the husks of the men they'd once been—and those scared by the woman they'd once destroyed.

"Stand your ground!" Mrs. Andrews's voice is rough and brimming with hatred as she rushes forward on the platform. Standing on the edge, she scowls, wincing with disgust. Her posture is hunched and her eyes black. "Fools! Hold your ground!"

Someone lets out a "*tssh!*" as the Dirty dead make impact. There are thuds like raindrops as collision after collision starts all the stranglers screaming.

Mouse is standing next to the Grimm. She looks up at him and takes his hand, and he leads her back around to the rear of his coach where the door stands ajar. Expectantly, they wait.

One by one, the stranglers fall in a frozen collapse. There're no bloody wounds. No clang of weapons. Just what looks to be paralyzing fear. Since stranglers don't blink, can't close their eyes, they're forced to simply see. And whatever they see apparently sets each off clumsily running for his life. Being pursued by the ugly remains of women from their pasts, hunting them with merciless fury, must be terrifying. Each strangler takes off running but inevitably trips, floundering, childlike, as though their feet have met mud and they're incapable of navigating anything other than driving themselves violently into the ground.

Turning over to look up at their hunters, they each raise a hand defensively and cry for mercy, but none is given. Hands gripping their chests, they roil and contort, flailing on the ground, before the sheen in their eyes dulls over. Whether it's guilt, self-loathing, or a spell of another kind, the effect is permanent. They die.

Slowly but surely, trails of heavy soot-black smoke rise, sucked in the direction of the Grimm's coach. The scent on the air is putrid by the time the black cloud grows to the size of a great willow. Rabbit, Rook, and the others are left covering their faces for protection. The black pollution, spirits of the stranglers, curls and balloons before it reaches the vacuum of the coach where it briskly gets drawn inside. The Grimm closes the door. Standing at the Grimm's side, Mouse brushes her hands together, like she's done with some work.

"Fools!" Mrs. Andrews screams. Turning back to Whitetail, she feverishly begins snapping her flint, looking for it to flame. She knocks at it, and it sparks but dies. Again, she strikes it, and it sparks but flickers and dies. Frustration makes her back hunch. She's quivering.

"*Agh!*" she cries, her voice echoing off the hills, cueing her that the clearing has grown quiet. Her hands fumble with the flint as she turns to look over her shoulder. Her mouth gapes at the sight of the clearing filled with the Dirty dead. They're all silently watching her. She freezes.

"You," she hisses to no one. "You all stand there judging *me*?" Her bottom lip trembles as her eyes dart along the crowd.

Who knows what she sees in them. Whether it's the women she's hurt along the way or herself when she lived as a toothless and battered wraith in the mud, it forces a horrible, angry scream from her chest that echoes through the valley.

"Bitter? Jealous? You're all just mad you didn't have the balls to do what I did and play the game to win." Black tears stream down her cheeks. She throws her fake teeth away. As she huffs, exasperated, her mouth hangs lopsided. "Ugly cowards. You weren't smart enough to keep yourselves out of trouble, and you got what you bought. Messed with the Dirt, and it was a fist full of soil on your own graves!"

Angrily she turns, throwing down the antlers. They each smash into shards that slide across the rock ledge. With only a quick look back at the antlers' broken pieces, she again starts working on the flint. She hammers again and again, but each time she draws a flame and holds it to the pyre, the wind blows it out.

"What is it?" Rook asks. It's almost inexplicable why the flint isn't catching. It's the most reliable flame in existence.

"The will," she whispers, turning to look at him. "The will of the wilds."

Whitetail lets out a low groan as finally, with a snap, the flint catches, and Mrs. Andrews holds a blazing flame out to the pyre's stack. There's a rushing sound as all the idling Dirty dead blow as one. In a flash, instead of the pyre, it's Mrs. Andrews's shirt cuff that's on fire.

Mrs. Andrews mumbles a noise of surprise before she lets out a shriek in panic, shaking her arm furiously. Spinning, she turns, and a drifting ember, like a comet from her coat cuff, lights her skirt, igniting it. Her full skirt lights up like a torch as she spins. What was purple cloth is quickly turning black. Intermittently Mrs. Andrews arches her back, then bends, cowering as she tries to smother what's blazing and avoid being completely engulfed in flames. Mrs. Andrews lets out a chilling wail as the flames meet her chest and the high neck of her dress. A black flap violently bolts out of her skull, thrusting her head back, as the noises she's making stop sounding human. Something else thrusts from the other side of the woman's head, then waves, flapping. *They're wings. The winged creature from Tituba's prophecy.* There are two in total. They've emerged from her skull looking black and shiny as oil. Then two more burst out, these looking speckled with small white dots, but as each spot quickly darts open, they reveal in turn what appear to be red, glistening eyes. Rabbit remembers Whitetail's talk of the biggest threat to Dirt. The woman against women. This isn't just any old bird, this is a grotesque vulture.

"*Ahh!*" she screams. "*Ahh!*" Her dress crumbles, becoming ash. Her face is completely transformed into a winged black skull as she staggers, spinning. Teetering toward the back edge of the platform, Mrs. Andrews leaps in an apparent attempt to take flight before falling heavily off the edge in a heavy lump, casting trails of smoke and large flakes of black soot up on the breeze.

Up and running toward the platform now, Rabbit sprints for Whitetail. The sea of Dirty dead parts, letting Rabbit and the other orphans through their pack. On the stage, Rabbit heads for the pyre as Rook sprints to find Mrs. Andrews. Rabbit rips off Whitetail's black hood.

"Ms.!" Rabbit says, her voice cracking. "Mama!"

"Run off! Kept woman's gone!" Rook yells from the far edge of the platform where Mrs. Andrews's flaming body had just fallen. "There's just a trail of black ashes!" A dog-like howl sirens once in the distant woods.

"Untie her wrists!" Rook commands Pheasant as he runs closer. Back at the post, he gets to work with Pea at Whitetail's ankles. As Pheasant succeeds in unknotting Whitetail's wrists, Whitetail collapses in a quiet heap.

"Whitetail," Rabbit says, putting a hand on Whitetail's cheek. "I'm sorry." Rabbit begins to cry. Up close she sees just how skeletal Whitetail has become. Her eyes don't open. Her mouth doesn't move. Her chest, its movement, is nonexistent.

"No," Rook whispers.

"She's gone," Pea says in a quiet voice. As she says it, a large tendril thrusts Whitetail's face skyward. Red shoots out of Whitetail's gray mouth. It's dark, like blood. Smells like it too. Reaching, almost defensively at first, the red tests the air before more of it floods out in a shot of misty spray, some of which spills, pooling down Whitetail's front.

Whitetail's letting Hyena go.

As Hyena drips down Whitetail's front, her spray erratically collects in beads of coagulating vapor, joining the bigger plume hovering in the air above.

The Dirty dead look at one another.

Rabbit sees there's a morose look of knowing on each of their faces.

The horses stomp their feet nervously with unease. Their harnesses squeak, and their chains clank as they shuffle.

A new noise sounds. Rabbit stands up, exhausted and numb. Whatever is coming, she's failed to save her own mother's life. There's a low rumbling, sharp and crackling. Popping like dust at the hearth. Some crocuses emerge through the soil around the trees in the fringes. Rabbit can see them, violet and abundant. The noise cues the Dirty army to head for the coach. The Grimm opens the door for them, and one by one they pile by the hundreds into the coach that apparently has a limitless capacity. At the tail end of the Dirty dead, Rabbit spots Whitetail's spirit. Mouse's spirit is reaching for her hand. The Grimm continues to hold the door open for the pair, but gently Whitetail grabs the handle and closes the coach door.

Mouse raises her arms, ready for Whitetail to pick her up. Whitetail scoops Mouse up and walks toward the driver's seat at the front of the carriage. The Grimm nods knowingly before he follows and offers her a hand up into the coachman's seat. Whitetail refuses, choosing instead to hoist her and Mouse up into the driver's seat on her own.

The Grimm rounds the coach with heavy steps and climbs up onto the right side of the seat, ready to ride, this time as a passenger.

As the sun breaks through the cloud cover overhead, the sky brightens.

Rabbit would cry tears for Whitetail, the person who mothered her, who loved her enough to want to save her from this coming rebellion, who always sat in the shadows so she could walk in the sun . . . but her time has come for summer. The will of the wilds has decided it, just as they decided to grant Rabbit the coming of the Grimm, forcing all other elements not into an ideal, but into a reset in their rightful place.

Mouse is sitting in Whitetail's lap. Turned around to face the children, Mouse's chin rests on Whitetail's shoulder. As her face tilts, Mouse smiles. She waves. Recalling Mouse's last words to her the night she was murdered in the kitchen at Andrews by Hyena: *We'll wave.* It's a small open-and-closed grab of a farewell that takes Rabbit's breath away as it burrows like a worm into her deepest of regrets for ever being cruel to the child.

Mouse holds up one finger as a drawn-out signal. Rabbit remembers it: "*Don't forget.*"

The ring. Rabbit remembers Mouse's gift from the night she died. Opening the tin, she slides it on her pointer finger.

Whitetail turns, too, eyeing Rabbit hard. She mouths something. One last utterance?

She repeats it. Whitetail presses her fingertips to her lips, then draws them away with a last wave—exactly the same as the kiss Mouse had blown Rabbit the night in the kitchen after she'd cursed the Beard.

All at once, Rabbit knows what Whitetail just said . . . *So proud of you, Rabbit.*

Whitetail takes up, then cracks the coach's whip, calling "*yah!*" A violent thunder sounds. As quickly as the coach arrived, the horses rear and bolt, cantering thunderously down into the earth, down a road only they know how to tread, off to deliver the stranglers to winter. But Rabbit knows Whitetail will drop herself and the other Dirt off at summerland first.

And Hyena is blowing away overhead. Taken on the warm wind, she's tracing along the sky, a blood-red streak staining the sunset.

The children all gather around Rabbit, and together they're quiet for a long time. There's no sniffling, no tears, just the feeling of being whole again. All of them together. Rook finally lifts his chin off the top of Rabbit's head. He looks around.

"What now?" Rook asks her as he watches each little girl pick up a piece of Ms.'s antlers.

Rabbit weighs the threats of the past and those yet to come. She's been set on fire, but not by any flame. Looking at the dirt under her fingernails and feeling that small shard of antler, the piece of Whitetail's spirit in her chest as it burrows a little deeper, she decides: "The war has begun."

It is the will of the wilds.

* * *

ACKNOWLEDGEMENTS

I owe so many thanks.

To my grandfather, Harold, the storyteller. And Michele Zackheim for taking my writing so seriously all those years ago. To Tracy Auerbach, for reading the earliest draft of this novel. And to Abigail F. Taylor for helping me hone it.

Thank you to Elizabeth Kilcoyne for introducing me to Erin Clyburn, my incredible agent. All my gratitude, Erin. You championed this novel! And you helped it find a perfect home. Thanks to my publisher, Amanda Manns. You've made a dream come true.

Also, to my boys, Oz and Shep. Thanks for playing in the Beaverkill and letting Mum work, guys. I love you always. XO

MEG RIPLEY was born in Ontario and raised in Newfoundland, Canada, surrounded by whales and icebergs. After an MFA in illustration from SVA, NYC, she worked as an illustrator for a decade before realizing her love of writing fiction could no longer be ignored. She lives in Brooklyn with her husband and two children.

CREATURE PUBLISHING was founded on a passion for feminist discourse and horror's potential for social commentary and catharsis. Seeking to address the gender imbalance and lack of diversity traditionally found in the horror genre, Creature is a platform for stories which challenge the status quo. Our definition of feminist horror, broad and inclusive, expands the scope of what horror can be and who can make it.